Sweeney

Sweeney

Robert Julyan

University of New Mexico Press | Albuquerque

Library of Congress Cataloging-in-Publication Data

Julyan, Robert Hixson.
Sweeney / Robert Julyan.
p. cm.
ISBN 978-0-8263-5033-6 (pbk. : alk. paper) — ISBN 978-0-8263-5034-3 (electronic)
1. City and town life—Fiction. 2. Country life—Fiction. 3. New Mexico—Fiction.
I. Title.
PS3610.U5375S84 2011
813'.6—dc22

2011004418

TO MY FAMILY,
for their love and support,
and for keeping keen
my sense of humor and the ridiculous.

AND TO DOUG AND NANCE,
who were there from the beginning,
and whose encouragement, caring, and wise advice
made this book possible.

Chapter One

●▶ WITHOUT BOTHERING TO LOOK FOR TRAFFIC, Dave Daly stepped from the cracked sidewalk onto Main Street. He'd long ago taken for granted that in Sweeney no vehicles would be bearing down on him, yet as he stepped onto the empty street today a memory arose of crossing the street on his bicycle as an eight-year-old, his mother yelling, "Be careful. Watch for cars," and him feeling bold as a pirate as he steered his Schwinn among the lumbering Fords and Chevys and Oldsmobiles and pickups pulling in and out of parking places on Main Street.

Today the only thing moving on Main Street was a halfhearted late-afternoon dust devil pirouetting in the hot, dry wind of the High Plains. The only kind of visitor Sweeney got these days.

He angled across the street and headed for the Chick 'n' More Restaurant down the block. Saturday, and he was late for the monthly luncheon meeting of the Sweeney Rotary Club. The Chick 'n' More wasn't much on cuisine or décor, and like Sweeney it had seen better days— Dave could remember the restaurant's aquarium before the fish died— but at the moment it was all Sweeney had.

But at least it had that. Jones Drugstore, where he'd squatted on the floor and read Superman and Captain Marvel comic books, had closed long ago and now was boarded up. So was Johnson Shoe Store, where he'd acquired his first sneakers, and the Metropolitan Movie Theater.

Lifeless, they moldered behind weathered plywood graying from years in the harsh High Plains sun. It did the same to people. He glanced at the sidewalk. A sprig of ragweed pushed about three inches above a crack in the pavement—completely safe from accidental trampling.

He entered the Chick 'n' More. He nodded greetings to the clutch of old-timers—Eddie Fowles, Ben Lambert, and Tony Gallegos—seated as if by natural law at their usual Formica-topped table in the corner. His nose experienced the usual mixed feelings about the pervasive smell of mature grease frying. He quick-stepped to the small back room where the Rotary Club members sat around a larger Formica table.

"I'll have the special," he said to Helen, the waitress, who was leaving. He didn't bother to ask what the special might be. He knew: a slice of well-done roasted beef that had drowned in a pool of dark, tasteless gravy, which oozed over the top of equally tasteless mashed potatoes next to gray-green string beans fresh from a can. On separate plates would be foam rubber rolls and a salad of iceberg lettuce leaves and two slices of a gas-ripened tomato. The Chick 'n' More special never varied.

"I'll have coffee, too," he called after Helen. Then he murmured greetings to his fellow Rotarians and took a seat.

"I have sad news to bring to you," intoned Sweeney Rotary president Ron Suffitt solemnly as he stood to open the meeting. Ron, who sold insurance out of a tiny office in his home, had been born in Sweeney—about the same year as Dave—and as Rotary president he was at the apex of a long career of mediocrity. But when intoning and solemnity were required, he could deliver. He was deeply solemn now.

"Ed has just informed me that he and Edna inherited a bit of money after her mother passed away last month—she wisely had bought life insurance—and they're thinking of buying a motor home and moving to Florida. They've tried to sell the Chick 'n' More—I know you've all heard about that—but they've had no takers, so they're shutting the place down and hoping things will look better later."

Dave groaned. Everyone looked at him as if he'd yawned in church.

"This is the last time we'll be able to meet here," Ron continued. "We'll have to find a new meeting place."

Dave groaned again. Again everyone stared at him.

"There isn't a new meeting place," he said, louder than he'd intended. Then after an internal what-the-hell, he continued. "Let's see, shall we go to the new Ramada Inn and Conference Center, down near the

Interstate exit? Or perhaps the Hampton Suites, near the mall. Or more realistically, maybe we can use Chester Smith's garage, now that the Cub Scouts don't meet there anymore."

"If you attend all the meetings, you get a merit badge," guffawed Tom Binks. Binks, a Sweeney native who worked for the natural gas company, was known as a blowhard and professional lowlife whose off-work time primarily was spent neglecting his large family, who lived in an undermaintained double-wide at the edge of town. For Dave he performed the useful function of dampening excess sentimentality about small-town wholesomeness. Dave wished the gas company would appoint another representative to the Rotary Club, one who would contribute more than noise.

Ignoring him, Dave continued, "What's wrong with us? We act as if everything is just fine, when we all know this town is dying under our feet."

Uncharacteristically, everyone was silent.

Then Nettie Wilkin spoke. The oldest of the Rotarians, she was the owner of the Style Salon, where Sweeney's elderly women went to have their hair done in colors rarely seen outside of glaciers. Adjusting her glasses so she could look squarely at everyone, she said, "Dave's right. I remember when Mount Dora was a lively place. Now it's all but a ghost town. So are most of the other towns in Kiowa County. That's where Sweeney's headed. And we all know it. We just don't want to talk about it."

People shifted uneasily in their seats and shot glances at each other.

"But people are starting to talk about it," said Leland Morton finally. He was a longtime local rancher who also served as town manager. "They complain to me about it, want to know what I'm going to do about it. I don't know what the hell to do."

From the silence it was apparent that no one else in the room did either. Underscoring the situation's gravity, for the first time in memory Ron had neglected to call the meeting to order and read the minutes from the last meeting.

Dave stared at the meal that had appeared before him. Then he surveyed the restaurant as if seeing it for the first time. So this was the end? Never again would he gaze at the restaurant's faux-walnut paneling, balance on the wobbly vinyl seats, taste the mint-flavored toothpicks at the counter, add his gum to the ancient strata stuck beneath the tabletop, layers dating to when he and his high school friends had ordered burgers and fries and Cokes. A lifetime spent in this wretched little restaurant, now it would close? He was flummoxed to realize he would miss it.

He asked, "What will Helen do?" Helen was the cafe's only waitress. She'd started at the Chick 'n' More when she was in high school more than thirty-five years ago, and she'd gotten old and rundown along with the restaurant. Now she was raising her three grandchildren while her daughter was in California tagging after her latest worthless boyfriend, who was about to achieve rock stardom any day now. What would Helen do when the Chick 'n' More closed?

"If this town's going to survive, we've got to do something," Dave said flatly.

"Why didn't Billy the Kid come by here, so that we could tell tourists how he shot up the town, or at least slept here," said Fred Yoder as he poured spilled coffee from his saucer back into his cup. For more than forty years he'd been the town's barber, operating out of one of the few shops still open on Main Street, yet even his business was dwindling. His only customers were elderly ranchers and other locals who usually wore hats and didn't care how they looked. Sweeney's young boys insisted on having their hair cut anywhere else.

"Look at what Fort Sumner's done with Billy the Kid," Yoder said. "It's too bad Billy didn't pass by Sweeney."

"Screw Billy," said Roger Rollins, the local veterinarian. Looking around the table as if daring anyone to contradict him, he continued, "Nobody goes out of their way for Billy. And what tourists? Let's face it, ladies and gentlemen, we're ninety boring miles from I-40, and Tucumcari is the closest town—we are way out of anyone's way. Besides, Sweeney didn't even exist when Billy was around."

It was true. Like many High Plains New Mexico towns, Sweeney had been born after 1900 during a brief homesteader boom that coincided with an ephemeral rainy cycle. Hopeful farmers arrived to lay out 160-acre farmsteads all over the plains, post offices sprouted in general stores and ranch headquarters, and towns such as Sweeney sprang up like mushrooms after a rain. But then the rains failed, and most of the farmers moved on or became ranchers whose stock could survive on the tough, short grass. When the dirt roads were paved in the 1950s and the remaining population could travel elsewhere for cheaper goods and services, the little communities wilted and died. Yet somehow Sweeney had survived. Until now.

"Okay, so what *would* bring people here?"

"Nothing ever happened here."

"We happened here."

"That's my point."

"Too bad aliens didn't come here, like they did in Roswell," said Yoder, slurping his coffee. "Make a few of those crop circles, like they did over in England . . ."

"If we had crops," sniped Roger.

" . . . or make something like that Stonehenge. I'm told that's a fierce tourist attraction."

"Built by pagans!" The Reverend Wayne Fall rose from his seat to protest. He was pastor of Sweeney's only Protestant church. It had a denomination, but no one was quite sure what it was. Everyone was fairly sure it wasn't Seventh Day Adventist or Jehovah's Witnesses or Mormon, but after that no one knew or cared. The general theology ran toward Bible-quoting, sin-condemning—and lots of music. "Wishing we had pagan monuments is what happens when we don't open our meetings with a prayer and a Bible reading. As I have proposed on many occasions . . ." But his incipient sermon was headed off by Suffitt, who rose to ask for a report from the Civic Improvement Committee.

After the Rotarians heard that the flowers planted in front of the town offices had not yet died, the meeting settled into the comfort of "old business" before the desultory motion to adjourn. Ron said he would notify the members of the location of the next meeting, when a site was found. "Try Chester," someone said.

Before everyone left, Dave said decency demanded that the club give Helen a much larger tip than usual. Everyone agreed.

It took Dave five minutes to walk home, not that he needed to time it. He knew by instinct the walking time to everything in Sweeney. Once, in high school, he had bet that he could find his way from the school to the drugstore wearing a blindfold. He'd made a few miscalculations, but he'd made it. His instincts were even more finely tuned by now. Too bad he wasn't a Peeping Tom. He could prowl unseen without a flashlight throughout Sweeney—looking into boarded windows.

A metaphor for his life.

"Knock it off," he told himself as he walked through the front door of the Daly bungalow on Mangrove Street. "No more negativity."

The first sound he heard in the house was the mindless nattering of the TV, driving his spirits even lower. "Hi, team," he said with false cheer as he entered the living room, where his daughter and wife slouched in chairs. "The Rotary meeting lasted a little longer than usual."

Traci heaved a deep, obnoxious, teenage sigh and rolled her eyes. Joanie, his wife, just rolled her eyes.

Suddenly Dave felt he could not simply walk into the kitchen and read the newspaper. "Anybody feel like taking a drive? We could go up the road to Conejo. We could look for . . ." He didn't know what they could look for.

Traci looked at him like he'd suggested they go watch cans rust at the dump. "Wow! Conejo! All three buildings of it. Won't the kids at school be excited when I tell them I went to Conejo! Maybe we'll see a tumbleweed too." The sarcasm in her voice was as thick as used motor oil. She rolled her eyes again and returned to watching the TV. Traci never let a day pass without reminding her father how much she hated Sweeney and held him responsible for her being imprisoned here.

Dave looked at Joanie. Unlike Dave and Traci she had not been born in Sweeney; she'd been born in Los Angeles, a fact their daughter resented deeply. Responding to the pleading in Dave's voice she sighed and said, "Well, I guess I could stand to get out a bit." Then added, "To see the sights." The temptation was too great.

They drove the family's blue Chevy pickup down Main Street and turned left at the feedstore, onto County Road 49. At the junction at the end of town, Dave nodded toward a gnarly cluster of large, oddly shaped boulders. "Good old Indian Rocks," he said. Joanie ignored him.

Dave wondered whether he'd unconsciously chosen to go this route because Indian Rocks was the most conspicuous feature—no, the *only* conspicuous feature—on the otherwise featureless landscape. Though he was the local high school science teacher, he never understood what geological process had created this odd anomaly on the plains, but like all Sweeney natives over forty he was inordinately fond of it. As a child he'd clambered on them and played hide-and-seek around them. Locally, half a dozen stories circulated about the origin of the name: the rocks reminded people of a group of Indians watching the town; Indians had lived here; Indians had ambushed settlers here; an Indian chief had been killed at the rocks; Indians had a buffalo-hunting camp here.

As for the rocks themselves, Dave's favorite explanation was that the rocks were the fossilized droppings of a colossal dinosaur.

"Have you ever considered painting Indian Rocks?" Dave asked, hoping to break Joanie's icy silence. Aside from her parenting and part-time work at the Sweeney health clinic, Joanie had only her horse to occupy her time—and the horse had recently died. He'd been suggesting that Joanie take up painting, which she'd once studied in college.

"No, I think Albert Bierstadt said everything that could be said about Indian Rocks."

Dave dropped the subject.

After Indian Rocks, the drama of the land became more muted: endless swells on a sea of short-grass prairie stretching without interruption to a distant, level horizon. To most people, the plains were the epitome of monotony, but he saw beauty and variety in the grasslands. The grass changed color with the seasons, even a blush of green in a wet year. Subtle depressions known as playas became ephemeral lakes, then brief grasslands, attracting antelope. Prehistoric Indians had once stalked game here, leaving behind projectile points. With the seasons passed the slow parade of High Plains wildflowers—mahogany-and-yellow coneflowers, yellow sunflowers, white milkweed, pink-purple bergamot, blue-violet asters, and many, many more—species that in wet times could turn the grasslands almost gaudy with color.

Dave allowed that Joanie would have been justified in saying it didn't matter which road they took because from her perspective all the roads looked the same. He also knew he couldn't explain to her how to him each road was as distinct and familiar as the face of a relative. Up ahead on NM 49 was where he and Carl "Furrball" Furr had gotten Furrball's pickup stuck in the borrow pit and had to walk the three miles back to town with a High Plains blizzard at their backs. Farther up the road was where Uncle Willard had taken him pheasant hunting. In the field across the road he'd helped a friend's father bring in a crop of hay. And how could he forget the site where a car stuffed with him and his fellow teenagers one Halloween had gotten stopped by the deputy sheriff on suspicion that perhaps, just maybe, they had been involved in hurling pumpkins at the high school's front door.

Just beneath the darkening horizon were the decaying remains of the Henderson homestead: mud stucco dissolving in the infrequent rains, adobe bricks showing through. Near the home stood the skeleton of a dead windmill. Old Man Henderson had still lived there when Dave was a child.

On the opposite side of the road was a subtle rise topped by a crude, weathered wooden cross. No one knew whose grave it marked, but it too was a landmark in his personal geography. A local high school tradition required English teachers to ask their students to write stories based on the grave. Dave's story had told of a Buffalo Soldier separated from his troop who was killed by Comanches. Then he recalled Traci showing him the story she had written when her English teacher gave the same assignment; in it the cross marked the grave of a homesteader's daughter who had died of boredom.

"Look, an antelope!" exclaimed Dave, pointing to a pronghorn standing motionless on the prairie, the white of its rump and tan of its coat contrasting with the straw-colored grass. Mentioning the animal was a weak diversion, Dave knew; antelope were more common than jackrabbits on the plains around Sweeney, but despite that he never tired of seeing them. They reminded him that after all the years of farming and ranching here, the plains remained ancient and wild.

Joanie didn't bother to look. Instead she turned and looked hard at him. "It's time you told me why we're here."

Dave stopped the pickup and turned toward her. "The Chick 'n' More is closing. Sweeney is dying. We talked about it in the Rotary meeting." He briefly summarized the discussion.

"Look, honey," said Joanie, "I know you love Sweeney, and I respect that. But the town today isn't the town you knew. It *is* dying. It's sad, but things change, and we have to accept and adapt. I hate to say it, but we have to begin thinking about our future—and Traci's. Can we really ask her to spend the rest of her youth in a place she hates?"

Dave's shoulders sagged. She was right. But once he left Sweeney, he would never return. The town and all the memories it held would be lost to him forever.

Memories of his mom and dad. Together they had run the local newspaper, the *Sweeney Oracle and Independent*, "Serving Kiowa County and Beyond," until it folded in the 1960s. His parents kind of folded too, lingering on in town for a few years until heart disease eventually claimed them both, five months apart. Dave's sister, Diane, six years older than him, had built upon her newspaper experience to get a journalism degree and now was a Pacific Rim correspondent for a British financial publication. At least that was what she was doing the last he'd heard. She never returned to Sweeney after their parents died, and she and Dave had little in common—least of all caring about Sweeney. Like his parents had.

"I don't know what to do," he said to Joanie. "I suppose I should be looking for jobs, sending out applications. And I have been looking at what schools have openings, I really have. But it's like looking through catalogs for ways to spend money you're going to inherit from a dear relative who isn't dead yet."

"But do you really want to be the last one left standing when everyone else has moved on?"

He thought of his parents after the paper died. Why *did* he stay? Was he hiding from something? "No, and I don't want Traci to be either."

"I knew you'd feel that way."

"But, you know, there are advantages to living in a small town," Dave said, starting the pickup. "It's not all bad. We don't have to worry about crime or safety."

"Neither do the people at the South Pole."

"Cold, that was cold."

Dave and Joanie returned home to a catastrophe. Traci was hysterical. "This can't happen! This is the end!"

While Dave and Joanie were gone one of Traci's friends had phoned with the news that Jeff Wiggins would be moving. His parents had sold the ranch, and they were all moving to Florida. Since early childhood, Traci, like all the local girls, had worshiped Jeff. And now that he finally was beginning to show an interest in her, he was leaving forever. For a teenage girl, it was an asteroid striking the earth.

"I can't believe this is happening! Now . . . now there's . . . nothing. Nothing! I hate this stupid town. *I hate this stupid town!*" She dissolved into tears and fled weeping to her room. Joanie looked at Dave.

"Hey, it's not Sweeney's fault his folks sold the ranch," Dave protested. But he knew that in fact it was Sweeney's fault. And he knew the time had come to begin sending applications.

Dave sought oblivion in a football game on TV. Sometime in the third quarter, having failed to find a reason to care which team won, Dave dozed. The phone rang. He answered it.

Dave had known Roger's voice since high school, where he had a reputation of being wild, despite also being the valedictorian of his tiny class. That was among the advantages of a small town school: you could be the class rowdy, the class clown, and the most-likely-to-succeed all at the same time. That certainly had described Roger. And despite going away to college and returning as a respected veterinarian, he hadn't lost a certain outlaw sense of humor that in most people rarely survived adolescence. Dave suspected that one reason Roger chose to return to Sweeney, meager pickings even for a vet in ranch country, was that here he could preserve remnants of that outlaw part of himself. He also was the closest Dave had to a best friend.

Now he listened as Roger said, "I've been thinking about what you said this afternoon, at the meeting. It was all true, we do have to do something—and I think we can. But it can't be everyone."

"What do you mean?"

"We need to talk. I can think of a couple of other people who might be receptive and should be involved. Let's get together."

"I don't know what you're talking about."

"Tomorrow morning at 8:30 at the Chick 'n' More."

"Dammit, Roger, you don't have to sound so conspiratorial."

Roger chuckled. "The Chick 'n' More, 8:30. Be there. The password is 'I'm a dipshit.'"

Nettie was depressed as she walked back to the Style Salon after the Rotary Club meeting. So the Chick 'n' More was closing? Well, perhaps it was inevitable. She could remember when Sweeney had four restaurants—and five saloons. And a clothing store, a drugstore, a station for the railroad that ran through the town on its way to the coal fields near Raton, four churches, two banks, and even a local newspaper.

One by one they had withered and vanished. She looked at where the fanciest restaurant, the Cattle Car, had been, now a vacant lot, the long-abandoned building bulldozed about five years ago. One of several vacant lots along Main Street, the stigmata of hard times and poverty, like missing teeth.

How had it come to this? The same way she'd gotten old, so gradually she hardly knew it was happening until one day she looked in the mirror and her grandmother looked back.

The farms had gone first. The wet cycle had been followed by drought.

Then plummeting demand for coal sank the railroad. Drought and the Depression winnowed small ranches into fewer, bigger ranches. When the rural roads were paved, local people drove to places like Tucumcari and Las Vegas for more and cheaper goods and services. Gradually the town began drying up, shutting down.

But, dammit, towns weren't people. Towns didn't have to die. They could grow and thrive as they got older.

Her depression deepened as she opened the door to the Style Salon—locking it had never entered her mind—and reversed the "Closed" sign to read "Open." Except for her years on the rodeo circuit with Johnny, she'd spent her entire life in this little town. And unlike the meeting's other Rotarians she could remember a vastly different Sweeney: Main Street filled with cars on Saturday when farmers and ranchers came in to do their shopping, dances to live fiddle music in the Grange Hall, Fourth of July parades and barbecues in the park, rodeos at the county fairgrounds, the townwide celebration when Robby McPherson led the Sweeney football team to a state championship. He'd gotten a college football scholarship, flunked out, and never returned.

Now the only time Sweeney's citizens got together was for funerals.

Dave and Roger were right: Sweeney had to do more than just survive, it had to recover. Otherwise, it wasn't worth it.

As she was leaving the Style Salon later that afternoon, little Sammy Edwards rode up on his bike, handed her a folded note, and rode off. It read: "Important meeting tomorrow morning, 8:30, the Chick 'n' More. Sweeney needs you."

Leland Morton shoved a George Strait tape into his pickup's tape player as he steered the vehicle out of the town offices parking lot. He didn't bother looking for traffic, but before driving away he paused to look at the little building. It was older than he was, built by the federal Works Progress Administration during the Depression. They'd built well then; the solid stone structure had withstood almost eighty years of High Plains seasons and even a small tornado. It likely would outlast Sweeney itself.

As the early evening lights of Sweeney receded in the rearview mirror and George sang of other heartaches, Leland reached into the glove compartment, found the familiar round Skoal container, opened it, and extracted a joint. He lit it with the truck's cigarette lighter, took a deep toke, held it, and then exhaled. He took another hit, butted the joint, and put the roach back in the Skoal can.

Leland had first tasted pot when he went away to the state agricultural school, back in the late fifties. Pot was several years from being popular, but a few people had tried it, and he was one of them. He liked it. He also found that pot was a welcome alternative to the most popular drug on campus—alcohol. By graduation he knew he and alcohol were not going to have a good relationship, and having weed around made it much easier to break up with booze. He kept in touch with a few pot suppliers from college, friends who were making the most of their horticultural education, and he bought what he needed on occasional trips. He hadn't smoked when Ruth was alive and Grant still lived at home, but after her death seven years ago and with his son living in Chicago, he welcomed its company on the long drives home and the longer nights.

He rolled down the window of the pickup, stuck his elbow out, leaned back, and as George crooned he thought about Sweeney.

Without Ruth and Grant, Sweeney was all he had. Leland had entertained fantasies of Grant getting his college degree, then returning home to run the ranch with him, eventually continuing the line of fathers and sons to own the ranch since his great-grandfather established it in the 1920s. With Grant's degree in economics perhaps he could even figure out a way to make the ranch profitable.

But instead Grant had sent home a letter from college announcing that he was gay, had always been gay, and thus would not be returning to Sweeney. Leland and Ruth had been stunned. Looking back they could see that while Grant had seemed to enjoy many aspects of ranching, he never fit into the ranching community, was withdrawn around people, and had no close friends, except for school classmate Kathy Larkin, a year younger. After the initial shock, Ruth had gently guided Leland to as much acceptance as he was capable of. Grant hadn't been effeminate, had even wrestled steers in the local rodeos—how could he be gay? And how could Leland explain that to the ranching community? When Grant returned twice a year to visit, it was an extremely awkward time for both of them; by mutual unspoken agreement they seldom went into Sweeney or visited other ranches, and upon departing Grant left no doubt he would not be returning to become a rancher. Especially as he made more money as a financial consultant in a year than the ranch did in decades.

So now the ranch would follow Sweeney—and even Leland him-self—into an empty future.

But not yet. He had no trouble balancing his roles as ranch manager and town manager. Neither the cows nor the people—both dwindling—made many demands upon him these days, and he was determined to do what he could to keep the town alive, even if he didn't have a clue what that might be.

George Strait's mournful ballad ended and was followed by another. Leland's mind slipped into the familiar rut of wondering just what might keep Sweeney alive. He felt he was letting the people of Sweeney down, though he knew they were too decent to blame him. Actually, Sweeney had lasted longer than most High Plains towns. But people still came to him for answers—and he didn't have any. He knew where to get a good price on tires for the town's snow plow, but how to keep Sweeney alive. . . .

Not that he hadn't tried. He'd applied for state and federal rural assistance programs and even got money to buy new equipment and hire kids to clean up the playground, but those were like putting tape on a shredded paper bag.

He'd considered "rural economic development," but he couldn't imagine the industry that would locate in Sweeney. He grimly imag-ined the pitch: "Come to Sweeney, Sweetheart of the Plains, Gateway to Anywhere Else. We offer a small, aging, and technologically illiterate workforce, declining and underperforming schools, staggering trans-portation costs, remoteness from markets, no amenities, and no busi-ness infrastructure. On the other hand, you can have lots of abandoned buildings for a song." No, a business locating in Sweeney would be like a kayaker moving to the Sahara.

On many nights as he drove he thought about what possibly could resuscitate the town. He thought of Roswell, where the crash of a stray, and secret, weather balloon during the Cold War had kicked up an ever-expanding cloud of bullshit about a crashed spaceship and a top-secret cover-up of alien bodies. Now Roswell with its hokey UFO museums had a modest tourist industry. But no aliens had landed near Sweeney, unless you counted Scratch 'n' Sniff, the town eccentric.

Leland thought of Marfa, Texas, which had made a cottage indus-try out of mysterious lights floating in the distance on certain nights. Many people said they were just car headlight reflections, but that didn't stanch the flow of people who came to see for themselves.

Nor could Sweeney play the famous outlaw card. Clayton, New Mexico, had created a minor industry out of being the place where robber Black Jack Ketchum was clumsily hung and decapitated. But nothing like that had ever happened in Sweeney.

Leland thought of the British film, *The Full Monty*, in which a group of unemployed and desperate men in a grimy and decaying English industrial town had chosen to raise money by stripping, full frontally nude, before an audience of the town's women. "Hell, that's nothing," thought Leland. "I'd never wear clothes again if I thought it would keep Sweeney alive."

Stonehenge. Yoder was right. There was a tourist attraction. Low maintenance, doesn't need advertising, and all the heavy lifting was done millennia ago. But Neolithic monument builders had been scarce around Sweeney. Maybe centuries hence people would come to marvel at the ruins of the town's concrete silo, but he doubted it.

He'd thought about staging an old-time cattle drive and inviting noncowboys to come along. The ranching community could get behind that idea. But a little asking around revealed that other communities had beaten Sweeney to the punch, with better accommodations and probably more cattle. Still, the temptation lingered. . . .

"Come experience the cattle drives as they *really* were: hot, dusty, uncomfortable, and boring. You'll drink the same wretched coffee as the real cowboys, freeze in your blankets just like they did, have your nostrils filled with the scent of cow shit day after day, and when the whole adventure is over, get blind drunk in a cheap saloon and wake up broke and with gonorrhea just like they did. It will be the best night you won't remember."

Sweeney had nothing. Leland occasionally wondered if that wasn't what made it unique. Towns that truly had nothing distinct about them actually were quite rare. No native son who became famous, no well-known natural disaster, no huge concrete sugar beet sculpture, no notorious chile recipe, no world's biggest ball of baling wire—nothing. Maybe that would be Sweeney's portal to fame: Nothingville. For the most jaded of travelers, when you've seen and done it all—come experience the ultimate Zen travel destination, the town with nothing.

Nothing. Through his pickup's pitted and bug-spattered windshield he gazed at the evening sky. For more than sixty years he'd watched as the vast High Plains sky turned from day to night; he never tired of it. Tonight a few high horsetail clouds were like pinkish-yellow brush-strokes across a pale-blue canvas. Beautiful. Nothing?

Leland sighed. He returned to the Skoal can and took one more deep hit off the roach.

Following well-worn ruts in a dirt road, Leland finally arrived at an open gate, and then after a quarter mile the ranch house. Climbing from the pickup, he paused and glanced upward. Could anyone ever tire of seeing the Milky Way in the clarity of the High Plains sky at night? The stars were so thick and bright they obscured the constellations. As far as his eye could see, the only competing light was the dim 25-watt bulb above the entrance to the barn.

Leland strolled there and entered, savoring the uniquely blended smell of livestock, hay, feed, and manure, listening for the reassuring stir of the animals waiting for him. A horse nickered in its stall. A goat nuzzled the boards of its pen. A long-haired yellow cat, Amarillo, rubbed against his legs as he scooped feed from a bin.

Ruth had loved the animals. Now they allowed Leland to believe that she was still here, a gentle buffer against the emptiness, like the light above the barn.

Inside the house, after feeding the cat, Leland noticed the message light on his phone. The message was short: "The Chick 'n' More, tomorrow morning, 8:30."

Kathy Larkin rubbed her temples as she drove her vintage red Ford Mustang toward Sweeney from the east, directly into the setting sun. The backlighting silhouetted the thirty-foot-tall water tower on which big black letters proclaimed Sweeney. "The Sweeney skyscraper," she thought for perhaps the thousandth time. Sweeney also was proudly introduced by the town's booster sign: "The Sweeney Rotary Club welcomes you to Sweeney—Come to Play, Come to Stay." Beneath that was another sign put up by the high school spirit club: "Sweeney, Home of the Stompin' Cowboys." Beneath were smaller signs for the 4-H Club, the Kiowa County Extension Service, the High Plains Soil and Water Conservation District, the Sweeney-Conejo Homemakers Club, and the Sweeney Community Church. Once a sign had proclaimed the population, but it had been removed when the population dropped beneath one thousand, a third of what it once had been.

Kathy slowly shook her head.

She'd had a hard day and was eager to get home. She'd had to help move ninety-year-old Mrs. Gonzalez out of her home in San Jon. Mrs. Gonzalez had not gone quietly. But High Plains Mental Health Services, the social services agency out of Tucumcari for which Kathy worked, had determined that Mrs. Gonzalez could no longer care for herself and was, in fact, a menace to herself and others. She'd taken to leaving her house and wandering about the streets of San Jon stark naked. She'd been blamed for at least one traffic accident. When citizens tried tactfully to intervene in her Godiva-like wanderings, she became belligerent. Mrs. Gonzalez had been clothed when Kathy and her coworkers arrived to move her to new quarters; that was not the case when they left.

A hard day.

When Kathy had joined High Plains Mental Health Services, she'd insisted that none of her clients have any connection with Sweeney. She couldn't bring herself to delve into the inner demons of the people she'd grown up with. Besides, she told herself, she already knew how crazy they all were.

So she worked in other High Plains towns, most of which were as much like Sweeney as one dried husk of corn to another. "Husk towns," Kathy called them. Withering. Just like the people in them. Kathy hadn't really wanted to work in eastern New Mexico, but her parents' rapid health decline had coincided with college graduation and a failed relationship, so she'd accepted when a high school acquaintance had pulled strings and found her a job with High Plains. It was to have been a temporary option, until things changed. But things didn't change, and now she'd been with the agency for ten years, which she felt made her just as dysfunctional as her clients.

She drove down Sweeney's Main Street, then turned left onto Honeysuckle Street. She was proud of the Mustang. It was by far the classiest, sexiest car in Sweeney. And she didn't care that people in Sweeney no longer were impressed or knew she'd inherited it from her father when he'd stopped driving. Her sexy red Mustang was a bird flipped in the face of her present life.

She turned the car into the driveway of the two-story Victorian house where she lived with her parents. Someday she should hire someone to paint the house; it deserved better care than she gave it. She'd lived in this house her entire life, and as long as her parents were alive and needed her, she would continue living in it.

"That you, Kathy?" came a creaky female voice from the living room as Kathy entered the kitchen.

"Just me," answered Kathy. She wanted to say, "No, it's Dorothy from Oz, and I just wanted to tell you that Toto and I will be taking a vacation." And her mother would answer, "That's nice."

Her father, she knew, was upstairs in his den. She wasn't sure what he did there. Probably slept. But he always came down for meals.

"You wouldn't believe the terrible things people said and did on the TV today," clucked her mother as Kathy came into the room. Mother, a retired teacher, spent most of her time now watching trashy TV. Unfortunately, lately she'd been mistaking TV for reality.

"I just hope that poor young woman someday will learn the true father of her baby," Mother continued. "I'll think about her and pray for her."

"That's kind of you, Mother," said Kathy, adding to herself, "Maybe you can introduce her to that nice young man you met yesterday who doesn't know how many kids he's fathered. What's one more?"

Kathy went back into the kitchen to begin preparing dinner. She scowled. She hated her elderly parents' rigid schedules. Dinner had to be exactly at six or they would begin asking about it.

Around her feet curled her old gray cat, Rasta. She'd adopted him following a phone call from Roger Rollins saying a hard-luck kitten had made his way to the veterinary clinic and needed a good home. "I'll bring him right over," he'd said before she could refuse. "This is definitely a quality cat." And he'd been right, despite the cat's scroungy appearance and king-of-the-road attitude. She admired that about Rasta, that he lived life on his terms. But he also was a good friend and faithful companion. He slept on her bed at night, and many evenings, when the air and the silence in the house were desperately dead, she would take Rasta for a leisurely walk around the block. The neighborhood dogs long ago had learned that Rasta was not a fun cat to chase.

After dinner and the dishes she was finally free—to do what? A few friends from high school had never left Sweeney, but they were married, with children. They reminded Kathy that she was still single, and her dependents were in their seventies. Not much they could talk about except Sweeney—Kathy's least favorite topic. If only Sweeney had a good bar where she could meet new people, talk, listen to music, shoot pool—*anything* but endure another night in this house with these old people.

Kathy recalled the time she told her mother that she was going to spend the weekend in Santa Fe, just having fun. Her mother had clucked and said, "Do you think that's sensible? You never know what kind of people you'll meet in those places." And Kathy had blurted, "Why do you think I'm going?" The humor of the recollection faded as she washed the dishes.

"All the burdens of marriage," she said, "and none of the joys."

After dinner, the dishes, and seeing that her parents were in their usual stations—her mother in front of the TV, her father in his room—she retired to her room—and the rest of the world.

As she waited while the computer booted up she reflected that if she had no real life, neither did millions of other people. And through the miracle of the Internet, they could all interact.

One visit to a relatively safe chat room had convinced her that she did not want to run away and join that circus. But she faithfully checked several news sites each day, if only to reassure herself that a larger world existed beyond Kiowa County. As a child she'd been a grizzly for knowledge, ravenous and omnivorous. Now she roamed the Internet pursuing her many interests as she once had ranged through the public library, currently open only one night a week.

As Kathy finally prepared to shut down the computer, she heard a knock on her door. It was her parents. Her father had in his hand a slip of paper. "While you were at work a man called."

Kathy raised her eyebrows in surprise. "Did he leave a message?"

"Yes, he did. I wrote it down." Her father handed her the slip of paper.

It said: "The Chick 'n' More. 8:30 tomorrow morning. Be there. The Phantom."

"That's a very strange message, Kathy," said Mother. "I'm not sure you should be meeting a strange man who calls himself a name like that."

"It's okay, Mother, I know who it is." Yes, she growled inwardly, the tasteless, inappropriate humor was as good as a signature.

When Rudd Torgelson arrived Tuesday morning at the sprawling corrugated tin building that was Torgelson Farm and Ranch Implements, he was surprised to find the light blinking on the answering machine on his cluttered desk. By choice he had no close friends, and most business contacts had learned that phone messages were not appreciated and rarely answered. Rudd let the phone light blink while he changed into his grease-stained work clothes, and only after he had poured from a grease-stained Thermos a cup of the bitter coffee he made at home did he finally pick up the phone.

Immediately he recognized the thinly disguised voice insisting he attend a meeting at the Chick 'n' More at 8:30, a half-hour away, but he had no idea why. He couldn't imagine any local project about which he gave a shit, and besides he had to replace a valve in Willy Trujillo's tractor.

Still, the mystery of the call sufficiently intrigued him that he gruffly closed the garage doors and began walking toward the Chick 'n' More. He didn't bother changing his clothes.

And sure enough, as he strode into the back room of the Chick 'n' More, his suspicions were confirmed. There was Roger Rollins. He recognized the others too. Rollins, Dave Daly, Kathy Larkin, Leland Morton, and Nettie Wilkin. But it struck Rudd as he grunted a greeting and sat down that perhaps the greatest anomaly in the group was himself. His family was the oldest and most respected in Sweeney, once holders of vast tracts of near-worthless farm and ranch land. Now he ran the local heavy equipment dealership, though increasingly his income came from repairs and parts, not sales of new equipment. An immensely tool-savvy man, he was the first and last resort any time a serious mechanical problem struck in Sweeney. He'd never been to college, or lived anywhere but Sweeney, but he was well read, well informed, and had good sense. People sought his advice for nonmechanical problems as well. Despite this, he kept to himself, belonged to no community organizations, and was known for being gruff.

"Thanks for coming, Rudd," said Roger. As Rudd pulled up a chair Roger got up and closed the door. Everyone exchanged "What the hell?" glances. Returning to his seat, Roger continued. "I'll cut to the chase: Sweeney is dying. Those of you who were at the Rotary meeting yesterday know what I'm talking about. Am I correct in assuming you're with us on this, Rudd?"

The big man nodded.

"So, we know we've got to do something, but we don't know what we can do." Nods and skeptical looks all around.

Dave spoke, "I must say that while I want Sweeney to survive, lately I've concluded it needs to do more than just survive. I don't want Sweeney to just be on life-support. The kids here hate this place, and I'm not sure I blame them. If we're going to do something for Sweeney, I want it to bring the town back to *life*. Make it worth living in again."

Kathy Larkin, who had loathed the town as a kid, spoke. "I second that. I have a certain fondness for Sweeney too, but as you know I'm not here by choice right now. I don't want Sweeney to die either, but it's got to become better than *this*."

"Sweeney wasn't always like this," huffed Nettie. She was by twenty years the oldest person in the room, and her fierce loyalty to Sweeney was well known. "Sweeney used to be a lively place."

"Agreed," said Roger. "Look, this isn't your average Rotary Club meeting. We're here to *do* something. I have a plan. It will take each of us to pull it off—but only if you agree to it and swear, really swear, confidentiality."

"Do we have to decide now?" asked Nettie.

"I'm afraid so. The moment of decision has come. And even if you choose not to participate, you have to swear confidentiality or leave now."

Dave arched an eyebrow as he looked at Rollins. He didn't know what his friend had in mind, but at least this part of it was no joke.

"I'm in," Dave said. "For the whole pot."

"Me too," said Kathy.

"Well, I don't want to be left out," said Nettie.

Leland nodded.

They looked at Rudd. He scowled and then shrugged. "Well, I'll probably regret this, but . . . what the hell."

Afterward, as Nettie, Dave, Leland, Kathy, and Rudd left separately from the meeting, they were united by a single thought: "That's the most harebrained idea I ever heard."

The meeting at the Chick 'n' More had gone well, Roger thought as he walked back to the All Creatures Veterinary Clinic. No one had balked, everyone had agreed to his plan. Even Kathy Larkin, who he knew had little fondness for Sweeney—and even less for him. It was a cockamamie plan at best, with a minuscule chance of succeeding, but at the least it would shake things up a bit—and Sweeney definitely needed to be shaken up.

Perhaps that was his role in life, to shake things up, to initiate the enlivening events that good taste and good sense prevented others from attempting. That certainly had been his role in high school. His pranks and antics greatly relieved the school's almost fungal dullness. Of course, some of his stunts had been ill-conceived, and one had been cruel. He'd never ceased regretting that one.

But he nonetheless clung to his renegade, often adolescent persona, and perhaps he'd stayed in Sweeney because here people knew what to expect of him.

He couldn't think of many other reasons. Even after his father had a stroke, and his parents moved to Arizona—he'd stayed. When he brought his bride, Kim, here after getting his veterinary degree, he'd entertained fantasies of the two of them setting up a statewide network of animal rescue missions, but Kim had announced one day that Sweeney was all she'd expected—and less. Much less. She left, and he'd stayed.

He hadn't thought the marriage could be saved even if he'd gone with her, but Sweeney didn't have that much for him either. Certainly not if he wanted another mate. Sure, cowgirls were plentiful, and as a native-born vet he was eminently desirable. But he'd found them a little parochial for his taste. He recalled one girl who, when he said he hoped one day to visit Paris, had replied that she'd been there, and had been unimpressed by the shopping malls. She was referring to Paris, Texas.

So why did he remain in Sweeney? Was it because it was comfortable? He hoped that wasn't the reason.

Chapter Two

● RETURNING ALWAYS WAS THE HARDEST, physically and emotionally. For what seemed the hundredth time Joanie Daly tried to find a comfortable position in the back seat of the van. Long miles of straight, empty road, with Sweeney at the end. Was the trip worth it? Probably not, but did she—did any of them—have a choice?

They called themselves the Get-out-of-Dodge Girls, and once every four months a klatch of Sweeney women got out of Sweeney. Two days, one overnight. It was arranged with their employers and spouses. If they didn't like it, they would suffer subtle but severe repercussions. Early Saturday morning the women would pile into a van owned by one of the women and take turns driving to Santa Fe. There they'd begin with some power-shopping, then go out for a decadent dinner, followed by a visit to an Indian casino, before finally returning to a hotel suite where they would drink, play cards, tell jokes, and laugh until consciousness faded.

When Joanie was invited to join the group, she found the idea repellent, but she agreed to go, just once. Sure enough, it was just as loud, crude, boozy, and exhausting as she'd imagined—and she hadn't missed a trip since.

Now she slouched in silence, taking only slight comfort in knowing that most of her companions felt worse. No one said much on the trips home. Everyone was tired and short on sleep, a few were hung over. Joanie wasn't among them, at least not this time. Instead she sat in brooding dread of returning home, to the inevitable conflicts with Traci, to frustration with Dave, to the emptiness of Sweeney.

Returning after a weekend in Santa Fe was like painful drug withdrawal for it reminded her that once she had been part of the larger world, a young woman in southern California, instead of just another bored housewife stuck in nowhere.

She recalled her feelings upon first arriving in Sweeney. She'd been excited when Dave had told her they'd be living in ranch country, that the family house had a barn and corral behind it, that she could have a horse. During her childhood in Los Angeles, having a horse had been a fantasy, like becoming a movie star, and she'd been ecstatic when Dave told her that if they moved to Sweeney, she definitely could have a horse. She'd tried to temper her expectations, but she couldn't completely repress the TV image of the Ponderosa Ranch—high mountain pastures, split-rail fences, a log cabin framed by aspen groves and snow-capped peaks.

Instead, she found a two-story white frame house on a dusty street in a decaying little town on the dry plains of eastern New Mexico, the barn a dilapidated shack with just a couple of stalls, the corral a small pen enclosed by posts and wire. No split logs, no high mountain pastures, no snow-capped peaks.

Through Roger, Dave's high school friend and local vet, she'd acquired a horse, and also through him she'd found a soul mate, Roger's wife, Kim, who also had been brought to Sweeney as an innocent, hopeful young bride. Over countless cups of coffee they'd salved their disappointment by ridiculing Sweeney—"And then that guy made of petrified wood drove by the Chick 'n' More for the fourteenth time to check on whether anything had changed since the last time he'd been there. . . ." But when Roger and Kim had split up and Kim had bailed out of Sweeney, Joanie had stayed.

She told herself it was for Traci, that if nothing else Sweeney was a safe place to raise a young girl, in contrast to Southern California, but the safety came at a high price.

She looked at her companions. Each also was traveling the dark path of resignation.

They were an odd agglomeration. Two were natives of Sweeney, three, including Joanie, were from elsewhere. All but one were married, but following an unspoken rule they didn't talk about their husbands. Karen Suffitt was married to Ron Suffitt, her high school sweetheart, and she was comparably bland and colorless. Joanie had often reflected that Karen and Ron were among the few couples whose reputation would be enhanced by a sex scandal.

Connie Nesbitt, divorced, was Sweeney's realtor-in-residence. Her husband had decamped long before Joanie arrived in town, leaving Connie marooned in Sweeney with a young son. Joanie had wondered why Connie didn't return to Minnesota, from whence she had come, but all she would say was that the winters were better in Sweeney. Joanie was sure that was not the reason.

Vickie Gallegos, an elementary school teacher originally from Santa Rosa, was married to a local rancher. Together they were related to half the Hispanics in eastern New Mexico.

And Nettie Wilkin, a longtime widow, was the glue that held the group together, partly because of her venerable age but also because as proprietor of the Style Salon she knew the pulse of Sweeney better than anyone. Assuming Sweeney had a pulse, thought Joanie. Nettie actually professed affection for Sweeney. Tactfully, she seldom talked about it, except gently to keep things in check when sentiments regarding Sweeney were especially bitter. "Remember, Sweeney's just gotten old, as will we. At least you will. I'm plannin' on not being home when old age calls."

Now Joanie noticed Nettie was uncharacteristically somber on this trip. She knew the others also were wondering why but were reluctant to ask. They hoped Nettie would say something, if something needed to be said.

Now Nettie's funk had devolved into anger, and Joanie heard her muttering spitefully as she steered the van toward town.

"Nettie, what is *wrong*?" asked Karen.

"Oh, it's, it's . . . you ever go to the horse track?" Most of the women allowed they did not, at least not on a regular basis.

"And you see one horse in the paddock that you really like, that seems really special, so you bet on that horse, and then it doesn't just not win, it comes in dead last. You're mad at the horse for betraying you, for letting you down, even though the horse hadn't agreed to anything. And you're mad at yourself for being so naive and gullible. That's kind of what I'm feeling right now."

"And the horse might be . . . ?" Joanie let the question hang.

"Ladies, trust me. It's someone we all know, its name begins with S, and I don't want to talk about it."

That seemed to end it, and Joanie sank back into her slouch as the van pulled into town. Suddenly she was jolted upright by Nettie slamming on the brakes and gasping, "Oh my. Oh my, oh my, oh my."

"What is it, Nettie? Are you all . . . Omigod!"

Ahead, framed by the receding lines of Main Street, was Indian Rocks—but with a difference. The largest and longest rock had been upended and now pointed skyward. With two round smaller rocks at its base, it looked exactly like a giant phallus.

Joanie felt like simultaneously screaming and laughing.

Nettie stomped on the accelerator and raced into town. Dula Roberts, the town marshal, sat in his car on Main Street. Nettie pulled up beside him and through the open window shouted, "What happened?"

"What do you mean?" replied Roberts.

"With *that!*" screamed Nettie, pointing at the rocks.

"I don't know. Nobody does. It's all anyone's been talking about since this morning."

Nettie glowered at the man and muttered an uncomplimentary reference to Roger Rollins. Joanie didn't have a clue what that was about.

Roberts, starting to get a little offended, said, "Look at the size of that rock! It's not like it was shoved up there by high school kids in their pickups. And it gets weirder than that. I'd send you up there to see for yourself, but I'm treating it as a crime scene."

"A crime scene?!" And with that Nettie sped off to take each woman home to consult her own information sources.

In Nettie's case, that was her sister, Vera, who had lots of time on her hands and used it to be current about *everything* in Sweeney, though lately that took less time than it once had. It took four busy signals before her sister answered.

"You're calling about the rocks."

"Of course I am. I asked that underinformed officer on Main Street, and all he could say was that no one knew what happened, that they were treating it as a crime scene."

"Oh, Nettie, it's all true. The first anyone knew about it was S&S running up and down Main Street raving about aliens and things coming to pass. Then everyone else saw it." "S&S" was the acronym by which

Sweeney's resident raving loony was known. It stood for "Scratch 'n' Sniff," inspired by the man's aversion to personal hygiene. No one knew his real name. He'd been S&S ever since he arrived in Sweeney years ago. S&S lived a simple, humble life of sleeping in sheds, wearing cast-off clothes, and scrounging for liquor and food, in that order. The booze often took him to a quasi-mystical and semiclothed state. Harmless, but you definitely didn't want to get downwind from him.

"Nettie, they say that rock weighs thirty tons, and overnight it went from lying down to being upright. I don't think even the Egyptians who built the pyramids could do that, and they had Moses and miracles to help them."

Nettie let that pass. "The cop suggested there was something else weird about the rocks."

"That's right," said Vera breathlessly. "There are strange holes up there, gouged into the ground. But there's nothing else. No tire tracks, no footprints. Of course, there's people who say they found other stuff up there, but they're keeping it quiet."

"They? Who is they?"

"Sheriff's office. Someone notified them. They sent a deputy out here to look around."

"What did he say?"

"He said, and I quote, 'Damnedest thing I ever saw.' That's it."

"Vera, do you know what that thing looks like?"

"Well, Nettie, I wasn't exactly born yesterday," Vera huffed. "I was married for forty years . . ."

"I didn't mean that. I mean, have people realized what we've got sticking up at the end of Main Street?"

"Nettie, I don't think there's a man, woman, child, or domestic animal anywhere near Sweeney who doesn't know what we've got here."

"Well, I hope nobody outside notices until we can do something about it. The very idea. . . ."

Nettie's next phone call was to Roger Rollins. "You said you were going to do something to Indian Rocks to attract attention. Is that . . . that . . . that *thing* what you had in mind?"

"Honest, no one who had seen the rocks in the ground would have noticed the resemblance. It's not apparent until you see it . . . erect like that." He started to giggle. Nettie hung up on him.

Dave Daly heard a car door slam and female feet running toward the house. Odd, Joanie never ran returning from one of her trips. "Dave!" she shouted. When he poked his head around the kitchen corner, she said, "You won't believe what I just saw!"

"Could it possibly have something to do with Indian Rocks?"

She stared at him, and then stammered, "Well . . . well . . . well . . ."

Dave shrugged. "Well, what can I say? S&S noticed it first, and the word spread pretty fast. No one seems to know anything about it." Dave recoiled at lying to Joanie, but he had taken an oath of silence, and the deception was well intentioned. The knowledge that most deceptions were well intentioned only increased his misgivings. To distract himself, he asked, "Want to see it?"

"Can we?"

"Sure, everyone else has."

As they walked to the rocks, Dave explained that, crime scene or not, everyone in Sweeney had been to gawk at the rocks. Finally, the sheriff's office posted a deputy at the site to keep people from disturbing the unexplained marks. These consisted of three holes, about four feet in diameter and three feet deep in the hard, caliche soil, tapering downward like inverted cones. At the bottom of each was a single black volcanic rock. The holes were equidistant from each other, each exactly fifty feet from the uplifted stone and forming a triangle. Fifty feet beyond these holes were six smaller but similar holes, again equidistant from each other and aligned with the inner holes to create a hexagon enclosing the triangle. Each also contained a black rock. It was not the work of prairie dogs.

People were still milling around the site when Dave and Joanie arrived. They had invited Traci, but she and her friends already had visited the rocks. Regardless of how they felt about the rocks, nothing would keep the local youth away, especially when there were rumors of mysterious signs. This was far more exciting than Derrick Jensen's claim to have found a human bone in the old cemetery.

Dave said hi to a few friends. He echoed the deputy when asked his opinion. "Damndest thing I ever saw."

By this time S&S had established himself as the local authority on the phenomenon, strutting around like a drunken ostrich, holding forth to anyone who would listen. "I was walking down the street, minding my own business, when there it was, risin' like a miracle at the end of the street. It was kind of eerie-like, and it seemed to put off a kind of power. Nasterdormus predicted something like this. It's comin' to pass. It's all comin' to pass."

Dave and Joanie circled the site, peering into the holes and gazing at the monolith.

"Well, well, . . . I'm speechless. Sweeney didn't prepare me for this," Joanie said as she stood before the towering stone. "It sure wasn't what I expected when I woke up this morning." She shook her head. "That trip to Santa Fe seems a long time ago. What do you make of it?"

"Beats the hell out of me," said Dave, stuffing his hands in the pockets of his jeans.

She pointed to the pits.

"What could make something like that? Couldn't highway construction equipment do something like that?"

"Not without leaving obvious tracks and signs—and I don't see any."

"But you don't believe this was made by unnatural forces, or aliens, do you?"

"Of course I don't, but I don't know what to believe. This phallus stone has got me stumped."

She elbowed him in the ribs.

As they drifted around the site, Dave sampled peoples' opinions:

"It's a cross."

"No, it's a pentagram."

"Notice how it points north."

"Look how the pits are aligned with the rock."

"I think it's a hoax."

"Okay, then tell me how that rock got uplifted like that? I've never seen the piece of heavy equipment that could raise something like that. Road crews come to a rock like that, they blast it. It's too big to be moved intact."

"Well, the Stonehenge people did it."

"Yeah, and it took hundreds of men working for years. I haven't seen any ancient Britons working at Indian Rocks lately, have you?"

"This happened overnight. While we slept."

"Makes you wonder."

As Dave and Joanie were leaving, Dave noticed a TV crew setting up near S&S. "Uh-oh, let's to be sure to catch the news tonight."

"I think I'll take a walk," Dave announced not long after supper, though neither Joanie nor Traci was listening. Traci at the kitchen phone had just embarked upon the second of many long, intense conversations with her friends. Joanie, who also had calls to make, was badgering Traci. Good time for a walk.

He wasn't sure where he was going, he was just restless. The late May night was warm, the air as soft as rabbit fur. He walked down Main Street. There he noticed that he wasn't alone. Sitting in cars and lounging in doorways were dozens of his fellow citizens. They all faced the Rocks. (Already, the townspeople had ceased calling them Indian Rocks and now simply said the Rocks.) They were waiting for something to happen, perhaps the appearance of the aura S&S claimed to have seen. A few people wandered around, sampling rumors.

Roger Rollins ambled by. Nodding toward the Rocks he asked, "What do you think, an aura will appear?"

"Anything's possible," said Dave, "anything's possible. I think the strangest thing of all is Main Street tonight. When was the last time we saw this many people on Main Street in Sweeney?"

Roger surveyed the street. "As I recall, that would be when the state police set up a roadblock trying to catch that escaped homicidal maniac, 1967 I believe that was. Long time ago. This part of the state just doesn't get its fair share of escaped murderers."

"It's definitely an issue for the Chamber of Commerce."

"Yep, those were the good old days," added Roger.

Ken and Katy Watson wandered by, led by their young son. Ken worked at the county vehicle maintenance yard and repaired windmills on the side. Katy taught Christian preschool in her home.

"I don't put no stock in anything S&S says," stated Ken, "'specially about the Rocks glowing. But something made those pits out there. That's what troubles me."

"Are UFOs real, Dad?" asked the young boy.

"I don't know," said Ken.

"Are they, Mommy?"

"Well if they are, I wouldn't worry about them," pronounced Katy, ending the discussion.

Suddenly a collective gasp arose from Main Street. The Rocks! Circles of light were playing on them, moving over their surface, especially the uplifted one.

"It's aliens!" someone shouted.

"It's flashlights," someone else replied.

Abruptly the lights ceased as someone on Main Street trained a car spotlight on the Rocks. In the background could be seen fleeing adolescents.

"Damned kids," said Ken, shaking his head and smiling.

Suddenly another gasp swept the watchers. There, visible when the spotlight was turned off, was a definite glow, an eerie bluish-green.

"That ain't flashlights!"

No one was eager to approach the stone. And then, as subtly and as softly as it had come, the glow faded to darkness.

"Damn!" said Ken. Katy, her mouth wide open, was too stunned to reprove him for swearing.

Dave returned from his walk in time to catch the ten o'clock news. Traci and Joanie already were seated in front of the set. Neither greeted him as he sat down.

Apparently it was a slow news night, and Dave could imagine the TV producers saying, "Sweeney? This state has a Sweeney? Where the hell is that?" So this night they gave the town and its rocks a full ninety seconds. The newscasters, sensing that S&S's theories were more colorful than the "Beats me" comments of the town manager and police, featured him in their segment. Especially as he had been the first to see the "Sweeney Event" as the newscaster called it. S&S basked.

"It was glowing like it had a kind of halo or an aura about it. I could feel a kind of electricity coming from it." S&S hadn't mentioned that in his early accounts. "There's a power emanatin' from those rocks. They was chosen. This was predicted, it's things comin' to pass."

Mercifully, the phallic resemblance was lost on S&S, and the cameramen had been discreet in choosing angles from which to photograph it.

Not that Traci cared. Watching the news with her parents, she was beside herself.

"Just when I thought things couldn't get any worse!" she wailed. "How will all you parents react to mass teenage suicide? Now we not only live in a nothing town, but when we finally get noticed it's for an obscene rock.

"Oh, Dad, do we *have* to live here?" she pleaded. "Can't we leave?"

She turned and glared unspoken accusations at her mother. *You* were from Los Angeles. I could have been born there—exciting, trendy, glamorous—but instead *you* agreed to come to Sweeney. It's all *your* fault.

Joanie simply sighed. Maybe Traci was right, maybe agreeing to move with Dave to Sweeney was a mistake, maybe she should have held out for another New Mexico town, Albuquerque or Santa Fe.

Traci intensified her glare, then broke into sobs and fled to her room.

Chapter Three

♣ TWO WEEKS AFTER THE ROCK'S ARISING, a man in safari khakis and an African bush hat strode into the Sweeney town offices and stood before Leland Morton, who had been busy leaning back in his oak chair and staring at the clutter on his desk.

"Good morning, sir, I am Henri Barré, independent filmmaker, from Montreal." The man had an accent Leland was sure he'd never before heard in Sweeney. The man didn't extend his hand, so Leland didn't get up. Besides, no one he knew wore sweet cologne like that, and Leland feared contamination.

The man spoke again. "Would you be so kind as to direct me to the Druid Stone and the ley-line holes."

"Come again?" replied Leland.

"The stone that was uplifted in the center of pits laid out in a sacred Celtic geometry of cosmic energy points."

"Beg pardon?"

Then it dawned on Leland that the stranger was inquiring about Indian Rocks and the holes. "Oh, them. They're at the end of Main Street, look to your left, you can't miss 'em."

A half hour passed before the next independent filmmaker appeared, a deeply tanned young woman with black hair who clearly bought her clothes in the women's section of the same store as Monsieur Barré. "Is it true that the gentleman who first saw the Rock uttered words about this being connected with Nostradamus?"

"That would be a fact," answered Leland, leaning forward in his chair.

"And you, sir," asked the woman airily, "do you have reason to suspect this was part of Nostradamus's plan?"

"I don't rightly know, ma'am, but I assure you and the rest of the public that if Nostradamus is planning anything more in Kiowa County, our law enforcement will get him."

Kathy Larkin had hardly entered the front door of her home when the phone rang in the kitchen. Kathy got it before her parents. "Larkins, this is Kathy," she said, as if a call to the household could be for anyone but her. She recognized Leland's voice.

"Oh, hi, Leland. What's up? Er . . . sorry, perhaps that isn't a good phrase to use in Sweeney right now." Despite the difference in their ages, she'd always been close to the elderly rancher. In high school she'd been friends with his son, Grant, and had stood by Grant when in his senior year rumors circulated that he was gay. She'd remained friends with Grant when at college he confirmed the rumors were true. It was to Kathy that Leland had turned in his distress upon learning his son's orientation—they still were the only two people in Sweeney who knew about Grant—and she'd helped guide him through the difficult process of acceptance. He in turn was the only person with whom she could talk candidly about being trapped in Sweeney.

"Very funny. Kathy, I've just had my fourth 'independent filmmaker' come in since the Rock went up. And they aren't all little outfits. They've got rigs bigger than Minnesota snowbirds. We're getting noticed."

"And the problem is? Are they drunk and disorderly?"

"Change is coming, Kathy. This noon I went to the Chick 'n' More and couldn't even find counter space!"

"Hmmmm. That *is* serious. Imagine, Helen getting decent tips for a change," she said as she sat on a chair near the kitchen table and began removing her shoes.

"They say Will Diggs is renting space on his land to all the rigs, letting them use his shower and toilet."

"I always knew that man was a born entrepreneur."

"Yeah, well now that things have been set in motion, I thought I'd remind you that you once offered to be a temporary deputy if needed. I'm just letting you know it could happen."

"Thanks for the warning, Leland. And please keep me posted."

"Like I said, the word is really getting out about our . . . what did that French guy call it, our Druid Stone?"

"Druids in Sweeney? Imagine that. By the way, have you heard from Grant lately?"

"Can't say I have, but I've been pretty busy, haven't been home much, though I expect he'd leave a message."

"But as far as you know he's still planning to make his usual summer trip home?"

Leland paused, and then said, "I haven't heard otherwise. I'll let you know if I hear anything."

"Thanks, it'll be good to see him, lots to talk about."

Another pause, then, "You going to the meeting tonight, Kathy?"

"I'll be there."

The phone rang in the maintenance garage of Torgelson's Farm and Ranch Implements. With practiced patience Rudd Torgelson extricated himself from the engine compartment of a John Deere tractor, wiped his hands upon a greasy red garage rag he pulled from the back pocket of his work suit, and answered the phone on his cluttered desk.

"Torgelson's."

It was Roger Rollins. "We need to talk."

"I suppose we do."

"Tonight, my clinic, at six."

"I'll be there," Rudd said. He hung up without a parting and returned to the tractor.

Then he stood up, brushed pale-brown hair from his forehead, and returned to the desk. He sat in his old swivel chair and poured a cup of coffee from the Thermos. He didn't make coffee in the shop, because it encouraged people to come around and talk. As if his demeanor wasn't discouragement enough. The only person who ever got past Rudd's gruff demeanor to hang around the shop was S&S, on whom normal social cues were lost.

The coffee was black and bitter. That was okay; he didn't drink it for the taste. He wasn't much for the niceties of life. Though equipment and parts dealers routinely gave him calendars and posters, the garage's walls were bare except for the tools hanging everywhere and the shelves crowded with cans of motor oil and solvents, containers of nuts and bolts, and the countless other odds and ends that went with servicing heavy equipment.

Why had he agreed to join this quixotic project of Rollins's? He certainly wasn't a joiner, didn't seek camaraderie. And he doubted he had done it for love of Sweeney. Despite his family's pioneer history here, they had always been on the margins of what passed for town society. Now he was his family's last surviving member, living alone in the decaying three-story wood-frame house at the end of Tupelo Street. Rudd had observed how he and the house resembled each other: big, isolated, and not to be replaced when gone.

Rudd knew everyone in town but had no close friends. He had never been married; his high school classmates could not remember him ever having a girlfriend. The low-level rumor around town for years had been that he was gay, but his bachelorhood was the only evidence anyone had. He might be asexual, but he was not effeminate. He'd never come on to anyone, he had no local partner. He fit in well at rodeos.

Rudd knew about the rumors—he knew just about everything in town. As for the rumors, he ignored them. His response to whatever anyone thought about him, from his huge size to his sexuality, always was the same: Screw 'em. In the most profound sense, he simply didn't give a shit.

So why had he allowed himself to be roped into this affair? He didn't really know, but as he sipped his bitter coffee he realized that it might be important to find out.

"Finally gettin' some respect, yessiree, we're finally gettin' some respect." Rudd looked up as the gravelly voice of S&S echoed off the garage's corrugated tin walls. In the two weeks since the raising of the Rock, Rudd had endured S&S's increasingly incoherent ravings with a stoicism born of long practice.

"Who's finally getting some respect?" asked Rudd perfunctorily, not bothering to greet his visitor. S&S often stopped by about this time of day. The turgid smells of diesel fuel and oily metal masked most of S&S's odor, and S&S never minded that the big man ignored his ramblings. Rudd even paid S&S for small chores around the garage, picking up rags and sweeping the floor.

"Sweeney and me," crowed the scrawny tatterdemalion, who resembled a skinny rooster that had wandered onto a highway and been hit by an oil truck. "People finally payin' attention, comin' from all over."

"What do you mean?"

"Moviemakers, that's what I mean. I've heard they're startin' to swarm on Sweeney like flies on shit" —Rudd winced at this— "I seen one of 'em, down by the town offices, and I've heard there are others. That Rock's been here all along, and I been here all along, and now there's people payin' attention."

Rudd shuddered at the thought that Sweeney and S&S might be metaphors for each other, especially as he suspected there might be something to it.

"What do you think raised up that rock and dug those pits?"

S&S squinted at Rudd suspiciously. "I never said I knowed. I haven't."

"I heard you were saying this had been foretold, maybe by some ancient guy in Europe or Egypt."

"And who's to say it ain't so?" S&S raised his chin defiantly as he sauntered to where a broom leaned against a wall. "There's lots of stuff in this world that ain't explained. Lots of things that was prophesied that are comin' to pass. As Nosterdomus said in the Book of Reservation, when the whores of Babylon get linked up with the beast of Egypt, then there's going to be marvels and mysteries. And if you don't think the whores o' Babylon ain't been active, well, let me tell you . . ."

Rudd decided it was time to return to work.

By six o'clock sharp, all those summoned—Dave, Leland, Nettie, Kathy, and Rudd—were seated around the table in the small conference room of the All Creatures Veterinary Clinic. From adjacent rooms came the sounds of animals stirring in their cages, hopeful of release, or at least attention, as well as the smells of animals and antiseptic. On the conference room walls were photos of cherished animals along with inscriptions from their owners.

"Well?" Nettie huffed at Roger, glaring at him through her silver-rimmed glasses. It was a demand as much as a question.

"Why are you looking at me?" Roger retorted. "I didn't exactly raise those rocks by myself."

Nettie's glare didn't waver. "I figured this nonsense would all just blow over, but it hasn't. It's just gotten bigger—don't none of you make any cracks about that."

"Wouldn't dream of it," said Dave, then paused and added, "Roger's right. We're all in this together. None of us could have predicted what would happen with that big stone and what it would look like."

"A likely story," Nettie humphed.

Leland spoke. "For better or worse, what's done is done. I admit I was kind of shocked when I saw that Rock in the full light of day, and I still have mixed feelings about it . . ."

"Mixed? How?" exclaimed Nettie.

Leland hesitated. "From certain angles it doesn't look like . . . well, what it looks like. In fact, the media seem to be ignoring that aspect of the Rock. Most concentrate on the Mystery Holes, as they're calling them. Most of the people that come by the town offices haven't even mentioned the resemblance at all. They all seem to regard it as some kind of alien project."

"Sorry, Leland," said Kathy, "they're just being tactful, or they have another agenda. There's not a soul in Sweeney who doesn't know what that Rock looks like, and I'm sure everyone else does too."

Dave leaned forward on his elbows and looked around the table. "Now, I agree this is a complication we hadn't counted on, but let's face it, the resemblance has garnered the Rock more attention than if it wasn't there."

"It's not necessarily the kind of attention we want," said Rudd, leaning back and crossing his arms, speaking for the first time.

"Do we really know what kind of attention we want?" argued Roger. "Who was it that said, there's no such thing as good publicity or bad publicity, there's only publicity? So far, no harm's been done by the resemblance, and let's face it, things have been different around Sweeney these days. If one of our goals was to shake things up a bit, we've succeeded."

A dog howled plaintively from a nearby room. "Excuse me a minute," said Roger as he got up and left the conference room. Soon the dog ceased howling, and Roger returned.

"Roger's right," said Kathy, looking at Nettie as she spoke. "The truth is, when you set something in motion, you can't know where it's going to go, and you can't always control it."

"And we do know what was going to happen if we'd done nothing," said Dave. "Sweeney was going to die. Sometimes being scared and out of control is the price you have to pay for taking charge and changing things."

Nettie sighed, and then nodded sagely. "Well, it does remind me of what Johnny used to say during our rodeo days: It doesn't matter how rank the bull turns out to be, when you're on his back and the chute gate swings open, you've got to ride him. By the way, Rudd, just how did you all dig those holes and raise that rock, without leaving marks?"

The big man stared at her, and smiled. "Smoke and mirrors and the miracle of hydraulics. Them, and heavy-duty posthole routers."

Seeing bewilderment still on Nettie's face, Dave added, "We shouldn't forget the contribution of Sweeney High School, which gave the project temporary use of leftover scraps of AstroTurf from its football field and which protects the ground underneath from such things as tire tracks."

"And that eerie green glow that was seen that one night?"

"Well, as the local science teacher," Dave said, "I'll only mention that certain phosphorescent chemicals briefly give off a green glow after light is shined on them."

Nettie shook her head. She knew that was all she'd get from them, at least for now.

"Hey, Leland," said Roger, as the group began to break up and Leland was almost at the door, "before you go I've got something to show you."

"This wouldn't be a stray dog, would it?"

Roger bridled. "Well, I wouldn't exactly call Trixie a stray. Not with her qualities. No, a dog like this doesn't just wander around. Tragic circumstance separated this quality dog from her owner."

"Trixie, huh? Definitely a classy name." Leland slowly shook his head and reached for the doorknob.

"No, wait, this dog really is special. Just take a look at her."

"If she's so special, there'll be lots of people wanting to adopt her."

Roger looked wounded. "Do you really think I'd let a dog like this go to just anyone?"

Sensing defeat, Leland let go of the doorknob and said, "Okay, let's see her—but I'm not promising anything."

Later, as Leland drove home, he glanced at the decidedly well-mixed-breed terrier-sized dog sitting with a big smile on the seat beside him. Trixie. Not exactly a name Ruth would have chosen. The dog looked at him with soft, adoring eyes and a big, eager smile. Grant would like a dog like this. He'd tell Grant about the dog when next they spoke on the phone; it would give them something safe to talk about, a small link between their separate worlds.

"Well, Trixie, if you really are extraordinarily precocious, you'll show it by getting along with the other animals at the ranch, starting with a big, yellow cat who's under the impression the ranch is his."

A warm, dry, prairie wind was moving dust and dried leaves around as Nettie walked down Olive Street toward her modest, one-story frame house. She was angry, and a little depressed, both arising from confusion about the Rock. She didn't like being confused, especially not in Sweeney. Security and predictability were virtues that supposedly compensated for the town's monotony.

She blamed Roger. She didn't at all believe he had been surprised by the Rock's shape—and even if he had, he still didn't have to be so damned smug about it. Restoring Sweeney to life didn't involve having a giant penis at the end of town. The town could use a little excitement, but it didn't have to get *that* excited.

She started to chuckle, then caught herself. She had to admit that the situation had sizable humorous potential.

And now she'd been thrust into the awkward position of channeling the moral indignation of the town's elderly women and simultaneously ensuring that nothing came of it. Everyone knew they had formed a committee to do something about the Rock—they formed committees about everything, from starving children in Africa to flowers in the Sweeney park. Given their history, keeping the women busily ineffective shouldn't be difficult, but she nonetheless felt uncomfortable with her dual role.

And as a leading member of Reverend Fall's congregation, how was she supposed to handle him? His righteous opposition to the Rock would only intensify, would only accelerate his descent into obnoxious fundamentalism. Was that why she'd been included in the conspiracy, to act as a mole and covertly thwart opposition? To something she herself opposed? Or at least she thought she did. Actually, she didn't know what she thought. Damn that Roger!

Why couldn't the Rock have been shaped like a bone? Well, in a sense it . . . Stop it! If she wasn't careful she'd be as bad as all the rest.

She wondered what Johnny would have thought about the Rock. She had a pretty good idea, but it only confused her more.

She was still thinking about Johnny as she entered her home. The wind and dust tried to follow her inside. She closed the door, switched on the lights, and walked into the kitchen. With a sigh, she took out a glass from the cupboard, then went to the pantry, retrieved a bottle of Wild Turkey whiskey, and poured herself about two inches. Then she sat at the kitchen table and took a long drink, grimacing afterward. She rarely drank; she kept the bottle primarily for guests. But mentioning Johnny at the meeting and their rodeo days together had exhumed the old loneliness. The house was cold and empty.

She took another sip of the whiskey and grimaced again. Damn, that stuff was vile! She knew there were better brands out there, but she still chose Wild Turkey out of nostalgia. It was what the rodeo cowboys and cowgirls drank. At the end of a rodeo, when everyone was leaning against the slats of the arena, tired and dusty and beat up, someone would produce a bottle and a little tin cup from one of their rodeo bags, and everyone would pass the cup around and talk. About what had gone wrong, what if anything had gone right, the bull that twisted the wrong way, the calf that bolted the chute too soon, the horse that missed a step in the barrel turn. How things would be different in the next go-round, everyone knowing they wouldn't. And before long the whiskey and the talk would dissolve most of the hurts, and everyone would drift back to their pickups and leave for their motel rooms.

Nettie looked through the kitchen door into the living room and the glass-and-wood case that held the rodeo trophies. Most were Johnny's bull-riding trophies. The rest were hers, won in the barrel racing. Even from the kitchen she could identify each trophy, could recite exactly which rodeo it came from. Johnny had been a damned good bull rider— and she wasn't half-bad at barrel racing. They'd made a good team.

Her parents had been furious when she ran away and married him. "Marrying a cowboy is the worst thing you can do—and a rodeo cowboy at that! They're just plain no good."

But they'd been wrong. Johnny had been good. He'd never run around like a lot of the cowboys, and he didn't take to drink. And, oh, the times they had, knocking around all over the West, going to this town and that, following the rodeos, having good times and bad.

Until the inevitable happened: a contrary bull kicked Johnny in his lower back, and he became just another stove-up ex-bull rider. He took it well. They returned to Sweeney. He got a job at the stockyards, she opened the Style Salon. She was unable to have children, but that was okay; they had each other. And then he up and died of esophageal cancer, from too many years of dipping snuff.

She took another sip of the Wild Turkey. The whiskey was bitter, but the memories were sweet.

Though the Sweeney Rotarians' regular meeting was not for two weeks, several members felt an emergency session was called for, so on a Monday night, two weeks and one day after the transformation of Indian Rocks, Ron Suffitt summoned everyone to his garage, in lieu of the Chick 'n' More. He couldn't provide food, but he did offer coffee and store-bought cookies.

To everyone's surprise, Rudd Torgelson walked in the door just as Ron was about to call the meeting to order. As owner of one of the town's most important surviving local businesses, Torgelson had officially been a Rotary member for years, but he never attended meetings or worked on projects. He was greeted heartily. He just grunted in reply.

"Great timing, Rudd," quipped Roger Rollins. He was perched on a pile of *Insurance Today* magazines. "For the first time in recent history the Sweeney Rotarians actually have something to talk about."

Ron huffed. "I like to think that many of the projects we've discussed have been quite valuable to the community."

"You're right." Roger held up his hands. "I withdraw the statement."

"Thank you," Ron stated solemnly, then, clearing his throat, he continued. "We all know why we're here—"

Fred Yoder interrupted. "I heard them ghostly lights were seen again, pointing in the direction of an Indian burial ground."

"Oh, come on," objected Tom Binks. He sat unsteadily on the seat of a lawn-mower tractor. Dave, balancing on a fender, recoiled from the sour stench of beer on Binks's breath.

"We're not here to swap rumors," boomed Binks. "We've done nothing else for days. Let's start talking about what this means for Sweeney. About our public image as a town."

"We have a public image?" said Roger.

Binks fumed at the interruption. "Damned right we do, certainly now. We're the town with a big dick-shaped rock" —several Rotarians winced at Binks's indelicacy— "and it's a gawdammed disgrace. Nettie, I understand the women of Sweeney have formed a committee to look into this?"

Covert glances were exchanged all around. Soon after the phallic rock had arisen, a small clutch of elderly women of high moral standing had coalesced around Nettie. They were dedicated to de-erecting the offending formation. Within hours the group was called the Saltpeter Patrol. The committee called themselves Citizens United against Nudity in our Town, but they quickly changed the name when people noticed the acronym. The new name was People for Decency by Nature. No one could quite explain what this meant, but the goal was clear. PDN charged into action by forming a subcommittee to investigate the creation of a set of bylaws, along with another subcommittee to nominate a slate of officers.

"Yes, we have a committee, and we're working on it. That Rock's an embarrassment," said Nettie. She glared at Roger. "The town's a laughingstock."

"At least it's a living laughingstock," rejoined Dave.

"Those rocks are blasphemous and obscene," said the Reverend Wayne Fall from his seat at a card table, his hands folded over a Bible. Suddenly everyone seemed to feel a simultaneous need to shift position, followed by an apprehensive silence. It was inevitable that Reverend Fall would inject religion into any discussion, usually as fiery rants and interminable sermons. "As the Lord saith," he began, "when iniquity—"

Roger interrupted. "Have any of you Googled 'Sweeney' lately?" He looked around the table like a blackjack dealer. He savored the bewilderment on Nettie's face as she mouthed the word "Google?" Reverend Fall glared at Roger; he wasn't done yet, but all eyes were on Roger.

Not waiting for an answer, Roger continued. "It's a search of the Internet, and I have done a Google search for Sweeney. Before the Rock, you'd get, maybe, five hits, and those would be for the electric coop and census records, lists of schools and clinics. Maybe eight hits. Google 'Sweeney' now and you're likely to get a couple of hundred hits—and some of them are pretty strange."

"Details, details," urged Dave.

"Easy now. We've all had our strangeness thresholds raised lately. What I was getting at is that Sweeney suddenly is on the map. Actually, on a lot of maps."

Binks boomed again. "I heard that we're listed by the Druid Society of America and the Burning Man and Rainbow Nation hippie tribes. More motorcycle clubs than you want to know about. We're listed in a directory of 'fun places to get naked in the U.S.' by the Naked Hogs Motorcycle Club in Texas. I'm surprised we haven't had a bunch of queers coming here."

Leland flushed angry red, but before he could respond Reverend Fall said, "That's just what I was getting ready to talk about—"

Dave interrupted. "Actually, we don't need Google or Giggle or Goggle or whatever to tell us that things are different in Sweeney these days. All we need to do is walk by the Chick 'n' More—if you can get across the street. Look at where we're meeting. Did we ever dream we'd be bounced from the Chick 'n' More to a garage—a very nice garage, Ron— because the Chick 'n' More of all places was overbooked? Another film crew, I suspect."

"Come on, Dave," said Ron, "Ed said that because we were longtime customers he'd cancel the other booking, even though he'd lose two hundred dollars doing it. We couldn't let him do that, especially after what he was willing to do for us."

Dave gave up, nodded.

"Our loss is Ed and Edna's gain," said Ron grandiloquently. "Maybe they won't move away now."

"My business has picked up, I can say that," said Yoder. Dave winced in sympathy for those who chose the haircut and not the shoeshine.

Nettie allowed as how she had sold more cosmetics and hair products in the last week than in the previous year. And to people she'd never seen before. "Who knows what kind of people would travel to see a . . . well, one of *those*."

Roger said, "Will Diggs is installing electrical hookups on his property where people have been parking trailers. And he's brought in Port-a-Potties until he finishes his toilet and shower room."

Leland added, "Our local law enforcement has been busier than usual. You'll say I'm lying, but our patrolman has given two speeding tickets in one day."

"So, what does this mean?" asked Ron.

Connie Nesbitt, Sweeney's only real estate broker, who could no longer remember exactly how to draw up a purchase offer, stood, smoothed her peach-colored dress, which she wore only when serious business was pending, and said, "To me, that up-ended rock is the second most beautiful thing I've ever seen shaped like that." Several Rotarians gasped; none dared ask what was the first.

"I mean it," continued Connie. "The other day one of our visitors asked about buying land near the Rock. Can you believe it, buying land in Sweeney instead of trying to sell it? If this is embarrassment, I'll gladly be embarrassed all the way to the bank."

"For what it's worth," said Roger, "most websites don't focus on the Rock's anatomical aspect but rather its mysterious arising, and the pits around it. A few make fun of it, but when most refer to its shape they talk about it as a fertility symbol—they ascribe pagan symbolism to it."

"Hmmph!" snorted Nettie.

"Not everyone is willing to overlook its shape." Reverend Fall's time to speak had come. Trembling with indignation and clutching his Bible, he rose and glowered sternly around the garage. He was lean and austere, but his patriarchal presence was compromised by his dark hair sticking out at crazy angles, the result of Yoder's barbering. This time he would not be silenced. "There are hundreds of God-fearing people in this town who are not happy to have their community associated with this piece of geological pornography. Or with pagan fertility symbols either."

Roger remained seated as he responded. "Hundreds of God-fearing people in this town? I didn't think we could find hundreds of people of any kind in this town."

Reverend Fall glared at Roger, who unabashedly continued, "Seems to me that the fact it's there, without anyone having put it up, argues for God having given his consent."

"To *that?!*" gasped Reverend Fall. "All you can think of is how much money you can make from it, but it's clear God did not put that there, unless it was to test us."

Into the roiling waters stepped Ron. "Now, now. Nothing has to be decided immediately, and besides, we're the Rotary Club, not the town council."

"We have a town council?" asked Roger.

"It doesn't matter," said Dave. "We have Nettie's fine committee looking into the issue."

Chapter Four

ON MOST MONDAYS TRACI DALY PLODDED miserably to the front steps of the Kiowa County Consolidated School, but today she all but skipped. This Monday was the first school day since the filmmakers had arrived. For once her friends had something important to talk about.

Traci headed instinctively, like a salmon to its birth site, to her personal clique by the concrete railing along the steps, keeping a discreet distance from other groups seated nearby. Delayed by an argument with her mom, Traci was the last to arrive.

Traci often had noted that theirs was an eclectic clique. The girls had little in common except having grown up together in Sweeney, but that was enough. There was Christie, product of the rancher community, who wore blue jeans and a patterned shirt with pearl snap buttons. She was borderline attractive and never lacked for young cowboys to accompany her to the church and ranch events that were her social life.

Kimberly was in her uniform as well: black pants, black shoes and socks, and a black T-shirt that said something about a Hags of Hell concert tour—as if any rock group, goth or otherwise, had ever played in Sweeney. Her clothing always reeked of stale cigarette smoke, not entirely due to both her parents being heavy smokers. Concealed beneath her clothing, Traci knew, were a couple of piercings and at least one tattoo. Traci was never sure how deep Kimberly's rebellion ran. The only potential goth boyfriend for Kimberly was Jeremy Land, and he was two years younger, four inches shorter, and had tastes inspired by computer games.

And Heather—did she *have* to wear that fuzzy pastel stuff her mom picked out for her at a K-mart somewhere? Totally dorky, though the clothes did conceal Heather's extra weight. Her personality matched her clothing, Traci thought. Cheery, fuzzy, and totally lacking in style. Still, she was fun to be with and had lots of friends in school. Her current boyfriend was Freddy Simms, whose father worked for the highway department. A month from now it would be someone else, perhaps a former boyfriend. In an environment of finite male resources, recycling was important.

Too bad her friends didn't dress like her, Traci thought, the apex of trendiness and cool, but when it came to cliques, in a place like Sweeney you couldn't be choosy. Traci currently was without a boyfriend; she'd set her sights on Jeff Wiggins—until his family yanked him out of the boyfriend pool. Compared to him, the remaining alternatives were just unacceptable.

Just as Traci approached, the bell rang, and her friends were swept away in the flood of students entering the building. "Lunchroom!" she cried after them.

During the past weekend, as on every weekend, phone conversations had kept the youths of Sweeney in touch with each other, but for true fulfillment nothing equaled face-to-face gossip in the school lunchroom. Traci endured her morning classes, oblivious to the teachers and the lessons. In the halls she caught snatches of conversation—brief, tantalizing.

Like seismic waves emanating from an earthquake, the transformation of Indian Rocks sent rumor shocks through the student body. Soon it was simply taken for granted that a major movie was to be made in Sweeney; the arrival of the independent filmmakers all but confirmed it. Immediately, in tiny clusters around the school, in smoke-filled bathrooms, on school steps, in the parking lot, wherever students gathered, the words were the same: "We can work on the set. We can be extras. We'll be in the movies!"

Sweeney's adolescent males nurtured fantasies of beautiful Hollywood nymphets, bringing to Sweeney a culture of uninhibited, aggressive sex. Abundant flesh, shameless seduction, steam on the windows of movie set trailers.

The female adolescent fantasies at their core were pretty much the same.

So by the time the lunch bell finally rang, Traci already had a full cargo of gossip to deliver and questions to ask. Dodging other students, she sprinted to her locker, dumped her school books, and dashed to the lunchroom.

To the untrained eye, the lunchroom might seem just a bunch of kids sitting at tables eating, but to Traci and all the other students it was like a continent, with each table representing a different country. They spoke different languages, had different customs, dressed differently, and like neighboring nations everywhere, they all hated each other. Order was maintained by a rigid status-based hierarchy. For a student from the Nerd table to attempt to sit at the Popular table was . . . well, just unthinkable. Traci and her friends inhabited the Almost-but-not-quite-popular table, and as she made her way there the girls swiveled toward her.

"Hi, everyone," she said. Then she looked closer at her friends' faces. They seemed stricken. "What's wrong? Has something happened?"

"*He's* here!" stammered Heather, with the stunned look of someone who has just achieved enlightenment.

"Who's here?" asked Traci. "Jesus? Is Jesus here?"

Heather was too stricken to respond, so Kimberly intervened.

"Keener! Heather saw him this morning, standing by a car near the Chick 'n' More. Then he got in the back seat of the car, and it drove off." Keener was the current teen idol, who like other celebrities resided in a remote, quasi-mythical realm unattainable by mere mortals. His presence in a place like Sweeney was akin to God sitting in a pew in the local church.

"It was him, I swear it," insisted Heather. "They say he's here to consider Sweeney for a TV segment. Or maybe a DVD. Or maybe a movie."

Traci glanced around the lunchroom. The kids at the other tables also were locked in intense deliberation. Had they also heard of Keener being in Sweeney?

"Hey, guys," said Traci to the group, "the Nerd Herd over there just heard a rumor that Kermit the Frog was coming to town."

"Who are the Jocks hoping for?"

"The Dallas Cowboy cheerleaders!" said Heather. Everyone laughed until they realized it might be true; then it wasn't funny. Too bad the other cliques didn't have a real celebrity, like Keener.

"We should ditch class this afternoon and go see him," stated Kimberly, a slight edge in her voice making it sound like a dare.

Skipping class was unprecedented and dangerous, but . . .

"I say we do it," Traci heard herself saying. "There's nothing happening in class, everyone's just staring out the window thinking about what's been going on. I don't think anyone will even miss us. And what if this is our *only* chance?"

"I can't . . . I just can't," protested Christie. No one was surprised. In school Christie was Snow White, the model child, the perfect student. For her, even seeing Keener ranked beneath keeping her perfect attendance record. She looked as if she was going to cry.

"It's okay," Traci consoled. "We understand." And they did, too, for while Christie was Snow White in behavior, she also was fairly plain in appearance, which landed her in this group, whose members discovered that she was a genuinely nice person, a sincere and loyal friend. "Just don't tell on us. Okay? Just don't say anything, and you can be part of us, without actually skipping class."

Christie beamed. "Agreed."

"How about sixth period?"

As Traci, Heather, and Kimberly all had gym that period, that too was agreed. And as they all were nonathletes, they had only to answer roll and then slip out the door, never to be missed.

But when the girls entered the gym during sixth period, they found a sign telling them not to suit up but to report to the auditorium, where attendance would be taken. Upon entering the darkened room, the girls saw teachers and school officials standing by the doors, barring escape. On the stage a film screen had been pulled down.

"Oh, no!" moaned Heather.

"It can't be . . . oh, let it not be . . . it *is* . . . a gawdammed sex ed movie," wailed Kimberly.

"Ah, shit!" said Traci. "We're going to miss Keener so we can look at photos of gonorrhea sores? Shit, shit, shit!"

"No we're not," said Kimberly. She explained her plan to them.

"Hey, Rachel, wait up," Kimberly shouted as the girls filed into the auditorium. Ahead of them a tall, skinny girl wearing a long, deeply out-of-fashion dress turned and gazed at them through square glasses from beneath dark bangs. Rachel Rowe was a singularly strange girl whose oddness was aggravated by a desperate desire to belong. Her academic intelligence was stratospheric, but her social intelligence was subterranean. She was not a member of their clique. She was not a member of any clique, but in a clinging, obnoxious way she'd made clear that she wanted to be one of them. She also had no sense of boundaries; she could be talked into doing almost anything.

"Hi, there," answered Rachel, clearly excited to be spoken to.

"Hey, Rache," said Kimberly, "it's a real bummer to have to watch a stupid sex ed movie."

"Yes, it is a bummer," said Rachel, apparently not sure what a bummer was or how it related to a sex ed move but eager to agree. "It's a bummer, all right. A bummer."

Traci and Heather rolled their eyes.

"Listen, Rache," Kimberly continued, "I've got a plan that can have fun with this, that is, if you're willing to go along, if you're one of us."

"Oh, I am," agreed Rachel hastily. "I am."

"Great," said Kimberly, "I knew we could count on you." Then she whispered her plan in Rachel's ear.

"I have to do that?" gasped Rachel. "That's disgusting."

"Yeah, but it'll be funny. Come on, Rache, you can do it. Then we can all laugh about it tomorrow when you have lunch with us in the lunchroom. At our table. You'll be one of us, right?"

Rachel's face brightened. "It will be funny. We can laugh about it together."

"Way to go, Rache. We knew you'd come through for us."

As they separated upon entering the auditorium, Traci turned to Kimberly. "I don't know about this, I really don't. This had better work." She had no feelings for Rachel, but this seemed cruel, predatory, like taking advantage of a retarded person. Which in a way Rachel was, at least socially. But then Rachel had agreed to it, and if it worked the girls might get to see Keener. Traci vowed to make it up to Rachel, though she wished the girls could do it without accepting Rachel into their group, even temporarily.

Ms. Leslie Rogers, or "Coach" as she preferred to be called, stood at the front of the auditorium like a drill sergeant and gave a perfunctory introductory lecture about changing morals and the need for "today's teens" to be informed. Then the lights dimmed, and the film began.

There was the predictable dramatization of the young teens who weren't careful and got the clap or chlamydia or something appalling. This was followed by the required avuncular medical expert who presented horrifying statistics—"Even petting your cat can give you an STD"—followed by the inevitable horror show of symptoms and consequences.

It was at the beginning of this, as a huge, ulcerating sore was on the screen, that the sound of retching rent the darkness. "I'm sick," moaned Rachel. She heaved again.

Suddenly, another girl's voice: "Omigod, she's puking! It's running down the floor." Then the sound of more puking.

"I can smell it!" screamed a girl on the other side of the room. At this point mass regurgitation erupted throughout the auditorium. The lights went on, teachers rushed to the aid of the stricken—and three girls slipped unnoticed out the doors.

"That was *awesome*," effused Kimberly, as the girls sauntered toward Main Street. "I mean, that was, like, totally, unbelievably, shit-faced awesome."

"That will indeed live forever in the annals of Sweeney High," said Heather with pride.

"I know Rachel is weird—she proved that again today—but we owe her," said Traci. "It wouldn't have happened without her. We wouldn't be here without her."

"Resolved," said Heather. "Rachel's status has been officially raised."

"From creepy to just strange," said Kimberly.

At Main Street they scanned for any celebrity-looking cars but saw nothing. They saw several cars they didn't recognize but nothing like what Keener might ride in.

"It was here, I swear it," said Heather. "It was right by the Chick 'n' More."

"We believe you," said Traci. "It was only a slim chance he would still be here anyway."

"Maybe he'll come back," said Kimberly. "Let's hang out here for a while to see if he does. As long as we're here."

They walked the length of Main Street twice, taking note of unfamiliar cars—it was still difficult grasping that concept. Most just contained sightseers willing to drive all the way to Sweeney to take a few photos "for the folks back home."

Then an elderly van with the words "Exotic Productions" stenciled on its side drove by, just as they were preparing to return to school. The van pulled up beside them and a tanned young man with surfer-blond hair leaned out the window.

"Hi there," he said, beaming. "We're part of a movie project that will be filmed here. We're doing promotion shots. Maybe you girls can help us—are you from here?"

Yes! exulted Heather inwardly. Vindicated! It might not be Keener, but this was still it!

Traci said, "Yep, we're from here. Actually, we're supposed to be in the high school right over there, but we're ditching." As one, the girls giggled.

"All right!" seconded the tanned young man. "Say, would you girls mind showing us around the rocks? We'd like you to be in some of the pictures. Seeing as you've got time on your hands." He winked.

The girls giggled again, and then looked at each other. Someone nodded.

"Great, get in," said the tan.

"Uh, why don't we meet you at the rocks," said Heather.

"Sure, sounds good," answered the tan. "See you there," he added as the van drove off.

"It's just a minute away, and I don't like getting in strange vans. I hope that's okay with you," said Heather.

Everyone nodded. "Good call." "Quick thinking."

The young man and his two partners, who weren't as young or tanned, were unloading photographic equipment at the rocks when the girls arrived.

"What do you want us to do?" they asked.

"For now, stand next to the rocks," said the young man. "Just kind of position yourselves around on them."

"What's the name of the movie?" Heather asked.

"Don't know," answered the tan. "It's way too early for the movie to be named. The script hasn't even been written."

Heather nodded, embarrassed.

The two other men, having mounted cameras on tripods, began taking pictures.

"We're trying to get local color," crooned the tan. "Say, you girls look great! I'll bet you've modeled before, am I right?"

The girls giggled a no.

"Could you stand closer to the Rock, the big upright one?" one of the cameramen directed Heather. "That's it, now give me a big smile."

Heather obliged.

"Now, if you can take your right arm and put it around the Rock, kind of hugging it."

Heather, suddenly reminded of what the Rock looked like, felt uncomfortable, but she nonetheless put her arm around the Rock and smiled.

"That's it, that's great. Now can you stand a little closer to the stone, put your arm a little farther around it? That's it, that's great. Now with your other arm lift up your blouse. . . ."

As they walked back to school, they savored their indignation.

"We should have known when they tried to get us in that van," said Heather. "Exotic Productions! Exotic my ass!"

"Actually, that was exactly their intention," quipped Kimberly. The girls laughed.

Traci walked for the most part in silence. She knew their absence from school almost certainly would be noticed, that they would be busted. And she didn't care. The consequences, if any, were likely to be minor. In fact, she suspected her father would secretly be proud of her. After all, he often had told her of the time he and his high school friends had ditched school to get an early start on what was rumored to be the party of the century, to be held at the remote ranch of a friend whose parents were away. Her father had made clear that the intended moral of the story was that the party was the disappointment of the century, with the only memorable event being Will Lightener, profoundly drunk, falling on a fresh cow pattie. But while her dad didn't condone ditching, the relish with which he told the story suggested that for him as for her, the memories made the crime worth it, despite the disappointment.

As for her mother, Traci remembered her alluding to having ditched high school once in LA; Traci heard no relish in her mother's voice, but still . . .

As she walked, Traci basked in warm satisfaction. She and her friends had stepped outside their boxes and experienced an adventure, albeit a ludicrous one. She was happy.

"Don't forget," said Traci. "We owe Rachel."

As Traci expected, when she and her friends returned to school they were told to report to the principal's office. There they sat silently on hard wooden chairs as the principal delivered the pro forma lecture about skipping school. Traci suspected that with principalship came a folder containing the scripts of all the standard lectures the office entailed: tardiness, horsing around in the lunchroom, smoking in the bathrooms, forging notes from home, the list was long. And because the principal's lecture seemed truly perfunctory, Traci assumed that the consequences would be minimal. In fact, as she passed her father in the hall after leaving the principal's office, he gave her a sly wink.

So Traci was completely unprepared for her mother's reaction when she got home, tossed her school books onto the floor beside the sofa, and settled in for therapeutic TV watching.

"Turn that off!" Joanie shrieked. "Listen to me! Don't you *ever* do that again. *Ever.* Do you hear me?" Traci goggled. She'd never witnessed her mother like this, almost hysterical, with fear in her voice.

"Hey, chill."

"Don't you tell me to chill," shouted her mother before Traci could say more. "If you ever so much as think about leaving school again and wandering around . . . around God knows where, you'll be grounded for the rest of your natural life."

"Hey, it's not like we do this all the time—and it was no big deal anyway. All we did was walk around Sweeney looking for a movie star—who wasn't there."

"What about those men who tried to pick you up? I heard about that from Heather's mother. You knew nothing about them, yet they were trying to get you into their car."

"But we didn't go," protested Traci, still flummoxed by her mom's intensity.

"Yes, and the fact that you didn't go is the only reason you're not severely grounded now."

"I don't understand, Mom. Yeah, ditching is against the rules, but Dad ditched once, and so did you, didn't you?"

Her mother's face darkened. "Well, didn't you?" Traci pressed.

Suddenly her mother wrapped her arms around her daughter and began crying. "I did ditch, and I guess that's why I'm so upset with you now. I've seen what can happen."

"What did happen?"

"I don't want to talk about it." Then, realizing she had to talk about it, having broached the issue, she continued, "We were seniors, three of us, and we thought we were so sophisticated, so worldly. Ditching was kind of a tradition for seniors, so we ditched, went down on the Strip, to cruise, look for excitement."

She paused and wiped tears away with the back of her hand. "Some guys in a red Camaro convertible pulled up, surfer types, blond, tans. They said they were going to an awesome party, said the Beach Boys, some other rock stars, would be there."

She grimaced, as if the memory physically pained her, then resumed. "There were no Beach Boys, and we were to be the party. Mary Lou and I were able to get out of the car at a traffic light, but Jenny still thought she was going to an awesome party. They dumped her in a parking lot on the Strip. Her parents found her wandering bruised, bloody, and dazed. She never talked about what happened to her, and her family moved away soon after."

Traci reached out and took her mother's hand. "That was terrible . . . and I guess I understand better why you were so upset. But, Mom, that was LA, this is Sweeney."

Her mother stared at nothing for a moment and then said, "Yes, this is Sweeney."

Later, on the porch, while Traci was on the phone inside, Joanie talked to Dave about what had happened.

"I know I overreacted, but I couldn't help myself. All those horrible memories of that time in LA came back to me. I was unprepared. I'd taken for granted that Sweeney was safe—and when it wasn't . . ."

"I'm sorry, and I understand." Dave put his arms around Joanie's shoulders. "I guess I've come to take Sweeney's safety for granted too— and I know better."

"What do you mean?"

"When I was young, about fourth grade, there was a horrible murder here. A hired hand on one of the ranches, down near Conejo, raped a local girl, then killed her and tried to hide her body in an arroyo. When she went missing it electrified the town, because we all knew her and her family. Everyone was pretty sure something bad had happened. As kids we kept our eyes open as we went around town, half hoping we'd find something, half hoping we wouldn't. Parents told us to be careful, they were worried. It was all anyone talked about.

"Then a rancher shot at a coyote, and when he followed the animal into an arroyo he found the body. It was horrible. As editor of the local paper, Dad went along with the recovery crew. He was stricken when he returned. He never talked about it.

"It didn't take the state police long to figure out who did it. He was arrested, confessed, and sentenced to life. It took people a long time to get over it, but eventually they did. Memories faded, a new generation came along. It became old history among the few people who remembered it. I never thought to tell you about it.

"But I'm afraid that if rock-solid safety is what you want from Sweeney, this sorry town can't even come up with that."

Overhead in the crystalline night sky of the High Plains were the familiar, comforting constellations of summer: Aquila the Eagle, centered on the first-magnitude star, Altair; Lyra the Lyre, crowned by regal Vega; Scorpius the Scorpion, with the angry red giant Antares at center; the fainter outline of Hercules, with its globular star cluster; and her favorite, Cygnus the Swan, with Deneb radiant at its head.

Rachel Rowe knew them all, even the smaller ones, like Delphinius the Dolphin. She knew the names of their brightest stars, knew their magnitudes and distances, and much, much more. For as long as she could remember, they had been her best friends—beautiful, endlessly fascinating, always there when she needed them.

She needed them now.

She sat alone, her back against the Rock at the edge of town and gazed upward. An evening breeze whisked away remnants of the day's heat. The air smelled of dry grasses and dust.

She was humiliated by what she'd done that afternoon in the school auditorium. She'd overheard a few kids refer to her as Rachel the Regurgitator. Why had she done it? She knew the answer but took little comfort in it. She'd done it because girls she hoped would be her friends had asked her to. Because perhaps finally she could belong.

She'd never belonged. She was different. She knew that, and to a degree accepted it. From the time she and her father had moved to Sweeney, when she was in fifth grade, she'd felt isolated. It wasn't just that she got far better grades than the other students, it was that while she knew the answers to all the questions and problems, she didn't know anything else. The subtle, unspoken rules, codes, taboos, and scripts that everyone else knew—all were opaque to her, like text in a foreign language. Her mother had departed when she was an infant—her father never discussed the details. As for her father, he had chosen to live in Sweeney because it was far from the turmoil of urban life—and he didn't have to interact with anyone. He wrote software applications for tiny groups of scientists in obscure fields. He rarely left the house; in fact, he rarely left his office. Thus, Rachel had grown up with no feminine presence, no sense of clothes or fashion or personal style, no one with whom to make girl talk, no one to guide her through growing up. Her father wasn't a bad man. He loved her and taught her what he knew, but he had no social skills to impart.

So she had always remained an outsider. She'd been happy to move to Sweeney, for the same reason as her father. Though she had no friends here, her peers weren't actively vicious, as in the city school. She suspected that was because the kids here knew they were outsiders as well, adrift far from the main currents of American adolescence. Also, she liked her teachers here, especially Mr. Daly, the science teacher. He shared her love of astronomy, and seemed genuinely interested in hearing about her nighttime observations.

She'd tried to fit in here, but her attempts had just been an embarrassing series of missteps. In junior high she once offered to take a group of girls stargazing, to teach them the constellations and show them all the cool stuff in the cosmos. They'd laughed at her. So she gave up trying, but not yearning.

That was why she'd agreed to the puking stunt. And now students were laughing at her again. But at least her new friends weren't laughing—were they?

She gazed at Deneb, at the head of the swan, frozen in graceful, eternal flight northward along the Milky Way. Deneb had a magnitude of 1.25, a white, class A supergiant. That's what she liked about the stars: they were knowable. Unlike people.

Chapter Five

◆ "DON'T BE LATE, JUNE," Wayne Fall shouted over his shoulder to his wife as he clomped down the front steps of their bungalow home. He couldn't see June in the kitchen rolling her eyes and mouthing "As if I could."

During each Sunday church service June sat at the organ and provided the music so essential for attendance, but Wayne was the pastor and would deliver today's sermon—the first to address the satanic manifestation at Indian Rocks. The previous Sundays after its arising he'd ducked the issue and only spoke in a general way about sin, hoping that perhaps God would make the Rock disappear or at least fall back down, but God hadn't acted, a clear sign that the Almighty had delegated responsibility to him.

Usually Wayne rehearsed his sermon as he walked, but today, for the first time, he didn't really know what he was going to say. His mind refused to focus on anything but the outrage—no, the blasphemy!—of the Rock, but he simply did not know how or even whether to bring it up to the congregation. Would they resent him for reminding them of it? Or would they look to him for spiritual guidance?

None of the courses he'd taken at the small Bible college in Lubbock, where he'd received his ordination, had prepared him for this, but they had told him he could expect to be tested. At first he thought his long wait for a pastorship was his test, but then he'd finally received the call from the church in Sweeney. Since then he'd taken his responsibilities most seriously, visiting the sick and shut-ins, but his training had dictated that his highest service to his flock was to save them from the temptations of Satan and the torments of Hell.

Serious sin, however, was hard to come by in Sweeney, especially among his increasingly geriatric congregation. How could he preach a sermon on lust to people who used walkers to get into the pews? Now, however, Satan's handiwork was rearing its . . . its . . . whatever, just outside Sweeney for all to see. *This* was his test. *This* was why the Lord had called him here.

He raised his chin and tried to put righteous determination in his steps as he strode the two blocks to the church, tugging at the buttoned collar of his starched white shirt and wishing that his solemn role as pastor didn't require him to wear a black suit in such hot weather.

Reaching the little white frame church, an incongruous bit of the Midwest on the New Mexico plains, he entered the vestry by a back door and began the ritual of donning the black, pastoral robes. He used a white handkerchief to wipe sweat from his brow, sweat he suspected was due as much to nerves as to heat. He didn't need to prepare the main chapel; Ed Teeds would see to that, as he had for the past fifty years.

Wayne slumped in the vestry's well-worn overstuffed chair. The 9:00 a.m. service hadn't even begun, and already he was exhausted, an emotional wreck. What *should* he do? What would Jesus do?

Wayne couldn't imagine. After all, Jesus had never had to confront geo-pornography like this. Nor had the prophets nor the disciples, as far as he knew. But Wayne always told his flock, "Seek ye the answers in the Bible"—he was fond of King James speak—so he decided now to try it himself. Taking the Bible he always carried with him, he closed his eyes, opened the book, and jabbed his index finger onto the page. Then he looked. It was the Book of Jonah: "Arise, go to Nineveh, that great city, and cry against it; for their wickedness is come up before me."

Wayne was dumbstruck. "God couldn't have spoken plainer if he'd handed me a note," he muttered. He glanced at the clock. It was time.

With head erect and chin forward, Wayne opened the vestry door and prepared to mount to the pulpit—then faltered. There in the church, almost like a miracle, was a phenomenon he'd never seen before: all the pews were filled. Panic clutched at him, but he was saved by the passage from Jonah. It was a sign.

But first the congregation had to sing a few hymns and recite a few Bible verses and listen to church announcements. By the time he finally began his sermon, Wayne was raring to go.

"Welcome, my brethren, to God's house. And well you might come here, because it's one of the last holy places in Nineveh—I mean Sweeney. Wickedness! Wickedness has come to our town!"

Someone in the congregation uttered, "Yes, brother."

"And sin! Yea, I say unto you, the Devil, Satan himself, has come to Sweeney!"

More murmurs of "Tell it, brother" and "Amen."

Lowering his voice for dramatic effect, Wayne continued. "You know what I'm talking about." His voice was rising again. "I'm talking about *those rocks*! Those obscene, blasphemous rocks!

"We don't know who erected"—a titter swept the room, Wayne paused and scowled, then resumed with a crescendo—"we don't know who did this, but I think we can safely assume it wasn't God!"

"Amen, brother." "You tell it, preacher."

Wayne had his audience for a full twenty minutes, and he did not waste a second. Satan and the forces of darkness never received such a tongue-flogging. Sin had never been condemned so soundly. He thundered, he erupted, he flung his arms around like a broken windmill, and at the end he was weeping. So was much of the congregation. It was a profound struggle to pull himself together for the offering, followed by the final blessing and hymn. Regrettably, June concluded the service by playing the old favorite, "Stand up, stand up for Jesus," which Wayne thought was an unfortunate choice. He'd have to speak to her about it.

After the service, as Wayne greeted departing parishioners outside the church, he basked in their praise and support. "Good job, Reverend." "That's telling it like it is." "I'm glad someone has the courage to speak up." A couple of the women gave him hugs.

The eleven o'clock service was even better.

"Did you see the church this morning?" Wayne crowed to June as she began fixing lunch for them in their home's kitchen. She nodded absently as she spread mayonnaise on bread slices.

"I guess I told old Satan what's what," he continued as she set a plate of bologna sandwiches on the Formica tabletop in front of him. When the children were still living at home, she'd always prepared a full Sunday dinner for the family. Then, after Wayne said grace, they all would talk, but since Luke and Sarah had moved away she'd withdrawn to fixing just a light meal. Wayne still said grace, however, and as June perfunctorily bowed her head she caught herself doubting that the Prince of Darkness had been sitting in the pews of the Sweeney church that morning. At least she hadn't seen him.

She didn't question that the Rocks were obscene, but she was more concerned about their effect on Wayne. She'd known he was unhappy working as a supervisor at a truck depot in Tucumcari, and she'd been pleased when he was called to be pastor in Sweeney, though it wouldn't have been her first choice of a place to live. The move had been good for Luke and Sarah, who thrived in the small pond of Sweeney and won scholarships to good colleges.

But she'd also seen Wayne exhausted after his long commute daily to Tucumcari, where he continued to work. More troubling lately was his immersion in the darker waters of Christian fundamentalism, especially radio preachers. His parents had been deeply conservative Christians, with no social life outside the church, and the only friends he'd ever had were from church and Sunday school. "If only Wayne had had a more normal upbringing," June often thought. "He doesn't really know how to relate to people or how to have fun." Now she feared the Rocks would lead to a hysterical crusade that would only alienate people further.

Grace finished, Wayne continued, "Yesirree, if Old Scratch thinks he's got a free hand in Sweeney, he's got another think coming, at least while I'm around. Yep, this is a church vigilant and armed with the truth of the Holy Spirit. As Jesus said in scripture, 'Get thee around to my back side, Satan, for it is—'"

"Behind me," June interrupted.

"Huh?" asked Wayne, irritated.

"He said, 'Get thee behind me.'"

"Whatever. And because of the power of the spirit that was in the Lord—"

"Pass the mayo, please," June interrupted again. Wayne frowned and handed her the jar.

"These are trying times for Sweeney," Wayne resumed, "and in these times of tribulation a leader will rise up, one who will lead the people out of iniquity—"

"Could I have the salt, please?"

Frowning again, he passed her the shaker.

"I didn't think Agnes Jenkins looked well this morning, did you?" June asked, hoping to change the subject. "I heard she'd been to the doctor in Tucumcari. I don't know what's going on with her, do you?"

"No, I don't, but I do know that if Satan—"

"Excuse me," June said, finishing her sandwich and gulping the last of her milk. She rose and went into the living room. In the corner stood a Hammond upright piano, the grain of its oak finish rich from repeated oilings and polishings. She walked to the piano bench, lifted its top, and took out a collection of popular tunes from the '60s.

Her parents in the small West Texas town where she'd grown up had always encouraged her music, and that had been her major at the Lubbock Bible college where she'd met Wayne. She'd played church music there, but she'd also earned money playing secular music at weddings, anniversaries, receptions, parties—she loved playing almost any kind of music almost anywhere.

Closing the bench's top, she sat at the piano, opened the keyboard's cover, then leafed through the collection until she found a selection she liked. Putting her fingers to the keyboard she began playing the old Beatles favorite, "Yesterday," humming the words softly to herself.

" . . . all my troubles seemed so far away, oh I believe in yesterday . . ."

"I think God would be happier if you played something glorifying Him and His kingdom," said Wayne entering the room, "instead of these songs from a sinful world. After all, didn't King David tell the people to play their horns and instruments and praise the Lord?"

With resignation June dropped her shoulders, closed the piano, put the music back in the bench, and returned to the kitchen to do the dishes.

Chapter Six

❧ AS LELAND STROLLED DOWN MAIN STREET toward the town offices, he savored the contentment lingering from a Thursday afternoon doughnut and cup of coffee at the Chick 'n' More. The preceding week had been relatively quiet. School had closed for the summer, and the end-of-school pranks had been no more than expected, aside from senior boys painting "Our Class—Pointing the Way to the Future" on the Rock. A little scrubbing removed that. The independent filmmakers had departed, as well as most curiosity seekers. Sweeney was old news in the media, and he'd begun to hope the town was settling back into its familiar routines. That was among the consolations of living in a place like Sweeney: comfortable routines.

It was when he stopped to breathe a contented sigh into the peaceful air that Leland noticed a subtle tremor in the pavement. He looked down the street. Entering the town, like a column of tanks, was a line of enormous RVs. Leland's mouth dropped, as if he'd seen a herd of elephants.

The lead RV stopped when it reached him. The passenger window rolled down, and a sixtyish woman with a reddish, round, cheerful face and bleached-blond hair in curlers leaned out. "Hi, there, could you direct us to the Natural Wonder Campground?"

"What? . . . Natural Wonder? . . . Oh, you must be meaning Will Diggs's place."

The driver, a man with an even rounder and redder face, leaned over. He wore a ball cap with the slogan "World's Best Grandfather." "Yeah, Will Diggs, that's the name it said on the website."

Leland recited the directions. The grandmotherly lady chirped, "This is a nice little town you've got here."

"Well, thank you," said Leland. "We're proud of it. Welcome to Sweeney." He smiled broadly. Yes, it was good to have regular, down-home folks in Sweeney for a change.

As the RV began pulling away to lead the caravan to the Natural Wonder Campground, Leland glanced at the sign painted on the vehicle's side: "Let It All Hang Out Senior Nudist RV Club."

"Oh, shit."

Later, back in his office, Leland eased himself into his familiar wooden chair and picked up the phone that had been ringing ever since he entered.

"Have you heard?" asked Nettie.

"I was there when they arrived, I expect everyone's heard."

"Well, what are you going to do about it?"

"Nothing I can do about it, or want to," he replied, leaning back. "I took a stroll down to the campground to see what their plans were. They were circling the wagons, so to speak, just like an old-time wagon train. I told them we didn't have any ordinances against nudity but said I hoped they'd be discreet. They assured me they'd dealt with this before and never had any complaints. They said they weren't a bunch of exhibitionists and would only be naked within the confines of their encampment. If anyone was offended, it would be because they went out of their way to be."

"Well, in that case, I guess it's okay."

He leaned forward. "Nettie, as I was standing there among the RVs, a lady, seventy if she's a day, comes up to me wearing only a purse. She asks where she can buy postcards that she can send to her grandkids. Then, she reaches into her purse and pulls out some photos. Nettie, I'm standing there with my face hanging out while a woman, bald-naked as a baby bird, is showing me photos of her grandkids!"

Nettie laughed. "Well, I hope you said they were cute."

"Said what was cute?"

Before the sun set, every soul in Sweeney, even the normally bedridden, had driven or walked by the LIAHOSNRVC encampment. Everyone, including Reverend Fall and his parishioners, was profoundly disappointed. A wall of screens surrounded the RV enclosure. There was nothing at all to be seen, nothing at all scandalous. From inside came the scent of meat roasting on portable grills, the sounds of people laughing and talking.

"It's an orgy!" pronounced Reverend Fall, but no one was convinced.

"It's a barbecue," people replied. They recognized the smells. Townspeople drifted back to their homes. When darkness fell, the local male teenagers attempted to creep up Indianlike on the nudist encampment and peer in, but the nudists had dogs.

Only Ronnie Sparks claimed to have made it to the perimeter for a quick peek. "It was horrible! Imagine your grandma and grandpa and all your aunts and uncles standing around *naked*."

But then no one ever paid much attention to Ronnie, and most of the boys remained convinced the nudists were traveling with their teenage nieces.

The following morning Roger and Dave sat at a tiny table in the corner of the Chick 'n' More. They'd fetched their coffee themselves and now were waiting for Helen to get around to them for their breakfast orders. Normally she was fairly laid-back, but then the Chick 'n' More wasn't normally full. Today she was jumping around like a chicken on a hammock. A few locals shared the counter while people from the RV camp dominated the tables. They'd all ordered massive breakfasts and were chatting and laughing heartily.

"Can't say I'm regretting waiting for Helen," said Dave. "If half those people give her a decent tip she'll be able to quit this joint."

"The price of success," answered Roger. "And speaking of mixed feelings regarding success, I hate to say it but I can't stay long, I've got a busy morning ahead. Do you have any idea how many cats and dogs and birds and god-knows-whatever are living in that encampment? And every one of their owners called last night to make an appointment for their pampered pet. I suspect the best cure for what ails most of them is just letting them out of those mobile cages. I hope the dogs hanging around Sweeney are aware of how good they have it."

"I'm sure they are," said Dave, with exaggerated solemnity, "I'm sure they are."

Roger glanced at the stack of manila envelopes in Dave's lap. "Doing a mass mailing?"

"Mass mail, junk mail, whatever." He took a long pull on his coffee and turned toward Roger. "I'm applying for teaching positions elsewhere."

Roger's coffee cup hand halted halfway to his mouth. He met Dave's eyes.

"Joanie and Traci hate it here. They're only here because of me, because they have no choice. That's not how I want them to remember me, how I want them to remember Sweeney and their lives here."

Roger nodded, and then asked, "Where are you applying?"

"Albuquerque, Carlsbad, Roswell, Santa Fe, you name it."

Roger winced. "I'm sorry."

"I suppose I should envy you, being unattached, not having two other people calling the shots in your life."

Roger returned the coffee cup to his mouth, took a long drink and said, "No, don't envy me. Remember, I didn't choose to be unattached. It has its moments, I'll admit, but on cold lonely nights a house full of sick animals is no substitute for the warm body of a good woman."

"You ever thought of finding someone?"

"All the time. But I want someone whose commitment isn't conditional on where we live—and since I live in Sweeney that's a tough requirement. Remember, when Kim left me because of Sweeney, Joanie could have left you—but she didn't."

Dave sighed. "Yeah. I guess that's why I'm mailing these now."

Helen's eventual arrival interrupted their conversation. "I'm sorry, boys, but, well, you can see what it's been like all morning." She jangled the pocket of her apron. "But I ain't complaining, no, I ain't complaining. Now, what'll you have?"

As they waited for their order, Roger stood up and began walking among the tables, extending his hand.

"Welcome to Sweeney, folks. Where you all from?"

They eagerly told him. Pretty much everywhere.

Then Roger asked, "Say, I'm interested in the nudity. Hell, I've been naked once or twice myself. Actually, as I recall some of my best times in life were when I was naked." Roger grinned as everyone laughed, then said with feigned offense, "What are you laughing at? I meant being born. What did you think I meant?"

The red-faced man who led the RV caravan into town spoke from a table across the room. "This nudism ain't about sex, it's about being out free in the natural world, as God intended us to be."

"Well, that's certainly how he chose to bring us into the world," Roger replied.

From a seat at the counter came a question from Jim Biddle, an elderly rancher who lived south of town. "What kind of places do you go to? Most of 'em warm, I reckon."

A woman from another quadrant of the room, a stout woman wearing a Fort Lauderdale T-shirt and a Sedona, Arizona, ball cap, replied, "Oh, we go all kinds of places. 'This land is your land, this land is our—'"

"Cork it, Betty," said yet another RVer, triggering widespread laughter among the others, one of whom asked, "By the way, where's the name Sweeney come from? In all our travels I've never encountered another place with that name."

Helen, overhearing the question, replied, "I heard it came from a place in Texas with that name, early settlers came from there."

Biddle said, "I heard it was the last name of an old buffalo hunter who settled in these parts, before the homesteaders arrived."

Roger looked at Dave, who raised his eyebrows and shrugged.

Before a dispute could flare, another RVer asked, "What kind of stock do you raise out here?"

"Well," replied Bill McGinnis, another rancher, "we raise hell when we can, but most of the time we have to settle for looking after the world's scrawniest coyotes and tending to our purebred jackrabbits. They're all free-range, you know."

"Got any buffalo around here?" an RVer asked.

Jim Biddle spoke up. "Matter of fact, we do. I've got a herd on my land." After a pause he asked, "Want to see 'em?"

As the RVers were making arrangements to follow Jim to his ranch, Roger and Dave just looked at each other.

"Sweeney may not have much of a future," Roger said, "but at least it finally got interesting."

Dave hefted the envelopes. "Let's enjoy it while we can."

Closing the door behind him, Dave left the comforting conversation of the Chick 'n' More to walk down the street to the post office. A mailbox was on a nearby corner, but Dave had distrusted mailboxes ever since he and a mid-school coconspirator had deposited an envelope containing a road-kill skunk, addressed to the school's principal. That stunt had turned out to be far less funny than they'd expected.

Dave paused before ascending the three poured-concrete steps leading into the tiny lobby of the Sweeney Post Office, 86002. The diminutive brick building with its flower boxes stuffed with red-blossom geraniums, real in warm weather, plastic in cold, had always reminded Dave of a midget wearing a tuxedo.

Someday, perhaps soon, he reflected, this post office will close, like so many others in similar towns all across America. He recited the names of several High Plains towns that had lost their post offices in his lifetime: Bueyeros, Hayden, Quay, Glenrio, Cameron, Bellview, among others. Scores more had closed earlier, and only a dwindling number of old-timers even recognized the names of the towns they once served. When an isolated community lost its post office, it was like taking a terminal patient off life support. The town became like the ancient, decrepit relative whom no one visits anymore, eventually dying with no one noticing.

As Dave entered the lobby with the applications under his arm, he felt that he was betraying Sweeney. But Joanie and Traci had no such sappy attachment to Sweeney. He often wondered if Traci, having been born and raised here, would develop a sentimental fondness for the town. At the moment—not a chance.

He looked at the envelopes' addresses. Many were going to High Plains towns whose only advantage over Sweeney was that they were larger and more likely to remain alive, at least a little longer. But all were empty of memories for him. Towns of no attachments, a shallow past, and an impersonal future. It was Sweeney's future, or lack of one, that reminded him why he was here in the post office.

Dave knew Albuquerque or Santa Fe offered the best chances of landing a position, but he hoped he'd get a reply from one of the High Plains towns, if only because Joanie and Traci wouldn't regard it as much of an improvement over Sweeney. If that was so, and if he was offered a position, maybe they'd reconsider staying in Sweeney.

"Sure," he muttered as he approached the window.

Suddenly he was stopped by a cheerful voice. "Hi, Dave. Hot enough for you? We've still got a few of those Elvis stamps, if you're interested."

Rita Gallegos, the postmistress. Her round, pleasant face framed by graying black hair peered out at him from the opening in the wooden partition separating the customers from the postal business behind it. Dave glanced over Rita's shoulder and saw a pile of celebrity magazines on a table.

"Sure, why not? Give me half a dozen." As Rita searched the drawers Dave wondered what he should tell Rita about his mailings. She was sure to notice the addresses and inevitably would ask. Then everyone in town would know.

"Here you go, put your mail on the wing, with the face of the King." She laughed loudly at her rhyme. "What're you mailing today? Looks serious. Too heavy for these Elvis stamps."

"Oh, just school business, you know." In a sense, it was.

"That damned paperwork never ends," she said as she accepted his envelopes and affixed postage to them.

As Dave walked out the door he wondered what would become of Rita when the post office closed. For her family, running the post office was akin to owning a ranch. Her father had been Sweeney's postmaster, and his father before him. Through good times and bad they had been part of the neural network that kept the body of Sweeney functioning.

As Dave stepped down the concrete steps, he decided not to pursue the analogy further.

Dave was still depressed from mailing the applications when upon entering home Joanie greeted him by saying, "Well, did you do it?" His depression deepened.

Before he could answer, the phone rang in the Daly kitchen. Dave answered it, then with a puzzled expression turned to Joanie, "It's for you—Roger."

Joanie returned Dave's puzzled look as she took the receiver. "Hi, Roger," she said tentatively. She liked Roger, though she always wondered whether his marriage to Kim might have survived if he hadn't been so stubborn about staying in Sweeney. She and Kim had kept in touch for a while, but they drifted apart as their worlds became more alien to each other. Joanie still missed Kim, and tried not to blame Roger for her loss, but this became more difficult as her own resentment of Sweeney grew.

"Hey, Joanie," Roger said, "I understand you're without a horse at the moment."

Joanie allowed that she was, especially as she was aware Roger already knew it. After all, he had been the one who had put down Scout, her beloved horse, when he had become too old to go on living. For Joanie, being able to keep a horse in a tiny barn and corral behind the house was the only good thing about living in Sweeney.

"Listen, Joanie," Roger continued, "I know you've got a tender heart" —and a soft head, Joanie thought, sensing what was coming— "and you're a good judge of horses—"

"Since when?"

Roger pushed on. "So I knew I'd feel bad if I didn't call you about a horse I got in a couple of days ago. I won't hide anything from you. She's been abused, badly, and not just physically, you know what I mean."

Joanie did.

"But for all her problems, there's good in her, Joanie. She's beat up but not broken, she's still got a good heart."

"Where'd you get her?"

"Guy down near Santa Rosa got arrested for animal abuse. Horrible case. The authorities had to do something with the animals that were worth saving, so they called a few vets to see if they'd take them. Most said no, I said yes. It was that or put her down. She really is a quality horse that doesn't deserve what life has given her."

Joanie's resistance was melting into a puddle around her feet. "I'll take a look."

As she started to hang up she asked, "What's her name?"

"Flicka."

After breakfast, the "tourists," as they were politely called, fanned out to see the sights, primarily the Rock. Local people remarked that S&S conspicuously was not in residence spouting off, until someone mentioned that S&S was scheduled to give a talk that night in the encampment. "Will he be nude? Nah, that would be . . . unthinkable, even for nudists!"

After long moments of appropriate awe, of almost religious respect, and the recording of the moment in countless digital images, the RVers drifted back into town, and many of them went to Adelino and Judy Baca's Baca Mart, the local convenience store and gas station.

The Baca Mart hadn't started out as a convenience store. Adelino, like his father, had set out to run a regular old-time gas station, that pumped gas, fixed tires, undertook miscellaneous repairs, sold oil, antifreeze, and fan belts, and had posted on the greasy walls of the garage girly pinup calendars donated by oil companies. *That* was what he regarded as a gas station.

But Adelino had seen the future, and it looked like a self-pump convenience store. He concluded that the only sure way to forestall a convenience store opening in Sweeney and putting him out of business was to open one himself. So with a hefty loan from the bank in Tucumcari, he gritted his teeth and did just that. He kept the garage and still did quite a bit of work there. It was where he hung out. His wife, Judy, managed the convenience store.

"Let's see, you've got two large sodas, a twelve-pack of Miller Lite, a bag of chips, two candy bars, and lip balm," Judy Baca said to the mountainous, sunburned woman at the counter. She tried to concentrate as she tallied the list. She had never been so busy. So was Adelino, fixing tires and selling oil and hydraulic fluid and what all.

"You don't have any ball caps?" asked the woman. "Or T-shirts? I've just got to get something as a souvenir. You wouldn't believe the collection I've got. No? Oh, dear, if you did, honey, you could sell a million of them. And at about any price. We RVers just love ball caps. We trade them, you know, and a ball cap with the Rock on it—well, that would be a hot item."

Judy thanked the lady for the advice, gave her a soda on the house, and resolved to order T-shirts and ball caps before the day was over.

"What should I put on them?" she wondered as she watched another RVer cradle a bag of chips and a can of outdoor grill lighter fluid in her arms. The caps couldn't show, well . . . the infamous resemblance. Maybe they shouldn't show the Rock at all. She shuddered as the phrase "Between the Rock and a Hard Place" entered her mind. How about "I rocked at the Rock. Nature's Unsolved Mystery. Sweeney, New Mexico"? Yes, that would do it. Fifty ball caps and fifty T-shirts, before the day was over.

As the woman was going out the door, she turned and said, "You know, honey, you people here need to get the word out about this town. There's lots of RVers who'd love to come to a nice little place like this. 'Course, most of 'em would be 'covered.'" The woman spat the word.

Judy took this to mean non-nude. "Oh, that'd be great . . . I mean, we're pretty tolerant around here."

At the Style Salon Nettie faced a minor crisis. On Saturdays she catered primarily to the dwindling number of local nonretired women who couldn't come during the week, but today the small waiting area was crowded with RVers, as well as locals. These latter included Iris Gerber and her neighbor, Harriet Moggs.

Iris and Harriet lived across from each other on Magnolia Street. Iris was a slob. Nettie often tried to excuse her friend by referring to Iris's upbringing by a timid, colorless mother and a drunken, abusive father, both now departed, but she suspected Iris had been born a slob. Iris lived alone in a huge, unkempt house she inherited from her parents, and there she lived a contented life of slovenly hedonism based upon television and junk food abuse. Unkind people in Sweeney said she resulted from the mating of a hippopotamus and Bozo the Clown, but it was true that next to S&S, the most horrific sight in Sweeney was Iris waddling down the street in a sundress. Where she got her clothing was a mystery, as no one could recall ever seeing anything so gaudy in an actual store. Nettie suspected that the reason Iris had never left Sweeney was because here she was under no pressure to be other than who she was. Nettie also suspected that Iris was aware of what people said about her appearance, but like Rudd Torgelson, she simply didn't give a shit.

Harriet, in contrast to Iris, was small, withered, and inconspicuous, like a long-dead spider in an attic. And so old that no one could remember a time when she had not lived alone in her antique three-story house. She went nowhere and did nothing except putter in her garden and once a month go to the Style Salon. There she had Nettie dye her hair a hideous orange that Harriet insisted was her natural color. Nettie knew that wasn't true, because she'd seen the color only once before, on an orangutan at the Albuquerque zoo.

Nettie knew why Iris at least was here today: for the gossip. Iris wanted to hear what the nudists had to say. The waiting area didn't have enough chairs, so Nettie got a couple from the back room, as well as wooden boxes. Iris occupied two.

"It's a pleasure to welcome you to Sweeney," Nettie remarked to the woman in the chair, who was old enough to have voted for Roosevelt— either one—and had requested purple tint on her short-cropped hair.

"It's a pleasure to be here," bellowed a heavy, sixtyish woman wearing yellow, red, and black Capri pants and a sans-bra T-shirt saying, "I Got the Burn at Daytona Beach." Her voice matched her clothing.

"What's the news in a place like this? I imagine you people gossip, just like anyone else."

Nettie briefly imagined an anthropologist saying to a member of an isolated Amazon Indian tribe, "I imagine you eat food, just like ordinary people?"

"Well, the gossip here can be lean, especially as it gets used up pretty quick in a place this small."

"Aw, come on," persisted the woman.

"Oh, things are pretty quiet around here," Nettie replied. Too quiet, she thought, but she'd be damned if she'd admit that to a stranger.

"Of course, there's S&S," volunteered Iris.

"Who?" said the woman in the chair.

As she wiped excess purple tint from the woman's hair, Nettie briefly sketched a portrait of S&S. "Yep, you can pretty much count on S&S doing something outrageous just when things start getting a little slow."

Iris, squirming on her seats, blurted, "There was one time—you remember, Nettie—when he got lickered up on the Fourth of July and went parading down Main Street playing a flute like one of the Continental Soldiers, at midnight, stark naked."

The RVers laughed. "Sounds like our kind of guy," said the loud woman. "I'm glad he has no inhibitions about nakedness, because he's going to speak to the group tonight about discovering the Rock."

Iris gasped. "Oh, no, you can't allow that. There are sights a body wasn't meant to see, and S&S naked is one of them. Believe me, I'm speaking from experience." Nettie nodded.

"At least make him wear underwear," Iris insisted.

"Underwear!" Nettie guffawed. "Since when has S&S owned underwear?"

"Well, you must have other things going on," pressed the loud woman.

"Oh, we have our share of local scandals: people getting divorced—not too many affairs, hard to keep anything secret in a place like Sweeney—people drinking too much, kids at the school trying drugs, getting tattoos . . ."

"Speaking of tattoos," said the woman, "I've got one here you really should see." And with that she stood up and started reaching for the waist band of her pants.

"No, no, that's okay, another time," Nettie replied desperately. "I don't want to get distracted. I might slip, and we don't want that, do we?"

"Certainly not," said the woman in the chair.

"Well, what about you?" asked Nettie, changing the subject. "You travel all over the place, you must have had some real adventures."

"I'll say we have," said the woman in the chair.

The loud woman jumped in. "Remember the time that Arthur—he's one of our older members and gets pretty absentminded sometimes—"

"Addlepated," inserted the purple-headed woman.

"And one time he forgot he was naked, he spends so much time that way, and he got in his car and drove to the supermarket, walked across the parking lot, and started shopping."

"And he wasn't even embarrassed when they pointed out to him that this wasn't casual Friday at the store," offered the woman in the chair.

"That's right," the loud woman continued. "Of course, being naked is nothing to be embarrassed about, but still. . . . And when they escorted him to his car, all he kept saying was 'Can't I just go get my pickles?'"

Iris guffawed. Harriet said, "Why couldn't he get his pickles?"

Other stories followed. Of members traveling to the annual motorcycle rally in Sturgis, South Dakota, and discovering that riding naked there barely raised an eyebrow. Of nude beaches in southern California. Of nude fishing trips out of Key West—"You don't know what danger is until you've tried to land a barracuda in the altogether!"

Reluctant as Nettie was to admit it, the tales evoked memories of her rodeo days, and she began sharing them with the RVers. "There was the time when some fool left the gate to the calf pen open, and there were calves running up and down the bleachers with all these cowboys trying to catch them. And when they did, there were lots of folks who watched the rest of the rodeo standing up, if you know what I mean."

"By the way," asked the woman in the gaudy dress, "where'd that name Sweeney come from? I don't believe I've seen it anywhere else."

Nettie started to reply when Iris interrupted. "It's from Horace H. Sweeney. He was a U.S. senator for Missouri who did a lot of promoting of this area. Folks say he'd bought a lot of land here and was hoping to make a killing." Nettie had never heard that story before, but she figured it was as plausible as the other stories she'd heard.

Normally Nettie closed the Style Salon at noon on Saturdays, but when the last customer finally left she looked at the clock and saw that it was past one. The time had just flown by.

As the last customer, an RVer, walked out the door, Nettie yelled after her, "Take to heart what we said about S&S."

Leland sat at the counter of the Chick 'n' More and through its unwashed windows watched daylight fade from Main Street. He watched Fred Yoder lower the blinds in his barbershop. An elderly Ford pickup rolled lazily down Main Street. Old Abe Martinez going home from the feedstore.

He sipped the dregs of the restaurant's last coffee pot of the day. He was the only customer left, and Helen was starting to clean up and empty the cash register. Time for him to go home too, but he knew he had time for a few more minutes of conversation before the lonely drive.

"So business hasn't been too bad lately?"

Helen turned and gave him a stare that said, "Is the sky blue?"

Leland chuckled.

"We can't keep the kitchen stocked. We're buying every piece of produce anyone brings in, anything good, that is. You don't raise anything at your place, do you?"

"Sorry." Ruth had kept a garden, and each evening at supper during the growing season he had listened patiently as she gave her daily detailed gardening reports—how the tomatoes were doing, disappointment with the new variety of snap beans, rabbit raids on the carrots, the strawberries almost ripe. He missed eating fresh produce, but what he really missed was Ruth.

"I've taken in more in tips in the last day or so than I did the whole of last month. I'm blistering my bones I'm so busy, but I'm not complaining. If this keeps up, I'm going to have the house roof fixed—and maybe buy a new TV."

"How about Ed and Edna, how're they taking this?"

"Well, let's just say they're not complaining either."

"They still fixing to move?"

"They hope this all will last, but they're trying to be ready if it doesn't. Me too. I do hear, though, that they've told their real estate agent in Florida to pull in the reins for a bit."

Suddenly from outside the Chick 'n' More came the rumble of a pickup whose failing muffler Leland identified as Jim Biddle's, accompanied by the smoother sounds of Jeeps of the type typically towed behind RVs. The restaurant's doors burst open, and Jim Biddle and half a dozen RVers barged in.

"Helen, I know you're about to close, "said Biddle, striding up to the counter, "but you remember that ground buffalo meat I gave you some time ago. You froze it, I believe?"

Helen nodded.

"Well, if you and Ed and Edna could see your way to frying up buffalo burgers for me and these nice folks I'm sure we could make it worth your while."

From the kitchen came Ed's voice, "The answer is yes . . . if that's okay with you, Helen?"

"Fine by me." She shot a look at Leland that said, "See what I mean?"

Biddle was talking to the red-faced leader of the RVers. "So it's settled then, we're going to do it. And here's the man we need to talk to." They approached Leland, whose lean, bland face suddenly tightened in perplexity. He was about to have something put to him, and he had no idea what.

"Leland, we're going to have a rodeo for these nice folks," Biddle proclaimed. "They've never seen or smelled a real, live western rodeo, and we're just the westerners that can show 'em one. We haven't had a chance to show off Sweeney hospitality in . . ." His voice trailed off. "Well, in too long. I'll put the word out to the ranchers, and we'll round up enough hands and stock to have a good little rodeo by late Sunday afternoon. You can help by making a few calls yourself and making sure the water and electricity are turned on at the fairgrounds."

Leland sat stunned. Then he smiled and slowly nodded. "Hell, yes. It's been way too long since we had a welcome mat rodeo. I'll get working on it."

As Leland left he heard Biddle saying to Red-face, "Remember, now, buffalo ain't cows, they're wild animals, so if you ever go to Yellowstone you know not to trust 'em, no matter how docile they look. . . ."

So instead of going home after the Chick 'n' More Leland returned to the town offices and their phone. Logistically, staging a spur-of-the-moment rodeo was like launching an impromptu invasion. The stalls and chutes and fencing and announcer's booth and bleachers all had to be checked and repaired. Stock ranging from horses to steers to calves to Brahma bulls had to be rounded up, as well as cowboys. Word of the rodeo had to be disseminated throughout the region. Fortunately, that wasn't much of an issue here, where publicity sort of happened on its own, though in this emergency a few key people made sure everyone was called. He also had to recruit stock handlers, judges and timers, a technician for the PA system, and an announcer and rodeo clown.

In the kitchen of the Larkin home the phone rang. Kathy ran downstairs from her computer to answer it. "Who the hell at this time . . ."

"Kathy, Leland."

"Leland, if you're calling to tell me there's a rodeo Sunday, four others have beat you to it. I had no idea I was on so many people's Rolodexes in Sweeney. That's a lot of trips up and down the stairs."

"Actually, my call does involve the rodeo. I need you to be the announcer."

Kathy's heart stopped. "What? *Me?*"

"That's right. And I'm not scraping the bottom of the barrel. Our usual announcer comes from Moriarty, but we don't have time to get him up here. Locally, you're my first choice."

"Surely you're joking." His silence told her he wasn't. "But . . . there's got to be someone besides me? I mean, I've never done it before." Suddenly panic replaced fatigue. She began pacing.

"To answer your first question, there's Ron Suffitt."

Kathy groaned.

"Right," Leland continued, "it would be like injecting everyone with Novocain as they entered the rodeo grounds. As for whether you can do it, hell yes you can. You've been to enough rodeos, you know the routine by heart."

Kathy said nothing. He was right, at least about knowing the routine. But it was one thing to know what rodeo announcers did, another to do it yourself. And in front of half of Kiowa County. Since returning to Sweeney she'd stayed aloof from the community. It helped preserve the illusion that living here was only temporary. Announcing for the rodeo certainly wasn't a long-term commitment, but it would change things, in ways she couldn't predict. That frightened her.

In the pause, Leland pressed his case. "Look, I've known you all your life. You're lively and witty and enthusiastic."

"Leland." Kathy sighed and leaned against the wall. "I'm flattered by you saying that, I genuinely am, and those words might have been applicable at one time . . . but when I look in the mirror these days I don't see lively and witty and enthusiastic—"

"I understand, believe me, I do. But I also believe you should do this. The idea just came to me, I don't know from where, but the more I've thought about it the more I'm convinced this is right, that not to do it would be wrong. But whether it makes sense or not, I'm willing to give it a go if you are."

"Oh, Leland, I don't know what to say, I just don't, my wit fails me."

"And besides, I'll be up in the announcer's booth in case you need me."

"Leland, I need to think a few minutes, can I call you right back?"

"Sure."

As she hung up the receiver, the magnitude of the decision struck her. She sagged onto a chair; it wobbled and creaked, just like her confidence. Being a rodeo announcer, speaking to more than a hundred people, acquaintances and strangers, keeping them entertained, keeping things moving—her? What the hell was Leland thinking?

He'd called her lively, witty, and enthusiastic. She sagged deeper. Yeah, and Bob Hope is still alive.

But had she once been so? Actually, for most of her youth people would have described her as Leland had. She'd always been at the center of whatever fun was going on. In college, she organized the dorm room joke sessions. Nor had she been afraid of public speaking. She'd been a class officer in high school—who hadn't?—and always enjoyed making presentations. In college she'd been the spokesperson for the ecology club.

But that was a long time ago. The dried up lake west of town had water during the Pleistocene.

Suddenly Kathy recognized the situation, one she knew too well. She stood at a junction, with one path leading to fear, the other to depression, for she had no doubt that if she turned Leland down, depression would follow. And bitter experience had taught her always to choose the path leading to fear, never the one leading to depression.

The phone fell from her fingers as she dialed Leland's number. As she retrieved it from the floor he answered.

"Hi, Leland, just as long as I don't have to be nude. . . ."

Where *were* they? The antacid tablets. When she needed them, they were always hiding in the folds of her purse. And she definitely needed them now.

Standing on a street corner midway between her home and the Chick 'n' More, June Fall rummaged again through her purse and eventually came up with half a roll of big, white tablets. She extracted three and popped them all in her mouth. She knew she took too many, that they weren't Life Savers, but lately she'd come to depend on them more and more, especially around Wayne, the one-man reform movement.

He hadn't always been like this. She recalled that he'd been lively and fun—sort of—when they were students together at Faith Bible College. Admittedly, he'd been a bit of a party-pooper, and she recalled the time he'd insisted on saying grace before some of his dorm buddies tapped a keg in their room.

She should cut back on the antacid tablets. No wonder her stomach was upset so often. She'd never taken three before, she really should cut back—but not today. She only hoped the three would be enough for what she was facing.

It began with stopping to chat with Nettie Wilkin outside the Chick 'n' More just now. Nettie was a stalwart in the church, had been for years. June liked Nettie and sensed Nettie felt similarly. They'd chatted, then suddenly Nettie had said, "Well, heavens yes, why didn't I think of it before?"

Before June could react Nettie looked directly at her and said, "You know about the rodeo." It wasn't a question. June nodded.

"And the reception?"

June shook her head.

"Well, right after the rodeo there's going to be a little reception in the agriculture hall at the fairgrounds. There'll be food, drinks—no alcohol —live music, maybe a square dance or two."

"They won't be naked, will they?"

"No, of course not," Nettie scoffed, "though with the clothes some of them wear you'd almost prefer them naked."

June's eyes widened.

"Don't you worry. They're nice people, just ordinary folks—except for being nudists—and in just a couple of days they'll have done this town a world of good."

"Well, I do hear that the Chick 'n' More might not be closing after all."

"But what I need to talk to you about is playing the piano at the reception—"

June gasped, her hands flying to her face. "No," she squeaked.

Nettie bored in on her. "You can do it. You've got to do it. The alternative is having Karen Suffitt sing." June paled. The rumor in church was that Karen Suffitt had taken voice lessons from coyotes. "Besides, nobody in town can play the piano like you. You're the best, dear. Especially as all you need to do is belt out a few easy oldies."

"But Wayne—"

"I'm not asking Wayne, I'm asking you." Nettie's eyes narrowed. "You can play a lot more than hymns. I've heard you playing in the church by yourself. You're good."

June knew she was. In college she'd always had more requests to play than she could accept, not that she didn't try. She *loved* playing popular music for people. It was fun. Music was supposed to be fun. But she hadn't played anything but hymns for years, except for herself. Wayne frowned on nonreligious music. The pain of her loss festered.

"Besides," pressed Nettie, "you can tell him I coerced you into saying yes. You can tell him I wouldn't take no for an answer, and he should respect the wishes of one of the church's most senior members." Nettie was ruthless.

June was speechless. She wanted to say yes—oh, how she wanted to say yes—but Wayne would never agree, certainly not with the nudists being involved. There would be a huge argument; Wayne would shout and rant and quote scripture, getting ever louder and more adamant until eventually she would fold and withdraw into sulky silence. But why couldn't Wayne let her win, just once, especially when it was about something as dear to her as her music?

Sensing victory, Nettie pressed on. "It would reflect poorly on our community church if you and the pastor turned the town down."

Maybe, thought June. It just might work. . . . And it would all be true.

Nettie pleaded, "Just say yes. You'll be doing a good deed for your town. This isn't an evil thing, it's a good thing."

And June knew Nettie was right. "Well, if you put it that way . . . okay, I'll do it. Yes. If it's okay with Wayne, that is." She chided herself for adding that, a bad habit.

Nettie hugged her. "I'm proud of you, and so is Sweeney."

June wasn't reassured, especially as it reminded her of what generals told their troops before sending them into battle.

Now with Nettie gone, June stood by herself at the corner and waited for the tablets to dissolve in her stomach. But to her surprise, anger, not fear, welled up. She had been humiliated by admitting to Nettie that she needed Wayne's permission to play. Like hell she did. She instantly regretted the swearing, but she still seethed at admitting that Wayne did indeed have the final say in everything she did—including her music.

She ached to play the piano at a party again, where music was making people happy, not putting them to sleep. And she knew that if she rejected this chance, she'd likely never get another. The rest of her musical life would be spent mechanically pounding out the same hymns she'd grown weary of twenty years ago, wondering where she'd gone wrong.

"Well, it won't be here," she said, and strode off toward home, her steps becoming shorter and shorter.

Surprisingly, Wayne seemed to take it pretty well. June had approached him and said, "We need to talk. Let's sit down."

At first he'd been fearful as he took a chair, but then he appeared almost relieved when she told him about the rodeo reception. June briefly suspected he thought she was going to leave him, and the rodeo reception was a lesser disaster.

Before he could recover and reject the idea, she replayed all of Nettie's arguments.

"Wayne, this could be serious. Nettie said that if we ruined the town's only reception in years by my refusing to play, that the whole congregation would leave the church—and she would lead them. She said they might become Catholics, or Mormons."

Wayne blanched.

"I know this is hard, Wayne, but the church needs to do this for the community. Everyone knows what a burden this is on . . . you. And on the church. But the town will respect us more for it."

"But, but . . . those people are nudists!"

"They'll be clothed! Nobody will be naked. They're just a bunch of old folks. There haven't been any problems since they've been in town. I wouldn't be surprised if a couple of them came to church tomorrow morning. Wayne, you might be able to bring them to Jesus."

Wayne looked up.

"Think about it. All over the world Christian missionaries are God's word to the strangest people. We can be a witness unto the nudists, show them they don't have to be naked to have a good time."

"Nettie and the others wouldn't really leave the church and become Mormons, would they?"

June nodded. She had him. She went to her piano and began playing a John Lennon favorite of hers, "Imagine."

A late-evening thunderstorm, unusual for this early in the season, roiled over the horizon, the dark land below accentuating the silent lightning within the white-gray clouds above. In all his years on the plains, Leland had never tired of what people called "lightning shows." And perhaps this one presaged an early monsoon season—and a wetter than usual summer. The homesteader farmers had seen the summer monsoon storms as both blessing and curse, for the rain often came with hail that could flatten their crops, usually just before harvest. But the farms had been abandoned during the droughts of the 1930s, and the ranchers welcomed any moisture-bearing storms.

Today had been a good day. Leland liked Biddle's rodeo idea; it was just the sort of thing Sweeney needed to pull together and do right now. He hoped he'd done the right thing by convincing Kathy to be the rodeo announcer, but as he'd said, his instinct had guided him, and like her he'd faced a choice between uncertainty and regret. What he hadn't told her was that he'd watched with dismay as her youthful brightness slowly faded after she returned to be with her parents: he couldn't bear to see her grow old and bitter. Sweeney did that to many young people who stayed, but perhaps announcing the rodeo would open a door for her, or at the least get her out to have some fun.

The thunderstorm was heading the wrong direction, receding, when he finally parked the pickup in front of the ranch house. Trixie followed him to the barn to tend to the animals and then into the house. He switched on the kitchen light, and as Amarillo wound around his ankles he noticed the blinking light on his phone.

He hesitated. Lately the messages had not been from people wanting to help him save money on long-distance phone service. He temporized by feeding Amarillo and Trixie. Then he returned to the phone and stared at it a moment before picking up the receiver. His anxiety was justified.

"Hi, Dad." It was Grant. Leland tried to enjoy talking to his son on the phone, but the awkwardness inherent in their relationship persisted. That relationship was likely to get even more awkward, given the object now unabashedly upright just outside town. He didn't want to talk about it, and certainly not about his role in its . . . raising up. Dammit, just how the hell did a straight person talk to someone of Grant's orientation—he couldn't bring himself to say gay or homosexual—about something like the Rock? It was a minefield of unintended offenses.

The message continued: "It's me. I wanted to firm up plans for this summer's trip to Sweeney. Ray won't be coming this year, big social work conference he has to attend, but I'm looking forward to it. Maybe around the end of July? Give me a call. Love you."

Grant ended all his phone calls with "Love you," and Leland always echoed the farewell, though it too was awkward for him. Not that he didn't love his son, but he hadn't grown up in a culture where men said "Love you" to one another. Affection was expressed in more subtle ways, like sharing a dip of snuff. Still, Leland knew he would be disappointed if Grant ever omitted the farewell.

What the hell was he going to do? He was in deep waters, and he was a dry-land cowboy. He needed help, and knew of only one person who might provide it. He picked up the phone again.

"Hello, Larkins. This is Kathy."

"Kathy, it's me again, hope I'm not calling too late."

"Oh, hi, Leland, no, I'm just wasting time on the Internet," Kathy replied. "You're calling about the rodeo?" She couldn't decide whether she'd be relieved or depressed if he said the announcing deal was off.

"Actually, I'm not." He paused and then said, "This is hard. I need your help. I've never talked to anyone about this. It's not about the rodeo or any town business. It's about Grant."

Kathy sucked in her breath. "Is he okay?"

"He's fine, but he's fixing to make his annual summer trip back to Sweeney—and Sweeney's undergone some changes since the last time he was here. Specifically, one big geological change."

"I see," Kathy said slowly. "Have you talked to him about what's been happening here?" She pulled up a chair and sat down.

"I haven't. I don't know how to. I'd cut my tongue out before I'd say anything to hurt or embarrass him, and I do want him to visit, but this damned Rock is a minefield, what with him being . . . well, you know. You're the only person besides me who knows."

"Yes, I do know. And you need to start feeling comfortable using terms like 'gay' and 'homosexual,' you need to be able to really talk to Grant and not just hide behind small talk."

Leland breathed deeply. "It won't be easy. I'll work on it. But even if I don't say something hurtful, there's always someone like that fool Tom Binks who will. Let's face it, Sweeney hasn't had a lot of practice with sexual diversity, and like most rural small towns it has some dark closets best not entered. The last thing I want is for Grant to have a bad experience here and not want to come again. We don't get together often enough as it is. I don't know what to do. That's why I called you, you know him better than anyone, probably better even than me."

"And you say Grant called today?"

"Yep, so I need to call back pretty soon."

"Look, you relax for a bit, do some chores, whatever, give yourself a couple of hours, then if you don't hear from me, give him a call. And Leland, when you talk to Grant, be straightforward and honest. That's your way. And you have to trust Grant to be able to handle whatever you say. You're both good men, wanting to do the right thing. It'll work out."

"Thanks, Kathy."

"And if Grant asks why you took so long getting back to him, tell him you were attending a meeting of the Sweeney Opera Council."

"Straightforward and honest. Thanks again, Kathy."

Leland puttered around the house, giving Amarillo an unexpected second serving of cat food, going through mail that he'd let pile up, watering houseplants threatening to die, watching the clock hands move ever so slowly. And amid the trivial activity a question arose that he'd been dodging for a long time: in wanting to protect Grant from hurt and embarrassment while he was in Sweeney, wasn't he seeking to protect himself as well?

He knew the answer—and he didn't like it. In many ways life was easier when Grant wasn't around. He couldn't imagine telling his fellow ranchers, some of whom he'd known all his life, that his son was a homosexual. Sure, they wouldn't say anything overtly cruel, but the relationship would be permanently altered, he would forever be isolated. He hated the ranchers for this, and he hated himself for not having the courage to buck it.

Half an hour before the deadline he'd given himself to call Grant, the phone rang.

"Hi, Dad, sorry I missed you before. Is this a good time to talk?"

"Well, I hate to interrupt the discussion I was having with Amarillo about federal cat food subsidies, but I guess that will be okay."

"That cat is a born lobbyist, but then, all cats are. I wanted to talk about my trip this summer, and I understand that Sweeney is, shall we say, different than when I last was there."

"Yep, Sweeney is now anatomically correct. Son, I assume you've talked to Kathy and have been told what's been going on lately?"

"I have."

"And if she didn't tell you, I will: I had a major hand in it, and still support it, though I swear I didn't know what that rock was going to look like before we got it out of the ground."

"Dad, I'm proud of you for it. It's one of the things I've always admired about you and tried to emulate: when you see something that needs to be done, you do it."

Leland cringed. *I wish that were true regarding you.* Then he asked, "How do you feel about coming home with that thing sticking up?"

"You mean because I'm gay? Well, yeah, there are some gays who would make a big deal of it, just as there are straight people who would, but I'm not one of them. To me it's just a rock with an interesting resemblance, no different than a rock shaped like a skull or a nose or buttocks . . . well, maybe a little different.

"But, Dad, do you have any idea how many mountains and hills around New Mexico and other places are shaped like tits? Even named for them? Tetilla Peak near Santa Fe, the Tetons in Wyoming, Squaw Tits Mountains in Arizona—geology is mimicking the human anatomy all the time, though I admit geology usually stays above the waist. No, I'm looking forward to seeing the infamous Rock in Sweeney, but only in an abstract way."

Leland relaxed into his big recliner chair and began petting Amarillo, who jumped on his lap.

"Thanks, I'm glad to hear that. I'd have felt horrible if that damned thing had kept you away."

"And as for fools like Tom Binks, he won't be the first homophobic lowlife I've encountered. They're just a fact of life gays have to learn to deal with. But what I am worried about is how you'll feel if someone makes an antigay remark around you. I don't want you to be embarrassed or feel awkward because of me."

Leland cringed again, paused a long moment, then said, "Decent of you to feel that way, but if I'm not to worry about you, then you shouldn't have to worry about me. I've been thinking it's time I came out of the closet, as the father of a gay man. I'm proud of you, gay or straight. I don't give a shit about the likes of Tom Binks, and if he gets offensive, I'll just deal with it."

"Sounds like we should have an exciting time together. But please, don't start a fight with him or anyone on my account. That might feel good at the moment, but in the long run it will only make things worse. Now about those federal cat food subsidies. . . ."

After they hung up, Leland continued sitting in his chair, Amarillo on his lap, Trixie at his feet. He felt good about the conversation, felt he'd said the right things to reassure Grant. But had he reassured himself? He was ashamed to realize he still wished Grant's visit would come and go without Grant's orientation being an issue . . . no, dammit, that was just another dainty dodge. What he really meant was without anyone knowing Grant was a homosexual. Life would be so much simpler, but lately life in Sweeney had been anything but simple.

Chapter Seven

➤ THE SWEENEY RODEO ARENA DOMINATED the Kiowa County Fairgrounds; the only other structures were two plywood-and-tin buildings, one for livestock, the other for agriculture and everything else, from homegrown chiles and prize peonies to hand-sewn quilts and drawings by local children of their pets and favorite TV characters. As rodeo arenas went, Sweeney's was rather small, just a truncated oval less than fifty yards long and twenty-five yards wide, with bleachers along one side, a gate at the rounded end, and gates and chutes at the other, topped by a rectangular wooden announcer's booth reached by steep wooden stairs.

Curious, thought Kathy as she surveyed the arena from the announcer's booth, that so ordinary a setting could evoke such terror. She'd been to dozens of rodeos in Sweeney—they highlighted the community calendar like Fourth of July parades—but aside from helping cowgirl friends during high school, she never before had been a participant, and certainly not the central participant.

"Howdy, Kathy," said Ollie Biggers, one of several cowboys busy around the chutes. "Looking nice today."

"Thanks," she replied, deciding to take it as a compliment. For this occasion she had overcome her normal indifference to western attire and worn a bright turquoise-and-white blouse with faux-pearl buttons.

On her head was a gray-felt Stetson with a beaded turquoise-and-orange hat band. It all made her feel even more awkward. Her new blue jeans felt tight as she climbed the stairs, and her seldom-worn cowboy boots pinched her feet. She wasn't sure her sweaty forehead was due to midafternoon heat or anxiety.

From below and behind her came the sounds and smells of men and animals jostling in a maze of pens and chutes: cowboys' grunts and shouts, calves bawling, bulls bellowing, hooves kicking boards, and the blended odors of dust and sweat and cow and horse manure. Along one side of the arena a line of cowboys leaned against a board-and-wire fence in the fence-leaning stance of cowboys everywhere, as if only they could keep the fence from falling down. The back right pocket of each pair of Wrangler jeans bore the cowboy emblem, a pale circle worn by a can of snuff.

At the far end waited the parade participants, obscured by a gate and a cloud of dust kicked up by horses and other animals. The parade, involving the whole community, was as much a part of rodeo as the bull-riding. In the stands, in the shade of a wooden roof, sat the spectators, fanning themselves, sipping cold drinks, talking, and waiting. To Kathy it was all so familiar—yet so stomach-knotting.

She turned toward Leland, who had just entered the booth. He returned her sickly look with a broad smile. "Great day for a rodeo, ain't it?" Clearly it was—marshmallow clouds in a brilliant-blue New Mexico sky, with just enough wind to blow away the dust but not enough to raise any more. Was it just her imagination or was Leland enjoying her discomfort? Her weak smile betrayed her skepticism. He patted her on the back. "Don't worry, you'll do fine."

Just then Red-face and Loud-woman from the nudist RV camp arrived in the announcer's booth. "Howdy, howdy," Red-face bellowed. He wore a broad-brimmed straw cowboy hat obviously on its maiden voyage outside the feedstore where he'd undoubtedly bought it. The hat band was as yet unstained by the sweat streaming down the man's face, and the price tag was still on it. Loud-woman wore her trademark Capri pants and a T-shirt reading "Rodeo naked." Where she got that was anyone's guess.

"I invited them to be up here," explained Leland as he introduced them to Kathy, "to give us a sense of what things our out-of-town visitors might want to know about."

"Great," said Kathy as she shook their hands. *Gee thanks, Leland, as if I didn't have enough to focus on.*

Just then someone at the arena's far end waved a red bandana. "That's the signal that everything's ready to begin," explained Leland to the guests. "We always start with the parade."

"By the way," Kathy asked, "what's in the parade?"

"Beats me," said Leland.

As the gate swung open, Kathy tentatively took the microphone, cleared her throat, and began speaking.

"Welcome everybody to the first-ever Sweeney Hospitality Rodeo, and we'd like to give a special welcome to our guests, in whose honor this rodeo is being held. It's going to get pretty wild and western here, so everybody hold onto your hats and prepare to have a real good time."

In the stands, Traci Daly began fidgeting with the settings of the camera that hung from her neck. "Hurry," said Heather, "she's coming out now."

Traci raised the camera to her eyes and focused as a regal palomino pranced out of the gate at the arena's far end, leading the parade. Brightly colored ribbons dangled from all the tack. On the horse's back, in a saddle resplendent with silver studs and long leather tassels, sat Christie. Seeing her friends, she waved.

"Did you get that?" asked Heather urgently.

"Relax," said Traci in exasperation. "We'll have ten times more pictures than they'll actually use."

Because Dave Daly was the sponsor of the school's yearbook, Traci and her friends had been drafted into acquiring photos. "Great," Traci had said at the time, "nothing ever happens here. It will be like documenting a chess tournament."

But the assignment had turned out more fun than the girls had expected, especially as they had taken the school's dullness as a mandate to capture any bizarre or ridiculous thing that happened. When the school cafeteria catastrophically had served cabbage Jell-O one day, the resulting food fight had been duly recorded for posterity.

Traci in particular enjoyed photography. Sensing this, her parents had bought her a good quality digital camera, and in addition to sharing ridiculous school photos with her friends on Facebook, she experimented with more serious photography, visiting sites on the Web. She stubbornly resisted the idea that anything in Sweeney was worth photographing, but she'd taken photos of especially dramatic sunsets.

"Too bad they didn't ask me to lead the parade," snarked Kimberly. "I'd have given them something *really* memorable."

Traci looked at Kimberly's multiple piercings. "Well, you do have as much metal on you as that horse."

Heather waved wildly to Christie, then turned to her friends. "Beautiful, just beautiful. Isn't she beautiful?"

"Oh, yes, she really is," said Rachel Rowe, now an honorary, if temporary, member of the group. "I'm so glad she's my friend."

"She meant the horse," said Traci. Rachel looked confused and hurt.

"I'm just kidding, Christie *is* beautiful out there."

In the announcer's booth, Kathy spoke into the microphone. "That's Christie Herwig, folks, and her horse, Fury, a purebred palomino. Christie's a thoroughbred herself, with the best attendance record in the history of our local high school, and since she lives thirty miles out on the plains, that's no slouch of an achievement.

"Now, let's see what's coming along next."

As if on cue a gaggle of little kids, mostly local 4-H Club members, marched into the arena, leading their colts and calves and lambs. One tiny girl had a bunny on a leash hopping behind her. It was achingly cute.

"And now—" Kathy paused, looked hard toward the far gate, then said to Leland under her breath, "Please, tell me it isn't, not after last time." Leland squinted down the arena, frowned, then shrugged. Kathy again addressed the microphone, "And now, it's Abe Martinez and his team of oxen. You don't see oxen much anymore, but it's animals like these that brought the settlers' wagons over the Santa Fe Trail and helped populate these parts. Let's give a big hand to the little ones and to these big ones. Keep 'em moving, Abe." As applause rippled through the arena Kathy whispered, "Please, Abe, whatever you do, keep them moving, please don't let them stop."

But stop they did, when the little girl with the rabbit dropped the leash, and the bunny bounded away. Half a dozen cowboys ran to catch it as it hopped frantically around the arena. In that dreadful pause in the parade, the oxen halted. Then one of them, slightly the larger, began urinating.

And urinating. And urinating. And urinating. Then the other ox began.

A hush fell over the crowd as they waited to see just how long the urination would last. Beneath the oxen the piss became a puddle then a pond. And still it continued. Abe tried to prod his team into moving, but they were stubborn as oxen. Finally the yellow flood became a stream became a dribble, then nothing. At last, the oxen began plodding forward. Applause erupted from the audience.

From the announcer's booth Kathy proclaimed, "There you have it, folks, one of the great wonders of the animal kingdom, the bladder capacity of a fully hydrated ox—and you witnessed it in Sweeney. When folks around here talk about flash floods, this is what they mean."

In the stands, Kimberly urgently turned to Traci. "Did you get that?" Traci nodded smugly.

The rest of the parade was an anticlimax, even the appearance of S&S riding into the arena behind Rudd Torgelson on a huge front-end loader with a bucket of dirt to cover the oxen-bog.

"Say," said Red-face in the announcer's booth, "isn't that the guy that was supposed to speak to us last night?"

"From what I heard, that's him," Kathy replied.

"How'd it go?" asked Leland.

"Let's just say he didn't quite meet our dress code," said Red-face.

And you're nudists, thought Kathy.

The first event in the rodeo was the saddle-bronc riding. Kathy turned to Leland, "Who's the rodeo clown?" Introducing and interacting with the rodeo clown was part of the role of rodeo announcer.

"Roger."

"Ohforgod'ssake . . ." But she could not say more, because just then Roger the Rodeo Clown was entering the arena. Dressed in baggy hobo clothing and Emmett Kelley makeup, he bowed grandly to the crowd.

Kathy smiled evilly as she introduced him. "Our clown for the Sweeney Hospitality Rodeo today is none other than Roger Rollins, our local veterinarian." More grand bowing from Roger.

"Yep, it's not easy being a rodeo clown," Kathy explained. "You've got to have just the right combination of low intelligence, lack of good sense, absence of self-respect, and tasteless humor—but here in Sweeney we've got one of the best."

Roger glowered at her through his makeup.

"The goal of saddle-bronc riding," she continued, "is to stay on the horse for eight seconds, the longest eight seconds in a cowboy's life."

"It should be easy to stay on them," said Loud-woman. "After all, they're sitting in a saddle."

"Sounds easy, doesn't it?" Kathy said into the microphone. "Just stay in the saddle for eight seconds. Well, there's stove-up cowboys out there who can tell you it's one of the most challenging, difficult events in all rodeo. It's where rodeo began, cowboys breaking wild horses to the saddle. Unlike bareback riding and bull riding, you can't grab onto a secure cinch around the animal, you just have the rein attached to the halter."

"And saddle broncs are meaner'n piss," said Roger-the-Clown from the arena.

"What's that," said Kathy, "they're meaner than the Swiss? That's not a very nice thing to say."

Roger took off his tattered hat, threw it on the ground, and stomped on it. Everyone laughed.

Roger's description proved correct; only two of the four riders were still on their horses when the buzzer sounded, and one of them was halfway off.

"I think it's cruel," pouted Loud-woman.

Kathy answered into the microphone. "We've got a question here as to whether rodeo is cruel. I know cowboys who sure think it is—at least to them. Actually, injuries to the stock are far, far less common than injuries to the cowboys. You don't see saddle broncs carrying around bags of pain pills. In fact, if I was livestock, I'd rather be in rodeo than most other places that livestock wind up. That's because I'd live longer than most animals. My owner would take better care of me, because I'm more valuable, and I'd live a more natural lifestyle, out on the range rather than in a pen, because then I'd be more wild.

"Our next event's the steer wrestling. Here a cowboy on a horse chases a running steer. The cowboy leaps off his horse onto the steer beside him, grabs the animal by the horns, then tries to wrestle the steer to the ground and onto his back. Now doesn't that sound like fun?"

"Just what is a steer?" asked Red-face.

"And for those of you who are unclear as to what a steer is, our wise veterinarian clown will explain."

"He's a bull that's been balloxed."

"You say he's a bull that's been flummoxed? What on earth do you mean by that?"

"He's been castrated."

"Educated? Well, that's a little better."

"They're where we get Rocky Mountain oysters."

"We get blisters from them? You're not making much sense, Roger."

Roger again grounded his hat and stomped on it.

"Oh, I get it, Leland just told me. You know when you take your male dog to the vet to be neutered, well that happens to some young bulls. Are any of these steers here your doing, Roger?"

He stuck out his tongue at her.

The steer wrestling went smoothly, followed by the calf roping. The rodeo organizers had decided to skip the bareback riding in the interest of time and the absence of stock.

When the last calf had been untied and had scampered out of the arena, Kathy said, "Well, since we're featuring little ones, here's an event that everyone loves—the mutton bustin'."

And with that the chute gate beneath the announcer's booth swung open and out leaped a sheep with a little boy on its back.

"Ride him, Stevie," someone yelled. Unfortunately, little Stevie's cinch had come loose, and by the time the buzzer sounded he was hanging under the sheep and had to be rescued by Roger.

"That was Stevie Gallegos," said Kathy. "That kid will go far—he's got his own unique way of doing things."

Other kids and sheep followed. A little girl, McKenna Collins, stayed on her sheep the whole time, but the others slid off.

"It's harder than it looks. Let's give them all a big hand," Kathy said. The crowd responded with a loud cheer. "It's from kids like these that future rodeo cowboys come. Don't tell their mothers I said that."

She turned to Leland and grinned. She didn't know exactly when it had happened, but her fear had evaporated. She and the crowd were having fun together. Leland nodded and grinned back.

"The next event," Kathy announced, "is the barrel racing. This is women's chance to shine in rodeo. It's an event that features skill, sensitivity, grace, a close connection between horse and rider, and—dare I say it?—intelligence."

From the arena Roger made exaggerated angry gestures toward Kathy.

"See what I mean?" Kathy said to the crowd's approval. Roger responded by again dust-stomping his hat.

Loud-woman asked, "Does that mean women aren't allowed to compete in the other events? Can they only do the barrel racing?"

Kathy answered into the microphone. "We have a question as to whether a woman would be allowed to compete in the other events. The answer is, sure they can enter. They might even do fairly well, but I like to think that sticking to the barrel racing is proof that women just plain have more good sense than men."

Down in the arena cowboys were setting up three barrels at measured locations. Kathy looked down and saw Roger take a notebook from his baggy pants, scribble on it, and then pass it to a boy who ran it up to the announcer's booth and handed it to Kathy. Into the microphone she said, "I've just received word that we've got something special for you today. To give a quick demonstration of what barrel racing is all about we've got our own barrel racing queen, Nettie Wilkin. She's got a house full of trophies that she won all over the West. Let's give her a big hand."

And with that a gate opened beneath the announcer's booth and out rode Nettie astride a beautiful chestnut mare that Kathy recognized as coming from Roger's stable of spares. Nettie wore jeans and a fancy red-and-white western blouse. On her head was her broad-brimmed, Sunday-go-to-rodeo cowboy hat. She rode easily in the saddle.

"Did you know about this?" Kathy whispered to Leland.

"Hell, no, we're all just making this up as we go."

Kathy resumed announcing. "In this event, a rider enters the arena at full speed, quickly rounds each barrel in a cloverleaf pattern, and then exits where she entered."

As Kathy announced, Nettie guided her horse at a canter through the required course around the barrels.

"Speed is what counts in this event. They're racing against the clock, and a few hundredths of a second can make the difference between winning and losing. The riders steer their horses as close as they can to the barrels trying to shave precious seconds. If they knock over a barrel, a five-second penalty is added to their total time."

As Nettie returned to the gate from whence she'd come, she took off her hat and waved it to the crowd.

"I know her!" exclaimed Loud-woman. "She did my hair yesterday. She told me stories about her rodeo days, but I thought she was just making most of them up."

"Oh, no," said Leland. "She's the real deal. If she says it happened, it happened."

Suddenly from the chute beneath them a horse and rider burst into the arena. The rider, a girl who looked to be preteen, urged her horse at breakneck speed toward the first barrel, swung around it, then the next, and finally the third. The last barrel wobbled but did not fall.

"That's Katie Simms on Warpaint," Kathy announced to the crowd, "and, let's see here, her time was 16.3 seconds. That's a mighty good time, folks. Katie's just twelve. She's been working with that horse since she was nine, and it shows. Let's hear it for Katie and Warpaint."

None of the horses and riders that followed had the same knack—two of them toppled barrels and one horse decided to skip the last barrel altogether. At the end of the event Katie and Warpaint had the winning time.

"Our final event," announced Kathy, "is the one you've all been looking forward to, the bull riding. It's the wildest, toughest, most dangerous event in rodeo, and I know our rodeo clown has been looking forward to it too, because it allows him to exhibit his talent as bull bait."

Roger stuck out his tongue at her.

Kathy smiled, stuck out her tongue back, and continued. "We've rounded up five of the meanest, rankest bulls in Kiowa County, and we've got five of the county's craziest—I mean bravest—cowboys willing to try to stay on them for a full eight seconds."

"I'm glad it isn't more, for the sake of the cowboys," said Loud-woman.

"Actually," Kathy explained into the microphone, "the eight-second time limit in the bull riding and the bucking horse events isn't to protect the cowboys but to protect the animals, because they start getting tired and out of adrenaline after eight seconds. Nobody gives a damn about the cowboys because they're not worth nearly as much as a good bull."

The announcer's booth shook as a bull goaded into the chute below tried to demolish it. Cowboys pushed on all sides trying to contain the bull and calm him down so the rider could climb on his back.

"Our first rider out is Billy Baca from over near Chupadera." With that the cowboy nodded, the chute swung open, and out leaped an angry bull, made even angrier by a jolt to his haunches from an electric cattle prod. The bull leaped, spun once in the air, and when he came down Billy was on the ground.

Immediately, Roger was in front of the bull, waving his hat, distracting the bull while Billy scrambled out of harm's way. In a cloud of dust and with the bell around his neck clanging angrily, the bull charged Roger, who deftly leaped inside a barrel that had been left in the ring from the barrel racing. The bull rolled the barrel with his horns before running out the open gate at the arena's end.

"Let's have a big Sweeney hand for Billy Baca, I know that looks easy, folks, but don't try this at home. This should only be done by cowboys with certified training on a barrel behind a barn.

"Next up is Toby Nelson, from right here in Sweeney," Kathy announced. Toby was able to stay on his bull the full eight seconds, primarily because his bull was more interested in running than jumping.

"Remember, folks," said Kathy, "if more than one cowboy stays on the full time, the cowboy with the rankest bull wins. Now we've got Manuel Baca, Billy's big brother."

Manuel also had drawn a nasty-tempered bull, and unfortunately he was airborne when the whistle blew.

Jim Switzer, the next rider out, did little better.

"And now, our final rider of the day is . . ." Kathy turned to Leland. "I can't read this. It looks like it says Bare-assed Bob."

Before Leland could answer, the gate swung open, and out leaped an enormous bull on whose back clung a cowboy wearing only boots and spurs, a bandana mask, and a jock-strap.

"Yep, I guess that's what it says," replied Leland.

The bull leaped and spun and sunfished, but Bob clung like a cocklebur. When the buzzer sounded, a cowboy on a horse rode up to Bob, who grabbed onto the rider and swung himself behind him. The two immediately rode through the gate and out of sight.

Cheering and pandemonium erupted from the crowd.

"I'll be damned," said Leland. "I'll just plain be go to hell, I ain't never seen anything like that."

Red-face and Loud-woman both clapped him on the back. "That was great!" exclaimed Red-face. "That just absolutely beats all."

"That takes the prize," said Loud-woman. "You didn't have to do that just for our benefit, but we do appreciate it."

Before Leland could stammer a response, Kathy said into the microphone, "Folks, that was Bare-assed Bob. Yep, that's what it says on the program list, and sure as I'm standing here that was indeed Bare-assed Bob.

"I'm sure that ride was in honor of our esteemed guests, and I'm sure we all can agree it was a memorable one. Yep, this was one for the record books. And remember, you saw it at the Sweeney Hospitality Rodeo."

"Did you get that?" Heather prodded Traci.

"You bet I did, every second of it."

"I think I know who Bare-assed Bob was," gasped Christie.

"Just *how* do you know?" sniped Kimberly.

"Well, certainly not the way you think."

With the exit of Bare-assed Bob, all that remained of the rodeo was the reception, and before the dust settled in the arena the crowd flowed toward the agriculture hall. Nettie clapped Leland on the back as the two approached the entrance. "We did Sweeney proud."

"We did indeed."

As they entered, they heard two visitors arguing.

"I say that Bare-assed Bob was the best part. You just can't beat that. Imagine, the people here talking a cowboy into doing that, just for us."

"Yeah, that was good, but the image that will always stick in my mind is of those oxen pissing. I didn't think they'd ever stop."

"That was impressive. I don't know how they arranged that, maybe shoved hoses down their throats."

Leland and Nettie just looked at each other and shook their heads. Preoccupied with the visitors, they missed another argument taking place nearby.

"Please, Wayne," June Fall pleaded as the two stood outside the agricultural building. "The piano's here and everything. Everyone will be disappointed."

"No! Absolutely not! That naked cowboy at the end proves what I've been saying! If you think either of us is going to have anything to do with this, this . . . obscene, sinful event . . ."

Desperate, June looked around for Nettie, hoping for support, but Nettie was gone, and given the height of Wayne's dudgeon perhaps not even Nettie could have any influence.

"Please, Wayne, this means so much to me. This is just a harmless little reception, with our friends and neighbors. And our church members. Wayne, this means so much to me. And you promised."

"I didn't promise, and a profane dance shouldn't mean so much to you, serving the Lord should be your highest priority. How do we know someone won't streak naked through the dance hall? How do we know some of those nudists won't suddenly take their clothes off?"

To those questions, June had no answer. Wiping away tears, she acknowledged defeat. But this was not the end of it, she vowed, no, this was not the end.

Chapter Eight

◆ FLICKA. SURE, THOUGHT JOANIE as she peered into the stall where a scrawny, raw-boned horse cowered in wild-eyed terror in the corner, its dull red-brown hide marred by scars and sores. Yesterday evening Roger had delivered the horse—heavily sedated—to the barn behind the Daly home.

Flicka. The man who'd savaged this horse certainly hadn't given her that name. No, the name was Roger's doing, damn him, a name he'd come up with after rescuing the horse, a name he knew would dissolve Joanie's resistance to adopting the horse. How could she *not* adopt a pathetic, abused horse named Flicka?

As a child in Los Angeles, Joanie had nourished her young-girl horse fantasies with a rich diet of horse novels, and among her favorites, ranking with *Black Beauty* and *Misty of Chincoteague*, had been *My Friend Flicka*, the 1940s novel by Mary O'Hara in which ten-year-old Ken, living on a ranch in Wyoming, had resolved to befriend and tame a wild horse everyone said was beyond befriending. Damn that Roger.

Joanie always had felt that being born in Los Angeles had been a colossal karmic mistake, that somehow she'd been intended for a ranch in Montana or maybe Wyoming or Colorado but had inadvertently been rerouted to a dentist's home in the southern California megalopolis.

And as she experienced more of the dark side of Los Angeles, she was even more convinced that fate had simply screwed up. Dave's appeal as a potential husband had been considerably enhanced when he said he was from ranch country in New Mexico. She had never quite forgiven him for the ranch country turning out to be Sweeney.

And her Sweeney Flicka wasn't exactly the Wyoming Flicka either. Like her namesake, this Flicka was a chestnut mare, with a white blaze on her forehead. Unfortunately, the resemblance ended there. Where the fictional horse had been fiery and spirited, this Flicka was sullen and psychotic. Her bones stuck out like coat hangers on her malnourished body, and her open sores demanded treatment.

"She's in pretty bad shape, isn't she?"

Joanie turned as Dave entered the barn. She glared at him as he joined her at the stall.

"Hey, I didn't abuse that horse. In fact, I brought her an apple, thought you might need it." Dave nodded to the jar of salve in Joanie's hand. He handed Joanie a wrinkled apple that she recognized as having been in the family's refrigerator far too long. Nonetheless she took it and even muttered thanks. She knew that Dave had been skeptical about adopting the horse, but he had not pushed his objections, and for that she was grateful.

Joanie delayed offering the apple to the horse until Dave had filled the feed trough and replenished the stall's water. Then, when Dave had retreated to avoid overwhelming the horse but remaining close enough to help, Joanie unlatched the stall's door and slowly entered.

"Hello, Flicka," Joanie spoke in her most soothing voice. "I'm not going to hurt you. Those days are over. I'm here to help you, to make you feel better. I'm your friend."

The horse showed no signs of understanding. Joanie took another step forward. The horse took a step backward.

"Here, I've brought you an apple," she said as she advanced.

Suddenly the horse's nostrils flared, her eyes went white with terrified madness, and she reared, her forelegs pawing the air.

Joanie retreated, closing the stall door behind her lest the horse bolt.

"Are you really sure you want to do this?" Dave asked as Joanie caught her breath.

"What do you mean by that?"

"I mean, I've seen other horses like her, and usually there ain't no fix to 'em, as the saying goes. And horses like her aren't just unfixable, they're dangerous. They're unpredictable, they can eat out of your hand one minute and brain you with their hooves the next."

Joanie bristled. "That sounds more like humans, dangerous and unpredictable. She didn't start out like this, some damned human made her this way. Ken wouldn't give up."

"Who's Ken?"

Joanie ignored him and retrieved the apple from the ground where she'd dropped it. This time she approached the horse from outside the stall. Again the horse panicked as she extended her offering, so she tossed it onto the stall's straw-covered floor, in front of the horse. The horse paid no attention but stared at Joanie with fear and suspicion.

"I think we should leave now. Nothing more you can do here, and I'm late for the Rotary Club meeting," said Dave.

"Well, we certainly wouldn't want that. I'm sure the United Nations of Kiowa County have important things to discuss."

Dave scowled. "That wasn't called for. Look, I know you're upset about the horse, but that's not my fault. And I was serious about that horse being dangerous. Make sure Traci doesn't go near her."

"You make it sound like Flicka's a rattlesnake," retorted Joanie, "and God knows we've got plenty of those around here. I bet they don't have rattlesnakes in Montana."

Dave looked at her in bewilderment, then shook his head and walked away.

Dammit. Dave simmered as he strode down the sidewalk toward Main Street. He was angry with himself for being angry with Joanie for being angry with him. Concatenated anger is the worst kind. He knew what having a horse meant to Joanie, and that it was the only thing that redeemed Sweeney for her. So here he was, married to a woman whose only attachment to the town she detested was an animal that he detested. No, that was too strong a word. In fact, he felt pity for the horse and blamed her mental state on the abuse she'd suffered. But for all that, she still was a dangerous horse, and Joanie's obsession potentially was dangerous, too.

Dave wondered what Joanie would do about Flicka if they moved, say, to Carlsbad. If he was going to give up Sweeney, then she could damn well give up that crazy horse.

Thinking about moving led him to wonder how long it usually took school districts to respond to applications. He hoped the school bureaucracies would move with characteristic sluggishness. Even Joanie conceded that Sweeney definitely had been more interesting lately—but not *that* interesting. Sweeney needed more time. Like a couple of decades.

Quickening his steps not to be late for the Rotary Club meeting, Dave nonetheless glanced both ways on Main Street before crossing, noticing as he did so the contrast between the gesture now and a few weeks ago. Then the street had been empty, as usual. Lately, though, he had reason to look before stepping onto the pavement. Even the pavement smelled different; it smelled of tire rubber and oil leaks; it smelled of asphalt driven upon.

As if in corroboration, an ominous, throaty rumble warned him of several Harley-Davidson motorcycles rolling down Main Street, like bombers in formation. The riders, all late middle-aged men with salt-and-pepper beards and gray ponytails, waved to him as they passed. He waved back. Friendly folks, maybe he'd chat with them if they had lunch at the Chick 'n' More.

Dave entered the restaurant and went immediately to the back room that had been restored to the Rotarians with Ed and Edna's decision not to close the business, at least not now. "Hi," he said to no one in particular, and no one in particular said hi in return. He noticed a few new faces at the meeting—Rita Gallegos, the postmistress, and Kathy Larkin. He took that to indicate revitalized community spirit; they certainly hadn't come for the food. "I'll have the special," he said as he breezed past Helen, who was exiting with luncheon orders.

"Which one?" she asked.

Dave stopped abruptly. "Which one?"

"We've got the roast beef special"—Dave nodded in recognition—"and we've got the buffalo burger special, $8.95, with fries."

"I'll . . . I'll have the buffalo burger."

"Good choice," said Helen as she departed.

"Since when has the Chick 'n' More had more than one special?" Dave asked as he took his seat. "And buffalo burgers?"

"We're living in strange times," said Roger.

"We're living in the End Times," muttered the Reverend Fall.

Ron Suffitt ignored him. "They added buffalo burgers to the menu after they were such a hit with those RVers. Almost all the visitors these days order them. Ed and Edna are having a hard time keeping their meat locker stocked."

"I heard Ed and Edna are thinking of changing the restaurant's name to the Hard Rock Café," jibed Roger. Reverend Fall blanched. "Just kidding," Roger added.

"Last I heard, Jim Biddle bought a few more buffalo to put on his range," said Leland, "and he's talking about letting the herd increase. I've heard that buffalo will breed like jackrabbits if you let 'em."

"That's a fact," said Roger. "At least that's what I've read in the literature. And you don't have to worry about diseases or convincing them to live off the prairie grass."

"Wonder what that says about us," said Dave. He glanced at the meal Helen had just put before him. The greasy, stringy fries resembled deep-fried grama grass.

"I hear Adelino and Judy are planning on fencing in that pasture next to their place and putting a couple of buffalo in there," said Fred Yoder, "you know, kind of a tourist attraction."

"It's true," said Rita Gallegos, the postmistress. "From my window at the post office I can see them working. They hired my boy and a couple of his friends to help clear the land and put up the fencing."

"Employment in Sweeney is soaring," observed Roger wryly, sipping his black coffee.

"And I hear they've already got a bunch of souvenir T-shirts and ball caps in the Baca Mart," said Tom Binks. "They have 'Rock On' stenciled on them, and then something about Sweeney." Then he chuckled. "I suggested something like 'Hard—'" But Leland interrupted before he could finish. "It's past time that we kept conversations about that Rock serious and civil." He glared at Binks.

"Ah, what's got your dander up?" Binks retorted. "You act like that Rock was some kind of sacred symbol, like it is for the all the queers who'll be coming here to worship it." He chortled.

"I said, that's enough, Tom."

"And I asked why's it such a big deal?"

Leland looked around the table and took a deep breath. "I guess now's as good a time and place as any to announce this: I'm the father of a homosexual."

"Grant's a homosexual?" gasped Nettie.

"He is," said Leland. "He's a good and decent man, like I raised him, and I don't cotton to him being called a 'queer' or any other names. You can learn to accept him for who he is, just as I have."

Kathy gave a smile and a nod she hoped Leland would notice.

Binks guffawed. "And to think I been telling people we don't raise fruit around here!"

Leland lunged for Binks, but Nettie beat him. With her right hand she slapped Binks in the face so hard that Helen in the next room stopped what she was doing and looked in. "I've known that boy since birth, Binks, and he's worth ten of the likes of you."

Red-faced and sputtering, Binks started to rise, cocking his arm. "No damn woman slaps me . . ."

Suddenly Rudd's huge hand grabbed him by the back of the neck and lifted him off the floor. "Tom, you're about to get yourself into way more trouble than you can handle. Why don't you and me go outside and talk this over." And with that he frog-marched Binks out of the room.

The rest of the Rotarians sat in stunned silence. Leland remained standing, looking hard at everyone who dared meet his gaze. His eyes rested on Reverend Fall, who sat gape-mouthed and speechless. Then he sat down.

At that point Dave rose. He looked first at Leland, then at the other Rotarians. "I too have known Grant a long time. I taught him in school. He was raised well, and it showed.

"We're here today talking about the Rock and what it means for our town. Some good things, I hope, maybe some attention, more jobs, more money. But even if none of those come to pass I sincerely hope it will open our eyes to the wider world we all live in and the people of all kinds who live in it with us. Little towns like Sweeney aren't worth saving if they're nothing but prairie dog holes where people live isolated in ignorance and intolerance. We've just had a bunch of nudists here, and we did ourselves proud by welcoming them and getting to know each other. We don't know who else might be coming, but I hope we'll rise to those challenges as well. That's all I have to say."

"Hear, hear!" shouted Roger and began clapping. Tentatively, most other people around the table joined him.

In the awkward silence that followed, Reverend Fall stood. Avoiding Leland's gaze he said in a tremulous voice, "That Rock's still an obscenity. I know most of you would like to overlook that, but believe me, every one of our visitors knows exactly what it looks like. They aren't coming here to honor or respect our town, they're coming to laugh at it. To them it's a joke—and so are we."

As if in reply to his outrage the growl of barely muffled motorcycle engines reverberated through the restaurant. The boomer bikers were dropping in for lunch.

Leland turned to Dave. "Looks like one of the challenges just stopped by."

"That's what I'm talking about," persisted Fall, finding his stride. "Ever since that . . . that . . . that affront to God appeared, our little town has been beset by mayhem. Well, I for one—"

Fearing that an avalanche of a sermon was about to descend from the mountain of the reverend's indignation, Dave interrupted. "Hold on, this is what I was talking about. These motorcyclists aren't Hell's Angels or Satan's Slaves," —Fall winced— "they're just ordinary people like us who like to get out once in a while on their expensive toys and see the country. And I for one am delighted they've chosen to come to this part of the country. They come into town, ride around, see the sights, take pictures, spend some money, and then leave."

Fall gave it one last go, "They go home and laugh about us to their friends. Imagine what they said about that naked cowboy at the rodeo . . ."

Seeing snickers and grins all around, Fall slumped into sullen silence.

Sensing an opportunity to reassert control of the meeting, Ron said, "Actually, we need to discuss that at this meeting—"

"Bare-assed Bob?" asked Roger.

Ron sputtered, "No, I mean the economic ramifications." Ron said the word as if he'd been waiting his whole life to use it. "According to my survey and calculations, those RVers spent close to $1,200 in Sweeney last weekend, including gasoline, supplies, food, rental space at Will Diggs's place, and sundries. Maybe even $1,500. In one weekend."

Someone gave a low whistle.

"Don't forget haircuts," said Yoder. "I gave half a dozen haircuts over the weekend, about three times more than I usually give."

"Their wives were down at my place getting their hair done," added Nettie.

"Adelino and Judy say they could have done a lot more business if they'd known the RVers were coming and could have stocked up for them," said Yoder.

"Well, maybe we should discuss that," said Ron.

"We should indeed," said Leland, "but first I'd like to read you a letter I received from those folks." He stood and pulled a sheet of paper from his shirt pocket. Unfolding it he read:

"Dear Citizens of Sweeney,

We the members of the Let It All Hang Out Senior Nudist RV Club wish to express our deep appreciation for the great hospitality you showed us during our recent visit to your town. In all our travels we don't believe we've had as much fun or were welcomed as warmly as we were in Sweeney. The rodeo was a special treat, and having a nude cowboy in our honor was a gift we won't forget.

"Honest," said Leland as he looked at the questioning expressions around the table, "we didn't plan that. I told them that at the rodeo, but they didn't believe me." He continued:

"You people have a great little community with a lot to offer to groups such as ours, and we intend to spread the word. We hope you'll go to our website to see the photos we took during our wonderful visit. Thanks again,

Sincerely,

Ruth Roggins, President, LIAHOSNRVC"

"Well, did you go to their website?" asked Dave.

"I did, after pulling Rachel Rowe off the street to help. That kid's sharp with computers. The website lets you meet the club members a little more candidly than you might want, but it does say very nice things about Sweeney, and the photos of the town, the ones that weren't of the Rock, were pretty flattering. Actually, even the photos of the Rock were fairly tasteful."

"Hmmph," grumped Fall.

"I think we should send a nice reply," said Connie Nesbitt. Dave noticed that she was again wearing her formal realtor-in-residence dress, a sure sign of optimism in the business community.

"Do I hear a motion to that effect?" said Ron.

"Just do it," said Connie.

Ron humphed but let it ride, seeing Leland had more to say.

"I've been getting inquiries from other RV clubs. Not nudist ones, just regular clubs, wanting to come here, asking about accommodations, food, activities, that sort of thing."

"But we don't really have any of 'that sort of thing,'" said Connie. "Let's face it, we just kind of winged it with the nudists. We don't have any lodgings, any restaurants other than the Chick 'n' More, no activities—we can't put on a rodeo every time people come to town."

"For one thing, Bare-assed Bob wouldn't hold up," quipped Roger. Nettie glared at him.

Connie continued, "We've been caught off guard at being a tourist destination, and we're not really set up for it, but that doesn't mean we can't be. This is cause for celebration, not consternation. Last time we were here we were talking about Sweeney dying, now we're talking about buying britches big enough to fit. Look at the other little towns out here on the Plains, they'd give anything to be in our shoes. We're the Rotary Club, dammit, we're supposed to supply leadership."

Several voices proclaimed "Hear! Hear!"

"But it's all because of that obscene Rock," protested Fall. "The Bible says a house built on sandstone shall not survive."

"That's 'sand,' not 'sandstone,'" corrected Nettie.

"You know what I mean," Fall blustered.

"Connie's right," said Dave, ignoring Fall. "Whether we approve of the Rock or not, there's no denying it's brought changes to Sweeney. There's a different spirit in the town, a life that wasn't here before, at least not for a long time. You can even see it among the kids—and, man, they have really needed new life here."

Nettie spoke up. "I don't know about you all, but that rodeo was the best thing that's happened in Sweeney in years. It was Sweeney like it used to be. It brought people together and let them have fun, let them shine. Think about those little kids with their little animals, and Christie Herwig leading the parade. In fact, it could have allowed even more people to have fun and shine with their musical ability"—and here Nettie turned her gaze directly at Fall—"if it hadn't been for a certain closed-minded, mean-spirited—"

Ron, sensing a confrontation, jumped in. "By the way, Nettie, how's your committee coming with its work?" It was a tactless move, as everyone exchanged worried glances. After all, the committee's stated goal was to remove the offending Rock, which was at least partly responsible for the town's recent success.

"Oh, we're moving right along," said Nettie. "Our subcommittee on bylaws has formed a sub-subcommittee to discuss protocols for future meetings." A subtle sigh of relief went around the table.

Having been spared further conflict, Ron returned to his original subject. "I think we're agreed we need to do more to welcome our many visitors. Any ideas?"

"Well, we can promote ourselves via the Internet," said Connie. "You know, put good stuff on our town's website."

"We have a town website?" Dave asked Leland.

"Well, uh, no, never needed one, but I guess we do now. Anyone know how to create a website?" Embarrassed, uncomfortable glances all around.

Dave answered, "I admit I don't either, but there's kids at school who do it on their cell phones between classes." Astonished stares. "Just kidding, but it's no big deal to them. I'd recommend Rachel Rowe. She could do it faster than she could solve a quadratic equation—and that's fast. Traci and her friends could take photos to put on it."

Leland nodded. "We could pay them with state Rural Community Development money we've got in the town account. It's just been sitting there because we haven't had anything to spend it on. Actually, we probably could get more money if we had specific projects. The Rural Community Development Program is just aching to put money into this part of the state."

"See what I mean?" said Connie. "That's the sort of can-do attitude that led to the rodeo, and that's the attitude that's going to lead us out of the wilderness."

Abruptly, Reverend Fall rose to his feet, sputtering, "How dare you! Invoking the holy words of the Lord to promote that pagan obscenity. And mark my words, this town is selling its soul to the Devil, and the day will be terrible when he comes to collect."

And with that he rose from the table and stormed out.

"Funny how Satan never made us an offer till now," said Roger. "Now, back to that website. . . ."

On his way out of the Chick 'n' More, Leland stopped at the table where the boomer bikers were finishing their buffalo burgers.

"Howdy, gentlemen. I'm the town manager here, and I just wanted to welcome you to Sweeney. Where're you all from?"

"Lubbock," proclaimed one, who wore expensive black leather head to toe, including a black leather cap from which dangled a gray ponytail. "We're members of the Lubbock Chain Gang Harley Club. Usually we ride with our wives, but we decided to leave them at home for this trip."

"Why's that?" asked Leland, then regretted the question.

"Oh, you know . . . that Rock," another man answered. His black-leather jacket was open to reveal a Lubbock Lions Club pin.

"Didn't want them making any unfortunate size comparisons," said another. "Yessir, that Rock's really something. We've got nothing like that in Lubbock . . ."

"Unless you count 'Bull Pud' Lawrence," said a third. They all laughed.

Leland, eager to change the subject, asked, "How'd you come to hear about . . . Sweeney?"

"Oh, we keep tabs on the websites of quite a few biker touring groups. Sweeney's starting to get mentioned on several of them."

"Indeed?"

"The one that set us on the track of this trip is out of California. It's a big group. "

Leland's face brightened.

"They're out of San Francisco, Dykes on Bikes."

Behind his smile Leland's inner voice said *Damn.*

June Fall heard the front door slam, then angry footsteps approaching the kitchen. Apparently the Rotary Club meeting had not gone well. She sighed deeply and continued putting away the remnants of her blissfully solitary lunch. As she waited for Wayne to enter the room, her own anger reemerged. She had been so close to making music for fun again, so close . . . and then to have it snatched away at the last moment. She didn't know whether she was more resentful of Wayne or Bare-assed Bob. Wayne was more convenient.

"Sodom. Sodom and Gomorrah!" raged Wayne as he entered the room and began pacing around the kitchen table, too upset to sit down. "The City of the Plains. That's what we've become, the City of the Plains."

"It's 'Cities of the Plain,'" corrected June.

He grimaced in frustration and then paused to wait for June to ask why he was so angry. When she didn't he continued, "I'm talking about people willing to betray their morals for thirty pieces of silver. Making a bargain with the Devil."

"All right, Wayne," said June in a voice that did nothing to disguise her boredom, "why don't you tell me what happened." She didn't bother to sit down to listen but continued putting dishes in the cupboard.

Wayne glared at her, then sensing her indifference began explaining. "They're all talking about what a great thing last weekend was, a great thing, as if having a bunch of naked people come to town to see an obscene rock was a great thing. Going on and on about how much money they spent—thirty pieces of silver."

"Did they talk about how much fun everyone had?" asked June pointedly. "Or almost everyone, that is."

"Now, June, let's not get into that. There's ways of having fun that would be pleasing in the sight of the Lord—"

"Name three," June interrupted.

"—and besides, righteousness isn't about having fun."

"That's for sure," said June, "at least not in some people's version of Christianity. I wonder if that's why our kids don't want to come home for holidays much anymore, all the righteousness oozing all over the place. So much righteousness it's hard to breathe sometimes."

The mention of their children added heat to her anger. Wayne's waxing righteousness had been a wedge in the family since Luke and Sarah went to college. Luke studied architecture, a field Wayne suspected was dominated by homosexuals, while Sarah studied electrical engineering, which Wayne felt violated biblical gender roles. Now, as each had good jobs in their chosen fields, they returned home less and less frequently. June blamed reluctance to face inevitable conflicts with their father. Luke lived in Seattle, Sarah in Portland. She was married—the wedding had been in Portland, and not performed by Wayne—and now she was hinting about starting a family.

"I said, let's not get into that. We're talking about this town selling its soul to the Devil, for thirty pieces of silver. Oh, and speaking of sin, Leland announced that his son is a homosexual."

"Grant?" June hadn't really known Grant, as the Mortons didn't come to church, but she had talked to Grant a few times at 4-H events, and she remembered that once he had stopped by a church bake sale and bought some brownies that judging from an adolescent pimple erupting on his face he clearly didn't want or need. Seemed like a nice kid.

"So now you're going to go off on an antihomosexual crusade?" She recalled Wayne's antihomosexual rants when Luke had announced he wanted to study architecture. She'd been raised to believe homosexuality was contrary to scripture and at the very least was unnatural, but she'd never known any homosexuals, and she regarded as absurd Wayne's fears that Luke would be recruited to homosexuality if he studied architecture at a good school. Like his tirades against popular music.

"Someone has to care about decency and morality," he proclaimed.

"Oh, come off it, Wayne, can't you see that this town is dying?" She slammed the cupboard door shut, then stood in front of him, her hands on her hips, one hand clenched around the dishcloth.

"Can't you see that the people in this town have been dying too, shriveling up inside, stores boarded up, young people moving away, the church's congregation getting older, smaller? And then something comes along that brings a little life and a little money to this poor town—and all you can do is rant and rave and call everyone a sinner. Wayne, I'm telling you, if you keep this up you won't have five people in church."

And with that she threw down the dishcloth and stalked into the living room. She sat at the piano and began playing, a piece she hadn't played in years, an Everly Brothers classic, "All I Have to Do Is Dream."

Wayne started to follow her, picking up the Bible that rested on the table beside the reclining lounger in front of the TV, but before he could raise it she turned and skewered him with a don't-even-think-about-it glare.

After the Rotary Club meeting, Kathy Larkin strolled back to her home on Honeysuckle Street. For the thousandth time she promised to notice whether honeysuckles grew anywhere in Sweeney; she knew they didn't on Honeysuckle Street. Today she had taken a rare day off to attend the meeting, primarily to hear reactions to the rodeo. She was not formally a Rotary member, but then the club had always ignored membership requirements. Normally she ignored the club, but she actually had enjoyed this meeting.

And she was happy to have been there when Leland made his announcement. That had been as unexpected for her as she suspected it had been for him, but it seemed to have gone pretty well. No one rushed to Binks's defense—certainly not after Rudd intervened. Of course, it hadn't hurt that homophobia's champion was a lowlife like Tom Binks, but she had no illusions about the unanimity of the Rotarians' acceptance, nor about the difficult times ahead for Leland. Later she'd have to call him to congratulate him and give him support. He would need it. She'd also have to call Grant and tell him that now would be a good time to reach out to his dad.

But that would be later. Now she had time on her hands and was using it to walk along Main Street. Downtown Sweeney normally held few attractions—make that *no* attractions—for her, and she usually spent her time in town doing chores around the house. She didn't relish housework, but she did enjoy tending her little garden, and that was where most weekends found her, in earth-stained jeans, with Rasta her cat nearby, nurturing the few flowers and vegetables lucky enough to have a minor share of Sweeney's precious municipal water supply.

After today's meeting, however, she'd been seized by a curious restlessness, and when she approached her home, she paused and turned back toward Main Street. As she walked, she was newly aware of her neighborhood. She knew who lived in each house she passed. She waved to old Mrs. Perkins, who was out tending the morning glories that climbed the trellises surrounding her porch. The Dougherty twins were making a clamor as they raced their Big Wheels around on their driveway and into the street. Everyone else, however, either was not home or indoors, likely the latter. How sad, thought Kathy, for it was a beautiful day, the air still fresh and cool, a gentle breeze wandering around like an exploring cat. Overhead a few cotton-ball clouds relieved the harsh blank-blue so typical of the High Plains in early summer.

Back on Main Street Kathy saw the receding forms of men on motorcycles, and on the sidewalks a few more people than she would have expected on a normal day in Sweeney. Not everyone was indoors. Yes, today was indeed an unusual day.

She was midway in her stroll down Main Street, nearly opposite the Chick 'n' More, when she abruptly stopped. Leaving the restaurant were several people who had stayed after the meeting—including Roger Rollins. His head was down as he crossed the street so he'd have bumped into her if she hadn't moved. Except for the Rotary Club meeting, she hadn't seen him since the rodeo. She didn't welcome this encounter.

"Well, if it isn't the town clown," she said, then instantly regretted her sarcasm.

"I hope you're referring to the rodeo."

"Why, what else would I be referring to?" she said, then again regretted her inability to control her emotions.

"Kathy, that was a long time ago. Let it be."

"I'm talking about the rodeo." She felt diminished by lying. "I thought you were a perfect choice for rodeo clown, and I thought you did real well with it."

"Well, I suppose your repartee helped," he said, then added, "You were a great announcer. The best we've ever had. I'm not really surprised. Leland chose well."

"Thanks." Then changing the subject, she asked, "What did you think of Leland's announcement?"

Roger hesitated before answering. "That took guts. Leland's a tough old cowboy, but I'll bet that was harder than anything he ever faced on the ranch. Folks seemed to take it pretty well—except for that worthless Binks—but make no mistake, Leland's alienated himself from the community in a way he wasn't before. Oh, people will go on about their business with him like they always did, but now there'll always be a fence around him. 'His son's a homosexual.' Like I said, that took guts."

"I don't think we'll ever know just how much, but I have to say I knew about Grant before this. I talked to Leland about Grant yesterday. He loves that boy. And I think it's important that those of us who admire Leland for what he did stick by him."

Roger nodded.

"Speaking of that," Kathy continued, "I mentioned to Grant that while he's here this summer, he and Leland should have a barbecue at the ranch. Not quite a coming out party, just a get-together for friends. You should come, if only because Grant mentioned on the phone that he and his partner are looking for a cat, and I was reasonably sure you'd have one, a 'quality' one." She forced a smile.

A frown briefly clouded Roger's face. He started to speak, paused, then changed direction. "It's good that the RVers have spread the word about Sweeney being a hospitable place. Leland's starting to get inquiries from other groups. We need to get our act together if we're going to become a tourist destination. I'm glad we're getting a website."

"What about the reverend?" Kathy asked, relieved at the shift in the conversation.

"He's pretty marginalized. People in general approve of the changes that have come to Sweeney, they see positive things happening, and they want them to continue."

"Me too. I swear I saw signs of life on Main Street today."

Roger chuckled. Then he said, "By the way, that old cat of yours, Rasta, I just know he's lonely. Cats often do better with another cat around, and I do happen to have one, an extra high quality one—"

"Nice talking to you, Roger," said Kathy, ending the conversation and walking away.

She continued her walk for a few more blocks, then gave up and returned home. Try as she would she could not recapture the magic of the day after her encounter with Roger. She was angry with herself for how she'd been with Roger, snippy, borderline rude. And she was angry with Roger for reviving old hurts and resentments.

They'd been seniors in high school. Both were conspicuously bright—they were covaledictorians—but their identities and reputations were opposites. Roger was a renegade, a cutup, and a prankster. Kathy was compulsively responsible, a teacher's pet, a follower of rules. They despised each other.

Around Easter that year, Kathy got wind of a schoolwide plot, hatched by Roger, for the conspirators to enter the school's restrooms at a prearranged time and simultaneously flush every toilet repeatedly. He'd heard somewhere that the overload would blow out the plumbing system and shut down the school. Kathy had been appalled. Despite her reluctance to be a snitch, she felt an obligation to let the administration know what was planned, and without naming names she told them. They acted decisively to thwart the plot.

A week later Roger got his revenge. On Friday Kathy received in the mail a letter, on school administration stationery, stating that because of her good deed she'd been selected to receive the special GGTS award. The letters stood for Good Government Tremendous Service, and she was to receive the award at a special assembly at ten on Monday morning.

Kathy was thrilled. She told everyone about it. When the ten o'clock bell rang on Monday, she and several friends went to the auditorium, where she was greeted not by administrators, teachers, and her fellow students but by Roger and a claque of his buddies. They held a banner that read: "To Kathy Larkin, the GGTS Award—Goody-Goody Two Shoes." They laughed uproariously. She fled in tears. Word of her "award" spread throughout the school, and Good-Goody Two Shoes became permanently welded to her identity. Pain and humiliation had marked her final months in school.

Roger was right: it was a long time ago, but the memories still stung.

Iris Gerber entered the Style Salon sputtering like a chicken emerging from a stock tank. "Well, I never, never in my whole life, witnessed anything as thoroughly outrageous as, as . . ."

"Yes?" said Nettie, looking up from the woman whose hair she was touching up. Even without the RVers, the Style Salon was uncharacteristically crowded, all the back room chairs recruited for the visitors now occupied by locals. Nettie knew the reason: this wasn't about grooming but about gossip. "What's so outrageous, Iris?"

"Why, that rodeo, that Bare-assed Bob."

Nettie couldn't help herself. She burst out laughing. It spread among the other women. Soon Iris's protests were aborted by her own guffaws.

"Bare-assed Bob!" exclaimed Agnes Peterson, whose platinum hair was being lovingly retouched by Nettie, all remaining strands of it. "Since when have we seen the likes of him?" She cackled loudly.

"But it reflects poorly on our town," said Myrtle Evans, waiting her turn. She was a dour, humorless widow who lived alone on Tupelo Street. Her husband had died twenty years ago; people said it was the only way he could get shut of her. She was a regular at the Style Salon, where her particular tastes in gossip ran toward the malicious. She always wore an antique pink-and-blue dress that she had sewed in the remote past and that spoke loudly that her frugality exceeded her seamstress ability.

"Actually, it hasn't," said Nettie. In the rumor roundtable that was the Style Salon, it was Nettie's role to act as moderator, allowing each woman to express her opinions and to ensure that the line of out-and-out libel was not crossed. She also strove to mention actual, substantiated fact wherever possible or necessary. In that role, Nettie proceeded to relate Leland's report at the Rotary Club meeting. "Sweeney's getting noticed, we're getting a reputation as a nice, friendly place to visit."

"But it's all because of that Rock," protested Myrtle. "Reverend Fall says it's an affront to God, and we're provoking divine wrath by not removing it. He says the devil is at work in Sweeney right now."

Nettie humphed. "Reverend Fall needs an enema." Myrtle gasped. Everyone else laughed.

"That's blasphemous," said Myrtle. "He's a man of God; he's our minister."

"Okay, I'm sorry," said Nettie. "And I'm not saying I approve of the Rock. It's just that for the first time in I don't know when, Sweeney is starting to be how it used to be—"

"We never had a Bare-assed Bob before," interjected Iris.

"What I mean is that the town is starting to show signs of life again. There's people on the streets again. There's new jobs for the young people. And people are starting to have fun again, to talk about improving the town." Then, unable to resist, she added, "Reverend Fall's idea of improving the town is haranguing people about what sinners they are. I don't think he'd recognize harmless fun if it bit him on the—" She stopped there, as Iris tactfully interrupted.

"I'll allow that the quality of the gossip has certainly improved."

"Well, I don't think much of these modern times," grumped Myrtle. "People were a lot more moral back in the good old days, and I think we should try to get back to them."

Iris's face darkened. "I can't say I agree with you, Myrtle, not about people being more moral back then. I've heard tales about Prohibition here in Kiowa County, and there was more immoral, illegal stuff going on then than there is now. There were killings back then. And even after Prohibition ended men were getting drunk and beating their wives and children and nobody doing a thing about it."

Nettie smiled sympathetically to Iris. Her father had been an infamous mean drunk, and more than once Iris had slunk into school with a black eye.

"Well, I just say that people were a lot more God-fearing than they are now, and we're ignoring the warnings of Reverend Fall at our peril," stated Myrtle with finality, and with that she retreated into the pages of *Ladies Home Journal.*

"What about our committee?" asked Agnes, as Nettie applied the final touches to the woman's coif and handed her a mirror. "We're doing something about that Rock, aren't we?"

Nettie surveyed the room. Every woman present was a member of People for Decency in Nature. "Indeed we are." She assumed a posture of noble leadership. "We'll be discussing our bylaws at our next meeting, and then we'll be in a position to elect permanent officers."

"When is our next meeting?" asked Iris.

"Why, could be any day now," answered Nettie, then feeling this wasn't definite enough she added, "Could you all make a meeting at the end of next week?" She knew the women could make a meeting at *any* time in the week.

All the women said they'd be there. Then Myrtle added, "I think we should invite Reverend Fall to come speak to us."

Inwardly, Nettie cringed but in the face of consensus she could only say, "That's a good idea, Myrtle, would you go about inviting him? Tell him he'll have to keep his remarks brief, because we've got a lot of committee business to get done during the meeting." She hoped that telling Fall to be succinct would be so daunting that Myrtle wouldn't get around to the invitation.

As Agnes preened in the mirror and the next woman prepared for her appointment, Nettie wasn't sure whether she'd achieved anything at all this day.

When Dave returned from the Rotary Club meeting, he found Traci slumped on the sofa in front of the TV watching a weekend cable talk-show, one he found particularly distasteful. "Hey, Traci," he said, "turn that off. I've got something I need to talk to you about."

"Aw, Dad, can't it wait a minute? They're just about to show these people's tattoos that aren't allowed in supermarkets."

Dave grimaced. "Then they're not allowed here either—and I do need to talk to you now, so turn that off." Traci rolled her eyes and rose from the sofa. Dave persisted. "Actually, I think you might find this interesting." Traci rolled her eyes again as she switched off the TV.

"At the meeting of the Rotary Club this morning"—Traci started another roll of her eyes when Dave blurted angrily, "Stop that! That's just plain rude. Don't do it again if you don't want to be grounded this weekend." God! He hated trying to converse with a sullen teenager. And he took no consolation in knowing that Traci was at least as hostile to Joanie.

"As I was saying," he continued, trying to calm his voice, "at the . . . meeting we talked about the town needing a website. We're going to need photos for it, and I thought you and your friends could take some, since you're already set up and have been taking photos for the school yearbook."

Traci goggled. "Us? Take photos for the Sweeney website?" Dave nodded grimly, his anger rising again.

Traci blindly pushed on. "What would we take photos of? Oh, I know, we could take action shots of tumbleweeds. Or we could go to the Sweeney mega-mall, you know, the Baca Mart. Or how about a few scenics of the waterfalls cascading down the mountains, or at least grass withering in the breeze. And then there's always the Rock, our famous Rock—"

"That's enough. Nobody's going to force you. You didn't give me time to mention that we were going to pay you to do this, but if you'd rather spend your summer stocking shelves at the Baca Mart, that's fine with me. We'll find someone else who can use the money and the experience."

And with that he rose and stomped off.

"Wait, Dad," called Traci. She paused. She didn't want to apologize, but she knew that only an apology would bring her back across the line she'd crossed. She did enjoy photography and had begun to think about pursuing it in college. And almost anything would beat being a stocker at the Baca Mart. But most decisively, she feared the wrath of her friends if they learned she'd deprived them of a paying summer job.

"Dad . . . I'm sorry. I got carried away." Dave continued to glower at her. "It's just that, well, finding interesting photos of Sweeney to put on a website will be a bit of a challenge. Even you have to admit that, don't you?"

Dave softened. "Well, Sweeney's not exactly Yellowstone"—Traci started to roll her eyes again but caught herself—"but it's meeting challenges like this that makes for a true professional photographer. So you might do it?"

"I'll talk to the girls and see what they think, but, yeah, I think there's a good chance. You say we'll get paid?"

"The town's got money in an account for this sort of thing. You won't get rich, but you'll make more than at the Baca Mart, and you'll get to work on your own schedule and do it with your friends."

To herself, Traci screamed "Yes!!!"

"Oh, by the way," Dave said, "there's one other thing." Traci eyed him with suspicion. "We need someone to create and maintain the website. I thought maybe a schoolkid could do that too, and in all my science classes there's one student who really stands out as having the skills. This is going to work out well, because she's a member of your group, Rachel Rowe. I saw her with you at the rodeo."

As he turned to walk out of the room he saw the color drain from Traci's face.

"Well, isn't she?" he asked.

"Yes . . . but no. Not really, we only allowed her in temporarily, to kind of pay her back for what she did to help us ditch school. She's not really part of our group—how could she be? Dad, she's totally weird."

"So what are you going to do, let her think you're her friends for a couple of weeks and then dump her when you figure your debt's been paid?"

"Well . . . no, but Dad, she can't be one of *us*—she's, like, leprosy. What would the other kids think if they thought she was one of *us*." Traci shuddered.

"What would you think of yourselves if that's the kind of people you are?"

"Leprosy," said Traci as she addressed her friends whom she had summoned to an emergency meeting at the picnic table outside the Baca Mart. "We have leprosy, and it's in the form of Rachel. Once you get something like that you can't get rid of it."

"Herpes is like that too," offered Heather. Traci rolled her eyes.

She explained the Sweeney website photography proposal to them, and as expected, they accepted eagerly. Then she informed them of Rachel's involvement. "What are we going to do? We'll never get rid of her."

"I don't think she's so bad," said Christie. "She doesn't mean to be weird, not like some people I know who dye their hair weird colors and wear nothing but black."

"Or people who wear nothing but cheesy cowgirl outfits." Kimberly was in her Goth uniform.

"Come on, guys, cool it," Traci said. "We all have a little weirdness that we've adopted" —though she couldn't think of a single example in her own case. "But not meaning to be weird is the worst kind of weird, because you can't change it," Traci continued. "Rachel has geek in her genes."

"Sort of like a Wrangler sticker on your jeans," jibed Kimberly. "Sorry, Christie, I couldn't resist."

Further bickering was forestalled by Heather saying, "Watch it, here she comes."

"Dammit," said Traci, "it's like she's got radar that can locate us anywhere. See what I mean?"

"Hi, Rachel," said Christie warmly as the tall girl approached.

"Hi," said Rachel. "I didn't know you would be here"—Traci and Kimberly exchanged knowing looks—"my dad sent me here to get some coffee, but I was looking for you. Did you know that the conjunction of Mars, Jupiter, and the moon is happening now? I'm going out to observe it tonight—anyone want to come? You don't have to know anything about it, I can explain everything."

Traci and Kimberly rolled their eyes so forcefully their heads tilted back.

"Uh, thanks, Rache," said Heather, "but I've got something I need to do tonight."

"Me too," said Kimberly.

"Yeah, I'm scheduled for watching our garden grow tonight," said Traci.

"What?" said Rachel.

"Oh, nothing, never mind. I just meant I'll have to pass on the astronomy tonight. Maybe next time."

"But there won't be a next time, at least not for four hundred and seventy-five years. That's when the conjunction happens next."

"Well, that's a bummer," said Traci. "I guess I'll just have to learn to live with the disappointment."

Rachel looked confused.

"Actually," said Heather, changing the subject, "what we were discussing does involve you."

"It does?" Rachel brightened.

Traci, grateful for the chance to retreat from her sarcasm, explained about the website.

"Wow! That's great! Maybe we could set up a telescope and take pictures of the Andromeda galaxy. You can see it better from Sweeney than from almost anywhere in the U.S. That's because there's almost no light pollution at night here."

"You're sure right about that," sniped Traci.

"I think they'll be more interested in buildings," said Heather. "Yeah, buildings and, uh, maybe roads and, uh, well, I don't really know what we'll photograph, but we'll come up with something."

Kimberly snickered. "Maybe we'll get lucky and a tornado will blow through town."

"Oh, no," said Rachel, "that would be terrible."

"Just kidding."

"You know, there are some historic old ranches around Sweeney. I think those might be kind of interesting," offered Christie. Kimberly rolled her eyes, and Christie glared fiercely at her.

"But the first thing is the website," said Heather, again changing the subject. "Can you do it, Rache?"

"Oh, sure, it's simple. We can have hyperlinks and apps and Java script and—"

"Whatever," said Traci.

"I'll get our website up right away. I'll let you know. But right now I've got to get back with the coffee for my dad." And with that she turned and went into the Baca Mart.

As Rachel entered the store, Traci turned to her friends. "See what I mean? Leprosy."

When he heard the door shut in his equipment repair garage, Rudd barely looked up from his desk where he had been doing paperwork. It would be S&S, but in the moments that followed Rudd sensed that something was amiss. S&S seemed disturbed. No, Rudd corrected himself, upset; S&S was always disturbed. The skinny scarecrow had come into the shop in uncharacteristic silence, gone over to the corner where the tools were stored, grabbed the broom, and begun angrily sweeping the floor. Normally, he went straight to Rudd, following him around, running off his mouth until the big man could stand it no longer and thrust the broom into his hand and ordered him to get to work. For S&S to begin sweeping immediately—and in silence—yes, something definitely was wrong.

Rudd suspected it might have to do with S&S's failure to impress the nudists, but when he asked, "What did you think of Sweeney's visitors?" S&S replied, "They was nice folks, I told 'em a lot they didn't know," and then resumed sweeping.

Then what was it? Rudd wondered. Not that he had any reason to care, but to his surprise he did. It was one of several changes in himself he'd noticed since the rodeo. Another was the stirring of a paternal interest in Sweeney, which he never suspected existed in him. Having deep roots in the town meant nothing to him; he'd always been as indifferent to his native soil as a cactus. But he'd enjoyed himself at the rodeo, and most strange, he'd enjoyed other people enjoying themselves. Maybe raising the Rock had been a good idea after all.

"Hey, you want some coffee? You look like you could use a cup," Rudd asked from his desk.

S&S looked up, startled. Rudd had never offered him coffee before. "Yes, I would," he managed to answer. "Yes indeed I would." And with that he put aside the broom and approached the desk where Rudd had found a greasy cup and begun pouring coffee into it from his Thermos.

"That's good," said S&S as he sipped the steaming black liquid. Rudd grimaced. He knew the coffee actually was horrible, borderline undrinkable by anyone with any sense of taste. Apparently that was another thing he and S&S shared, Rudd thought sadly, no sense of taste.

Rudd sipped his own cup, and waited.

Not for long, however. "It ain't right," the ragamuffin started to sputter. "It just ain't right."

Rudd only raised his eyebrows questioningly. It was enough.

"I'm being evicted. That's right, evicted, from the only home I've got. That damned Will Diggs is going to tear down that shack of his that I sleep in to make room for his damned RV park."

Rudd's eyebrows went even higher.

"I ain't got no place to live now. That shack wasn't much, but it was all I had." Then he lapsed into eloquent silence, staring at the floor and shaking his head. This *is* serious, thought Rudd.

"Well, there's got to be a solution," said the big man gently. S&S just shook his head. "Maybe I'll go have a talk with Diggs," Rudd continued, "see if we can figure something out."

"Won't do no good," said S&S. "He ain't wastin' no time. That shack'll be gone by the time you get there. Bulldozed to oblivion."

Actually, Rudd was certain he would have a chance to talk to Will Diggs; he owned the only bulldozer in Sweeney.

"Honestly, Rudd, I don't see how you put up with that disgusting little rodent," said Diggs later that afternoon as the two men leaned against the metal tread of the bulldozer Rudd had just delivered.

"Well, he can be trying," said Rudd, "but he's harmless."

"Not if you're trying to make a living and improve your property, he ain't."

Rudd glanced around at Diggs's "property." Except for the dusty field of dry and trampled grasses where the RV encampment had been, the property consisted mostly of piles of warped and weathered lumber interspersed with clots of rusting equipment and machinery. To Rudd, these thickets of obsolete machinery, ubiquitous on farms and ranches and homesteads throughout the High Plains, symbolized the futile faith that things really hadn't changed, that eventually everything would become useful again, sometime. Rudd knew better. To Rudd, Will Diggs's property was Sweeney in miniature—and it definitely could use improving.

"Look," Diggs continued, "making room for more RV facilities is only part of the reason I'm tearing down that shed. It's one thing to have that varmint hanging around that garage of yours; it's another to have him around paying visitors. You never know what he's going to do, or what condition he's going to be in. Remember that Fourth of July?"

Rudd nodded. Who could forget?

"I'll tell you what," said Rudd, "if you'll give S&S a couple of days to find new lodgings, I'll give you a special rate on that bulldozer."

"Fair enough," said Diggs.

"Damn, but the sunsets are pretty here," muttered Leland as he drove his pickup down the dirt roads that led from Sweeney toward his ranch. Trixie, seated beside him, grinned in agreement. Whatever else that dog might be, thought Leland, she was undeniably agreeable.

The road network, laid out during the homesteader era along section and quarter-section lines, followed a complex pattern of straight lines and right angles. Leland long ago had given up trying to direct nonlocals—"I'll come and get you" was what he always told visitors—but the general direction to his ranch was toward the setting sun. There, streaks of brilliant crimson, orange, and gold radiated upward through an early summer sky of high, dry clouds. Did the sky seem especially extravagant this evening?

Or was it that for the first time in longer than he could remember he was in an ebullient mood?

The rodeo had been a success, and Sweeney was beginning to change. He could sense it in the same way he could smell rain in approaching storm clouds after a long dry spell.

Today had been a long day but a good one. The Rotary Club meeting. Making the announcement had been hard, but it had been followed by an enormous sense of relief, almost liberation. And thanks to Rudd he hadn't gotten into it physically with Binks. He knew that throughout Kiowa County, at kitchen tables, around corrals, beside the road, over the phone, wherever people talked, his announcement was all they were talking about. People would view him differently now. And for perhaps the first time in his life he didn't really give a damn.

When he told the Rotarians about inquiries from prospective visitors, he had not mentioned some that he'd received, such as the one from the gay bicycle touring group, Queers with Gears, who were considering including Sweeney as a stop on their planned Ride-across-America event.

"That would raise a few eyebrows, wouldn't it, Trixie?" The dog heartily agreed.

"Well, we'll just have to deal with it," he said. The men he had seen on the Queers with Gears website looked like ordinary, decent people. As he scanned their faces, he thought of Grant. He never thought of his son as "queer." That seemed an ugly, hateful term. He still had difficulty saying Grant was "homosexual," though he definitely was. "Gay" seemed the most innocuous term, but he avoided that as well. Grant wasn't any of these labels, he was Grant. That's how Leland always would think of him. Grant the little kid helping him mend fence, raising the calf for 4-H, wanting to hear stories about his great-grandfather who had settled here and established the ranch.

Grant would have loved taking over the ranch, but his sexual orientation, something he was born with, made that impossible—and Leland blamed Sweeney for that more than his son. Narrow and intolerant. If Queers with Gears came through Sweeney they'd be regarded as a bunch of freaks, perverts.

His fellow ranchers would be the worst. Dammit, cowboys had the reputation of being rugged individualists, but the truth was that they were the most conformist bunch anywhere. They all looked the same, talked the same, wore the same clothes, voted the same, dipped the same snuff—and had the same prejudices.

And Leland knew he fit right in, always had. That's how he was brought up. He was ashamed he had always concealed Grant's homosexuality from the ranchers and the townspeople, told himself that he was protecting Grant, making it easier when he came home on holidays, but Leland knew that was only part of it. He also was protecting himself. For the first time Leland understood what Grant had gone through in coming out of the closet.

Maybe it would be good for Sweeney if Queers with Gears or Dykes on Bikes visited Sweeney. It was a big world out there, and it held all kinds of people. For years Sweeney had been in a coma, oblivious of the outside world, and now that Sweeney had chosen to wake up, it was in for rough awakenings.

"Yep, once you put your boat in the river of change," said Leland aloud, "you don't get to choose where the river goes." Trixie agreed with that too.

The light was fading and the phone was ringing when Leland entered the kitchen of the ranch house. It was Kathy. "What's up?" he asked amiably, still aglow with optimism.

"Actually, I have a couple of things. First, I was proud of you for your announcement at the meeting today. I didn't expect it, but it took guts, and you should know that there are others who feel as I do."

"Thanks. I didn't plan on it, but when the issue reared up, confronting it seemed the right thing to do."

"Second, I need to thank you for pushing me to announce at the rodeo. I can't remember when I had so much fun."

"Well, I just knew you were the right person for it," Leland said, his satisfaction deepening. "I just had kind of an instinct about it, a vibe, as people say."

"I'm glad you believe in vibes and that sort of thing." The irony in her voice evoked a vague foreboding in Leland. Kathy continued, "Does the date June 22 mean anything to you?"

"I don't think so. Is it someone's birthday? Have I forgotten someone's birthday?" He never was good at remembering birthdays.

"How about the word *solstice*?"

"Is that what you're trying to tell me, that the solstice is coming up?"

"You got it. Falls on a Saturday this year. And we'd better be ready, because more than a few people have noticed that our Rock is first cousin to Stonehenge."

After he hung up, Leland looked at Trixie. "You know that river I was talking about? I forgot to mention that it does help to have a paddle."

Again, Trixie agreed.

Chapter Nine

✦ RUDD HAD ARISEN AN HOUR EARLIER than usual and now was seated—unshaven, in his slippers, with his belt unbuckled and his shirt-tails outside his grease-stained denim overalls—in one of a dozen chairs at the big oak table in his home's kitchen. In front of him was a large bowl filled with cold cereal, next to it a carton of milk and a bowl of sugar. A cup of black coffee completed his breakfast. Midmorning at the garage he would have a danish from the Baca Mart.

Despite his own large size, the table and the capacious, silent kitchen reduced him to seeming almost an intruder. He usually ate his breakfast in perfunctory haste, but last night he'd slept poorly, and his mental turmoil did not depart when he awakened. Now his early rising gave him an unwelcome opportunity to survey the kitchen he usually didn't notice. Against one wall stood an iron stove as large as a car. It hadn't been used in years; Rudd cooked with a microwave and a hot plate that looked like toys in the cavernous kitchen. Near the stove was a hulking refrigerator, and near it a two-door walk-in pantry dense with shelves. Only one held food—a few boxes and cans. Two enormous soapstone sinks interrupted the expanse of counter top; beneath were drawers holding kitchen implements. At least 90 percent of the kitchen was unused, he observed. About the same percentage of unused space in the rest of the rambling three-story house. Some rooms he hadn't entered in years. No reason to. Just as there were parts of himself he hadn't visited in years. No reason to.

Dammit! That was another reason he was disturbed. Too damned many metaphors cropping up these days, raising questions he didn't want to answer. Like prickly pear spines, they had a way of working their way into his skin and resisting removal.

And today he was especially upset with himself. He had violated one of his most firmly held principles, one that had served him well all his adult life: Don't take on other people's problems. Yet here he was, alone in the sanctity of his home, wondering how he was going to find a place for S&S to live. S&S, of all gawdammed people!

He knew it was no use asking anyone in town to take S&S in, and he wouldn't have imposed on them anyway. That was another of his principles: Don't involve other people. So he was stuck with the problem.

Actually, there was an unused shed among the outbuildings behind his house. It had once been a playhouse, when the main house had been home to a large gaggle of relatives and kids. He'd been one of them. But as the family had dispersed and the children had grown up, the playhouse was forgotten. Rudd couldn't remember the last time he'd been inside it. Curiously, however, he had a clear memory of how it had been when he was a child.

On impulse, Rudd rose, opened the door leading from the kitchen to the back yard, and went outside. There was the old playhouse, surrounded by waist-high weeds. Rudd pushed them aside and wrestled open the door. The knob and hinges were rusted and protested when aroused from their long dormancy. The door opened only partly, forcing Rudd to suck in his stomach to enter.

The playhouse had but one room, but it was all the children needed. Leaks from the neglected roof had imparted a damp smell to the place, the mustiness of abandonment. Stepping inside he tripped over a pair of ancient tennis shoes, caked with mud. He recognized them. They were his, discarded here when he and his cousins, Johnson and Sam, had a mud fight after a thunderstorm. Still here.

Then as he looked around, he froze. It was as if he had unexpectedly blundered into the past. He hadn't been here in decades, yet time had been suspended here.

On a table rested the cups and saucers of a tea set. Rudd remembered when his cousin, Annie, had arranged the setting and tried to cajole

Rudd and Johnson into acting civilized for a few moments. After the last of the Kool-Aid was poured from the teapot and the cookies eaten, Johnson emitted a wall-shaking belch, and Rudd laughed so hard that Kool-Aid ran out his nose, causing Johnson to collapse on the floor and sending Annie running into the main house to complain. Rudd wondered, was this the same place setting? Could it possibly be?

On a shelf along one wall was his rock collection. He walked over and looked at the individual specimens, not picking them up but rather regarding them as if time had sanctified their arrangement. The piece of limestone that bore the imprint of a clam shell. He had found it in the layered rocks forming the sides of an arroyo southwest of Sweeney. It was his first fossil, the first rock in his collection. A piece of shale had the imprint of a fern. One rock, a piece of red and yellow chert, had been polished by rushing water; he'd found it where no water ran today. The most colorful rock in the collection was a vivid blue-and-green piece of copper ore that he had acquired from Hank Whitlock after a show-and-tell session at school. It had cost Rudd a Boy Scout pocketknife with only one broken blade, but it had been worth it.

In the opposite corner of the room was the overstuffed chair that his parents had given to the playhouse when its stuffing began to spill out. Next to the chair was a sagging cardboard box and in it a stack of comic books. With tenderness bordering on reverence, he picked up the top one. Superman, but this was a special issue, the one that told the story of how Superman came to Earth, of his parents, Jor-el and Lara, of the destruction of their home planet, Krypton, of his arrival on Earth and adoption by the Kents. As a child, Rudd had prized that issue above all others, it was one that he never traded with his friends and cousins. It was still here.

Rudd sagged into the chair. He was unprepared for being ambushed by his childhood like this. Memories and emotions he hadn't known in years swept over him. The good times he'd had in this playhouse, with the other children, the laughter and goofiness.

And then he was overcome by a deep sadness. The playhouse had been here all these years, forgotten and neglected. This was his past—and he had abandoned it. He picked up the copy of Superman and thumbed the pages.

What had happened to him? He thought of his big old house, the once-occupied rooms that now he never entered. What had happened?

Nothing sudden or dramatic. One by one the old people had died. Grandpa Silas. Grandma Emily. Weird old Uncle Morgan, who spent his days looking for his misplaced false teeth and his nights somnambulating naked. One by one they had passed away, as people put it. And his aunts and uncles, whose farms and ranches had gone bust and who had lived with their families in the big old house waiting for something to turn up, his cousins—Johnson, Annie, little Ricky, others he could barely remember—living in the house. One by one they had moved on too. Then his father died of lung cancer, and a year later his mother died of a stroke. Gone, one by one, until only he was left.

Rudd stood up abruptly, squeezed out the door, taking care to push it completely shut.

The first thing he needed to do was repair the roof. He was shaken from his encounter with his past, and as always he sought refuge in work, fixing something. Yes, he would fix up the playhouse. That would help make up for years of neglect. He would make the place livable again.

Livable? By whom? Unbidden, the image of S&S appeared, and he was brought abruptly back to the problem of finding a residence for the ragamuffin. The playhouse? Unthinkable! He surveyed the rest of the property. Clustered around a large barn that now housed machinery were several smaller buildings, like chicks around a mother hen. One had been a chicken coop. Somehow it didn't seem right to put S&S in there, though Rudd doubted that S&S would object. Nearby was another shed that had been used for storing . . . whatever.

Rudd walked over to it. He sneezed as he pushed the weathered door open and dislodged decades of dust and cobwebs; rodents unaccustomed to being disturbed scurried frantically into hiding. Only a few window frames held glass; the rest were covered with chicken wire. And stains on the warped floor boards told him that the roof leaked. Yes, this would work.

Of course, it would need fixing. S&S could do much of the labor, under Rudd's direction. Scrounging secondhand furniture around Sweeney would be no problem. A pump spigot near the barn still worked, furnishing whatever water S&S needed, likely not much, certainly not for bathing. And also near the barn was an ancient outhouse. That, too, could be resurrected.

There would have to be rules—and S&S would have to obey them. The big house and all other buildings, including the playhouse—especially the playhouse—would be off-limits. And he would have to be fully clothed at all times. And severe intoxication would not be tolerated. But Rudd's experience with S&S at the garage made him hopeful. Erratic and incoherent as S&S often was, his survival instinct remained intact.

So there it was. Until his new quarters were ready, S&S could sleep in the garage. Rudd would inform Will Diggs on his way to the garage this morning.

Then after S&S was settled, he would turn his attention to the playhouse. Of the two projects, the playhouse technically was the simpler, but Rudd suspected that emotionally it was the more challenging.

Will Diggs was unloading portable toilets when Rudd arrived to tell him of the solution to S&S's problem. Wiping his brow with a dirty, tattered bandanna that would have done S&S proud, Will said, "This is good. This is damned good. Your timing couldn't be better."

Rudd eyed him questioningly.

"We've got a big weekend coming up. I've got two groups booked already. It'll be good to have that varmint out of the way."

"Two groups?" asked Rudd.

"Yep, we've got a bunch that calls themselves Druids, whatever the hell that means. And then we've got the Indians."

"Druids? And Indians?"

"I'm clearing more land and bringing in extra toilets in case anyone else wants to show up. It's looking like this sawl-steece is shaping up to be a big deal."

Quite a morning, Rudd thought as he drove his pickup to the garage. Yes, this had been quite a morning.

"Dave, what do you know about Druids?" Leland asked as Dave seated himself at the counter at the Chick 'n' More and ordered a cup of coffee. It was Friday morning, and Dave had lots of chores awaiting him at home, but lately things there had been a little tense. Joanie had been consumed by trying to rehabilitate that crazy horse, which in turn had aggravated her relations with Traci, already festering, especially since the ditching incident. He sensed the volcano might blow this morning, and he didn't want to be around when it did. Tranquility, he craved tranquility. In Sweeney, that meant the Chick 'n' More.

"Druids?" Dave replied, unsure that he had heard correctly. "You mean, as in . . . Druids?"

"Yep, those are the folks I mean. I admit it's kind of an odd question, but there's a reason."

"Well, since you put it that way, I guess it's okay that I tell you," Dave answered, then leaned toward Leland conspiratorially.

"Druids were the priests of the ancient Celtic religion that existed in western Europe and especially in Britain before the Romans came and wiped them out."

"Pagans, in other words," said Leland, shaking his head.

"Yes, you could say that."

"I was afraid of that."

"Look, Leland, why don't you just tell me what this is all about?"

"The Romans apparently didn't wipe them all out, because I think we're going to have Druids visiting Sweeney."

"It's the Rock, isn't it?"

"How did you know?"

"Stonehenge. The real Druids died out about two thousand years ago, certainly by the time Britain was Christianized, but their nature worship has always had a lot of romantic appeal among certain types, and modern Druids are obsessed by Stonehenge. It symbolizes the ancient religion of the Britons for them, even though Stonehenge was built at least a thousand years before there were any Celts or Druids in Britain."

"These Druids are from Santa Fe," said Leland, shaking his head. "I got a call from their priest—is that what they call them, priests? At any rate, it was their leader, and he said they'd be arriving today, the day before the solstice, because they want to be present at dawn tomorrow. Said it was important to be at the rocks when the sun comes up."

"The people who built Stonehenge aligned the rocks so the rising sun would appear over a certain stone on the morning of the solstice," explained Dave. "It was a kind of astronomical calendar device."

"There's simpler ways of telling the solstice."

"Well, they did other stuff, performed ceremonies, rituals. We don't really know. Did the Druid you talked to mention any ceremonies? Any human sacrifices?"

"No, he didn't. Besides, we've got a municipal ordinance against human sacrifices, requires a permit."

"Indians?" Roger asked from atop a stool at the counter in the Chick 'n' More recently vacated by Dave Daly. The news of the Druids had spread quickly, but he'd only just now heard about the Indians from Rudd, who had heard it from Will Diggs. "We have Indians coming?"

"That's what I heard from Leland, and he was just here," answered Helen from behind the counter, and of course, she was in a position to hear just about everything. "That's what they're calling themselves."

"I'm detecting skepticism. What do you mean?"

"Well, I can't claim to be an expert on Indians, but I've done a little reading—did you know that I'm part Choctaw?—and I've never heard of the White Wolf Band of Apaches. Mescaleros, Jicarillas, Chiricahuas, yes, they're all Apaches, but the White Wolf Band? You ever hear of them?"

"Can't say I have, but that doesn't prove anything. There's a lot of obscure Indian groups out there."

"True. Well, anyways, they're coming. They say that our Rock, with its mystical spiritual power, especially on the solstice, is the perfect place to perform their ceremony to bring back the buffalo."

Roger took a sip from his coffee cup. "That shouldn't be hard, given that they're already back." He looked at the handwritten sign on the wall behind the counter advertising buffalo burgers.

Helen chuckled.

"Anyone else coming?" Roger asked. "I mean besides the Druids and the Indians?"

"Not yet, but then the solstice isn't until tomorrow. For all I know a group of aliens might be arriving."

Neither of them noticed a mammoth travel van lumbering down Main Street outside the Chick 'n' More. On its side was stenciled in bold letters "From the stars we come."

Nettie and Joanie leaned against the stall that held Flicka. "Well, for one thing, you can't just walk up to a horse like this," said Nettie. "And it would be best if you could get her out of a confined place, to someplace where she doesn't feel trapped."

Joanie, at a loss for what to do about her adopted horse, had called Nettie, hoping her friend had encountered similar horses during her barrel-racing days. She could have called Roger—and he certainly owed her the benefit of his experience—but she was still pissed at him for seducing her—that was the word—into adopting this pathetic, crazy, dangerous horse. Not that she was less committed. Ken wouldn't give up; neither would she.

Joanie had been right about Nettie. She had seen horses like Flicka, though she allowed that Flicka was among the more extreme cases. "When you get her in a place where she doesn't feel confined, then you need to sit down. That way you'll be less of a threat to her. Then you need to do something that will arouse her curiosity. I always used to braid a lariat. That would get them interested. Horses are as curious as cats. Eventually her curiosity will overcome her fear, and she'll come over to see what you're doing."

Thus it was that on Friday afternoon Joanie squatted on the ground about fifty yards from the Rock while nearby Flicka, tethered by a long rope to a stake in the ground, grazed on the sparse prairie grass. Occasionally, the horse would raise her head in Joanie's direction, as if wondering why a middle-aged woman might be sitting on the ground fiddling with what a human would recognize as a dollhouse.

Joanie had been sitting there for about an hour, and while she wasn't sure it had any therapeutic effect on Flicka, it sure did on her. Growing up in LA she'd often found delight and refuge in the miniature world of dollhouses, and even in her teen years—especially in her teen years—she'd retreated into them when the larger world became too chaotic, too unpredictable, too dangerous. She made miniature furnishings for them, decorated them, peopled them with imaginary characters. Time slowed and the outside world vanished when she was alone with her dollhouses. For weeks after the terrifying incident with Jenny she'd spent almost all her free time in her room with her dollhouses.

In college she'd put them aside, not because she'd outgrown her interest in them but because she rarely had the large blocks of time required to enter their world fully. She also felt a little embarrassed explaining them to her fellow students, and especially to boyfriends. That was one reason why she'd never tried to share them with Traci, even though she'd speculated that they might help Traci adjust to Sweeney. Or probably not. So while her dollhouses had accompanied her to Sweeney, they'd remained in the attic, ignored if not forgotten.

Now, however, rehabilitating Flicka necessitated simply sitting and working with her hands, so she had retrieved a favorite dollhouse, the three-story Victorian, from the attic, and as she sat on the grass, hand-sewing tiny curtains, she relaxed into the same contented concentration she'd known as a girl.

"Mother!"

Joanie jumped at the urgent whisper behind her. She turned to face a very distressed Traci.

"Mother, *what* are you doing?" She glanced over her shoulder lest her friends, who were milling around the Rock, happened to witness this.

"Be quiet, you'll startle Flicka."

"Well, we certainly wouldn't want that," said Traci sarcastically. "A grasshopper would spook that schizie horse."

Joanie's withering glare made Traci lower her voice further.

"Mother, I just can't believe it. You're sitting out here in a field with a . . . a horse, working on—what is that, a dollhouse? Oh, it's just too much."

Joanie, aware now of the problem, said nothing, but her eyes narrowed.

"It's not enough that I have the dorkiest parents in New Mexico," Traci continued heedlessly, "but they have to be wacko as well."

"That's enough, young lady," warned Joanie.

Traci glanced over her shoulder. Her friends were still near the Rock. "Mother, we're here taking pictures of the Rock for the Sweeney website," pleaded Traci, still whispering, "and what will be in the background? My mother, sitting in a field with a horse working on a dollhouse! I've never been so embarrassed."

"I said, that'll be enough," warned Joanie, menace rising in her voice.

Just then the girls detached themselves from the Rock and began walking toward Joanie and Traci. Traci moaned in despair.

"Hey, Trace, what's up?" asked Heather as they drew closer. "Oh, hi, Mrs. Daly."

Traci, hoping that Flicka was the lesser of the two humiliations, directed their attention to the horse rather than to the dollhouse. "This is my mom's latest project. She inherited this horse that's got serious mental problems, and she's trying to rehabilitate it." Traci made it sound like her mother was trying to counsel a rattlesnake.

Joanie frowned at Traci, then continued the explanation herself. "She was abused by her former owner, badly abused. The vet says there's still a good horse in there, and I'm trying to get her out." Joanie then went on to explain her strategy as recommended by Nettie.

Christie, who knew horses, nodded approval. "That's what my dad did with an abused horse we had once. But it's hard to rebuild their trust."

Suddenly Kimberly exclaimed, "Is that a dollhouse?" Traci melted into a puddle of mortification, unable to speak. Unlike the other girls, Kimberly was capable of a hard-edged scorn that could be devastating.

"Cool!" continued Kimberly. "I *love* dollhouses." Traci slowly raised her head in disbelief. Kimberly was in her Goth uniform, all black with a spiked belt and dangling chains. She wore a Megadeth T-shirt.

"I had a dollhouse when I was a little girl, and I loved it," Kimberly continued, then added bitterly, "Dad ran over it with the car."

"A dollhouse?" exclaimed Rachel as she bulled her way forward. "I want to see." The other girls rolled their eyes. "I never had a dollhouse," Rachel said plaintively. "I always wanted one."

"I have several dollhouses," explained Joanie. "They're all in the attic. Each one is different. One is my English manor dollhouse, another is my Swiss chalet dollhouse. I've even got a haunted house dollhouse."

Kimberly's eyes widened. "Way cool. Could I see them sometime?"

"Me too?" pleaded Rachel.

"Absolutely," said Joanie. "I've even got a Little House on the Prairie dollhouse, but I don't know how to make tumbleweeds or dust." All the girls except Traci laughed.

Just then Leland appeared, striding toward them from the Rock, Trixie trotting by his side. Flicka raised her head suspiciously and began backing away. So much for sitting in a quiet place by yourself, thought Joanie.

"Hi, girls, hi, Joanie. Don't mean to bother you, but this seemed a good chance, since I happened to be here, to let you know that tomorrow this will be a busy place, and you might want to find another place to work with that horse. Nettie told me all about her."

"Busy place?" asked Joanie.

"Yep, seems tomorrow's the summer solstice, longest day of the year, and there's . . . groups coming in to hold ceremonies. Most of them are staying at Will Diggs's RV park, but they'll be here before dawn, so they can see the sun rise."

Kimberly's attention shifted to Leland. "What kind of groups, Mr. Morton?"

Leland hesitated, then said, "Well, I don't know all that might show up, but I know there's folks calling themselves Druids. And Indians.

And people from Arizona that . . . I don't know how to put this, but they say they're from another planet."

"Whoa!" exclaimed Kimberly as the girls exchanged excited glances. Leland wasn't sure he'd done the right thing by telling them, knowing that they now would head straight for Will Diggs's RV park, but he knew they'd find out anyway.

As if by prearranged signal, the girls excused themselves to return to their photography and began moving back to the Rock. They needed to talk. "Bye, Mrs. Daly," called Kimberly. "Thanks for offering to show your dollhouses."

"Stop by any time," Joanie replied. Traci, the last to leave, turned to her mother. "Do you really have a haunted house dollhouse in the attic?" Traci asked. Joanie only nodded.

In the Style Salon, just before closing, Nettie was finishing the unpleasant task of dyeing Harriet Moggs's hair the appalling shade of orange that the woman demanded. She'd tried often to convince Harriet to go with something more appropriate to her venerable age, something like Precambrian white, but Harriet always insisted upon the orange. "It's the color I was born with."

The only other person in the salon was Iris Gerber, who was just hanging around, like a bird around a granary, hoping to gather a few spilled grains of gossip.

Suddenly the door opened, and a tall, slender middle-aged woman in a long robe wafted in. The women in the salon noticed the robe first. It was a gauzy rainbow of soft pastels—pink, violet, yellow, rose—and it seemed to flow around the woman like a mist. Around her neck she wore a gold necklace from which dangled amethyst crystals and wire-silver charms twisted into astrological signs. Her hair matched her robe, pale yellow, long and flowing. A scent reminiscent of sandalwood accompanied the woman.

Nettie's hands and Iris's mouth both stopped in midmotion. Harriet simply goggled.

"I am Liriodendra Cassiopeia," the woman pronounced. It was a statement of title, not an introduction.

"Afternoon, Ms. Catheopia," Nettie finally managed to say.

"Cassiopeia," the woman corrected haughtily, "like the constellation."

"Oh, *that* Cassiopeia," said Nettie. Iris and Harriet just continued to gape. "What can I do for you? I'm just about to close, but I suppose I could fit you in, if it's an emergency and it's not too involved."

The woman bridled. "I'm not here for anything," and with her hand she lovingly caressed her long hair, as if to reassure it. "I'm here to invite you to an important event. Cosmically important." And with that she glided through the room handing each woman a flier. Nettie thought she detected the faint scent of gin on the woman's breath.

Iris glanced at the flier. "'Channeling the Chakras'? 'Ceremony to prepare for joining the Galactic Community'?"

"You likely don't realize it," the woman vapored, "but the raising of your Rock by Sirians was a crucial step in the evolution of your planet. The creation of a new vortex center, where star energy and ancient earth energy are integrated. It was a monumental event, one that has happened only a few times in your planet's history. It happened at Atlantis, it happened at the pyramids of Giza, it happened at Stonehenge, and a few other places—and now it has happened here, in Sweeney. You are truly blessed."

"We're blessed with chakras?" asked Iris. "What are chakras? Are they contagious?"

"Well, I can see that consciousness here definitely needs to be raised," sneered Liriodendra. "A chakra is a nexus of metaphysical energy. They exist in the body of the planet, but seven of them also exist in each of our bodies. The problem is that our chakras usually are out of alignment. That's the purpose of our ceremony, to bring all of Earth's chakras and our own chakras into alignment."

"I've got chakras and there's something wrong with them?" Harriet croaked, her voice heavy with worry. "I'll bet that's why my joints have been aching so much lately."

Nettie's eyes narrowed. "Tell me again how this Rock of ours came to be raised, and how you found out about it."

"You must understand that you came from the stars," Liriodendra said ethereally.

"I came from the stars?" Harriet croaked again.

Ignoring her, the star woman continued. "In long ages past, extraterrestrials from the Lyran, Sirian, and Pleiadean star systems came to your planet. They founded advanced civilizations on the continents of Atlantis and Lemuria. They were beautiful beings, with golden hair—"

"There weren't any brunettes or redheads among them?" Nettie asked.

"—and they were extremely wise," the woman continued, ignoring Nettie. "But then conflict among them caused a dislocation of the chakras. There were great earthquakes, Atlantis and Lemuria sank into the sea, and there was a great flood that you remember as Noah's flood. The star people retreated underground, where most of them remain to this day."

"Well, do tell," said Iris whose initial amazement was turning to skepticism.

"Since then, the people who remained at the surface regressed into a degenerate state and forgot their origins. Now, as the planetary systems begin to come into conjunction and as the earth approaches the cosmic convergence foretold by the ancient Mayan elders, I have graced your planet to prepare you for the coming new age and to remind you of who you really are."

"Who's that?" asked Iris breathlessly.

Stretching to her full height, Liriodendra proclaimed to the women in the salon, "You are goddesses!"

Iris gasped.

From her chair Harriet rasped, "I'm a goddess?"

Nettie's eyes narrowed. "Well, speaking as one goddess to another, I've got a question. You keep saying 'your planet.' What do you mean by that? Seems to me it's your planet too."

"I am Liriodendra Cassiopeia. I am from Sirius. The goddess whose earthly body stands before you has channeled me. She and I have become one."

"Well, I never would have suspected," said Iris. Nettie suppressed a grin.

"So what are you inviting us to?" asked Nettie, as she applied the finishing touches to Harriet's hair.

"I and several of my sister goddesses have come in our travel van from Sedona, Arizona, to perform solstice ceremonies at the Rock when the light of your star strikes it in the morning, The energy flowing then will be extraordinary, and you are invited to come and participate in this awakening of star consciousness."

"Dawn at the Rock—I'll be there," said Iris with a conviction that Nettie knew was sincere. "Is there anything I should bring—lemonade, chips, potato salad? I imagine that even goddesses have to eat?"

"Our tradition on Sirius is that on occasions such as this we pour libations on the sacred earth and then consume them in joyous fellowship with the Earth Mother."

"So I should bring lemonade?" asked Iris.

"I think a beverage with a more adventurous spirit would be more appropriate," Liriodendra answered, and with that she turned to leave. "I hope to see you all there," she said as she swept out the door. "Remember, you are goddesses."

"Well, I never," said Harriet as she climbed down from the chair. "This me being a goddess changes everything."

As Iris helped Goddess Harriet through the front door, she turned to Nettie and asked, "Will you be there?"

"I wouldn't miss it for the world . . . our world, that is."

For Wayne Fall, this Friday had been more difficult than usual. Relations with June had been tense ever since the rodeo, and showed no signs of getting better. He did know how much she enjoyed playing popular music for people, but then she had to know how much being Sweeney's spiritual leader meant to him—and allowing her to play for a bunch of nudists would amount to sanctioning their immorality. Especially after that Bare-assed Bob spectacle at the rodeo. Any lewd thing could have happened at the dance. All week long he'd replayed these arguments in his mind, but they did nothing to calm the turmoil.

Then today two of his workers had failed to show up at the truck depot that he supervised in Tucumcari. Throughout the day Fall had railed to himself, "I just know that Riley's not sick, he's just declaring a three-day weekend for himself—again. I've already got a backlog of shipments to log in, and having to move crates for him. . . ."

Wayne hated his job. It was mindless and godless. He certainly didn't feel he was called to it by the Lord. But the job paid reasonably well, and there weren't a lot of alternatives in the area, especially for someone whose only credentials were a degree from a Bible college in Lubbock.

Adding to the day's frustrations, when he'd switched on his car's radio on the long commute back to Sweeney, he'd discovered that a High Plains electrical storm made it impossible to receive his favorite radio program, Pastor Pete's Bible Hour of Power Prophecy. He'd been counting on Pastor Pete to provide some spiritual guidance in his conflict with June. Not only did Pastor Pete distract him from the tedium of the featureless landscape, but he also often inspired him. If Wayne escaped the tribulation of the coming End Times, much of the credit would go to Pastor Pete. Friday was one of many days when Fall took solace in knowing that on the day of Rapture, which could occur any time now, he would instantly be transported to his heavenly home—and the truck depot and Riley and everyone else would be left to suffer unspeakable torments. Served them right. He knew he should witness to Riley and the others to warn them to mend their ways while there was still time, but he was sure they would just mock him, as they always did when he tried to talk to them about Jesus. Well, they would see who had the last laugh.

As he entered Sweeney and was about to turn down his street for home, his cell phone rang. It was June asking him to pick up a half-gallon of milk on the way home.

So, sighing with irritation, Wayne turned the little car around and drove back down Main Street to the Baca Mart.

He was halfway between the dairy case and the checkout counter when he stopped abruptly. Next to the counter was a new display case, with baseball caps and T-shirts sporting various logos. The one that first caught the reverend's eye read "Born again pagan."

Not believing his eyes, Wayne hesitantly stepped forward, like approaching a rattlesnake. Oh, dear Lord, the other logos were just as bad:

Rock On
I got stoned in Sweeney
Stonehenge, Giza, Machu Picchu, Sweeney

And worst of all, Rock of Sages.

Sputtering righteous indignation, he stormed to the counter and confronted Judy Baca.

"What . . . what . . . what is the meaning of . . . this?"

"You mean the tourist souvenirs?"

"Tourist souvenirs?" Fall sputtered. "You mean you're selling these blasphemies?"

"Well, yeah," responded Judy, becoming indignant herself. "What did you think, that we were opening a T-shirt and ball-cap museum?"

"But what's on these 'items' is offensive in the eyes of the Lord. As Sweeney's minister, I have to protest."

"Yeah, well as a Catholic who doesn't go to your church, I have to tell you to mind your own business. Lighten up, Wayne. I really think the Lord has more important things on his mind than funny sayings on ball caps in Sweeney. Besides, we'll sell a bunch of them at the solstice events at the Rock this weekend. You got anything against folks in this poor town making a little money for a change? Who knows, maybe some of the money will wind up in your collection plates on Sunday."

"Solstice events? At the Rock?"

"Haven't you heard? The summer solstice is tomorrow, and there's groups coming into town to do ceremonies and what-all over at the Rock. Somebody said Droods were coming."

Fall gasped. "Druids!"

"Yeah, that's them," responded Judy.

"They're pagans! They worship trees!"

"I guess that's why our distributor sent us ball caps and T-shirts with 'Druids do it in groves' on them, not that we've really got any groves around here." Fall glanced again at the case. Sure enough, the "groves" logos were there.

"Pagans!" His mind reeled. "So that's what Sweeney has become, a Mecca for pagans. Oh, this is worse than I ever imagined. Old Satan sure knew what he was doing when he targeted Sweeney."

Sensing futility, Judy asked, "Is that milk all you have?" as she started to ring it up.

"No! I'm not buying that," Fall thundered in his most patriarchal voice. "I shall not contribute to the works of Satan by purchasing the milk of Mammon."

"Suit yourself," said Judy. "By the way, we're getting in non-fat milk of Mammon next week."

With a humph, Fall started for the door, but before he could open it he was halted by a rack of bottles. They held a clear liquid and had crude, computer-printed labels.

As he turned to Judy with horror on his face, she said, "Eloy and Molly Herrera brought those in, mostly as a joke. They've got a well not too far from the Rock, and they thought this would be fun, but we've already sold about a dozen bottles."

Before leaving the store, Fall cast one more disbelieving look at the bottles. Their labels bore a drawing of the Rock and read: "Sweeney Weeney Water. Nature's Own Viagra. Not for human consumption, for geologic use only."

Friday afternoon, and happiness is Tucumcari in your rearview mirror, thought Kathy Larkin as she steered her red Mustang onto NM 459 that led over the plains to Sweeney. The end of a difficult week. An attorney for Willis Neal had wanted her to testify to how bright were Neal's prospects for rehabilitation, if only he could stay out of jail after yet another arrest for public intoxication. Kathy couldn't quite go that far, but she did what she could. Willis was all but hopeless and would surely die a practicing alcoholic, but he was harmless and would not be improved by jail.

Then a woman in Logan had called to threaten suicide. Kathy recalled that this particular woman had made similar calls before, but that did not mitigate the urgency with which Kathy responded to the call. To every such call.

Then there had been the usual workload of the depressed needing a life, the relatives of demented elderly who were convinced their kin were a danger to themselves if they continued to live outside a nursing home, recovering alcoholics off the wagon, sullen and surly teenagers, gestating divorces—a few she could help, most she couldn't.

A difficult week. Kathy turned on the car radio. Usually she listened to NPR as she drove home, but occasionally the drive required music. Everything she listened to had to first pass what she called her "Kiowa County Test." The grading system ran from Don't Want to Stop Driving at the top, down through Cool and Toe-tapping, then down through Ho-hum before finally bottoming out at Driving on the Rims. Usually classic rock and classical got the highest scores, but lately she'd been listening to classic country. Residue from the rodeo, perhaps.

But not today. A High Plains thunderstorm scattered static over all the stations, so she turned off the radio and spent a few minutes upbraiding herself for not getting around to installing a CD player in her car. Then she lapsed into her predictable Friday afternoon ambivalence. Yes, a shitty week was over, and she looked forward to a weekend of respite. But on most Friday afternoons she strayed into mild depression, triggered by the realization that once again the afternoon would be empty. Once, Friday afternoon had meant calling friends, planning to get together, doing things, partying, laughing, and having fun. Now, Friday afternoon meant nothing fun at all. She resented the loss, and blamed herself. As well as Sweeney. She always blamed Sweeney.

She was swimming upstream in a river of recrimination as she entered Sweeney and thus almost missed what was happening at Will Diggs's RV park at the edge of town. An image flashed briefly on her consciousness: teepees.

What? She braked, turned her car around, and drove back. She wasn't alone in her curiosity. Leland's pickup, high school kids' cars, Rudd's truck, Roger's pickup—damn! Oh, well, so be it.

She parked as close to the teepees as possible—her parents disintegrated if she was more than a few minutes late—and strolled over. Most spectators had taken shelter from the late afternoon sun behind an abandoned storage shed, and Kathy, to her regret, found herself standing beside Roger.

"Evening, gentlemen," she said amiably.

"Evening, Kathy," they chorused.

"Are those really teepees?" she asked.

"Appears so," answered Leland. "These . . . Indians are here for the solstice, along with other . . . groups. Tomorrow should be quite interesting."

Across the dusty weed patch that was the RV park, Kathy could see people bustling around several pickups from whose beds extended bundles of debarked timber lodgepoles. A couple of teepees already were up, while others were having canvas draped over a lodgepole framework. For Kathy, the scene had a strangely primeval quality that briefly beguiled her. Then she thought how historically authentic it all was— the women were doing most of the work.

Seeing the onlookers, a large man detached himself from the group and sauntered over. As he drew closer, Kathy noticed an unconformity between his clothing and the body it covered. He was dressed as an Indian, in a Hollywood sort of way, with a beaded headband, leather jacket with dangling fringes, tourist trap moccasins, buckskin leggings, and a wolf amulet and small leather medicine pouch hanging from a thong around his neck. Another leather pouch hung from a leather strap wrapped around his ample waist.

Yet the man didn't look like an Indian. He was tall, with a large paunch of the kind common in truck stops. His hair was light-brown, certainly not black, though he wore it long, parted in the middle, and in two braids, tied with turquoise-colored ribbons. His complexion was florid, his puffy red nose hinting of long acquaintance with alcohol, and his eyes were blue-green. He definitely would have been rejected as an extra in an Indian movie.

He carried a wooden staff elaborately decorated with leather strips, feathers, and inlaid turquoise. The staff was topped by the carved head of an eagle. As he approached he raised the staff and said, "Howa-pu-ka."

"Cowabunga," muttered Roger under his breath. It was the faux-Indian greeting that Chief Thunderthud had spoken on the old Howdy Doody show. Try as she would, Kathy could not suppress a giggle, which grew more irrepressible the more she tried to smother it. Finally, she feigned coughing.

"I am Soaring Eagle," the man proclaimed, "and I am chief of the White Wolf Apaches. On behalf of our people I bring you greetings."

Leland stepped forward, offered his hand, introduced himself, and said, "Welcome to Sweeney, Mr. Eagle. I know we're a bunch of gawkers here. It's just that we don't get a lot of teepees in town. But we're a friendly place, and if you need anything I'm sure you'll find lots of people willing to help. What exactly are you planning on doing tomorrow at the Rock?"

"In our tribe we call the 'Rock' Wana-tabe, and we believe its rising is a sign that the buffalo will return." Roger and Leland exchanged glances. Oblivious, the man continued, "We'll be doing our buffalo dance, which is directed to the Great Spirit."

From the leather pouch at his waist the man took out a pack of cigarettes and a lighter. As he lit up, Kathy noticed that he was a Marlboro man.

"Yeah, this here has been a sacred site for a long time," the man said, beginning to lapse into his native dialect, which Kathy guessed was Texan. "If we do this right, there'll be Indians coming from all over to work on the buffalo returning—but we was here first. Remember that. The White Wolves have already staked this out."

The look on Leland's face told Kathy he wasn't quite sure what the man meant; neither did she. In the background, the teepees continued to go up, and Kathy thought she saw what looked like a huge drum being unloaded from one of the pickups.

"Say," said Roger, "I'm curious, where are the White Wolves from? Where's your reservation located? I've never heard of your tribe before."

Leave it to Roger, Kathy thought, to ask the impertinent questions everyone wanted to ask but didn't dare.

Soaring Eagle took a deep drag on his cigarette, exhaled, and said, "Our reservation is the sacred earth. We are from all over. The reason you've never heard of us is because our brotherhood has only recently been made manifest through secret signs and ancient tribal ceremonies. We also placed ads in certain magazines to locate our dispossessed tribal members."

In her mind's eye Kathy pictured a little classified ad at the back of *Tomahawk Magazine:* "You might be an Indian! Take simple test and find out! Send $5 and SASE to Soaring Eagle. A new life as a mystic Indian awaits you!"

Kathy glanced at Roger, who glanced back. They exchanged smirks.

"By the way," said Soaring Eagle, "we're going to need supplies while we're here. Is there someplace in town where we can get, oh, you know, food, snacks, beverages?"

Kathy instantly understood that the operative word was "beverages," spelled "beer."

Leland answered. "The Baca Mart out on the highway near the edge of town has what you need."

"Thanks," said the man, as he tossed his cigarette on the ground and turned to walk away. Over his shoulder he said, "Some of you might be Indians too. You should take the test."

"Thanks," said Leland, as he ground the smoldering cigarette out with his boot.

Kathy began walking back to her car. Suddenly, as in a Zen enlightenment moment, she became aware of the profound weirdness of the scene. She smiled. This is great! Friday afternoon, and I've actually been having fun! She knew that she was past the quarter-hour when her parents would begin to boil, but this was too good to miss; her mother's TV show reports could wait. Sometimes life sent a higher calling.

"This will be cool on the Sweeney website, won't it?" pestered Rachel as Traci was taking her final photographs of the White Wolves erecting their teepees. "Won't this be cool?"

"Yes, Rachel, this will be cool," replied Traci wearily. Mercifully, irony and sarcasm were lost on Rachel.

"Hey, Trace, look over there," said Kimberly, pointing across the field. "Something's happening over there."

Three former school buses, their once-yellow bodies now covered by crudely painted green forest scenes, had stopped and were disgorging people dressed in green-and-brown robes.

Heather began walking toward them. "Check it out!"

If anything, these visitors were even more bizarre than the Indians. Most of the people, men and women alike, were dressed like Friar Tuck, with heavy woolen robes and rope belts. They wore sandals—or nothing—on their feet. Most were in their forties or fifties. The men had long, untrimmed, salt-and-pepper beards, while the women had dyed their hair gold or red. Both sexes wore it long and unbound. Around their heads were gold cloth headbands into which were stuck twigs and leaves. From cords around their necks dangled Celtic emblems. They were Druids.

Traci already had deduced that because she'd heard rumors that Druids were coming. Also, the Druids had set up a banner near their vehicles that read: Druidic Order of American Amoricans. Beltane Prophecy Grove. Santa Fe Henge.

Though Traci still considered herself a neophyte working photographer, she nonetheless had learned that nothing attracts certain people more than photographic equipment. The girls had barely started for the buses before a giant sloth of a man lumbered toward them. He was tall as well as fat, far more than Soaring Eagle, and he rolled as he walked. His beard was long, dark, and curly; woven into it were little amulets representing magical signs. On his chest, dangling from a thong around his neck, was a large silver pentacle. He carried a dark, wooden staff, carved with leaf and snake patterns. Topping the staff was a huge translucent green stone, cut and faceted to refract light.

"Welcome to the Grove of Druids. Here you will be safe."

What did *that* mean? wondered Traci. And what about this "grove" business, there were no trees here.

The man continued, "I am high priest of the grove. I also am the official bard. I am Uther Pendragon—do you want me to spell that name for you?"

On cue, Rachel whipped out a notebook and began writing. The man appeared relieved.

Kimberly nudged Heather. "'Uther' my butt. More like 'Udder.'"

"Do you mind if I take photos?" Traci asked hesitantly. She hadn't intended to ask, but now it seemed the thing to do.

"By all means feel free," said Uther expansively. He seemed to swell before their eyes. "I assume you are members of the press and have questions you wish to ask. I imagine you are surprised to learn that there are still Druids in the modern age. Well, let me give you a little background—"

"Actually, we're working for the town of Sweeney," Traci tried to explain. "We're working on a website for the town, and we need photos."

The man deflated slightly, then quickly swelled again. "You're doing the right thing. If anything will put this place on the map, tomorrow certainly will."

"What do you mean?" asked Heather. Rachel continued taking notes.

"Tomorrow is Alban Heruin" —he paused to spell it for Rachel— "Sacred Summer Solstice of the Celtic race. Tomorrow, on that auspicious day, we will be dedicating a new henge. And performing a major sacrificial ritual that hasn't been performed, maybe, since the days of Stonehenge and King Arthur and the Holy Grail!" He swept his arm grandly to point to the Rock in the distance.

"Wow!" said Kimberly.

Rachel stopped writing and asked, "Aren't Stonehenge and King Arthur, like, a couple thousand years apart?" Everyone ignored her.

As he made his gesture, Heather nudged Traci and nodded with her head toward one of the school buses. Descending the stairs was a bulbous woman about fifty. She wore a robe of thin, gauzy material, in shades of pale green.

"You can see right through it," gasped Traci. "She's naked!" Heather nodded deeply.

"The emergence of a new henge on Earth is a major event," Uther continued, "and it certainly portends other events to come." He paused to make sure Rachel had resumed taking notes, though now her face bore skepticism rather than wonder.

"There will be ceremonies and singing and dancing." And at that the man attempted a little jig that made him resemble a walrus. The girls stepped back. "And there will be feasting and drinking. We'll have mead and whiskey and the traditional Germanic beverage of the forest, beer. And most important, the Alban Heruin sacrifice will be resurrected and blood again will be shed in the name of the Old Ones."

"What's he talking about?" whispered Rachel.

"I'm not sure," Traci whispered back as she focused her camera's lens. She briefly was grateful to Rachel for sharing her unease at what she was hearing. "What's this ceremony?" Traci asked Uther.

"The consecration of a new henge requires a blood sacrifice. A beast will be slaughtered."

"What kind of beast?" blurted Rachel.

"One of the cloven hoofed tribe. A goat will be offered."

Rachel gasped. The girls looked at each other, then toward the Rock. There a small goat on a long tether was grazing. But before they had time to react, Uther concluded the interview, turned, and walked away as airily as a man weighing three hundred pounds could.

"That's not right," pronounced Rachel with surprising vehemence. "And I think he's a phony; what he said doesn't make sense."

"I don't know about that," said Kimberly, "but these Druids *suck*."

"Can they really just kill a goat here?" asked Heather.

The girls all looked at each other. They didn't know.

"Well, they can't," stated Rachel. Again, the girls were taken aback by the intensity of her outrage. This was a side of her none of them had seen before.

"I have an idea," said Traci.

Chapter Ten

"SATAN'S ARRIVING TONIGHT—if he's not already here!" Wayne shouted to June as he marched out the door of their home armed with a Bible, cross, and bag containing flashlights. To the west, the sun was sinking into the horizon; inexorably night was approaching. "Are you sure you don't want to come with me, June? There'll be powerful witnessing for Jesus tonight, maybe even actual wrestling with the Devil."

"No thanks, Wayne," June replied. "Wrestling's not really my thing. Besides, I need to stay here, just in case."

"Pray for me."

"Oh, I will."

As he strode off he didn't hear his wife mutter to herself, "Loopy, the poor man is just plain loopy. If only he doesn't embarrass himself and the church too badly."

When Wayne arrived at the Rock he looked with foreboding at the relentlessly sinking sun. Soon the deep blue would turn to indigo, then to black. A little more light would have been welcome. He switched his flashlights on and off to make sure they worked. He shivered, though the temperature was mild. Thundering against Satan on a Sunday morning in church was one thing; confronting him alone at night was another. Perhaps he should have been more diplomatic in his condemnation of the archfiend.

No! What was he saying? He raised his eyes and asked forgiveness, then clutched his Bible and cross tighter.

I've got to scout the area, he thought. Switching on one of the flashlights he walked around the Rock. Abruptly, he halted. His heart stopped. In the dirt were fresh hoof prints—cloven hoof prints. He gasped. Wasn't that how Satan was always depicted, with cloven hooves? Admittedly, these prints weren't very large, but Satan's power didn't depend on physical strength alone. With his flashlight in one hand and his Bible and cross in the other, he stalked around the Rock shouting, "Begone, thou foulish fiend!" It might have worked because he saw neither goat nor Satan.

Still, seeing the prints reminded him that he didn't know exactly what to expect upon meeting, face-to-face for the first time, the Prince of Darkness. Regrettably, Bible College and Pastor Pete had always been a little vague about the specifics of personally rebuking the Devil. Fall wasn't entirely confident that his Bible and cross were enough to protect him.

It was a night of righteous valor but also one of trial and tribulation, battling one panic after another all night long—coyotes, an owl, assorted rustlings and scurryings. When he heard a suspicious noise he would arise and run around waving the Bible and cross.

Nonetheless, as dawn approached Fall experienced a grim satisfaction. Satan was nowhere in sight, and he was still alive, although he was chilled and exhausted, physically and emotionally, from challenging Satan, daring him to come forward and wrestle like a man, or whatever.

Reverend Fall was the first person Dave Daly saw when he arrived at the Rock about an hour before dawn. The good minister was railing at Judy and Adelino, who had just arrived and were setting up their snack-and-souvenir tent by their pickup's headlights. They were ignoring the reverend. Dave decided to do likewise.

Instead he went over to Leland, who also had left his pickup's headlights on and was connecting power to the site and checking on the Port-a-Potties that had been ordered. "Glad to see you," said Leland, "could you help me run this wiring over to the outlet there?"

Dave picked up the long orange strands. "We need to run a line over there too." He pointed to a grassy area between two of the Mystery

Holes. "The Rotary decided at the last minute to set up a table with coffee and water. A little hospitality. Roger's idea."

As they were dragging the wire, Rudd materialized out of the predawn haze. Try as he would, Dave could not suppress the image "Gorillas in the mist." More disturbing was the apparition of S&S close behind him, looking like the crazed ghost of a starved coyote. Terrifying, unless you knew who he was, then you just stayed upwind. Dave hoped the reverend wouldn't see S&S and mistake him for a demon. Rudd didn't look particularly pleased with his companion, and S&S soon lost interest in the wiring and drifted away. Nearby, Traci and her friends, having borrowed a digital video recorder to augment their still cameras, began erecting tripods. Soon Roger appeared to set up the Rotary Club's coffee table.

"Hey, Kathy!" he shouted as she appeared, wandering around waiting for things to happen. "Come on over and give me a hand. Best seats in the house."

Kathy paused, pulled her cardigan sweater closer around her. She was neither a regular Rotarian nor a friend of Roger's, but . . . what the hell. She answered, "What the hell."

"How'd you escape?" he asked as he handed her a huge coffee can and a can opener.

"I told Mom and Dad that there was a civic event going on in Sweeney, and I was needed to help. And it looks like I am," she said, as the can opener bit into the can's lid. "How'd you get away? The clinic's got to be pretty busy."

"Very busy, but one of the advantages of being a vet is that you've always got a pool of animal-loving volunteers to draw from to help you out. Young girls actually compete for feeding the horses while I'm away. And, of course, there's Jimmy." Jimmy was a widowed, retired, slightly stove-up rancher who had moved to town and was happy to be working with animals again.

"It's good you showed up," Roger said, "because it'll be good background for you."

"I beg your pardon?"

"For when you are announcer for this event next year." He laughed.

Kathy laughed and threatened to hit him with her hat. "And you'll be the clown?"

"Not a chance! I'm not that stupid. Pissed-off bulls are nothing compared to the weird and crazy people here today. I'm not that brave."

"Do you really think this could happen every year?"

"Beats me, but the solstice comes around every year, twice in fact, as well as a couple of equinoxes. And loonies like our visitors have been around since the beginning."

Other Rotarians began showing up to help. Ron Suffitt, wearing a suit and tie, appeared with the Rotarian banner, which he tacked to the table.

Connie Nesbitt arrived with a stack of impromptu fliers promoting Sweeney as the "Mystic Center of the West." She also had a stack of real estate fliers.

"Every rancher in Kiowa County is here," said Leland to no one in particular as he hooked up electricity for the coffeepot. "And there's folks I've never seen before. There's license plates from West Texas to Santa Fe. Who'd have thought there were that many people willing to get up in the middle of the night to go see the sun rise over a rock."

Nettie always had been an early riser, so getting up before dawn posed no hardship, but getting Iris Gerber up and out the door was another matter. Iris lived alone and spent her evenings abusing snacks and TV; she usually didn't pass out until midnight.

After banging on Iris's door Nettie resorted to shouted threats. "If you don't get up and get dressed *now*, then I'm leaving without you, and you'll miss all the excitement."

With that Iris dumped herself out of bed, threw on some loose-fitting clothes, ran a brush through her hair, and clomped out the door. "Why can't dawn be later in the day," she grumbled.

"In Alaska it is," countered Nettie, "in the winter."

Iris continued grumbling all the way to the Rock—until she stopped abruptly. "Look," she whispered, pointing to a strange figure approaching the crowd that was gathering around the Rock. Even in the predawn darkness, the orange hair was unmistakable.

"It's Harriet!" gasped Iris.

Nettie looked at the figure doddering toward the Rock. "I'm not surprised. In fact, that was one reason I wanted you to come with me this morning. I had a feeling yesterday that she might get besotted with that goddess and chakra talk. Someone needs to look after her."

They exchanged looks that said, "Oh, joy, that's us," then moved to intercept Harriet.

"Oh, Iris, Nettie, I'm so happy to see you. Isn't this just the most interesting thing you ever saw?"

"I'll allow that," said Nettie.

"She said I was a goddess," continued Harriet, "that lady in the shop. Me, a goddess."

"Oh, I wouldn't take all that talk too seriously," said Nettie. "After all, she said me and Iris were goddesses too." She laughed.

But Harriet was not to be deflected. "Maybe you are. Wouldn't that be something, all of us goddesses?"

Nettie gave a skeptical shrug.

"She said I had chakras," Harriet pressed stubbornly. "Nobody else ever bothered to tell me I had chakras. I never knew I had them. I just know they're the reason my joints have been acting up lately, those chakras out of alignment. Nobody else ever told me about my chakras."

"I understand," said Nettie. "Maybe we'll all learn something interesting today. Let's just stay together and enjoy it." In the background, Iris slowly shook her head.

Together they wandered around the Rock, watching people arrive, greeting those they knew.

"Did you know I was a goddess?" Harriet insisted on asking everyone. "You might be one too. Or a god."

A ranch wife looked at her corpulent husband. "Him? A god? Of what, gravy?"

Harriet was a slow walker, but they weren't in a hurry. They stopped at Judy and Adelino's tent. Iris and Nettie pretended to be scandalized by the T-shirt logos.

"Well, I never . . . Nettie, look at this!" whispered Iris, pointing to a T-shirt that read, "Visualize This!" with a crude sketch of the Rock.

They were even more deliciously shocked by the Sweeney Weeney Water.

"Hey, Harriet, look at . . ."

But Harriet had vanished.

An almost imperceptible glow over the eastern horizon summoned both the Druids and the Sirians simultaneously. With great solemnity, the berobed Uther Pendragon led his people forward from their encampment, holding his staff aloft, chanting in what could have been a Celtic language, or maybe not. The sacrificial goat was left tied to the bumper of one of the vehicles nearby.

Upon approaching the Rock, the Druids paced off a circle around the rock with a diameter of exactly 108 feet, the diameter of the lintel stones at Stonehenge. The Druids began sticking tree branches in the soil along the circumference.

From another direction, Liriodendra led forth her followers, all women. They pranced forward and like the Druids began forming a circle around the Rock. The Sirian goddesses were heavily bejeweled and dressed in gauzy lavender robes that in the early light made even the stouter goddesses seem ethereal. They held aloft large amethyst crystals, and they strung a purple ribbon between themselves to form a ring.

"Hey! You can't run that ribbon through our sacred circle," protested Uther.

"Your so-called sacred circle is as nothing beside the power of the galaxy," replied Liriodendra.

One of the burlier Druids picked up the ribbon and moved it outside their circle. The Sirians, muttering under their breaths, grudgingly increased the diameter of their ring.

Uther then lifted his arms and his staff, signaling all the Druids to be silent. Minus a hundred pounds, he could have been reminiscent of Moses. In deep, loud, solemn tones, his jowls quavering, he began reciting a Celtic incantation.

"Tiocfa tálcheann
tar muir mercheann
a thí thollcheann
a chrann crommcheann."

Suddenly a loud thud sounded. Then another. Then more and more in a strong rhythm. The Indians had arrived, late and hungover, and commenced drumming. They sat in a loose circle around an enormous drum, upon which several large men were thumping with the palms of their hands.

"Hey, gawdammit!" shouted Uther. "Knock it off. We're conducting a ceremony over here."

"Screw your ceremony," replied Soaring Eagle, flashing the ancient Indian middle-finger symbol of disrespect. The drumming continued.

The Sirians, led by Liriodendra, joined the Druids' protest. "Stop it! Stop that drumming at once! No one can concentrate with that going on."

"Screw your concentrating," rejoined Soaring Eagle. The drumming continued.

Just as the Druids and Sirians began massing toward the Indians, Leland stepped forward. "The drumming has to stop until the incantations are over. Then you can continue, but much softer."

"The hell you say," snorted Soaring Eagle. "You have no jurisdiction on our sacred tribal lands. We have sovereignty on our ancient tribal lands. You hear that, you gawdammed Druids, *we* have sovereignty."

"That's for people other than us to settle," said Leland, "but here and now in Sweeney, where this Rock is located, we have an ordinance against disturbing the peace. Based upon numerous complaints, I can have you arrested. If you resist, you'll face other charges. On the other hand, if you agree to respect other people's rights and tone down the drumming, then nothing will happen at all."

"It ain't right," Soaring Eagle whined, sensing defeat. "It's always the gawdammed Indians that wind up giving up their rights." But he ordered the drummers to desist.

Then, in relative silence, they all awaited the sunrise.

At the sun's first glinting, the Druids, the Sirians, and the Indians all scrambled to stake out a place along the shadow cast by the sun behind the Rock.

"It's the sacred shadow!" bellowed Uther.

"It's the sidereal tangent!" shrieked Liriodendra.

"It's the Great Spirit!" shouted Soaring Eagle.

In his booming voice, Uther pronounced, "Welcome, O ancient Earth Goddess of the Americans. We who have come—"

"The Earth Mother is a Sirian!" interrupted Liriodendra.

Soaring Eagle shouted, "The Earth is *our* mother, assholes!"

And seizing the moment, the Indians hoisted in front of the Rock a pole topped by a buffalo skull. They then donned buffalo robes and headdresses and began parading and dancing around to frenetic drumming, which had resumed, louder than before.

"Ey-yah hey-tah see-bo-lah-lah!" shouted Soaring Eagle in his most Indian voice. Then in English, "Let the buffalo return."

Suddenly, running amok around the Rock, was a dark-brown animal. A young cow, draped with a robe and with fake buffalo horns attached to its head. The terrified beast ran helter-skelter trying to avoid the people, who also were panicked.

Then, without giving a reason, the faux-buffalo charged the Indians. In their dazed and hungover state, the Indians threw down their regalia and fled, but before reaching them, the calf was captured by high-school boys, who were suspected of having released it in the first place.

Everyone laughed, even the Druids and Sirians, especially as Soaring Eagle attempted to reconstitute his tribe. "Hey, come back here, gawdammit! What the hell kind of Indians are you anyway, running away from a little buffalo? Get back here!"

When the laughter subsided, the Sirians began their ceremony. Standing around their circle, they raised their purple crystals over their heads. Then they began prancing around in a flowing ring, holding the ribbon and the crystals aloft.

Except that the stampeding cow had stepped on the ribbon and severed it. "What do we do, Goddess Liriodendra?" asked one ribbon bearer.

"Tie the damned thing," raged Goddess Liriodendra. The goddesses flinched.

The ribbon reunited, the ribbon-bearers resumed dancing around the Rock while in the center, as close to the Rock as she could get, Liriodendra stood holding aloft her staff, topped by a huge, clear, highly faceted quartz crystal that caught the light of the rising sun and sent its rainbow spectrum outward. Raising her voice to the heavens, she sang a beautiful lilting song in a strange language.

Finally, in English, she cried, "Goddesses, our hour has come!"

Upon hearing the word "Goddess," and nothing else, Harriet Moggs, from within the crowd of onlookers, decided her hour had come too. With a raspy voice, she lurched into the area shouting, "I'm a goddess too! I'm a goddess too! She told me I was." She pointed to Liriodendra, who stood stunned.

"Who *is* this woman?"

"I'm Harriet Moggs, and I was in the beauty shop yesterday when you came in with those fliers and saying we was all goddesses. Well, damn but I think I am. So now I'm here and ready to do whatever it is we goddesses do."

Liriodendra was aghast but also very agile. "Actually, Goddess Moggs, we do have need of you." Harriet glowed. "We goddesses have staked out the holes and the positions of the Zodiac, but unfortunately, we left Sagittarius uncovered. That's a vital part of the sacred geography."

"Does this have anything to do with chakras?" croaked Harriet. "I don't know, but it seems my chakras have been doing poorly lately, sore and aching, and I was hoping to clear 'em up."

The ribbon-bearers stared in disbelief. Why hadn't Liriodendra told them about this woman?

Liriodendra rummaged in the folds of her robe and came up with a crystal. She presented it to Harriet and told her to stand in the Sagittarius position, which happened to be a long distance from the Rock. "Just stand there," intoned Liriodendra as she pushed Harriet in the right direction. "Hold the stone against your head, and it will make your chakras feel better. Great, in fact."

Harriet began backing toward where Liriodendra was pointing. "Farther, a little farther," Liriodendra called, then, "There, right there." Harriet held her hand to her ear. "Stay there!" Liriodendra shouted again. This time Harriet got the idea and held the crystal to her forehead.

That done, Liriodendra returned to channeling the Mother Planet of Sirius. She sang mellifluous syllables that everyone assumed was the language of the stars. At the same time she continued sending light beams out from her crystal.

Taking advantage of the Sirians' distraction, the Druids recommenced their ceremony. It had gone into its free-form phase, with everyone weaving and bobbing and dancing and singing to a Celtic melody played on a pan flute. The rhythm was compelling, and soon even the spectators began moving to the music.

"Care to dance?" said Roger to Kathy, holding out his hand.

Kathy laughed.

"You don't think I'm serious, do you?" he said.

"No, the amusing part is that I actually do think you're serious." But she wasn't sure herself why she was laughing. Sometimes Roger just made her laugh.

Driven by the booming baritone chanting of Uther, the Druids' Celtic ecstasy intensified. They writhed and sang in an unknown language—the pagan equivalent of speaking in tongues. Louder grew the music and wilder their gyrations until suddenly a woman began a high-pitched ululation. Her eyes rolled back in her head, and she seemed in an agitated trance.

Then, just as abruptly, she began removing her clothes. First her semi-transparent blouse, then her dress. She wore no underwear.

"It's Bare-assed Barbara!" someone shouted.

Pandemonium broke out. S&S, arms waving and whiskey voice wailing, staggered drunkenly toward the Rock, then began removing his clothes.

"Stop him!" came a panicked shout. The sheriff's deputy began moving hesitantly forward, but Rudd was there first, gently but firmly leading S&S away, still partly clothed.

Simultaneously, several Druids rushed to the blissed-out woman. They tried to cover her with their capes and cloaks, with only partial success.

The local youths were in paroxysms of laughter. Between gasps and with tears running from her eyes, Heather managed to ask Traci, "Did you get all that?"

Traci, aware that she had perhaps experienced one of her life's peak moments as a photographer, had indeed gotten it all. "Every precious, wonderful second."

"Well, there's more to come," said Heather.

Uncontrolled seizures of laughter also gripped Nettie and Iris. Poor Harriet Moggs just looked confused.

At the Rotary coffee table, tears were running down Kathy's face, while Roger had sunk to his knees.

Leland was laughing with wide-eyed amazement, though he also was aware he was witnessing Sweeney history in the making.

Reverend Fall, however, was not amused. Waving his Bible and cross, he charged the Druids.

"Repent and depart, pagans!" Fall shouted. "In the name of Jesus I command you to repent and depart. All of you. You're all pagans."

"Kiss my ass, preacher," bellowed Soaring Eagle as he led the remnants of his tribe back to the Rock. "We have our own god."

"This is blasphemy against the Lord!"

"Our lord is the Great Spirit, and it's time you gawdammed white missionaries stopped coming into our territory and messing with our religion. Go practice your Jesus voodoo somewhere else."

"You're going to hell," screamed Fall.

At this Soaring Eagle lunged at Fall, and a shoving match briefly ensued before Rudd broke it up by taking one man in each huge fist and holding them apart.

Hoping to salvage something of the ceremony after the debacle of Bare-assed Barbara, Uther retreated to his RV and emerged carrying aloft a knife with a jewel-encrusted handle while one of his followers led the goat forward and tied it to a post.

Dave Daly, seeing what was about to happen, yelled, "Hey! You can't kill animals here." He turned to Leland, who also was stepping forward.

"Sorry, folks, can't have any animal sacrifices here, against town ordinances."

"I regard this as an infringement of freedom of religion and freedom of speech," countered Uther ex cathedra, bloated with priestly authority. "The ritual of the goat sacrifice is essential to our Alban Heruin solstice ceremony. It must proceed."

But before Leland could react, the crowd collectively gasped. Standing atop the Rock, dressed in white silk, her arms extended from her sides to form a cross, was an angel. She could be nothing else. The backlight of the rising sun surrounded her with a glowing nimbus.

No one moved. Everyone stood speechless. A few people began kneeling. Catholics crossed themselves and prayed. And Reverend Fall cried "Hallelujah"—then collapsed on the ground in a swoon of religious ecstasy.

Glorious, the angel spread her radiance over everything—then seemed to lose her balance.

She wobbled, then knelt to catch herself.

The radiance was gone. Like a fleeing mouse, Rachel Rowe scrambled down the Rock and fled into the early morning shadows. "We'll get her!" cried two girls running after the fleeing figure.

Someone in the crowd yelled, "I know her!"

Discovering that the miracle was a hoax soured the general mood around the Rock.

"That's what you should be doing, preventing stuff like that," bellowed Uther at Leland, "instead of harassing citizens exercising their constitutionally protected freedom of religion rights."

And with that he turned, raised his dagger, and pronounced, "The sacrifice will proceed. Lead the offering forward."

"Uh, the goat's gone."

"What do you mean, the goat's gone?"

But when Uther looked at the post where the goat had been tied, the goat obviously was gone. "Did it get loose and run away?" he thundered.

"I don't think so," said a shamefaced Druid. "Look." He pointed to a severed rope and what had been left in the goat's place: a giant stuffed purple Barney doll with a note pinned to its chest: "Sacrifice this!"

"This is the last straw, the final outrage!" bellowed Uther.

Leland was gape-mouthed. There was no doubt the goat had been stolen. "I apologize," he said. "I'll look into this. Don't worry, you'll get your goat back or we'll compensate you for it." He preferred the latter.

Uther scoffed. "This whole thing is a travesty. You can expect that we'll be raising the issue of violation of religious freedom with the ACLU and other authorities."

"Yeah, us too," interjected Soaring Eagle.

And with that both turned and led their respective flocks away. That left Liriodendra and the goddesses. But now the sun had risen above the Rock and was starting to get hot. Perspiration caused the goddess's gauzy gowns to stick to their skins. Liriodendra looked at her bedraggled constellation and said, "Screw it." Then she too walked away.

Chapter Eleven

➤ THE SHADOW CAST BY THE SOLSTICE sun rising over the Rock was shrinking as the last Druids, Indians, and Sirians left the area in disappointment and disgust. The spectators, however, saw a beautiful day in June just beginning. Many had come a long way and were not ready to leave quite yet, especially as they had much to talk about after what they had just witnessed. Many people had brought picnic lunches, and for those who hadn't there was Judy and Adelino's tent. By noon, all the Sweeney Weeney Water was gone, as were most of the T-shirts and ball caps.

Business also was brisk at the Rotarians' coffee table. "Kathy, would you open another can, please?" Roger asked as he prepared to refill the coffee urn.

Kathy, busy filling a customer's coffee cup, just nodded. She was alone at the table with Roger because Connie Nesbitt, feeling her fliers weren't moving fast enough, had taken a stack and was putting them under vehicles' windshield wipers. Kathy handed an opened can to Roger as the next customers shuffled forward.

"That was the damndest thing I ever saw!" A middle-aged rancher and his wife stood in front of the table, in no hurry to ask for coffee, just wanting to talk, to share the experience.

"Which thing?" asked Kathy, then regretted it.

"Why, Bare-assed Barbara," the man said.

"He's just kidding," interrupted his wife. "He means the angel. That angel was just beautiful. It's too bad the actress you people hired had to go and lose her balance."

"But we didn't . . ."

"Oh, it's okay, we would have discovered she wasn't an angel pretty soon anyway," the woman continued, "but I've never seen a pageant like you folks put on, it ranks up there with Graceland."

"Where'd you hire that Bare-assed Barbara?" the husband asked.

But before Kathy could answer his wife took his arm and escorted him away.

"We'll be back next year," he called over his shoulder.

"To see the angel," his wife added.

Dave and Leland stood near the Rock, each holding a Styrofoam cup of Rotarian coffee, surveying the scene.

"Just look at this," said Dave. Perhaps a hundred people and a third as many vehicles were arrayed in a loose circle around the Rock. A tape player in a pickup played a Willie Nelson ballad. Children ran squealing among the Mystery Holes and clambered on the smaller rocks. Adults reclined on plastic and aluminum lawn chairs. The smell of chicken roasting on a grill wafted across the area.

Leland smiled and nodded. "There's folks out there I haven't seen in ten years."

"Everyone's having a good time," said Dave. "Neighbors coming together, kids having fun, life interesting and exciting, stuff to talk about—none of this would have happened without the Rock."

Again Leland nodded. "I know." He seemed in a kind of reverie.

"Are you worried about the legal threats?"

"Hell, no. It's all talk. And even if it wasn't, it would be thrown out of court. Besides, would a person who witnessed the Second Coming complain about getting sunburned?"

"Come again?"

"In the entire history of Sweeney, however long this town shall last, there will never be another day like this. This day will live in history and legend."

"Listen, Iris," said Nettie as the two women sat with Harriet Moggs on one of the rocks, "when I get home tonight, I'm writing down everything I can remember from this day—and you should too."

"Why?" said Iris as she munched on a piece of fried chicken she had cadged from friends having a tailgate party.

"Because you're a member of the Sweeney Historical Society, same as me. The events of this day must be preserved in the historical record. Sweeney's never had a day like this."

"Damn, I never thought of it that way," said Iris, "you're right. This day does beat all." She stopped to chuckle at remembering the morning's events. "My favorite was that little fake buffalo running around and chasing off those phony Indians."

"Take my advice, write down every detail of this day. I'm not much of a writer, but it doesn't matter, this is history, not literature."

Harriet Moggs, still wrapped in her jacket despite the sun, sat bewildered, muttering to herself. "Am I a goddess or not? What's this all about? If this is all funny business, why do my chakras hurt?"

"But before we can do anything," continued Nettie to Iris, "we've got a mission that our Christian faith is calling us to." And with that she got up and began moving toward where Reverend Fall sat on the ground as a few friends tried to revive him and talk to him.

"Where's the angel?" he pleaded, his eyes watery, red-rimmed, not quite focused.

"Uh . . . she's not here right now," stammered one of the men.

"Well, she doesn't need to be, old Satan didn't stick around long once she came on the scene. It was a miracle. We've all seen an angel. In Sweeney. Praise be! Hallelujah!"

"But, uh . . ."

Just then Nettie arrived. "I'll take care of him. Come on, Reverend, there's nothing more to do here, let's go home."

"I don't think he'll accept it," Iris said to Nettie as they were walking back to her house after depositing Reverend Fall and Harriet Moggs at their respective homes. "I don't think she will either. He'll think he saw an angel, and she'll think she's a goddess. My feet hurt."

"You should get out and walk more. You're right, they won't accept it. But only time will tell whether any permanent harm was done."

"You explained it to June, what happened and all?"

"I did. It wasn't much worse than what she'd expected. She hadn't expected the angel part, though. She'll take good care of him, be gentle with him."

"Wayne, we can talk about this after you've had hot food and rest." June placed a bowl of beef stew in front of him at the kitchen table where he sat, dazed, his eyes bright with delirium. "You've had a hard night, and a hard day."

"But I saw an angel, June, and other people did too. And after the angel appeared, the satanic goat disappeared and all those pagans left. It was a miracle. An angel from the reams of glory—"

"That's 'realms,' Wayne, 'realms of glory.'"

"Oh, whatever. It was a miracle. That Rock has to be preserved. It can't be taken down. It was where God saw Satan at work and sent one of His angels down to intervene. That site is sacred."

"We'll talk about it later. Now eat your stew before it gets cold."

After June had shepherded her husband to bed, the phone rang. June answered.

"Nettie here. How'd he take it?"

"I'm not sure he did. He was calmer after he ate a bit, but he's still convinced he saw an angel, even after I told him it was a high school girl dressed up as one, and people even knew who the girl was. He sort of concedes that a high school girl might have been atop the Rock, but he says that doesn't mean an angel wasn't there too. 'I know in my soul that what I saw was an angel.'"

"Uh-oh."

"No, actually, this all has had kind of a calming effect on him. He now opposes removing the Rock, because it's a sacred site. I had to talk to him about other people having a different opinion, and how he should keep his own opinions to himself. I kind of nudged him into thinking that God had decided who would see an angel and who would see a high school girl, and that folks would feel bad if they were the ones that just got the girl. I think I've got him damped down enough that he's okay to be around people."

"June, you're a saint," said Nettie.

"Thanks, but at the moment I've had enough of religious icons. I'll take a piano and a hall full of happy people to sainthood any day. I think miracles are overrated. I . . . I didn't mean to be blasphemous."

"No, you're absolutely right. I'll be over later to see what I can do. In the meantime, why don't you go practice the piano?"

"We're busted," said Kimberly as the group of girls huddled behind the high school, in a corner they knew was safe from view. They knew because they'd come here to smoke purloined cigarettes in mid-school. "Where's Traci?"

"I don't know," said Heather. "She was talking to some people. She'll be along. What do you mean 'We're busted'?"

"Someone recognized me," Rachel said miserably. "One of the boys from school." She sat on a step of the iron stairs, her long face cupped in her hands.

"Uh-oh," said Heather. Christie turned white. Going to jail definitely would torpedo her perfect attendance record.

Suddenly Traci burst on the scene, her face beaming.

"We're busted," said Heather.

Traci didn't seem to have heard. "Listen up, we're going to be famous. We're putting Sweeney on the map."

"What's that supposed to mean?" asked Kimberly sourly.

"I got every second of this wonderful, miraculous, totally awesome day on CD, and the world is waiting to see it. I've already taken more than a dozen orders for copies of this CD. I'm asking $50—and no one's blinked. A TV station in Lubbock offered me $100 for it."

"Wow!" said Rachel. "That's $700!" No one was surprised that she'd been the first to work out the math.

"I've got to go make a copy of the CD for the TV guy. I'm not giving away the original."

"But we've got a big problem here," said Heather. "We're busted. Someone recognized Rachel."

"Oh, I see," said Traci soberly.

"Does stealing the goat count as rustling?" asked Christie. She came from a tradition where stealing stock had once been a hanging offense.

"We're not giving the goat back," pronounced Rachel.

"I hope we have a choice," said Traci.

"We're *not* giving it back, I didn't go through . . . *that* for nothing." Though she was fighting back tears, she looked each of her friends in the eye. "If I'm going to make a public spectacle of myself—again—then it has to count for something."

The girls stared at Rachel, then glanced at each other, shocked. They'd never considered that Rachel might be aware of how she appeared to others.

Finally Traci said, "Rachel's right. She's the one who stood on the Rock, it's her call. By the way, Rachel, you were awesome."

"Yeah," said Kimberly. "For a second I thought you were an angel—and I knew you weren't."

"Yeah," said Heather. "It was just, just . . . unreal."

Christie put her hand on Rachel's shoulder and beamed approval.

Rachel looked around surprised, then in a slightly less miserable voice asked, "Where's the goat?"

"Tied in that arroyo over there," Heather said, pointing.

"As soon as it's dark, I'll bring it over to our place and put it in our barn," said Traci. "We've got an empty stall there."

"You should do it now," said Christie. "Coyotes could get the goat. Or it could make a lot of noise and get discovered. You should do it now. No one's paying attention."

Traci nodded.

"What about your parents?" asked Heather.

"I don't know. They'll find the goat—but remember, Dad tried to stop the Druids from killing it, and you know how Mom is about animals."

"We're still busted," reminded Heather.

"At least I am," said Rachel.

Suddenly the girls fell silent as the implications of this hit them. If Rachel took full responsibility, the rest of them were free, at least of the angel impersonation—and Rachel was caught no matter what. Christie briefly saw hope for her perfect attendance record, then instantly regretted the thought.

"Hey, Joanie, let me give you a hand with that."

Joanie had just pulled the Dalys' old blue Chevy pickup into the driveway and was getting ready to wrestle a fifty-pound feed bag out of the bed. Before she could protest, as Dave knew she would, he already had hoisted it onto his shoulder and was staggering toward the barn. He needed to smooth relations with Joanie over Flicka, and perhaps this would help. She seemed in a relatively good mood after witnessing the events at the Rock that morning.

"Thanks," said Joanie reluctantly. "Just put the bag by the stall, I'll do the feeding."

Dave grunted assent. He knew Joanie preferred to be the one who actually put feed in the stall on the theory that it would create positive associations in the horse, but so far it hadn't worked. Whenever anyone, for whatever reason, came into the stable, Flicka bolted into the corral and stood quivering in panic. Dave had learned not to say anything to Joanie, but he privately resented the horse as being a lost cause and a waste of time—and a dangerous one at that.

Carrying the bag, he kneed open the stable door, heaved the bag against the stall, then froze. A moment later, he went out the door and yelled, "Hey, Joanie, come here, you need to see this."

A frown on her face, Joanie walked to the stable door and peered in. "Omigod. Omigod."

In the stall next to Flicka's was a goat. *The* goat.

But even more shocking was Flicka. She was standing calmly by the goat's stall, and through the slats in the wall separating them the two were nuzzling noses. When Joanie put her hands to her face in astonishment, the horse placidly raised her head to look at the humans and then resumed nuzzling the goat.

And Flicka stayed there even when Joanie walked over to the stall's gate and peered over. Then Joanie backed away.

"I don't want to push it. I just can't believe it, it's as if the goat was telling the horse that it's all right, that she's safe here."

"Well, this goat should know, considering how close she came to being a Druid sacrifice. And this goat didn't just appear here by accident." He went back to the door and yelled again, "Traci! Traci, we need to talk to you."

Traci appeared in the house's back door. Her face fell when she saw her parents standing outside the barn. Sullenly, she slouched toward them.

But to her surprise, they were smiling.

"You've seen the goat?"

"We normally don't approve of theft, but sometimes there are higher laws," said Dave. Joanie nodded.

"Why don't you just tell us what happened," said Dave. So she did, pointedly not mentioning her coconspirators by name. Her parents already knew their identities.

Several times Dave laughed as Traci described the Druids and the girls' reactions to them. "They were gross!"

When Traci was done, she looked at her parents and asked, "You're not mad? I mean, I know you tried to stop the sacrifice—Dad, you were awesome—but . . . I thought you'd be mad?"

"It turns out," her mother said, "there's more to this than just rescuing the goat. Go look at Flicka."

Traci's confusion deepened. "Why? I don't like that horse, and she doesn't like me."

"Just go," said Dave.

When Traci emerged from the stable, she said but one word: "Omigod."

"Quite a different outcome than if the goat had been killed," observed Dave. "Leland and I would have shut down the sacrifice at the Rock, but the Druids would have just taken the goat somewhere else and killed it there."

"And the goat never would have met Flicka," said Joanie.

"We'll have to pay for the goat, of course," said Dave. Traci's eyes widened at the pronoun *we*.

The girls had agreed to meet back at the school later that afternoon. Traci, as usual, was late.

"Hey, guys, remember when we used to smoke back here?" Heather asked.

"Yeah," said Kimberly. "Remember the time we forgot there was a class upstairs with the window open and the smoke rose up into the classroom?"

"That was great! We'd have been busted if Suzy Wilson hadn't leaned out and warned us. Traci almost ran into the principal as she was splitting." The two laughed.

"I didn't smoke back here," said Christie indignantly.

"I didn't either," said Rachel, but with more regret than indignation in her voice.

"What should we do?" asked Kimberly. "Let's face it: we're busted. The whole town knows Rachel was the angel, and it's just a matter of time before they know about the goat too."

Heather just shook her head. "Maybe Traci'll know what to do."

"I'll say I did it all," said Rachel. "I'm caught no matter what; there's no reason for all of you to get caught too."

"That wouldn't be right," said Christie. "We all planned this."

"What's not right?" asked Traci as she arrived out of breath.

"Rachel offered to take the fall," said Heather, "but we don't think she should."

"You're right," said Traci, "and she won't have to. Listen, I've talked to a few people, and my parents have told me what they've heard. There are people in town who want the angel to have been real, who don't want to hear about Rachel. And even those who do know about Rachel aren't really interested in pursuing it. Rachel's off the hook."

Rachel looked around, confused.

"But what about the theft?" asked Heather.

"I know I'm off the hook for the angel," said Rachel, "but you were willing to stand by me, so I'll stand with you for the goat. Besides, this is the first time I've ever done anything like this . . . with a bunch of friends." And with that she began to cry.

Traci went to her and hugged her, followed, albeit hesitantly, by the other girls.

"Don't worry, Rache, we *are* all in this together," said Traci, "but as it turns out, we're probably all off the hook. For most of the people in this town, we're not thieves, we're liberators." She told them about the goat and Flicka and her parents' reactions.

"Do we still have to pay for the goat?" asked Kimberly.

"Yes," answered Traci, "but there's lots of people who'll chip in. My parents will, for sure. Anyone know how much goats are worth?"

"About $75 for a good doe," said Christie. "I think ours would go for a little less."

"Let's offer to pay twice that," said Traci. "Make everyone happy."

The solstice sun was declining to the west as Roger and Kathy began closing the Rotarian coffee stand. They poured coffee for themselves and went to sit on one of the rocks.

"Quite a day," said Kathy as she sipped her coffee and gazed over the area around the Rock, now emptying of visitors. Across the way, Judy and Adelino were packing up their tent.

"What was your favorite event?" Roger asked Kathy.

She paused, looking out as if replaying in her mind the events that had occurred. Finally she said, "I think it would have to be the angel and the rescue of the goat."

Roger nodded. "That was brilliant. Kind of makes me proud to be a graduate of Sweeney High. Though I confess I'm a little envious; nothing I ever did in high school had that kind of class."

He saw a cloud pass over Kathy's face. Quickly, too quickly, she asked as if to change the subject, "Do you really think this will become an annual event?"

"No reason not to," he answered. Then he said, "Look, Kathy, for what it's worth—and I hope it's worth something—I'm genuinely sorry about what happened—no, about what I did, it didn't just happen—to you in high school . . ."

"Roger, that's okay," Kathy said, and she started to get up.

"Wait, please wait." He paused while Kathy sat back down. "It's not okay. I'm not sure there's anything I can do or say to make it okay. I was just a wise-ass kid trying to be funny, without a clue as to how my actions might affect other people, especially people as different from me as you."

"Roger—"

"No," he interrupted. "I wish I could undo the harm you suffered, but I can't—that's just one of the facts of life I have to accept—but I do want you to know that I am sorry for what I did. I've never stopped regretting it."

Kathy was silent a moment. Then she reached over and placed her hand on Roger's. "Thank you. Sincerely, thank you. And actually, it does help. I've probably needed to let go of that for a long time, and this will help. We were just kids then, I did things I regret too."

"My regrets can beat up your regrets," said Roger, then quickly added, "Sorry, another bad joke. It just seems to be a habit I can't break."

Kathy grinned at him. "I hear there's a twelve-step program for people like you."

Roger laughed. "Hi, my name is Roger, and I'm a wise-ass."

"Do you really think this event could happen next year?"

"I don't know. A lot can happen in a year. But there's no reason for it not to happen. It could never be the same as this year—an event like this happens only once, and we were privileged to witness it" —he glanced at Kathy— "together—and it wouldn't have quite the same cast of characters and would evolve in different ways. But yes, the word will spread. The pool of Druids and Sirians and phony Indians and the like is bottomless, and this was a good excuse for people in these parts to get together and have a good time."

"You don't think there are negative aspects to this?" she asked as she drained her coffee cup.

But before he could answer, Adelino waved from across the way, wanting help moving a table. As they started to get up, Kathy put her hand on Roger's arm and said, "Thanks, Roger. We *are* different people now."

Roger simply smiled and nodded. Then as an afterthought he said, "I'd never do anything like that again—at least not exactly like that."

She swatted him with her hat.

Not until the sun was setting did the last cars and pickups finally leave. Leland sighed contentedly as he leaned against his pickup and watched them go. It had been a long day, a memorable day. And all things considered, it had gone about as well as could be expected. The town would have to pay for the goat, but already several people had come forward with donations. Hell, before this was done the town could pay for a dozen goats.

Leland reached down, patted Trixie on the head, and was just about to climb in his pickup and call it a day when Les Whittington, one of the codgers who hung around the town offices, walked briskly toward him. Something was wrong, sensed Leland; Les *never* walked briskly.

"Hey, Leland, I've been over to the town offices, and . . ."

Leland flinched. "Yes?"

"There's been some Indians asking for you."

Leland relaxed, even smiled. "Aw, that loopy Soaring Turkey and his phony bunch. Tell 'em I'll talk to them in the morning, if they're still around."

"No, Leland, it's not them." The codger's eyes widened, and he stammered, "I . . . I think these are real Indians."

Time to go home, Rudd thought. He was tired. He started walking away from the Rock when he thought about S&S. Where was that ragamuffin? And why should he care? It should be no concern of his. But before the debate could proceed further he saw S&S's form sprawled on the ground just outside the ring of vehicles, looking like a road-kill rooster. With a sigh, Rudd strode over.

Whether S&S was asleep or passed out, Rudd couldn't tell. Probably both. "Come on, get up," he said gruffly as he prodded S&S with his boot.

"Come on, time to go home." He was concerned that a vehicle would back over the man, especially as he was barely distinguishable from the trash and weeds. "Get up, dammit." He prodded the man again.

"What? What?" S&S muttered as he struggled to open his bleary eyes. "Is that goddess still here?"

"Nah, she was looking for you, said she was hot for you, but when she couldn't find you she took off. Now get the hell up."

Rudd took the man by the arm and helped him as he struggled to his feet.

"She was beautiful, that goddess," said S&S as he finally found his balance.

"All goddesses are beautiful," said Rudd, "but don't worry, there's plenty more where she came from."

"She was especially beautiful when she took off her clothes."

Rudd looked at S&S in astonishment. It had never occurred to him that S&S might be talking about Bare-assed Barbara. He shook his head and started steering the man away from the Rock.

When they got to Rudd's property, Rudd escorted S&S to the shed and watched as the man flopped onto the cheap bed. The only other furniture in the room was a card table, a folding metal chair, and a beat-up wooden dresser, two of whose drawers hung open and empty. S&S's wardrobe was minimal.

After depositing S&S, Rudd headed toward his own quarters, reflecting as he walked that his own wardrobe wasn't much larger than S&S's. He thought of the big, blank table in his kitchen, the empty chairs at the table, the almost-bare cupboard. On impulse he changed course and went instead to the old playhouse.

The door opened more easily than it had a few days ago. He left it slightly ajar; perhaps the ventilation would disperse the mustiness and allow more light to enter. In two long steps he crossed the room, then sank into the overstuffed chair.

What a day it had been! He hadn't laughed so hard in years. He hadn't had so much fun in years. Sitting in the chair he chuckled as he replayed the day's events in his mind. He didn't really have a favorite incident; all had been delightfully ridiculous, though he especially admired the angel for the purity of its absurdity.

It was easy to sit and reminisce here, where he'd had so much fun as a child. The main house was cold and lonely. As he sat, he wished he had someone to reminisce with. Once his cousins had shared the play-house with him. He hadn't thought about them in years. Where were they now? Briefly he wondered if he could find them if he tried, then dismissed the thought. What was happening to him? He didn't need people in his life, didn't want them. They were just trouble. Like that damned S&S. Life was simpler without them.

Or at least it had been. He thought about the decision to join the conspirators. At the time he wasn't sure why he had done it, given his serious reservations, but now he was glad he had. The plot could not have succeeded without him, and he had to admit he was pleased with the results. After all, today would not have happened without the Rock. The image of Harriet Moggs joining the goddesses came to his mind, and he chuckled again.

Eventually, no more chuckles came. As he left the playhouse he made sure to close the door; he certainly didn't want S&S mucking about in there. On his way to his house, Rudd stopped by the shed to check on S&S. He found the man asleep on the bed, still in his clothes, snoring. Rudd went over and took a woolen blanket from the bottom drawer of the dresser. Gently, he draped it over the malodorous form.

Tonight, as so often, Rachel returned to the rocks and the night sky. A quarter moon dimmed all but the brightest stars, but that was okay. They were still there; she knew they'd reappear. Reliable, predictable, comfortable. Hard to imagine that just a few hours earlier this scene had been filled with noise and color and motion and mayhem.

Mayhem she had helped create.

She'd done it again, allowed herself to be talked into doing something ridiculous and embarrassing. Dressing up as an angel and posing on top of the Rock. Where did Traci get ideas like that? What kind of mind produced them? Certainly not one like hers, so accustomed to solving well-defined problems by applying proven methods. So why didn't Traci dress up as an angel? Why did it have to be her?

As she gazed upward, she estimated the moon's angle of altitude above the horizon, then calculated how long before it set. Long ago she'd learned to tell time by this method. Anyone could do it, but she knew no one else who did.

At least the angel scheme had worked. The goat was rescued. She was happy about that. And after all, she was the one who had been most adamant about it not being sacrificed, so perhaps it was appropriate that she be the saving angel.

Saving angel. An appealing thought, not that she believed in angels.

And her being the angel did seem to have solidified her friendship with the girls. She'd suspected that initially she'd only been grudgingly accepted, a kind of obligation in return for helping them ditch school. *She* hadn't been asked to ditch school with them. But this time their appreciation seemed genuine. Christie especially. She'd actually invited her to come out and visit the ranch. Curious, that despite having lived in Sweeney most of her life, she'd never visited a ranch, though the town was surrounded by them.

Suddenly movement caught Rachel's eye. A dark figure was walking toward the rocks. Instinctively she shrank, began moving out of view, but it was too late, the figure changed course and began walking toward her.

"Evening, Rachel."

"Evening, Mr. Daly."

"Looks like I'm not the only person strange enough to like to hang out here at night—wait, I didn't mean you were strange."

"It's okay. I am kind of strange. I like to come here to look at the stars."

"Me too. They're somehow reassuring. Things seem simpler when I'm out here."

Rachel said nothing. Dave continued, "That was a brave thing you did today."

"What?"

"I mean, standing on the Rock and pretending to be an angel to distract the Druids so your friends could rescue the goat."

"I made a fool of myself."

"The goat doesn't think so. By the way, the goat is doing well in her new life as crazy horse counselor."

"Huh?"

"It's a long story. Stop by the house, and my wife will be happy to explain it to you. She thinks you're a hero. So do a lot of people in town."

"Why didn't one of the other girls dress up as an angel? Why did it have to be me?"

Dave paused. "I don't have a good answer for that. It could have been Traci. Maybe it *should* have been Traci. Maybe it just needed to be you. But trust me, your bravery will be remembered in this town for a long time."

Rachel was silent. Then looking up she said, "Do you think there's extraterrestrial life out there? I mean, the mathematical odds are over-whelmingly in favor of it."

"There's no doubt in my mind. There's probably even intelligent life, perhaps countless civilizations far more advanced than our own."

"Then why haven't they contacted us?"

Dave thought a moment, then laughed and said, "If I was an intel-ligent, civilized alien, I'd think twice about contacting Earthlings after what happened today in Sweeney."

Rachel laughed in spite of herself. They sat long at the rocks, talking about the properties of space, intergalactic voids, and the improbabili-ties of intelligent beings actually communicating with one another.

Eventually Rachel had to go home. Dave remained. As he reclined against one of the boulders he noticed that the stones still radiated heat from the day, warming him as he reclined against them. A pleasant, lan-guid feeling. In an earlier time, he'd have smoked a cigar or a pipe, but he'd said farewell to them years ago. Only rarely did he miss them.

What a crazy day it had been. He chuckled at the image of Har-riet Moggs, holding the jewel and chanting with the other oddesses—oops, meant goddesses, though "oddesses" would be more accurate. He'd known Harriet Moggs all his life. Or more accurately, she'd been part of his personal landscape. He didn't really know her, even though he had mowed her lawn one summer. She had been nice enough, and always offered him lemonade and cookies. She had weird orange hair and looked gnomelike even then.

Actually, of all the people in Sweeney, how many did he really know—and how many really knew him? His mental list was short, but at least it had a few names on it. How many would be on it in, say, Albuquerque or Santa Fe or Carlsbad or Logan?

Could anything ever be the same after today? What had they set in motion here? It seemed to Dave that today a divide had been crossed. No going back. He was elated and terrified at the same time. Life had returned to Sweeney. They had succeeded.

Yet it all rested upon some rocks and shallow holes. How long would they remain a novelty? What then? Would the eventual death of Sweeney reek of bathos, denied even a dignified death?

Chapter Twelve

A WEEK AFTER THE SOLSTICE, Dave was at home indulging in a well-deserved, guilt-free afternoon nap on the living room couch when suddenly Joanie barged in. Ignoring the sanctity of the moment she announced, "Priority mail for you. From Santa Fe."

He glanced at his watch. Only two. He still had another hour before the Rotary meeting, but he couldn't sleep with Joanie standing there, staring at him expectantly. Realizing delay's futility, Dave hauled himself upright on the couch while Joanie plopped next to him, handed him the envelope, and waited for him to open it. This annoyed him. Didn't a man have a right to privacy? How did she know it wasn't a passion letter from one of his several mistresses in Santa Fe?

Dave knew the envelope wasn't from a mistress but actually a sender much more threatening: Santa Fe Public Schools. He opened it, withdrew a letter and several forms, and, with Joanie peering over his shoulder, read it.

They were offering him a position teaching eighth grade science in one of the local middle schools. Despite the sharp decline in status and desirability, the job in Santa Fe paid significantly more than his current job in Sweeney.

"Of course, the real estate in Santa Fe costs more, too," he added, then instantly regretted yielding to the temptation.

"It could hardly cost less than here in Sweeney."

"What do you think?" He hoped to stall, since he knew what Joanie thought.

"It's Traci's decision, too."

"We'll consult her—but what do you think?"

"I think you'd be crazy not to at least consider it. You don't have to give them a decision today."

"No, I have two weeks. So you're right. I should check it out."

"Soon."

The authoritarian way she said that irritated Dave even more, so he abruptly terminated the conversation by saying he needed to go to the Rotary Club meeting at the Chick 'n' More. Joanie rolled her eyes.

Santa Fe, dammit! Dave trudged miserably down Mangrove Street toward Main Street and the meeting. Why couldn't it have been someplace like Carlsbad? That would have been an easy decision, at least for him, and maybe even for Traci and Joanie. Carlsbad would have meant trading a small High Plains town for a larger one—but Santa Fe? Dave knew that to the young people in Sweeney, those under sixty, Santa Fe was like Paris—exotic, romantic, sophisticated, trendy—everything Sweeney was not.

Santa Fe. Dave admitted that the state's capital held appeal even for him: coffee shops, bookstores, art galleries, cultural events. He could hike in the Sangre de Cristo Mountains behind Santa Fe and pursue his interest in western history. He laughed bitterly when he compared the restaurants in Santa Fe with the Chick 'n' More.

He looked down Mangrove Street—what a ridiculous name!—toward Main Street. No bookstores here, no ethnic restaurants, no interesting little shops. Instead tiny abandoned houses with eroding gray stucco exteriors, windows boarded up, roofs and porches sagging, fences keeping nothing out, nothing in. Ragweed and cheat grass and other plants lacking even a native pedigree long ago had asserted squatters' rights in what once had been yards, though here and there a few pink hollyhocks testified to someone's hopes for beauty and order.

Houses utterly beyond rehabilitation. Relics from a time gone by, like the dead cars and discarded appliances rusting in the backyards. Like the tangles of chicken wire in backyards from pens whose chickens were as forgotten as the people who kept them. Did anyone keep chickens anymore? Relics.

While these houses still stood they helped maintain the illusion that Sweeney was more alive than it really was. Looking down Mangrove Street a visitor would not immediately suspect that most of the houses were empty.

All across the plains were towns whose actual population was just a fraction of what it seemed from a perfunctory glance. Like Conejo. It still was labeled on the state highway map, and a highway sign told travelers that the cluster of buildings they were approaching was indeed Conejo. But not a single residence was inhabited. To Dave who knew the reality of these husk towns, the abandoned buildings reminded him of headstones in an old cemetery.

Dave looked again at the abandoned houses on Mangrove Street. He'd known some of the people who had lived in them. His mother and father had known everyone who lived in these houses, but now they too were gone, the office from which they had run the county newspaper just another boarded up building on Main Street.

Why was he so resistant to leaving? Was it just loyalty to his home-town? What did Sweeney offer that compensated for missing out on life in the larger world, as his sister Diane had chosen? Was being a Sweeney science teacher really all he wanted out of life? In Santa Fe he could explore other opportunities, perhaps change careers.

Sweeney or Santa Fe? To Joanie and Traci it seemed simple, like trad-ing a dying old clunker that leaked oil for a shiny new sports car. But though trendy and stylish, Santa Fe also was by far the most expensive city in the state, the home of millionaires and trust-funders and cultural elites. As the family of a mid-school teacher, the Dalys would be second-class citizens at best. Buying even a modest home would exhaust all their savings and income. More likely he would have to commute from one of the outlying communities, whose real estate also was scandal-ously expensive. The family would be bereft of all status and identity. Why couldn't Joanie see that?

And teaching mid-school? He didn't like teaching mid-schoolers. It was a difficult age at best, and in Santa Fe it would be especially difficult. The children of the wealthy went to private schools, leaving the public schools for the less-than-wealthy.

Gangs were a problem in Santa Fe, and because the indigenous His-panics were increasingly marginalized as affluent Anglos moved in and forced them out of the city where their families had lived for centuries, ethnic tensions often were high. He knew teachers who had taught in Santa Fe; for many it had been their terminal position. He would be the new teacher on the block and would pull lots of lunchroom and parking lot duty. Teaching mid-school in Santa Fe would be a move downward, not upward. Yet if Joanie and Traci wanted this move, he would have to go.

Damn! Suddenly Dave realized that Joanie and Traci held his future in their hands—and he might have miscalculated in assuming he would be offered a position in a town like Carlsbad that they would dislike almost as much as Sweeney.

All he needed was one vote against Santa Fe. It might come down to Flicka, or whether Kimberly knew someone who knew someone who was kind of cool in Santa Fe.

Too bad school wasn't in session. He could give a vivid lecture on the high incidence of airborne venereal disease in the state capital. Or maybe he could get Roger to let drop to Joanie that moving horses to Santa Fe usually killed them within weeks.

Dave paused where Mangrove Street joined Main Street. Ironic that most of Sweeney's streets were named for plants that couldn't survive here. Curious that he had never noticed this before. He was sure this held a profound meaning, but he didn't have the mental energy now to dig it out.

He sighed as he stepped onto Main Street. A casual visitor would not immediately notice that most businesses were defunct, but at least most buildings were still standing. Along the Main Streets in many High Plains towns the gaps left by collapsed or razed buildings bespoke long poverty and neglect, like missing teeth. But how long would the empty buildings here remain standing? There was Jones Drug, where as a child he'd read comic books and purchased penny candy, now closed and boarded up. Zero chances of it ever reopening. The Metropolitan movie theater. How many B-grade westerns had he seen there? Traci had never been inside it. The Ilfeld Mercantile building. Once the pioneering Jewish family had stores throughout eastern New Mexico. The building here still bore their name, but the painted letters were faded almost beyond recognition. The offices of his parents' newspaper, the *Sweeney Oracle and Independent*, "Serving Kiowa County and Beyond." The paper ceased publication soon after the IGA grocery closed. Now folks went to Tucumcari for their news and their groceries.

But a few businesses survived. From the open door of the storefront labeled Antiques, Carla Trujillo waved to him. She and her husband, Tony, sold mostly junk scavenged locally, as well as honey from Willard Cox's hives and paintings and chapbooks of cowboy poetry by Lee Tomkins, who had returned to Kiowa County after a career in the military and now lived by himself far out in the canyon country. The antiques store was among the busier businesses in Sweeney.

At the V-intersection of Main Street and County Road 87 was the Raylene Johnson Memorial Park. Raylene, a beloved elementary school teacher and pillar of the community, had been dead for ten years now, but Dave noticed that the patch of grass in the tiny park was watered and mowed, with fresh flowers placed at the base of the memorial plaque.

Dave recalled the last time he had been in Santa Fe. The city was engorged with newcomers, feverish with new residential and commercial developments. On the outskirts, outside the historic core, were colossal big-box stores with parking lots half the size of Sweeney—Walmart, Kmart, Seismo-Mart, everything you could want to buy, at very cheap prices, scores of fast-food franchises, grocery stores with whole aisles devoted just to organic chips, car and truck dealerships, rampant growth and prosperity. Was poor little Sweeney really that much more desirable?

More desirable, no, but worth saving—hell yes, Dave decided as he strode along the all-but-empty street.

Ron Suffitt rose to his feet in the meeting room of the Chick 'n' More and tapped his water glass with his spoon. With his other hand he adjusted the tie he always wore to Rotary meetings. No one else in Sweeney ever wore a tie to anything but weddings or funerals. Dave thought wearing a tie into the Chick 'n' More was a bit pretentious, but then Ron took his Rotary responsibilities very seriously.

"Ladies and gentlemen," Suffitt intoned, "we've got a lot to cover today, so let's get down to business. We'll start with the minutes of the last meeting."

"Screw the minutes of the last meeting," said Roger. "I move we skip everything except what we're really interested in, that is, what's been happening in Sweeney. I think we need to talk about what we're going to do next."

"I second that motion," said Dave. "No offense, Ron."

"Motion carried," proclaimed Nettie.

"But we haven't voted," said Ron, flustered.

"Motions based on just plain common sense don't need a vote," retorted Nettie. "Wastes time."

"Hear, hear!" said Rudd, laughing, to everyone's amazement. He seemed to be enjoying himself. Could he be on drugs?

"Okay, Rudd," said Ron testily, "what's your take on things?"

"I think things have been great lately. Of course, that's speaking only from the heavy equipment perspective." He chuckled. Then more soberly, "It's good to see people having fun in Sweeney. First, we put on the best rodeo in memory, and then right after that we have an event that will live in legend. No one has gotten hurt. I think we're on a roll."

Judy Baca raised her hand. "I can tell you that this has been a godsend for us. We're making bank payments again, and getting caught up. We didn't want to tell anybody, but we were thinking of selling out if things got much worse."

Helen the waitress, going around the table taking orders, paused to say, "People, look at where you're sitting right now. If it hadn't been for all the hoo-raw that's been happening in Sweeney lately this place would be closed—and I'd be out of a job. Now running a restaurant is fun again."

"Nettie, how about you?" asked Ron.

"I'm with Rudd. I honestly never thought I'd live to see Sweeney come back to life like it has." She paused to adjust her glasses and continued. "I took a drive the other day to Holden to visit my cousin, Eva, and it reminded me of where we were only a couple of months ago—decay, hopelessness, despair. Eva's heard all about the goings-on in Sweeney. She's completely scandalized, but you know what? She's envious too. She even sort of mentioned getting a trailer and moving to Sweeney, 'just to be close to you, Nettie.' I don't hear anyone talking about moving to Holden.

"But at the same time it seems like we're riding a wild horse. It's a great ride, until you're thrown or dragged through barbed wire."

Connie Nesbitt rose from her chair. Dave noticed she was wearing a stylish peach business suit with a large peach chrysanthemum bouquet in its lapel. "There's two hundred and thirty-five people, at least, who went home last Saturday with information about business and real estate opportunities in Sweeney. Now, I can't say my phone's been ringing off the hook, but word gets around, as Nettie's cousin proves, and these things take time. Nettie's right. It's been a wild ride, and we don't know where it will end. But I'd rather have an erratic heartbeat line than a flat line."

Judy Baca spoke again. "Actually, our phone has been ringing off the hook. Mostly folks wanting to order souvenirs, T-shirts and ball caps and such. And especially the Sweeney Weeney Water. We're starting to sell that stuff by the case. There's people out there who think it really works. I guess it's one of those things where if you think a thing works, it does."

Tom Binks stood. Dave was worried. Tom never stood.

"Weeney Water! Is that what Sweeney stands for—Weeney Water? And Bare-assed Bob and Bare-assed Barbara?"

"Don't forget the nudist RVers," interjected Reverend Fall.

"Yeah, and nudist RVers. Some people are willing to ignore what that Rock looks like, for whatever reasons" —he glanced pointedly at Leland— "but there's plenty of people in town who aren't." He paused to allow people to voice their support. When everyone was silent, he scowled and then continued, "I'm not a prude, but this whole thing's gotten kind of sleazy." Reverend Fall started to rise, but Judy Baca beat him to the floor.

"Sleazy?" she sputtered. "If you think paying bills and keeping going is sleazy . . . you know how I spell 'sleazy'? I spell it 'bankruptcy.' Now that's sleazy."

"But we are doing Satan's work," said Reverend Fall, "opening the door to him that he may enter. I understand what a temptation a little money is in a place as poor as Sweeney, but that's what it is—temptation. Opening the door to iniquity—obscenity, nudity, paganism. Sin always looks good at the beginning, but there will come a time of reckoning, and it will be a time of wailing and gnashing of teeth. There's been more sin in Sweeney lately than there has been in all its history before."

"Lot of catching up to do," said Roger. Reverend Fall glared at him and then with a forced forgiveness proclaimed, "We're approaching Armageddon, and the Antichrist—"

"That's enough," said Ron. Everyone knew to cut Fall off when he started quoting Revelation.

"Sleaze or not," said Dave, "we've definitely seen new activity, new life, and even new money in Sweeney lately. You wouldn't believe how much Traci and her friends made from selling copies of the video from last Saturday."

"That's what I mean," said Binks. "Sweeney, the Porn Capital of Kiowa County. We could end this whole thing tomorrow with chains and a couple of bulldozers, put the Rock back where it belongs. Sure, we've had fun, but enough's enough. I say we take the Rock down and get back to normal life." He looked to Reverend Fall for support.

But to his surprise, the reverend's face turned white and he rose to protest. "No, no! That would be against God's will, because that Rock is where the angel appeared to chase away the heathens, where the miracle happened. It should be a shrine."

Nettie, who was seated next to Leland, turned to him and whispered, "It's like June said: he's been miracle-ized."

"Let's keep some perspective here," said Connie Nesbitt. "We're selling bottles of phony water as a joke, and maybe good-humored T-shirts. But this isn't Las Vegas, or Atlantic City, we're not opening brothels or casinos here."

At that moment, Leland, who had been sitting silently at the table's end, cleared his throat ominously. All went silent when he stood. "Folks, there's people sitting outside who are waiting to meet you. They want to talk to you about a lot of things, including a casino."

And with that he left the room. The Rotarians barely had time to look at each other in bewilderment before Leland returned with two men and a woman. "I'd like to introduce Lee Harris," said Leland, nodding to one of the men, "and Ginny Harris, his wife, and Eddie Wilson. They say they're members of a tribe of Indians. They contacted me last Saturday, and I'll save you all a lot of trouble by telling you that from everything I've been able to dig up since then, they really are Indians, not like that Soaring Eagle and his bunch. I'll let Lee do the rest of the explaining."

Dave watched as Lee Harris moved forward to speak. Slightly older than the other two, he was middle-aged, barrel-chested, and with a bit of a paunch. He had the mahogany skin of a man who had worked outdoors much of his life. His broad, flat face with high cheekbones did indeed appear Indian. He wore a checkered flannel shirt, jeans, a belt with a silver buckle inset with turquoise, and a bolo tie with a big chunk of turquoise in the center. On his head was a baseball cap with the logo "Ace Construction—we always get it up." He began to speak in a soft voice.

"a-HEY-thla," he said. "That means 'greetings' in our language. We're Cocoyes."

Dave looked at Roger, who looked at Kathy, who looked at Nettie, and so on. All shrugged in amazed ignorance.

"Don't look for our reservation on any maps, and don't look for us in encyclopedias," Harris continued. "We're not there. But we're real, as you can see."

He went on to describe his tribe's history. They were living on the High Plains and elsewhere in New Mexico when the Spaniards arrived in 1540. The conquistador Don Juan de Oñate mentioned them in the chronicles of his 1598 colonizing expedition. And then, like so many other minor tribes at that time, they simply seemed to disappear. They played no part in the history of the High Plains, so historians ignored them. So did the other tribes. Their minuscule numbers and lack of territory precluded them from having a political voice. They had no documentation, so the federal government denied them official recognition, and thus a reservation.

Miraculously, however, throughout all this they had clung together, stubbornly maintaining kinship relations and even much of their language. In the 1970s, most tribal members moved to Los Angeles, where there was work.

But Los Angeles was a maelstrom of assimilation, and lately they'd realized they were losing their identity. The only way they could keep it was to have a reservation. That was when they heard of Sweeney and its rocks.

"We understand that the rocks used to be called Indian Rocks before they were raised up," said Harris. "Well, we think there was a reason. Our oral traditions tell of clumps of rocks out on the plains. We think this might have been one of them. This was Indian land."

"Now wait a minute," protested Roger. "If you think you can pull off a land grab by coming in and talking about oral traditions—"

But Harris put up his hand. "This isn't a land grab. We know we can't prove ancestral title to this land, and we don't have the resources to try. Believe me, we've fought that losing battle before.

"No, what we want to explore is some kind of arrangement in which we all can benefit. Having a recognized Indian reservation here could be a good thing for Sweeney, especially if the reservation had an Indian casino or other businesses that shared their revenue with the town."

"A casino?" gasped Nettie. "In Sweeney?" She spoke for everyone in the room.

Roger and Kathy strolled along Main Street after the Rotary meeting broke up.

"I never in my life thought I'd say this," said Roger, "but I think Suffitt did the right thing."

"You mean tabling the issue until the next meeting and then calling the meeting adjourned? I noticed he didn't technically follow proper parliamentary procedure."

"Yes, I was alarmed by that too."

Late afternoon heat still radiated from the cracked sidewalk blocks. A desultory breeze rearranged dust along the curb. Roger and Kathy both knew that soon the harsh light would soften, the air would become velvet, and overhead the brightest stars would appear in the pellucid sky long before it turned completely black. But for now. . . . As they arrived at the town offices, Roger wiped his brow with his arm and adjusted his cowboy hat. He paused in the shade of the solitary tree, a Siberian elm that volunteered its services to passersby. "Sweeney, Climate Capital of the West," he said. "Visit our Desolation Theme Park. The Town of Four W's—weather, weirdness, and Weeney Water."

Turning slightly more serious, he asked, "What do you think of the Indians and their proposal?"

"Part of that question is easy. Their casino proposal is preposterous. As someone who drives to and from Tucumcari to Sweeney almost every day, I can say they'd have to be giving away Rolls Royces for gamblers to drive out here. They have too many alternatives; this state is crawling with casinos."

"Agreed," said Roger.

"The other part, what do I think of the Indians—that's tougher." She paused and then continued, "An instinct in me says Leland is correct in saying these are real Indians. Frankly, I find them sympathetic. They're a pretty sorry lot, but they've survived against staggering odds—in many ways, they're like Sweeney itself, bypassed by modern society, facing extinction, and responding with something completely ridiculous."

Roger chuckled. "Well said. The town and the tribe are sinking, grasping at whatever floats by. They're the underdog that overcomes overwhelming obstacles and wins the state championship."

Kathy laughed. "And the school nerd gets the head cheerleader for his girlfriend." She sat on the concrete railing surrounding the tree and the desiccated lawn in front of the building. Roger sat too.

"Are you sorry you proposed altering Indian Rocks?" she asked.

Roger seemed surprised. "No. Hell, no. Barring anyone getting hurt, this is probably the best thing that ever happened to this town, and I'm proud to have played a part in it. And you?"

She shook her head and laughed. "I never in my life thought I'd say this, but I agree fully with Roger Rollins."

"We do live in strange times."

Kathy turned to Roger, pursed her lips and asked, "Why do you stay? I'm trapped here, but you could make a comfortable living anywhere. I don't want Sweeney to die. I've got friends and memories here, even a few good ones, but I know all too well what it's like to be committed to following a loved one to the end of her life. And I have a keen sense of what I'm missing."

"So you'd leave if you had the chance? And sooner or later you will."

"Answer my question first."

Roger crossed his legs and clasped his hands over his knees. He thought a moment. "Why do I stay? I've asked myself that question lots of times, and never found a good answer. I've got good memories too, and some not so good. I've got a few relatives scattered around eastern New Mexico and elsewhere, but I'm not really that close to any of them. There's a big world out there, and I'm missing it for the Chick 'n' More.

"But whenever I consider actually leaving, I always come up short— no other place is quite right, I'll get around to it after the county fair, I'll send away for information and never do. There's a part of me that doesn't want to leave here—gawdawful though it is—and so far that part has always had the upper hand. So as to your question as to why I stay here, I'm embarrassed to say I don't know. Now you."

"I don't know either." She brushed a spiky goathead thorn from the heel of her shoe. "I could go back to school, get a degree in something interesting, start a new career, something besides sweeping up the wreckage of other people's lives." She paused. "I've had the luxury, if you can call it that, of avoiding the issue of leaving, and that's always bothered me. But you're right, it's going to find me. And then? I tell myself that I want to leave Sweeney, that I can't wait to leave Sweeney, but I suspect that when the time comes, leaving will be difficult—and I don't really understand why either."

Roger looked at her and nodded. Then he said, "It's like they say, you can pick your friends, but you can't pick your relatives—or your hometown."

She smiled at him as she stood. "And in a place like Sweeney you can't even pick your friends."

Suddenly she stopped and looked down the street. Sweeney didn't have an ambulance, so the state police officer assigned to the town performed that role, and his speeding car was now turning from Main Street onto Honeysuckle Street. Her street.

"Uh oh," she said, and started running in the direction of her home.

Immediately upon leaving the Rotary meeting, Nettie bustled over to Magnolia Street and Iris's house. She needed to talk, and Iris served that purpose well. But she'd have to hurry if she was to beat the light-speed rays of gossip radiating outward from the meeting. In fact, as Nettie approached the front door of Iris's house, she could hear a telephone ringing over the clamor of a television.

"Tell them you'll call back," shouted Nettie as Iris stirred herself to pick up the phone. "We need to talk."

"I'll call you back," Nettie heard Iris say, just before the woman appeared to hold the door open. On her feet were pink, fuzzy slippers that once had been much pinker and fuzzier. She wore a shapeless, capacious housecoat, in whose stained folds could be seen a faded print of blue goats cavorting on a green background with yellow lollipop trees. Not faded enough, thought Nettie. Nettie always marveled that Iris could even find clothes so hideous, but she conceded that these were what for Iris were "work clothes" and that Iris was dressed for *serious* TV watching. And sure enough, as Nettie entered Iris's slovenly living room she noticed that one of the courtroom shows was on.

"Turn that off," said Nettie firmly, refusing to compete with a sordid dispute involving motorcycle parts. "The people of Sweeney have interesting times ahead."

For once Iris didn't protest but turned off the TV then flumped herself down on her sofa. "Want some chips?" She offered a bag to Nettie, who waved it aside.

When Nettie finished, Iris momentarily was speechless. Then she said, "Indians! Of all the gawdammed things to happen, we've got Indians."

"I wouldn't exactly use the term 'got.' You make them sound like bedbugs," Nettie bristled. "They seemed just like ordinary folks."

"Oh, you know what I mean." Actually, Nettie didn't, but she decided to let it ride.

"I don't have anything against Indians," Iris said, "especially considering they were here since the dinosaurs"—Nettie let that ride also—"it's just that never in my life did I expect Sweeney to have Indians."

"We don't exactly 'have' them," said Nettie, settling into one of Iris's overstuffed chairs.

"And a casino . . . I've heard some of those casinos have never-ending buffets, you know anything about that?"

"No, though I've heard that people gamble in casinos." The irony was lost on Iris. "But I don't think we have to worry about a casino here"—Iris's mouth sagged into a slight pout—"because the idea of people coming to Sweeney to gamble, or eat, is just plain absurd. But that doesn't mean we couldn't work out something else with the Indians."

Iris took a potato chip and thought as she chewed. Finally, she said, "I wouldn't mind Indians living here, long as they tried to fit in. Actually, I always kind of wanted to be an Indian myself. I think I've got Indian somewhere in my background, I think I remember my mom saying something about that."

Nettie recalled Iris's mother, a small, mousy woman completely dominated by her abusive husband. Perhaps fantasies of Indian blood and noble but futile resistance helped her cope.

Nettie decided she wasn't going to elicit any more opinions from Iris, at least for now. But by talking to Iris, Nettie had ensured that Iris, and the people in her gossip network, could at least begin with accurate information, before they distorted it. "How's Harriet?" Nettie asked, to change the subject.

"Let's go ask her," suggested Iris, nodding out the window. Sure enough, in Harriet's front yard across the street the old woman was doddering around among her flowers. Nettie winced. She hadn't really wanted to spend time talking to Harriet, but Iris already was on her feet and lumbering out the door.

As Nettie stood to follow, she felt herself step on something crunchy on the floor. It was an orange Cheeto, with a green, fuzzy fringe.

"Oh, Nettie, oh, Iris," Harriet rasped when she saw the two approaching. "You're just the people I wanted to see." Nettie and Iris exchanged worried glances.

"If it's about those roses, I wouldn't be pruning them this early, give them a few more weeks." Nettie knew it wasn't about the roses, but she'd hoped it was.

"Oh, no," said Harriet. "It's about this." And with that she hauled out from inside her blouse a large amethyst crystal on a gaudy gold-colored chain. "It's the crystal the goddess lady gave to me."

"It's beautiful, Harriet," Nettie offered.

"But it's not mine. She gave it to me for the ceremony, but I didn't have a chance to give it back to her."

"And now you feel this isn't rightfully yours," interpreted Nettie. Harriet nodded her head miserably.

"Well, that's just plain gawdammed ridiculous," blustered Iris, but Nettie waved her down while she spoke softly to Harriet.

"That's very noble of you to feel that way, Harriet, and everyone knows you would never dream of taking anything that wasn't yours." Harriet looked at Nettie with the desperate hope of a drowning person offered a life buoy.

"But it *is* yours," Nettie continued. "The goddess didn't loan it to you, she gave it to you. You were meant to have it, just like all the other goddesses in the ceremony. They didn't give their crystals back. She gave it to you, because you were a goddess too and were meant to have it. It's yours, Harriet."

Harriet looked like she was about to cry.

"Damn right it's yours, Harriet," blurted Iris, slapping Harriet on the back. "And, oh, but it's beautiful. I don't know what kind of gem that is, but it's way prettier than what you see on the shopping channel."

Harriet leaned forward and whispered, "Don't say a word to anyone, but I put this under my pillow at night, and I do swear that my chakras have been ever so much better."

Nettie reached forward and touched the crystal. "There are scads of miracles in that crystal."

A dust-devil of thoughts whirled in Dave's mind as he walked home from the Rotary meeting.

A casino in Sweeney? Preposterous. But could there be something else? Another arrangement? He got the feeling the Cocoyes, all hundred or so of them, would be easy to work with. After all, they didn't have a lot of alternatives.

But then, neither did Sweeney. Sure, things had been looking up lately, but a few good days weren't a permanent solution. And inevitably the novelty would wear off. What then?

And would he even be around to see how it played out, or would he be living and teaching in Santa Fe?

As he approached his house, he smelled animal smells wafting from the stables. On impulse he went over to check on Flicka. As usual, the horse was standing by the fence, communing with the goat.

As Dave approached, he saw Traci leaning against the corral fence, talking on her cell phone, her back to him. Not wishing to eavesdrop, Dave veered off toward the house, but not before he heard the words "cool" and "Santa Fe."

Obviously, Joanie had already told Traci about the Santa Fe offer—a bad sign.

"So you'll come over and help me wrap the CDs that people ordered? Cool. Now, back to this Santa Fe thing . . ."

"I don't know much about Santa Fe," said Kimberly noncommittally. "I mean, yeah, I know about Santa Fe, but I've only been there a couple of times. I don't know what it would be like to live there."

"I've heard you can sit on the plaza and see celebrities—movie stars, rock stars. Someone said they saw Keener there. Cool, huh?"

"Right, and the celebrities come right up to you and ask you to hang with them."

You're just jealous, thought Traci. "Well, at least it's a chance to get out of Dweeby." Traci reverted to the name she and her friends had for Sweeney when they were in mid-school. Ever since they'd gained awareness of an outside world, "getting out of Dweeby" was regarded as life's ultimate achievement, like escaping from Alcatraz.

"Yeah, I've still got a year to go," said Kimberly.

"Listen, Kim, I've got to go. I'll see you later."

Traci suddenly had realized that she too had only a year to go. Only a year before leaving for college and then getting out of Dweeby forever. Her last year with her friends. She would miss them and all that had been going on—to start all over again, for just a year, in an unknown situation.

But then, that unknown situation was Santa Fe. She imagined returning to Dweeby for a visit, dressed in the latest trendy fashions, telling her friends about all the cool things she'd done, the parties she'd gone to, the edgy people she'd met. She tried to savor the envy she would trigger among her friends.

Her former friends. They would be, like, from different planets.

Rudd didn't feel like going back to the shop after the Rotary meeting, and he'd already locked up, so instead he strolled through the late-afternoon heat toward home and what lately had become his favorite after-work retreat, the playhouse. There he sat in the big overstuffed chair, put his feet up on a wooden stool brought from the main house, and basked in the contentment he found among the memories that lived there. Often he read comic books, even though after almost forty years he still recognized all the characters and plots. Sometimes he sipped a cold beer fetched from the house. Usually he just sat and relaxed.

Today he needed to think. An Indian casino—what the hell was anyone to make of that, implausible as it seemed on the face of it?

Rudd had been sunk deep in thought and the overstuffed chair for about half an hour when a knock sounded at the door. "Who is it?" he growled.

"It's me," returned the scratchy voice of S&S. "I got a question."

Rudd levered himself to his feet, then opened the door but blocked the entrance with his massive body. "What's your question?"

"Is it true that Indians are coming?"

Rudd didn't know quite how to respond to that. "We met with some Indians at the—" He was halted by the bewilderment and shock on S&S's face as he stared into the playhouse. Finally, still staring, S&S half-whispered, "I been here before."

Rudd started, then snarled. "Gawdammit, I told you not to come in here."

With that, S&S turned to face Rudd. "I haven't. What I mean is that I been here before, a long time ago. Can I come in?"

Dumbfounded, Rudd could only stand aside as S&S slid past. Rudd's mouth dropped as he watched S&S looking around in wonder, as if he had just beheld a miracle. "I been here before," he repeated.

Rudd started to protest, but S&S ignored him and walked to the wall between the chair and the rock collection. Kneeling, he pried up a loose floorboard. He inserted his fingers into the hole beneath and retrieved a small object. He held it up for Rudd to see. It was the notched base of an arrowhead. "I put that there when I was here before, a long time ago."

Rudd stood gape-mouthed. Finally he asked, "Can you remember when it was?"

"I don't recall much of it, just little things, like that arrowhead. I was pretty little. I think I was visiting a relative who lived here. Old guy named Mangan—no, that wasn't it."

"Morgan," blurted Rudd.

"Yeah, that was him. He was always looking for his teeth."

Rudd was dumbfounded. When he'd been a child, the Torgelson house had been filled with people, relatives coming and going all the time. He never knew who most of them were or how they were related to him. But he had known that crazy Uncle Morgan was indeed his uncle, and he vaguely recalled a skinny, awkward kid who arrived one time to visit Uncle Morgan, a kid who appeared at the family meals, didn't say much, and departed after a couple of days, leaving no ripple in the Torgelson family ocean. Could that really have been S&S? And if that was so, didn't that mean that he and S&S were related? Maybe even cousins?

He looked at S&S, whose wide-eyed stare confirmed that he too had figured out the implications.

Chapter Thirteen

❧ KATHY WAS CARRYING A BREAKFAST TRAY down the stairs when the phone rang in the kitchen. "Larkins," she answered after setting the tray on the kitchen table

"Hi, Kathy." It was Roger. "I just called to see how your dad was—and how you were doing."

"He's okay. The stroke left him slightly paralyzed on his left side, and he has trouble talking, but the doctor says those symptoms should gradually recede—somewhat."

"I know about the 'somewhat.' I remember when my mom had her stroke. How's your mom doing with all this?"

"She's okay. She's pretty confused about it all, but then she has her TV shows—Roger, can you hang on a second, there's someone at the door."

Soon she returned. "Sorry about that. It was a neighbor with a casserole. I won't have to cook for a month, judging from the food people have been bringing by. Judy and Adelino brought a coffee urn all primed and ready to go. I told them I didn't drink that much coffee, but they just smiled. And you know what, I've refilled that urn twice a day, what with all the people stopping by. School kids even offered to help with the yard work."

"Good people. And how about you, how are you doing? And don't just say 'fine,' because I've been there and know better."

"Hang on just another second." After a short pause she returned. "There, I'm back."

"Another casserole?"

"No, a trip to the coffee urn. Now I'm sitting down and can talk. How am I? Overwhelmed and confused."

"That sounds normal."

"The doctor says Mom and Dad really shouldn't be left by themselves while I'm away at work. They need to be in an assisted living arrangement. He recommended a couple of places, and from working with High Plains Mental Health I know of facilities in Albuquerque that are pretty nice that we can afford—barely."

She paused. "But . . . I don't know why I'm telling you all this, but Mom and Dad have lived all their lives in Sweeney, most of them in this house. The assisted living places are nice enough, but they're like waiting rooms for death."

"An assisted living home is where my mom ended up after her stroke. It's one of many things in my life I regret."

"But if I moved to Albuquerque I could visit them every day, or at least often, and, this sounds selfish, I could finally get out of Sweeney and have a life. This town is like a waiting room for me too. If I'm ever going to escape Sweeney, this is my chance. Deep in my gut I know that if I don't leave now, I'll never leave."

"I understand."

"How can you understand?"

"Because I've had to accept that I'll never leave, and that was harder than you might think. It's like having a birthmark that could be removed but that you keep because it's a part of you. Staying in Sweeney has closed a lot of doors in my life, and I won't lie and say I don't have regrets about what I've given up to stay here, that I don't wonder how my life might have been different if I'd moved away, but . . . this damned town is part of who I am."

He paused. "I didn't intend to unload all of that on you. Maybe I'm not as clear about things as I think. But this is a difficult time for you, and I do understand. All you can do is take it one day at a time. But you've got a lot of support here, as you're discovering—and I'm here too."

"Thanks, I appreciate that." Then, changing the subject, "Actually, one of the decisions I've got to make concerns you."

"Yes?"

Kathy couldn't tell whether she detected worry or hope in his voice.

"Yes, I got a call yesterday evening from a guy down in Logan. They're preparing for their annual Logan Days rodeo. He happened to be here for our rodeo and had a good time. They need an announcer for their rodeo, and he wants it to be me. They'll pay my expenses and two hundred dollars."

"That's great! You said yes, I assume."

"Not yet. I told him I'd think it over."

"Ah, come on, you're a great rodeo announcer, and you had a good time, admit it."

"I did have a good time, and I certainly can use any extra money I can get about now. But it's got a complication."

"Yes."

"He wants me to bring that rodeo clown, 'that goofy one' was how he put it. He thinks we're a team."

Silence. Then, "Hmmm. I think I understand. Listen, we'll talk soon, but you've got other things to worry about right now. Besides, I've got to go. Someone just walked in with an injured coyote I've got to tend to."

Three days after the Rotary meeting Nettie was still fielding questions and surveying the opinions of local women about the possibility of Indians coming to Sweeney. Most of her acquaintances were completely flummoxed by the Indians and their casino proposal, though few saw any likelihood of that succeeding. Reactions ranged from "I'd rather that Sweeney die poor but honest than turn into Sin City on the Plains" to "I'd hustle truckers on Main Street if it would keep Sweeney alive." Given the age of the woman who said that, its chances of succeeding were slim.

"Have you ever seen one of these High Plains towns that died and then came back to life?" that woman had continued. "They don't. I think this whole town should take a field trip around eastern New Mexico and take a good long look at what's facing Sweeney. Start with Mount Dora, if we can still find it. It was a hopping place at one time. Then we can drive down the road to Farley, have coffee with the residents at the restaurant—oops, there isn't a restaurant in Farley anymore, and hardly any residents either. Maybe we should swing by Abbott and catch a baseball game at the Newton High School, they had a good team—when they had students. Yeah, I think a field trip would be a very good idea."

Three days, and women were still calling to ask questions and voice opinions, so Nettie was not surprised when the phone rang after her supper, as she was sitting at her kitchen table sipping the Wild Turkey she lately had been enjoying after eating and doing the dishes. But the call was not someone wanting to talk about the Indians, it was June Fall.

"Nettie, can I come over? I need to talk to you."

"Of course, June. I'm right here."

When June hung up, Nettie, sensing that this visit wasn't about the church newsletter, tossed back the rest of the whiskey before going into the bathroom and rinsing her mouth with mouthwash. Then she filled a bowl on the kitchen table with red-and-white mints from the cupboard. She'd hardly finished when she heard a knock on the door. Opening it, she saw June standing there, wringing her hands, her eyes red. The cheerful yellow-and-blue pastel print dress she wore contrasted with her obvious distress.

"Come in, dear, come in," said Nettie, ushering her toward the kitchen. "Sit down. Would you like tea? Or coffee? No? Then be sure to have a mint. I hear they're good for the nerves." And she popped one into her own mouth. "Now, tell me what's wrong."

"Nettie, I'm thinking about leaving Wayne." She collapsed into sobs.

"Now, now, settle yourself down and tell me what's going on. You did the right thing to call. Take your time, I'm not going anywhere."

The sobbing gradually subsided. "Ever since that damned solstice—and I don't care that I'm cursing—he's just gotten worse. Before he just wanted to get rid of the Rock. Now he feels called to make it into a shrine, and to protect it from desecration. He hangs around it. Every time school kids get near it he starts ranting and raving and runs them off. He's just plain nuts."

"I concede he's been a little unraveled lately, but maybe a few of his parishioners can rein him in a bit, talk sense to him."

"But, oh, Nettie, it's not just the Rock. It's personal too." June paused. Nettie waited.

"All the love and joy has gone out of our marriage. I can't even play the piano without him railing against 'secular influences.' I haven't been able get over my resentment at him preventing me from playing after the rodeo. That meant so much to me, but he was so blinded by 'righteousness' that he couldn't see that. My feelings didn't count. And it turned out that nothing scandalous happened at the reception, did it?"

"No, it didn't."

"Most of the time he asks me to stop playing because he wants to listen to some religious program on the radio, Pastor Pete or Pastor Paul or Pastor Poompadiah—I can't keep them straight, and I don't want to. They're all the same. They get him all riled up, carrying on about the End Times and Armageddon and sin and Satan and how the world is going to hell. Sometimes I want to just smash that damned radio. I can't remember the last time we went to a movie, or even just sat and watched TV. It's all too corrupt for him. I can't wait for him to go to work in the morning, and my stomach knots all up when he comes home. I can't go on living like this. I can feel my soul withering, drying up like . . . like a tumbleweed."

"I see," said Nettie softly.

"He wasn't always like this. He's always been religious—so have I—but he used to be fairly normal about it. But ever since he became pastor he's gradually gotten worse, he's gotten fanatical, almost desperate, as if he's always being tested, as if God is always watching him, making sure he measures up. He can never relax.

"The kids don't want to come home for visits anymore; he makes them so uncomfortable with his tirades. Nettie, I haven't seen Sarah in two years. We talk on the phone, and now she says she's pregnant. I'll have a grandchild that I won't get to see, at least not very often. Since they won't come here, I want to move away and live closer to them, but Wayne wouldn't hear of it, now that he's on a mission from God to protect that damned Rock. I don't know what to do. I just can't go on like this." She broke into sobs again.

"And, June, you don't have to," comforted Nettie. "You've got a tough nut of a problem, no denying, and at this very moment I don't have an answer. But Wayne isn't the only person with religion, and right now my faith is telling me that there's a solution to this problem, even if we can't see it yet. You've already started things moving by talking to me. We just have to be a little patient—I didn't say a lot patient—and remember, I did say 'we.' You're not in this alone."

When June left, Nettie poured herself a little more Wild Turkey. She didn't have the faintest idea what to do about Wayne.

Midmorning in Sweeney. Ripples of heat beginning to rise from the pavement. Hank Johnson's pickup driving back from the feedstore. A car full of high school kids heading off to somewhere. Iris Gerber in her big old Oldsmobile driving out of town, most likely toward the Walmart in Tucumcari. Fred Yoder sitting in the barber chair in his barber shop waiting for customers. The antiques store not yet open, their hours idiosyncratic, at best. The slow, easy rhythms of summer in a small town.

Dave sat at the counter in the Chick 'n' More. Better than hanging around the house. Joanie and Traci probably were confabulating about how great it would be to live in Santa Fe. The early morning customers had departed, leaving only him and Roger. Helen had just brought coffee for them, and now he was improving it with as much cream and sugar as he could stand. Otherwise, the Chick 'n' More coffee wasn't really fit to drink, though he knew people in Sweeney who thought it was great. Showed how much they knew. In Santa Fe he would have his choice of coffee shops—and his choice of coffees. Gourmet Kona, rich Guatemalan, exotic Sumatran, robust Kenyan—he remembered the descriptions from a Starbuck's, coffees from places he didn't know grew coffee.

"Do you think there's truth to the rumor that the Chick 'n' More buys its coffee beans from coffee plants down in Conejo?" Dave asked Roger, while Helen was back in the kitchen.

"Wouldn't doubt it," replied Roger, not looking up from his own cup. "The coffee has an aged cow manure taste to it that could come from the old feedlot down there."

Dave looked at the wall behind the counter. There in a frame was the first dollar Ed and Edna had ever taken in at the Chick 'n' More. There also was a sign that read: "No Shoes, No Shirt, No Service." That didn't even exclude S&S, at least not most of the time. Class, the Chick 'n' More was pure class. Just like the rest of Sweeney. So why was he so reluctant to leave?

"You ever thought about leaving Sweeney?"

"Not in the last ten minutes," Roger replied sourly, then added, "Hell, yes, I've thought a lot about leaving Sweeney. It's the doing part that I'm not good at."

Dave shook his head. "What is it about us? There's lots of us who can't think of a convincing reason to stay in this town, but who never actually get around to leaving."

"I can think of one who did. I was married to her, until she left."

"Maybe I shouldn't ask this, but do you ever think you should have gone with her?"

"Nah, I settled that issue a long time ago. Sweeney was only the sharpest wedge between us. Staying in Sweeney made my life simpler. Not happier, but sometimes you just have to settle for simpler."

Simpler, thought Dave. His life with Joanie and Traci and their conflicts and issues was anything but simple. Sometimes bachelorhood had a certain appeal. "You ever think about getting married again?"

"Not in the last ten minutes." Roger paused. "Sorry, that was a bad joke the first time. Yes, I've thought about it. I'd be happy to find a partner. But cowgirls aren't my type, and anyone else would face the same disappointments and frustrations as Kim did. I couldn't go through that again. Still, I do check the personals in the Tucumcari paper occasionally: Single woman seeks long-term relationship in small, dying town. Likes long, moonlight walks on the prairie amid cacti and cattle dung, low-brow dining, coyote opera, and snuggling with sick animals."

Dave just nodded. "If Joanie and Traci want to leave, I'll have to go."

"Of course you will. Our situations are different."

"I honestly don't know what to do about this Santa Fe thing, especially regarding Joanie and Traci," Dave persisted, wanting more support and advice than he was getting. "Can't you at least tell Joanie that Santa Fe is unhealthy for horses and goats?"

"You mean, say that all the style and ambiance and lizard-skin boots makes them neurotic?"

"Something like that."

"Nice try, but I don't think my credibility with Joanie is high enough."

Dave sagged. "I was just kidding, but I really don't know what to do. I always wondered what it would be like to live in Santa Fe, but now that the opportunity to find out is here, I realize that I don't want to. I don't belong in Santa Fe, I'd be out of place there—I guess that says a lot about me. But I think Joanie and Traci wouldn't really fit in either, yet I can't make that decision for them."

"I understand. For what it's worth, I agree, at least regarding Joanie. The Santa Fe horse scene is different from what it is in these parts—*very* different. There the emphasis is on hiring the right trainer, finding one with the right credentials in, say, Jungian Holistic Horse Therapy—and Joanie wouldn't fit in at all, at least not at first. Eventually she'd link up with folks like her, but a horse like Flicka would be like . . . like S&S at Wimbledon. I could tell you stories . . ."

"But then she doesn't really fit in here. I never thought about it, but she doesn't really fit in anywhere, certainly not back home in LA. I always hoped that Sweeney would grow on her, but I suspect you have to grow up in a place like Sweeney to appreciate it. And I don't think Traci and her friends would even agree with that." He sighed.

Down at the end of the counter, Helen was seated on a stool, taking a break, sipping her own coffee. Dave turned to her and said, "Say, Helen, you hear a lot of stuff in here, what are people saying about the Indians and their proposal?"

"Yes and no."

"Say what?" said Dave.

"Yes, they're fairly kindly disposed to the Indians, except for a few narrow-minded bigots, but no, they don't think much of a casino here."

"Yeah, that's what I've been hearing too," said Roger. "Actually, I don't think anyone has to worry regarding the casino—that just isn't going to happen."

"But I wouldn't mind seeing the Indians here," Helen continued. "It just seems right, Indians coming back to the Plains, where they used to be. Of course, I'm a little biased." She paused so the two men could ask what she meant.

"What do you mean?" asked Dave.

"My great-grandmother was raised on an Indian reservation down in Oklahoma, the Choctaws I think it was. Her father was an Indian agent there. One of her husbands was part Indian, and I think he's the one I'm descended from, so that makes me part Indian too. I think that's one of the reasons I've stayed out here on the plains, because the Indian part of me feels at home here."

Dave started to say that the Choctaws originally were from Mississippi, then thought better of it and said instead, "I think a lot of us are in sympathy with the Indians."

Then Roger interrupted. Looking out the front window he said, "Say, not to change the subject, but there's perhaps the strangest sight you'll ever see in Sweeney. Far stranger than Indians, Bare-assed Bob, the Druids, or even the goddesses—none of them even comes close."

Dave followed Roger's eyes out the window just in time to catch sight of S&S passing by. At least he thought it was S&S. The man wore a clean blue shirt with new Wrangler jeans; on his feet were new cowboy boots, he was cleanly shaven, his hair was slicked down and combed—and strangest of all, he was walking with a steady gait.

"Is that really who I think it is?" asked Dave, his eyes wide with incredulity.

"None other."

At that moment two citizens passed by the window. They gaped at seeing the transformed S&S, their eyes goggling as they looked backward when he passed. One bumped into a fire hydrant.

"What on earth happened?" asked Dave. "I mean, this just isn't natural. Is he okay? Has anybody talked to him?"

"I haven't met anyone who's actually talked to him," said Roger. "Everyone's too shocked. They act as if he might turn into a demon at any moment. It's just too strange. Someone ought to go tell Reverend Fall—here's a genuine miracle if he needs one."

At that moment Rudd entered the diner. Dave turned to Roger and said, "He'll know, if anyone will. Go ask him."

Roger shot Dave a look that spoke, "Thanks a lot," then turned to Rudd and said, "Hey, Rudd, come on over and let us buy you a cup of coffee. Dave has a question for you."

As Dave glared at Roger, the big man slid onto a stool next to them. "What's on your mind?" he said to both of them.

"It's about S&S," said Dave. "We saw him a minute ago, and . . . well, he didn't look the S&S we know and love."

"Yeah?"

"You know him better than anyone," said Roger. "We wondered if you had any idea what might be going on."

"A man can change, can't he?" growled Rudd. "There's more to Edward than meets the eye."

"Edward?!" exclaimed Dave and Roger simultaneously.

"That's his name, and it's time people began calling him by it. I know what 'S&S' stands for. If he's going to embark on a new life, then he doesn't need to be saddled with that old slur. I'll give people about one week to get used to his real name, and then if I hear 'S&S' after that, there's going to be consequences."

And with that he left the counter without waiting for his coffee and huffed out the door.

"What the hell was *that* all about?" said Dave.

At that moment Helen appeared to refill their cups. "Rudd couldn't stay?" she asked. "Say, was that S&S I saw walk by a minute ago?"

"Edward," said Roger. "From now on he's Edward—especially when Rudd's around. And don't ask me what's going on."

Joanie was frowning at her computer when the knock came at the door. For the past hour she'd been surfing websites having to do with Santa Fe, and real estate, and horses. The good news was that Santa Fe had a very fine facility called the Santa Fe Horse Park. The bad news was that it was where Santa Feans played polo and where junior dressage Olympians and world-class show jumpers trained. Not exactly what she imagined for Flicka and the goat. Bitterly Joanie reflected that the horses Santa Feans now rode were a far cry from the raw-boned, half-starved ponies the early settlers and Indians rode for most of the city's history. Flicka would have fit in then.

The worse news was that one horse site stated baldly: "The cost of housing a horse or two is not cheap in Santa Fe like the rest of the country, and if you want more space for horses and their needs prices are even higher, usually much higher."

Did she really want to move to Santa Fe? She couldn't imagine wanting to stay in Sweeney, not after all these years of discontent, but she acknowledged that she had gotten . . . well, comfortable here. Of course, that was the worst of all reasons to stay. Is that what happened in these little towns, that people just got so comfortable they couldn't leave?

That certainly hadn't happened to the young people in Sweeney. Yet while the incident of the girls ditching had shaken Joanie's faith in Sweeney's safety, she was not sorry Traci had grown up here—and she had only one year to go before she left for the outside world.

The knock came again. "Traci, will you get it?" Joanie called out, then remembered that Traci had gone to the store to link up with her friends. "Okay, just a minute!" she shouted when the knock came a third time.

She exited her browser then went from her den through the kitchen to the front door.

"Oh, hi, Kimberly," she said to the high school girl standing there. "I'm sorry, Traci isn't here right now. I think she went to the Baca Mart. You can probably find her there."

Kimberly seemed uncharacteristically nervous. "Actually, Mrs. Daly, I came to see you."

"Oh?"

"You remember you said I could come by and see your dollhouses? Would this be a good time? I mean, if you're not busy. I should have called ahead . . ."

"No, no, Kimberly. In fact, this is an excellent time. Come in. Would you like something to drink? The dollhouses are upstairs, it might be kind of stuffy up there. I think I'll have iced lemonade."

"Yes, that would nice."

As Joanie led Kimberly into the kitchen she reflected on the disconnect between the girl's behavior and her appearance. Kimberly had always attempted to cultivate an outlaw image, rebellious, defiant, yet the black T-shirt with its Jaws of Hell logo and red Gothic lettering contrasted starkly with the shy, polite girl wanting to see dollhouses.

Joanie poured lemonade from a pitcher into two ice-filled glasses and said, "Follow me. Be careful, the steps are kind of rickety." *Like everything else in this house.*

Once in the spacious but stuffy attic, Joanie switched on the single light bulb hanging by a cord from the peaked ceiling and with a struggle opened the room's two small windows. A breeze swept in like a stray cat, tremored gauzy cobwebs, and startled the dust that lay dozing on the trunks and boxes stacked everywhere. Kimberly sneezed.

"Sorry," said Joanie as she led the girl to the corner where the dollhouses were. Except for the dollhouse Joanie had taken to the Rock, the half dozen dollhouses wore the same dust as everything else in the room. Joanie felt embarrassed, neglectful. She found a rag and began dusting them but only raised more dust. Kimberly sneezed again and then knelt before them.

"They're beautiful," she whispered in a voice too awed to be merely polite.

"Come on," said Joanie, "let's get them out of this old attic. You take one and I'll take one."

Tenderly Kimberly picked one up and followed Joanie down the stairs and out the front door, where they set them on the porch. Two more trips brought them all down.

"They're just beautiful," Kimberly said again as Joanie whisked them with a soft brush.

"This was my first." Joanie pointed to one resembling a Victorian house. "My grandmother gave it to me. The rest I built myself, from kits I ordered."

"You built these?"

"Sure, the kits are kind of expensive, but not compared to a real house. For several years I got a new kit every Christmas."

She pointed out the English manor dollhouse, then the Cape Cod dollhouse, the haunted dollhouse, the log cabin dollhouse, and finally the Swiss chalet dollhouse. "I don't really have a favorite. I would just play with whichever one fit my mood. Do you have a dollhouse?"

Kimberly's radiance faded. "I did. It wasn't much, just an old cardboard thing. It was kind of beat up, but I loved it." She fell silent.

"What happened to it?"

"One day I left it in the driveway after playing with it, and Dad drove over it backing the car out."

"That's terrible! Did you try to repair it?"

Joanie saw bitterness flash across the girl's face. "No, Mom threw it away before I even knew Dad had run over it. She said she didn't want the junky old thing around the house. She said I was too old to play with dollhouses. She didn't understand that I loved that dollhouse even more for being run over."

Suddenly Joanie understood. Kimberly lived with her mother and father on the wrong side of the feedlot, the Sweeney equivalent of the wrong side of the tracks, in a house that once had been attractive and respectable but now was brought low by neglect. As had her mother, who wore the hard, life-bleached cynicism of someone who long ago had surrendered to hopelessness. Kimberly's father was a part-time plumber and full-time drunk who probably hadn't known he'd run over his daughter's precious dollhouse—and wouldn't have cared. For Kimberly, trapped in that tawdry environment, a dollhouse would have been an escape into fantasy, a world of refinement and taste, one she could control, one that reflected her true nature. What a loss the dollhouse must have been!

Embarrassment spread over Kimberly's face, as if she suspected she had revealed too much. "It really was just an ordinary old dollhouse."

"Oh, no," protested Joanie. "It was where you lived, or at least a part of you did. Let's face it, we all live in dollhouses, it's just that most of us build them only in our minds. A few people like you and me are fortunate to get to build them in reality as well."

Then on impulse Joanie said, "You know, I haven't worked on a doll-house in a long time, too long. What if I order one and you order one too, we could work on them together. Over here."

Kimberly's eyes widened. "That would be . . . great!" Then, "What about Traci?"

"She's welcome to get one too, but I don't think she will. I don't think she's into dollhouses. This would be just us, or anyone else who wants to join in. What kind of dollhouse do you think you'd like to get?"

"An English country house, with lots of bay windows and fireplaces and a winding staircase and maybe a secret room," blurted Kimberly, with a revealing lack of hesitation. "What about you?"

Joanie really had no idea what kind of house she wanted. Unlike Kimberly, she hadn't thought about it at all. She paused a long moment and then said, "I think I'll get a Santa Fe style adobe."

And in that instant she realized the dollhouse was as close as she was going to get to living in Santa Fe—and that was okay.

Despite a mild hangover, Nettie was still pondering what to do about Wayne Fall when she opened the Style Salon the next morning. She had three customers already waiting, including Iris. That told her that some-thing had happened in Sweeney that needed discussing. She had barely unlocked the door before Iris barged in and announced, "Have you all seen S&S lately?"

"You mean Edward?" said Myrtle Evans. "Rudd's been telling every-one his name is Edward, and not to refer to him as S&S anymore."

"Edward?!" bellowed Iris. "Edward! That scrawny, stinking, drunken—"

"Not anymore," said Myrtle. "He's walking around in new clothes, with his hair plastered down like he was selling Bibles door to door. And people claim he's sober."

Iris gasped. "Will wonders never cease!"

"I hear that he was seen in Rudd's truck the other day, the two of them driving off to God knows where, and when they returned he was all duded up."

"I allow that Rudd has been acting differently lately," said Nettie, recalling his behavior at the recent Rotary Club meeting.

Iris's eyes widened. "Could he be on drugs?"

"Oh, for heaven's sake, no," said Nettie. "Why does everyone think a person who acts a little different has to be on drugs? Can you honestly imagine Rudd Torgelson on drugs?"

Iris looked a little shamefaced. "Well, no—but there has to be a reason for what's happened to S&S."

"Besides, drugs aren't famous for getting people like S&S—I mean, Edward—cleaned up and sober," added Nettie.

"Well, if S&S has gotten cleaned up," observed Myrtle, "that means Sweeney's only got Harriet Moggs for the town scarecrow."

Iris kneaded her fleshy face into a scowl. "Harriet's old, but she's a decent, charitable woman who doesn't wish ill for anyone," she said, glaring at Myrtle. "Besides, Harriet's not doing well. It's not right for people to be making fun of her right now."

"Harriet's not feeling well?" asked Nettie. "What's wrong?"

"She's been feeling low for some time. I talked to her this morning, and she said she was up vomiting last night. She looked awful."

"Oh, dear," said Nettie.

"Listen, Trixie," Leland said as he steered his pickup toward Sweeney, "you know I value your opinion, so what do you think about the Indians and their proposal?" The dog seated beside him grinned at the sound of her master's voice.

"Yep, me too," Leland said, reaching over to pat the dog. "We're of one mind, er . . . mind and a half. I don't know how this is going to play out, but I do hope there's some way we can come up with an arrangement that will work for everyone, including the Indians."

Lately Leland had found himself talking to Trixie often. At first it kind of bothered him, but he didn't really have anyone else to talk to, and talking to Trixie focused his thinking. She certainly didn't mind.

A cottontail rabbit darted across the road, and Leland swerved to avoid it. Trixie didn't notice.

"But I don't have a clue what we could work out with the Indians that would bring enough people and dollars out to this godforsaken place to keep us all going. Do you know, Trixie?"

The dog continued grinning.

"Yeah, me neither. By the way, did you know you're going to meet a relative before long? Grant's coming home this summer." Trixie beamed. "Yep, that's how I feel. This trip will be different from other visits." It will be indeed, Leland thought. It would be easy for the two of them just to stay at the ranch, to avoid the people in Sweeney, but Leland knew Grant wouldn't approve of that. No, this was one of those situations that needed to be confronted directly. He glanced again at Trixie. "You don't care at all whether he's homosexual or straight, you're just interested in whether he treats you well. Too bad humans aren't like that."

Leland reflected on how his own thinking regarding homosexuality had changed. Ranchers and cowboys didn't talk much about homosexuals, but when they did it was in a jocular, disparaging way. "Homos" and "queers" were the subject of jokes and insults. Of course, no one actually knew any homosexuals, much less was related to one. They were just part of that vast outside world that included Blacks and Arabs and Orientals and foreigners in general and half a dozen other groups whose lives were alien to cowboy consciousness. The cowboys didn't hold any particular grudge against them; after all, it wasn't their fault they weren't born on a ranch.

When Leland took a cultural anthropology class in college, he realized that the ranching community, of which he was a member, fit every characteristic of a tribal society, including the view that anyone not of the tribe was of a lower order of being. The cowboy tribe definitely did not include homosexuals. So when Leland learned that his son was a homosexual, his identity was shaken. He'd been angry, confused, resentful—and afraid. Afraid that Grant's orientation would become widely known, afraid that he wouldn't know what to say to his friends and associates, afraid that he'd be alienated from the community he'd known all his life. Afraid that he'd not measure up and would betray Grant.

It took Ruth's patient, gentle hand to bring him along, that and the reality of Grant as the son he loved. And Grant, too, had helped. He hadn't forced the issue, had never told anyone but Kathy Larkin, who was almost as isolated in her own way. Now, after several years of patience and love, the anger, resentment, and confusion were gone. And after the confrontation with Binks in the Chick 'n' More, so was the fear.

Maybe he should buy Binks a cup of coffee.

Trixie had just jumped down from the pickup after Leland parked it near the town offices when Leland saw Tom Binks striding toward the building, looking like he had something on his mind. Without greeting Leland, Binks began, "Now about that casino thing . . ."

"I wouldn't worry about that, proposal's not going anywhere."

"I'm glad to hear that. We've got enough sleaze in this town already lately without having a casino and all the riffraff they bring in."

"Specially as we have our homegrown riffraff," snarked Leland, before regretting his lack of self-control.

"What's that supposed to mean?"

Leland wanted to say that Las Vegas had no monopoly on beer-soaked ne'er-do-wells who neglect their families. Instead he said, "Only this: If nothing else results from that Rock and all that's happened, I hope it teaches people in this little town not to judge people by narrow stereotypes and labels."

Binks looked puzzled. Leland started to move on when Binks continued, "But you know, I feel kind of sorry for those Indians. There's not many people that know this, but I'm part Indian."

Leland looked at Binks in amazement—blond-gray crewcut, blue eyes, red face.

"I know what you're thinking, but my grandmother always said our family had Cherokee blood from back somewhere, and I've always felt it, my Indian blood."

Leland boggled. Just what did Indian blood feel like?

"Even as a kid I always felt bad when the Indians got whupped in the old cowboy movies, and I can't help feeling that here these Indians are getting whupped again."

"Well, for what it's worth, I feel similarly."

"You're an Indian too?"

Leland was still shaking his head as he and Trixie walked up the sidewalk to the town offices and through the door. It was unlocked, and when he entered he found Rachel Rowe seated at the town's computer working on the Sweeney website. She clearly was very good with computers, unlike him. When she'd started working and said the computer needed upgrading and maintenance, she'd laughed at him when he brought out a can of WD-40. He didn't mind. Now he used her for all kinds of things he couldn't do, Internet searches and whatnot. She at first had objected when he offered to pay her a part-time salary, but he insisted.

"Say, Rachel, I've got a chore for you, if you're not too busy."

"Oh, no, Mr. Morton, I'm just putting in hyperlinks. It'll just take a second."

Leland had no idea what she was talking about. "Indian Rocks," he said. A cloud briefly passed over Rachel's face. Leland ignored it. "It's occurred to me that we don't really know who owns them. They haven't been of any use to anyone, until now, but if we're going to be talking to the Indians about them, we ought to at least nail that down. We've got plats here somewhere—could you look them over and see what you can find? You might need to use that computer to track them down."

Rachel briskly tapped some keys and said, "Sure, I'd be happy to. Those records probably should be digitized."

"Thanks, Rachel, I'd appreciate it. Let me know what you find. But don't go putting digits into those records until we can copy them first."

Rachel stared at him in disbelief.

Leland and Trixie retreated to what passed for his office. He sat in the old oak office chair and shuffled through the papers on his desk. He really ought to deal with at least one of them. He picked up a copy of the New Mexico Economic Development Department's quarterly statistical summary. It showed Sweeney sinking ever lower in the state's municipal population rankings. It was only a matter of time before truck stops had more people; they already generated more revenue.

He tossed the paper back onto the desk, onto what he called his Maybe Tomorrow pile. Then he put his feet up on his desk and leaned back, a posture he'd always found conducive to deep thought. That or sleep, whichever came first. He was midway between the two when the phone rang.

"Town of Sweeney," he answered. "Leland here."

"This is Lee Harris." Leland immediately recognized the Indian leader's soft voice. "I hope I'm not disturbing you."

"Oh, not at all, Sweeney's pretty quiet right now, for a change. I'm glad you called."

"Me and the other Cocoyes have been thinking. That casino thing just isn't going to fly. We took a trip to Albuquerque and Santa Fe, drove up and down the Rio Grande, and looked at the Indian casinos there. Ain't no way in hell anyone's going to drive to Sweeney to gamble at anything we could put up."

"That's pretty much the same conclusion most folks here have reached."

Harris was silent a moment, then he said, "Well, anyway, we're sorry to have bothered you, and we're grateful for the polite hearing you gave us. You've got a nice little town."

Now it was Leland's turn to pause. Finally he said, "Look, we're both in the same boat, your tribe and our town. I can't speak for the rest of the town, but I have a strong sense, call it an intuition if you will, that somehow we can work together to keep us both alive. I'm afraid I don't have a clue as to what we might do, but I don't think we should give up just yet." Not hearing a response, Leland continued, "What are your plans for the next few days?"

"We were thinking about going back to LA, but we really don't have anything urgent pulling us there."

"Well, why don't you come on back to Sweeney for a few days. Bring everyone. We can probably find someplace for you to stay."

"That won't be necessary. We've got travel trailers."

"We've got an RV campground here, though it doesn't amount to much."

"We're Indians. Our ancestors camped in brush wickiups covered with buffalo hides."

"Well, why don't you come here, spend a few days, get to know the town, let the town get to know you."

After he hung up, Leland looked at Trixie. "I don't know whether I did the right thing or not, inviting them here, but like Nettie said, once the chute is open you've just got to go for it and hang on."

Trixie grinned a slobbery grin.

"I was hoping you'd feel that way."

Just then Rachel poked her head in the room. "Mr. Morton, I did it. I found out who owns Indian Rocks."

Chapter Fourteen

❧ "DON'T WORRY, TRIXIE, I'M HOT TOO," Leland said as he rolled down the windows of his old pickup. He'd been hot when he awoke at the ranch, and now the temperature was climbing even higher in the mid-morning sun as he drove from the Sweeney town offices toward Will Diggs's RV park, where he expected the Cocoyes would camp. A newer pickup, one with air-conditioning and power windows, would have been more comfortable, but a cantankerous part of him regarded that as sissified. He'd grown up with "cowboy air-conditioning"—rolling down the windows and driving fast as hell—and that was what he preferred.

Old and stubborn, he thought, with a foolish sense of pride. When he'd stopped briefly by the town offices to see if anything required his immediate attention—nothing did—Rachel Rowe sat at the town's computer, pecking at the keyboard, but Leland saw only a bewildering mass of numbers on the screen, and he hadn't wanted to embarrass himself by asking what they meant.

Leland parked his pickup in the shade of the large elm at the park's edge and climbed out, along with Trixie, who followed adoringly at his heels. Not for the first time did Leland say to himself, "Damn, that Roger was right: Trixie really is a quality dog."

As they approached the RV park, the yelping of other dogs exploded from among the dozen or so travel trailers scattered there. Lee Harris

210

emerged from one of the trailers and ambled over to greet Leland. He yelled at the dogs, who more or less ignored him but whose barking subsided nonetheless. Trixie, to her credit, hadn't barked once.

"Glad to see you made it," said Leland.

"Got in late last night," said Harris. "Mr. Diggs helped us hook up." He pointed to a standpipe with a red pump-head on it. Nearby was a row of Port-a-Potties.

"I'm afraid Will's not much on facilities yet," said Leland, "but he's working on it."

"It's okay, we knew what to expect, and we're pretty much self-contained anyway. Come on, let me introduce you to the folks and show you around."

Harris led Leland to a dilapidated travel trailer from which issued the sounds of a TV program. "The reason we've got so many trailers," Harris explained, "is that most of us used to work construction and preferred to live at the job site. We're nomadic Indians."

Beneath the entrance to the old trailer was a mat of green Astroturf with "Welcome" and "Wipe your feet" in white letters. Above the door was a crude wooden sign reading, "If this trailer's rockin', don't bother knockin'." The door was open.

"Hey, Chester, Willa, come out," Harris called. "I want you to meet someone."

A stocky, elderly man appeared in the doorway and gimped down the steps. He wore faded jeans and a T-shirt that read "Remember Korea"; on his head was a greasy ball cap with the label "Old Fart."

"Chester, I want you to meet Leland Morton. Leland's the town manager here. He's the one who invited us. Leland, this here's Chester Cohen. He's our tribal elder, sort of."

"Pleased to meet you, Mr. . . . Cohen," Leland said as he shook the hand the man offered.

"Call me Chester, and I know what you're thinking, Leland: what kind of a name is Cohen for an Indian? Well, my Cocoye name is Caca y'is'te, but I got tired of people calling me Caca. Besides, I wanted to connect with my Jewish roots—it's a long story—and I read somewhere that among Jews the Cohens were rabbis, the keepers of the tribal lore."

Leland noted that Chester looked only vaguely Indian and not at all Jewish. "Well, we're honored to have you folks here in Sweeney, and we hope you'll make yourselves at home here."

"Hey, Willa," Chester called, "come out and meet Leland."

Leland glanced at the trailer's door, where a fleshy, elderly woman appeared. In the shadows behind her was another woman, whom Leland would have sworn was Iris Gerber.

Chester Cohen introduced his wife as Willa Two Feathers, and Leland conceded that she at least had an Indian look about her. She wore her gray hair in two long braids, and outside her red cotton blouse dangled a huge turquoise squash blossom necklace.

"That's quite a necklace you've got there," opened Leland.

"Thank you, it's supposed to be genuine Navajo," she said as she held it up for Leland to see. "At least that's what the Mexican said that I bought it from at a swap meet in LA."

"Impressive," said Leland.

"N'tha-hle," she replied. "That's Cocoye; it's what we say to compliments."

"She speaks the language real well," said Chester. "I do too, but sometimes she'll get to chewing me out in Cocoye and rattling off stuff even I don't understand. Just as well." He laughed. "She holds classes for the kids."

Willa chortled. "Actually, they like speaking Cocoye, practice it on their own, among themselves. You know, there's a lot of advantages to speaking a language no one else understands."

Then Willa continued. "It's been nice meeting you, Leland. I hope you'll excuse me, I need to get back to my TV show."

As Leland walked away he wondered again, could that really have been Iris looking agitated in the trailer?

Lee and Chester took Leland around to meet other Cocoyes. There were Willie and Jenny Wilson and their four children: Kevin, Ronny, Shelley, and Carlos.

"They've all got Cocoye names too," Chester pointed out, "but they can be hard to pronounce, so in their everyday lives they usually go by their European names. Willie's an electrician, used to work for the phone company. Jenny's got training as a nurse."

Leland met other families, usually with multiple kids. The Cocoyes seemed to be a pretty fertile bunch. They could go a long way toward keeping the Sweeney school system alive, he thought.

"This here's Uncle Billy," said Chester, introducing a rotund late-middle-aged man seated at a picnic table. On a chair beside him sat Tom Binks.

"Pleased to meet you," said Leland. "Morning, Tom."

"Howdy," said Uncle Billy jovially. "Pull up a log and sit a spell. We're just sitting here talking Indian stuff."

Leland remained standing. "Indeed," he said.

"Yep," continued Uncle Billy, "Tom here has been filling me in on the town you've got here, and it seems y'all already have an Indian presence, even if it's gone unrecognized."

"Indeed," Leland repeated.

"Yep, Tom here tells me the town's name itself is Indian, comes from Kiowa Indian words, Tse 'ua nee, meaning 'place of rocks.' Of course, we can help with getting Sweeney known for its Indian heritage. Hold on a minute, I've got something to show you." He retreated into his trailer and returned with a large feathered headdress and a huge drum.

"When you folks have a rodeo or a fair or something, we can put on a hell of a show for you, dancing and drumming and wearing colorful costumes. We don't think our ancestors out on the plains here really did any of that stuff, but some Cheyennes we met at a powwow taught us some of their dances and sold us Indian gear, and, what the hell, most folks don't know the difference anyway."

"I suspect you're right," said Leland, who had noticed that Tom Binks was wearing a beaded bracelet and had a big feather stuck in the band of his gas company ball cap. "I hope that's not an eagle feather, Tom," Leland said, "because you can be fined for having one of those in your possession."

Binks looked sheepish. "Turkey vulture—but it's legal to have an eagle feather if you're Indian, which I am, and if it's for legitimate ceremonial purposes."

Leland eyed the feathers in Uncle Billy's headdress. "Turkey vulture," the man responded quickly. "We ain't got official recognition—yet—so we can't have eagle feathers either, but like I said, most folks can't tell the difference."

"Well, it's no business of mine anyway," said Leland, "and I'm very happy you're enjoying our little town. We don't have much here, but we are friendly."

"Just like us," beamed Uncle Billy.

Leland noticed Lee Harris frowning as they walked away.

"Is anything wrong?" Leland asked.

"Are you part-Indian too?"

Leland paused and then said, "I think I see what you mean. No, the only Indian thing in my line is the Mohawk haircuts I and some friends gave each other when we were kids—big mistake. I imagine you've met Indian wannabes before, and I imagine it can get pretty annoying. I apologize for all the 'I'm one-ten-thousandth Comanche' nonsense you're likely to hear. They're good people, but Sweeney doesn't give 'em much to build a romantic identity upon. If you were Scottish, they'd all be wearing kilts and saying they were Campbells and McLeods."

Harris chuckled. "Actually, I'm not really so much annoyed at them—it's a compliment, in a way—as I am at Uncle Billy and a few others like him. It's one thing to be proud of your Indian heritage, it's another to turn it into a circus sideshow. The drum, the headdress, all the other costumes and paraphernalia—they don't have anything to do with genuine Cocoye traditions, they're just movie props. It's embarrassing sometimes. And it gets in the way of people understanding who Indians really were, and are. But we're stuck with these characters, just as you are with yours. I am glad, though, to hear that you don't claim any Indian blood."

"Not a drop. Now, Trixie here. . . ."

Leland was just about to leave when he noticed Jim Biddle strolling around the encampment. Turning to Harris and motioning to Uncle Billy, Leland said, "I want you to meet this guy. I think you'll be interested in his ranching."

After introductions Leland said, "Jim here has a herd of buffalo out on his ranch."

"It started out as just a hobby," explained Biddle, "but ever since Sweeney started getting attention I've been selling quite a bit of the meat to the Chick 'n' More. The meat's delicious—lean, tender—but I guess I don't have to tell you guys how great buffalo meat is."

Harris laughed uneasily, then said, "You know, it's been, . . . oh, say, a few years since we've eaten buffalo meat—it's not a big item in the LA supermarkets. We can hardly remember what it tastes like."

"Oh, it's good, real good," said Biddle. "Of course, buffalo aren't cows, they're wild animals. You don't round them up and ship them off to the stockyard. At my ranch I hunt them, but even with a rifle they can be a challenge. I've got to admire how you Indians were able to do it with just bows and arrows and spears."

"And for centuries we did it without horses," said Binks, who had followed Uncle Billy. Biddle looked at him in bafflement.

Harris rescued the situation. "We didn't really have a choice. The buffalo were pretty much all there was out on the plains. You can't make much of a tent out of prairie dog skins. We even depended on the buffalo to keep warm, and I don't mean just their hides. It's been a long time since any Cocoye sat around roasting jackrabbit s'mores over an aromatic buffalo chip campfire."

Biddle thought a minute, then turned to Leland. "You going to be at the Chick 'n' More later? I've got something I want to talk over with you."

"I think the tall one is kind of cute," said Heather as the girls settled into the shrinking puddle of late-morning shade behind the Rock. Nearby a couple of Cocoye boys had to settle for the lesser shade of one of the smaller rocks as they arrived to eat a snack. In the distance Flicka and her goat-friend grazed contently on the prairie grass.

"Some of them don't look much like Indians, at least not as I expect Indians to look," said Kimberly. "The tall one kind of looks like Keener."

"I wonder if any of them have ever ridden a horse," said Christie. "I could teach them. I'd be good at it, I could connect with them, because I'm part Indian myself."

The girls goggled at the stunningly Nordic Christie, who answered their astonished stares by saying defensively, "My mom says one of our ancestors took an Indian wife when he arrived in Minnesota from Norway. Traci, I think your mom's horse there might be descended from an Indian pony. I've got an eye for such things." Traci pointedly ignored the comment.

Rachel said, "According to the laws of genetics, recessive genes—"

"Wouldn't it be cool if they went to school here?" interrupted Kimberly.

"My father says there's no reason why they can't; there's nothing keeping them in Los Angeles," said Heather. "Imagine, actually wanting to leave California to come to Dweeby!"

"We'd have to change the school's mascot from the Sweeney Cowboys to the Sweeney Cowboys and Indians," said Heather. Christie and

Kimberly laughed, as did Rachel, though it was fairly clear she didn't really get the joke.

Traci, who had been uncharacteristically silent, rolled her eyes, then attempted to change the subject: "Listen, guys, I've got great news."

"What, you'll be living next door to Paris Hilton in Santa Fe?" Kimberly sniped.

Traci glowered at her, then continued. "You know the photos I've taken of Sweeney and that Rachel put up on the Sweeney website. Well, the photo editor at *New Mexico Magazine* noticed them and has asked permission to use one in a spread they're doing about the eastern plains. I'll get a credit line. How cool is that?"

The girls were decidedly reserved in their reaction to Traci's news.

Traci continued, "The photo editor said, and I quote, 'You have a rare sensitivity to an area of the state that most people don't bother to notice. Anyone can take a picture of Santa Fe, but it takes a photographer with special talent to create good images in a place like Sweeney.'"

"Did you tell him you keep your Sweeney photos in a file called Dweeby?" Kimberly asked.

Traci forced a laugh.

Kimberly continued, "Has your mother heard anything from the dollhouse company?"

"Dollhouse company?"

Kimberly explained.

"You and my mom are going to be building dollhouses together?" Traci asked incredulously.

"Well, yeah," retorted Kimberly. "I happen to think your mom's cool, and there's nothing wrong with building dollhouses. I heard that lots of celebrities are into dollhouses." It was an obvious and unnecessary lie.

"I've *never* had a dollhouse," whimpered Rachel.

"Well, I bet Traci's mom would let you join us," said Kimberly, grasping for an ally, even if it was Rachel.

Traci began a sulk. Not only was her photographic achievement underrecognized, but it was upstaged by dollhouses—and with the connivance of her own mother, dammit! Well, it wasn't her fault if they were just a bunch of dweeby hicks whose idea of fun was hanging out at stupid old rocks and talking about—dollhouses. Someday she'd send them postcards from New York or London or Paris. Or better still, they'd see her photos in a magazine—and it wouldn't be *Dollhouse World.*

No one noticed Rachel glancing back and forth between her watch and the Rock's shadow, nor that when they all departed she took a twig and thrust it into the ground at the shadow's edge.

It was only two in the afternoon when Nettie went to the window of the Style Salon and reversed the sign reading "Open" to read "Closed." Her most recent customer had just left, and she had no one in her appointment book, though that meant little as most of her customers just stopped by and were more than content to wait if others were ahead of them. In fact, most preferred to wait. She then switched off the wire-cage fan that provided token cooling in the room. Standing on the sidewalk outside the building, she reeled from the heat radiating from the pavement, but instead of heading home for a much-needed rest, she began walking toward Magnolia Street and Iris Gerber's house.

All day Nettie had been unable to stop worrying about Harriet Moggs. The old woman had the durability of an Egyptian mummy, and she'd been a fixture in Nettie's world so long that Nettie had come to take Harriet's permanence for granted. Iris's news that Harriet appeared seriously ill required investigation. She wanted Iris to accompany her. She knew Iris would be home because *Lovers and Dreams*, a trashy TV soap opera to which Iris was severely addicted, would have ended about ten minutes ago.

So Nettie was surprised when her knock on Iris's door failed to evoke the usual gruff response. She knocked again, harder, and then again. No answer. She stood on the porch puzzled—and a little concerned. Of the few certainties in this changing world, among the most solid was Iris Gerber's devotion to her soap operas.

Nettie had just turned to leave when she saw Iris lumbering up the street. "Where've you been?" Nettie called out as the woman approached her home.

Iris paused on the front steps to catch her breath, fanning herself with her hands. "Down with the Indians." She paused. "I went down to check them out, and it turns out I have a lot in common with one of the tribal elders, a woman named Willa, in addition to both of us being Indians."

Iris? An Indian? Nettie's just shook her head. "So, what do you have in common?"

"Well, we both have the same taste in drama, such as *Lovers and Dreams*."

Drama? Since when was *Lovers and Dreams* "drama"? Ignoring this, she pressed on. "Iris, I've been very worried ever since you told me Harriet wasn't doing well, and I think we should check on her."

Iris pursed her lips into a cauliflower of concern. "You're right. I haven't seen her yet today. We should go see how she is."

So the two walked across the street and knocked at Harriet's front door. Hearing no response, they knocked again. On the third try they heard a feeble croak from within. Finally the door creaked open and Harriet stood there in a nightgown that seemed as old and worn as the house and its occupant. She looked terrible, her hair unkempt, her face shrunken.

"I'm sorry I took so long," she said weakly. "I was in bed. I haven't been feeling well. I don't know what's wrong. Come in. Would you like something cold to drink?"

"Sure," said Iris, "but I can get it, I know where things are. You just sit down."

Harriet shambled into the living room and collapsed into a maroon velvet chair that gave a small gasp of dust when sat upon. The curtains were drawn in the room, which resembled a nineteenth-century period display in an old-timer museum. Nettie gingerly sat on the couch opposite its chair counterpart. Iris soon appeared carrying three glasses of iced lemonade.

"Now, tell us what's been going on," she said as she plopped down next to Nettie, raising a dust cloud that made Nettie sneeze.

"I don't know, I just don't know. I've been feeling poorly for some time, but in the last few days it's gotten worse. I've been putting that crystal under my pillow every night, and I wear it every day." She tugged at a chain around her neck and withdrew the heavy amethyst the goddess had given her.

"Tell us exactly what you've been feeling," pressed Nettie.

"I've been sick to my stomach a lot, I can't keep food down, and I don't have any appetite."

"Hmm," said Nettie. "You need to see a doctor."

"Well, I think there'll be one at the clinic next week," Harriet said. Nettie noticed that she hadn't touched her lemonade.

"No, you need to see one tomorrow."

"How can I do that?"

"We'll call and make an appointment for you at the hospital in Tucumcari," said Iris.

"But how can I get there? You know I don't drive. I think I should wait and go to the clinic here when the doctor comes." She clearly was resisting going to Tucumcari.

"No, you're going tomorrow," said Iris in a tone that brooked no contradiction. Harriet cowered.

"Don't worry about transportation," said Nettie. "We'll take care of that."

Nettie and Iris walked in silence back to Iris's house. Iris flumped into her big overstuffed chair, while Nettie sat on the edge of the sofa nearby. Iris reached for an open bag of Cheetos and stuffed a handful in her mouth. Then she reached for the TV remote.

"No," barked Nettie, "don't turn that damned thing on. We've got to talk. Iris, the time has come to meet with Reverend Fall."

"Why me? I don't even go to his church."

"Because he's the only person we know who's going to Tucumcari tomorrow morning. He needs to take Harriet, and your presence will add weight to our request." Nettie instantly regretted her choice of words, but Iris seemed not to have noticed.

"I thought you said he thinks Harriet's a pagan, because of that goddess woman, and he wants her out of the church."

"I did hear him say words to that effect, but the time has come for him to grow out of that and start being a true Christian. I'll stop by for you around eight."

"But that funny game show will be on then."

"Iris, Harriet is more important than any damned game show. I'll be by at eight."

"Jimmy, will you get that?" came Roger's voice as the bell above the front door of the All Creatures Veterinary Clinic sounded.

Kathy tentatively closed the door behind her as she entered the clinic. She'd forgotten about the bell and would have preferred a less conspicuous entrance. She didn't know exactly why she'd come. She knew it had something to do with Roger, but she wasn't sure what, though lately she'd found herself enjoying his irreverent humor. Or maybe she just needed a friend her own age. She tried to recall the last one she'd had and realized it probably was in college.

"Hi, Jimmy," Kathy said to the older man who emerged from the swinging door behind the front desk. "Tell Roger I came to see him, and if this isn't a good time, I can come back later."

Before Jimmy could answer, Roger poked his head out. "Kathy," he said with surprise. "I hope nothing's wrong with Rasta?" he said, puzzled. Kathy had never just stopped by the clinic before.

"Are you kidding? A tornado wouldn't harm that cat. Lindsey Scruggs, the mid-school girl, is at home with Mom and Dad, giving me a break, so I took a walk. After all, it wasn't like I could go to the art museum, or watch people at the mall."

"Welcome, by all means, welcome. Come on back, I'm in the middle of something that won't take a minute, then I'll show you around."

Leaving Jimmy at the front desk, Roger led Kathy into a large room that smelled of disinfectant and animals. Along one wall were stacked cages holding dogs, while along another wall were cages with cats. Other cages scattered around held other animals—rabbits, birds, and rodents of various species. Inside a glass terrarium a large lizard lay motionless.

On an operating table a large yellow dog lay sedated, with one of his front paws grotesquely swollen, his fur stained with blood and disinfectant. Kathy recalled having seen him around town.

"What's wrong with him?"

"Bipolar."

"What?"

"Yep, he cycles back and forth between stupid and brain-dead. Actually, he got tangled in old barbed wire, foot became infected. He doesn't really belong to anyone, but Fred Yoder puts food out for him, and he noticed the problem and brought him in."

Roger then introduced Kathy to the other animals. "Now this rabbit here belongs to the Jenkins family, over on Tulip Street. Ate something he shouldn't have."

"And the lizard?"

"Joe Garcia brought him in because he thought the scaly fellow was lethargic, not understanding that being lethargic is what lizards aspire to."

"Do all these animals have owners?" she asked, pointing to the cages.

"Yes, they do," Roger said with uncharacteristic seriousness, "but some of the owners just don't know it yet."

Kathy recalled Rasta and how Roger had foisted him on her.

"You find homes for all of them?"

"Almost all. I don't euthanize any of them just because they're homeless, only the ones in pain and suffering." Then to change the subject he said, "How are your folks doing?"

"They're okay. Dad seems to be getting most of his functions back, though he has a hard time speaking and getting around. Mom does what she can. Having to care for Dad actually has been good for her, given her something worthwhile to do. She walked down to the Baca Mart the other day to get him snacks that he likes. But she's frail."

"And you?"

"I'm getting by. High Plains Mental Health has been good about giving me a leave of absence to sort things out."

"Mmmm," said Roger, as he lifted the yellow dog off the table. "Say, could you open the door to that cage over there?"

Kathy held the door open as Roger gently put the dog onto a blanket. Then he scooped dry dog food into a bowl and filled another bowl with water.

"Have you succeeded in doing that, sorting things out?"

"Not really. Actually, not at all, but I don't have to make any decisions immediately. I'm very good at not making decisions. And speaking of that, have you made a decision about being the rodeo clown in Logan?"

"I have. Let me show you something."

He led Kathy into a nearby room. There on the floor, squirming on a blanket and lapping at a bowl of milk, were three puppies.

"Their mother was a stray, down near Clines Corners, got hit by a car. Waitress at the truck stop found these puppies out back and brought them here."

"Very kind of her, and you, but what does this have to do with the rodeo?"

"No one can give away puppies to kids like a rodeo clown."

They chatted as Roger showed her the other animals. "This cat here has a thyroid tumor. It could be cured with a very expensive radiation treatment in Albuquerque, but her owners can't afford it, so we're trying medication instead. This dog was hit out on the highway. No one's bothered to claim him. He's got liver damage, not likely to survive. Just trying to make him comfortable." Each animal had a story, usually a sad one. Animals abandoned, animals too old to go on living but with owners unwilling to let go. Animals with terminal diseases or injuries beyond healing.

After leaving the clinic, Kathy needed just to walk—and think. Roger and the animals. How did he cope with such suffering every day? Was this why he so persistently clung to the adolescent humor that often alienated people? He wasn't trying to make them laugh, he was trying to make himself laugh.

And was her job with High Plains Mental Health so much different? Trying to help mend broken lives? And how did she cope?

As she left the clinic, Roger half-jokingly had again tried to foist an unwanted cat on her. "Miss Kitty. She's tough, but she's got a sweet disposition. Definitely a quality cat. I just know she and Rasta would get along."

Knowing Rasta as she did Kathy knew better, but for the first time she was tempted.

When Helen brought Leland his late afternoon burger and coffee at the Chick 'n' More, he noticed she was wearing a beaded bracelet and a silver pendant inset with a piece of turquoise. Beneath her apron she wore a colorful ribbon shirt.

"Nice," he complimented. "I notice there seems to be a theme."

"Well, yes," said Helen curtly. "I've had these at home all these years but haven't worn them, because I didn't know whether I'd be accepted, but having these other Indians in town has given me the courage to 'come out.'"

Leland blanched. Was Helen a Choctaw lesbian?

Seeing the expression on his face, Helen quickly said, "No, I'm not one of 'those.' I mean, you don't know who's a racist and who's not. And I've learned things. Did you know that both Ed and Edna have Indian blood?"

Before answering Leland pondered the implications of the word "those" and wondered if Sweeney could indeed be home to a lesbian or two. Then he answered, "No, I didn't, but somehow I'm not surprised."

Helen gave him a puzzled look and continued. "Edna says someone in her family has papers that trace them back to Chief Oshkosh up in Wisconsin. And Ed, he says he's certain there's Mohican somewhere in his past."

"The last of the Mohicans, here in Sweeney," said Leland.

"Well, why not?" bridled Helen. "This is a big country, with a long history; there's been a lot of mixing going on."

"I meant no offense. There has indeed been a lot of mixing, and tolerance is a good thing."

Somewhat mollified, Helen left for the kitchen just as Jim Biddle came in and hoisted himself onto a seat next to Leland. Without waiting, he said, "Look, having these Indians here has set me to thinking."

"I know, you're Sitting Bull's great-grandson."

"Huh?"

"Never mind, bad joke. Seems like everyone's turning Indian lately. What's on your mind?"

Biddle motioned to Helen for a cup of coffee and said, "I think the town should throw a barbecue for the Indians while they're here." Leland raised his eyebrows in interest. Biddle continued, "I'll donate the meat, buffalo meat. I'll even bring in a few animals so folks can see them. We could have the barbecue out near the Rocks. Hell, if we can throw a rodeo for a bunch of nudists, we can throw a barbecue for these fine folks."

Helen, who had been listening, as always, said as she brought Biddle his coffee, "I think that's a great idea. I'm sure Ed and Edna would contribute."

"How about this Sunday? We could pull it together by then," said Biddle.

"Yes, I think we could," said Leland. He heard Helen talking to Ed and Edna in the kitchen. "In fact, I suspect the chuck wagon's already rolling."

Leland and Biddle discussed plans for a few minutes. Then Biddle finished his coffee and got up to leave. "Lots to do between now and then."

As he started out the door he turned to Leland and said, "What you said about me being related to Sitting Bull would have been impossible. He was Sioux, and my ancestors were Pawnees."

A long day, thought Leland. One more chore before he and Trixie could head back to the ranch and watch the sunset together. With Trixie beside him, Leland drove down Main Street to Rudd's garage. Sweeney had only one barbecue grill large enough for what was shaping up as the largest public barbecue in the town's history. The grill was a huge, wrought-iron contraption that looked like an artifact from the early Industrial Revolution, and while it technically did not belong to Rudd— no one knew who owned it—it was stored behind Rudd's garage, where it waited patiently with other seldom-used heavy equipment.

"I think a barbecue for the Indians is a great idea," said Rudd as he raised his head from the bowels of a backhoe. "Want some coffee?"

Leland knew better. "No thanks," he said as he watched Rudd wipe his hands on a red rag and pour himself a cup. Toward the back of the garage, Leland noticed a broom being pushed by a man he once would have taken for S&S. "Afternoon . . . uh, Edward."

"Howdy doo," cawed the scrawny man, who despite being covered in dirt and grease nonetheless looked more presentable than Leland had ever before seen him. Edward continued pushing the broom with uncommon industry.

"Yeah, I think a barbecue's just the thing," continued Rudd. "I'll load the grill onto a trailer and haul it over to the rocks tomorrow morning."

"I can swing by and give you a hand," said Leland.

"Won't be necessary, Edward can help."

Leland reflected that just a short time ago no one in their right mind, least of all Rudd, would have let S&S—Edward—within ten feet of heavy equipment.

"Actually, I kind of like the Indians, the little I've seen of them," Rudd continued. "One of them stopped by this morning to see about getting a broken trailer hitch welded."

The idea of Rudd admitting to liking anyone seemed to Leland almost as strange as S&S's transformation. "I hope you're not going to tell me you're part Indian too," Leland said. "Everyone else in this town seems to have suddenly discovered that they have Indians in their background."

"You mean like Tonto Binks?" Rudd stopped working and bellowed a huge laugh. "Nah, there ain't Indians in the Torgelson line." He paused. "We're Eskimos."

Leland's mouth dropped and then formed a sheepish grin as he realized that Rudd had pulled his leg. Imagine, Rudd Torgelson, joking. It seemed the current strangeness in Sweeney had no bottom.

As he started to leave, Leland turned back to Rudd and said, "Oh, there was one other thing I stopped by to mention. I had Rachel Rowe do a title search of the land with Indian Rocks, to see who actually owns them. That kid's a whiz, because she found out that the last owner was a guy named Morgan, who, it appears, was a Torgelson relative. I guess that makes you the owner."

"Well, not exactly," replied Rudd.

"What do you mean?"

"Leland, I think you'd better sit down."

The first, brightest stars had appeared in the sky when Nettie, Iris, and a couple of elderly women who belonged to Reverend Fall's church approached his home on Mimosa Street. Nettie tried hard not to be distracted by the vivid orange Cheeto stains around Iris's mouth. Tonight could be pivotal, and she needed all her concentration. Though she didn't like to admit it, she was apprehensive about confronting Fall. He was, after all, their minister. Moreover, lately he was borderline psychotic. She tried to recall what he'd been like when he first came to town. He'd always been a strict Bible-quoting fundamentalist, but then his congregation expected nothing else, and he and his family fit well into the community. Everyone liked June and the kids, and if Wayne could be a little self-righteous at times, he took his Christian calling very seriously. Perhaps that could bring him back from the pit of fanaticism.

June answered the door. Behind her, in the kitchen, Wayne stood puzzled. A covert glance of understanding passed between June and Nettie as June said, "My, what a pleasant surprise. Please come in." Nettie had called ahead.

June led them into the home's living room. When they all were seated, Nettie looked at Fall firmly and said, "Reverend, we're here to talk about Jesus."

Fall's face lit up. "Oh, that's wonderful. Just a minute, I'll go get my Bible, and it'll help me answer any questions you have. I'm always happy to bring the message of Jesus to souls who are seeking him."

"No, don't get your Bible, and we're not here to ask questions or seek your advice. We're here to give it." The other women sat stolidly as Nettie spoke.

Bewilderment replaced the eagerness on Reverend Fall's face.

"Reverend, how did Jesus spend his time?"

"What do you mean?"

"When Jesus got up in the morning, after he went to the bathroom, brushed his teeth, combed his hair, put his robes on, fed the cat, and ate breakfast, what did he set out to do during the day?"

Fall hesitated, grappling with the image of the Son of God taking a piss and brushing his teeth. Finally he said, with dignity, "Why, he went about preaching, spreading God's word."

"And what else did he do?"

"I'm not sure I know what you mean."

"Okay, we'll get right to it. He went about practicing what he preached—doing good, healing the sick, comforting the afflicted, ministering to society's outcasts, making himself an example of how God wants us to be, demonstrating love and compassion and forgiveness."

Fall's puzzlement deepened.

"Reverend, what we're trying to say is that there's more to being a Christian than quoting scripture. Any TV preacher can do that, and we know how much they're worth." Fall's face darkened. He wasn't sure he liked where this was going. Nettie continued.

"Jesus talked about caring for his flock, about being the good shepherd. Well, we're your flock, but frankly we don't feel you've been the best shepherd lately."

Fall looked stricken. This was not at all what he'd expected. "But I've tried as hard as I can to protect this town from Satan. As it says in the Book of Revelation—"

"Gosh darn it all, that's exactly what I'm driving at. Jesus asked people to look into their hearts. You've gotten so hung up on what certain parts of the Bible say that you've forgotten what Jesus said. And more importantly, what he did.

"You've turned into a fanatic. Your rantings and ravings are turning people away from the church. That's why we're here."

Fall bridled. "I don't have to listen to this. I'm your minister."

"Not for long, not if you don't wake up and mend your ways. We're here to tell you that unless you start being a real Christian and stop being a community nuisance, we the church elders will find us a new minister." Actually, Nettie hadn't discussed this with anyone in the church and was taking a huge risk, but she was encouraged by the continued silence of the two other church members with her.

Fall turned white. Nettie continued.

"There's people in the church who need love and compassion, who need ministering in a true Christian way. People who are sick and afraid and lonely, but you're so obsessed with that stupid Rock that you don't get around to visiting them anymore."

"But that Rock is where God's angel appeared."

Before Nettie could respond Iris wiped her mouth with her sleeve and spoke. "Reverend, people have tried to tell you: That was no angel sent by God. It was a high school kid playing a trick on people."

Fall looked at Nettie desperately.

"I'm sorry, Reverend, it's true. I didn't want to tell you at the time, because I didn't think you were in any shape to take it. That was wrong. But now I'm here to tell you it wasn't an angel. It was Rachel Rowe, and if you need more proof, we'll get her to come here and tell you herself."

Outrage, betrayal, and denial contorted Fall's face. He cast a pathetic look of appeal to June.

"Wayne, it's true," she said as she went and stood beside him, taking his hand gently in hers. "It's all true. They're right, Wayne. You need to listen to them, they're your friends, your real friends. There are people in the church who miss you, who need you, the real you." She glanced at Nettie, who glanced back.

Fall sagged in confusion. Where was Pastor Pete when he needed him? "Like who?" he finally asked.

"Like Harriet Moggs," said Iris. "Poor Harriet's got something wrong with her, seriously wrong, and she needs to go to the clinic in Tucumcari, and since you have to go there for work, you could take her."

"What's wrong with her?" Fall asked, genuine concern in his voice. Nettie found that reassuring.

"We don't know—but it's serious, whatever it is. She needs to be seen by a doctor. Tomorrow. I've made an appointment at the hospital."

"I wonder if it could have anything to do with her adoption of paganism at the solstice, a kind of retribution."

"No, it couldn't," stated Nettie. "God doesn't go around punishing decent people just because they get old and goofy, at least not the Christian God I believe in."

"Wayne, Harriet needs you," said June gently. "She's a member of your congregation, and she needs you to take her for help tomorrow."

"Well, of course I'll take her," stated Fall. "Can you get her ready to leave by six?"

"Swing by her house at six, and we'll have her ready," said Nettie. "And Reverend, pray that there's a lot of healing for all of us in this."

Chapter Fifteen

⬥ THE EARLY MORNING AIR WAS COOL AND FRESH when Wayne Fall arrived at Harriet Moggs's house, but his disposition was hot and sour. He hadn't recovered from the indignity inflicted upon him by Nettie and the others last night. The last people he wanted to see this morning were Nettie and Iris, yet there they were waiting on Harriet's front porch, their arms around the old woman, supporting her, while from the blanket wrapped around her she stared with confused, fearful eyes.

"Now, don't you worry about a thing," Nettie told Harriet, as Iris did a final check of Harriet's cloth travel bag. Then they helped Harriet down the steps and maneuvered her toward Wayne's Ford Fiesta. They greeted Wayne pleasantly; he glowered at them. How could they expect more? In silence the three helped Harriet into the car's front seat.

"Give me a call when she gets home," Nettie said to Wayne as he went around to the driver's side. "I want to hear what the doctor had to say." Wayne just nodded curtly.

As they drove out of town Wayne glanced at Harriet, who stared silently ahead. "Are you okay?" he asked. She merely nodded feebly. Wayne didn't know what to do or say. Though she was a longtime member of his congregation, she existed in his consciousness as just someone in the pews. He didn't really know her.

She continued sitting in stolid silence as they drove across the plains. That was okay with Wayne, as he was in no mood for conversation. He and June had had an ugly fight last night after Nettie and the others left, perhaps the only real fight in their entire marriage. She'd started it by siding with Nettie and the church members—and Iris. Iris, who wasn't even a member of the church—who was she to come into his home and talk about religion to him?

Who were any of them, for that matter?

And then the revelation about the Rock. . . . He was embarrassed, humiliated. June had known the figure wasn't an angel, they'd all known it, and yet they'd let him run around making a fool of himself.

Last night, when he'd attempted to quote scripture to June, she'd rebuked him, saying she could quote scripture too but that she was tired of scripture-quoting ruining their marriage.

He'd been shocked when she said their children didn't like returning home because of him. What was wrong? Hadn't he raised them in a proper Christian environment?

He'd been staggered when she implied that she was considering leaving him to move closer to them. Finally, and in deliberate defiance of all the righteousness he'd attempted to achieve in their home, she had stalked over to the piano and played an Elvis Presley song, "Heartbreak Hotel." When he protested, she'd simply ignored him.

As he drove he tried reminding himself that the early Christians also had suffered scorn while walking the path of righteousness, but he was disappointed that he wasn't able to wring more martyrdom from "Heartbreak Hotel."

Nine in the morning. Still pleasant, still about an hour before the tidal wave of High Plains summer heat swept ashore in Sweeney. Walking briskly, Roger turned the corner onto Honeysuckle Street and then slowed as he approached the Larkin home. If Kathy could drop in on the clinic, he could drop in on her. She was sitting on the home's front steps, a coffee cup beside her.

"Hi," he called as he turned onto the sidewalk toward the house. "I just happened to be passing by and thought I'd stop to say hello."

"Do you always walk around town with a plate of cookies in your hand? You don't have Miss Kitty concealed in there, do you?"

"I'm shocked that you could think such a thing. I just thought I might happen to be near here, so I brought something. For your parents. And for you." He handed her a plate covered with clear plastic wrap. "I baked these myself this morning."

"Touching," Kathy said as she accepted the plate, took a cookie, and bit into it. Holding it up, she said, "Very good. Remarkable, that you and Keebler have the same recipe."

Roger just grinned.

Kathy got up and took the cookies inside, then quickly returned, followed by a woman Roger hadn't seen before. She was middle-aged, with long, black hair in braids; she wore blue jeans and a blue, short-sleeved blouse.

"Roger, I'd like you to meet Jenny Wilson. She's with the encampment down at the RV park. I met her there yesterday, after I talked with you. She's a nurse, and when I told her about Mom and Dad, she offered to come by this morning and be with them while I ran a few errands."

Roger shook the woman's hand. "That's very kind of you, very neighborly. I'd offer to help, but I'm afraid I'd just toss her parents a dog biscuit if they got hungry."

"Roger's our local vet," Kathy explained. "He's also a widely acclaimed rodeo clown."

"Actually," said Jenny, "minding your folks is a good chance for me to get a little peace and quiet. All the kids and dogs down there at the RV park are bad enough, but that damned Uncle Billy hauled out that big drum of his, and he's been beating it for anyone who stops by."

Kathy finished her coffee, set the cup down on the step, then turned to Roger. "I've got to walk over to the Baca Mart and get a few things. Want to come along?"

"Sure, seeing as how I was just out ambling about anyway."

"I won't be gone long," she said to Jenny. "Help yourself to the cookies. Roger baked them himself—with a little help from the Keebler company."

Jenny smiled knowingly. "Take your time. I'm in no hurry to go anywhere."

"So," said Kathy as they strolled down Main Street, "you're committed to being rodeo clown when I announce at the rodeo down in Logan?"

"Yep, I am indeed," said Roger. "Those puppies need homes."

"Noble of you."

"You're going, I assume?"

"Yes. I did have a lot of fun announcing at the rodeo here, and I can use the money right now. Of course, I don't expect the Logan rodeo to have the same . . . the same special quality of our rodeo here, not unless Bare-assed Bob has decided to turn pro and hit the rodeo circuit, but it still should be fun."

Sweeney had not yet fully awakened as they turned onto Main Street. Only one vehicle was moving, Leland's pickup heading toward the town offices, though three vehicles, all familiar, were parked in front of the Chick 'n' More. As Roger and Kathy approached the boarded-up front of the Metropolitan movie theater, Kathy stopped.

"I wonder if there are still movie posters behind those boards," she said. Then with a trace of melancholy she continued, "My parents have told me that going to the movies here on Saturday night was the biggest event of the week in Sweeney. People would drive in from all over, do their shopping, and go to the movies. Kids would go to the matinee. There would be a cartoon, a newsreel, then the main feature, which usually would be some B western. I don't know why I'm telling you this, you know it as well as I do, and besides, the Metro was pretty much on its way out by our time. It really wasn't part of our growing up."

Roger nodded. "I was pretty small when the 'last picture show' occurred, but I still have a few memories. The popcorn, the jujubes. Those two kept the town dentist in business. When Sweeney had a town dentist. I can't remember the movies, but I loved the cartoons. For me as a kid the big thing was to go to a neighbor's house and watch television—until our family got its own set."

Kathy reached out and touched one of the weathered boards, like touching the glass frame of an antique family portrait, as if trying to establish a connection with what was forever unreachable. "Was it television that killed the Metro? Or that people didn't come here for shopping anymore? Or both?"

"Both. It couldn't have been the quality of the entertainment. One of my last memories of the Metro was getting up after the movie and realizing I couldn't move because the soles of my shoes were stuck to the floor by dried spilled soda. You just don't get those experiences watching TV at home."

He paused, then continued, "Actually, it was a lot of things, like paving the roads."

Kathy looked at him, puzzled. "What did paving roads have to do with the Metro?"

"Before the roads were paved in the 1960s, it was a long, tough drive to go to Tucumcari or Las Vegas for shopping, so folks came to Sweeney instead. When the roads were paved, downtown Sweeney started its decline. TV had brought the Metro to the edge of the pit, and the paved roads kicked it in."

"Paving the roads," said Kathy, shaking her head. "I remember my parents talking about how excited everyone was when it happened. They never dreamed it would be a nail driven into the coffin of our little town."

"No one did. The law of unintended consequences. But who knows, maybe the same law can pull the nail out."

Kathy walked up to the ticket booth, where dust and trash and tumbleweeds waited patiently. "What was the last movie that played here? Do you remember?"

"Actually, I do. It was *Planet of the Apes*. Appropriate, somehow."

Their reminiscences were interrupted by someone striding down the sidewalk toward them. He carried a brown paper bag and walked with the gait of an ostrich. He wore dark-green work pants and a matching shirt. His hair was firmly plastered to his scalp with what could have been axle grease.

"Howdy-doo," the man crowed as he approached. "Mighty fine morning."

"Morning, Edward," Roger answered. "It is indeed a fine morning."

"I been down to the Baca Mart, runnin' errands for my cousin, can't stop to chat, gotta get back." And with that he strode off.

Roger and Kathy stared at each other. Finally Roger said, "I guess you heard that 'Edward' turned out to be Rudd's cousin."

Kathy nodded. "That explained a lot. It seems to have improved both of them."

"Yep, from scroungy and hopeless to self-respecting and with a future, all in a relatively short time. Kind of like Sweeney itself."

"I like to think that Sweeney before the Rock was in a little better shape than S&S, but your point is well taken."

"There's an example," said Roger, nodding toward a shiny, pale blue SUV driving through town. "Recognize that car?" Kathy shook her head. Roger continued, "Those people, whoever they might be, are likely headed to see the Rock. Before its erection—if you'll pardon the expression—Sweeney *never* had unfamiliar cars on Main Street."

"True, but the odd tourist is pretty thin soup for the town to survive on."

"You're right, but the main lesson of this whole thing is that we can't predict how this will eventually play out. What's important is that we got things moving."

Kathy nodded thoughtfully. "Well, if S&S can turn into Edward, I guess anything's possible."

They said little more as they strolled down Main Street, finally arriving at the Baca Mart. Only one vehicle was in the parking lot, an unfamiliar silver Dodge pickup that seemed curiously at home in the oil-stained parking lot. As they opened the store's aluminum-and-glass door, Roger noticed that Weeney Water was still prominently displayed for sale near the entrance. Inside they found Judy Baca behind the counter, in animated conversation with a large, elderly woman they didn't recognize. She had a bag of ice under one arm, a bag of chips under the other.

"Hi, Kathy, hi, Roger," said Judy. Then, nodding to the woman, said, "This here's Willa Cohen. She's with the Indians down at the RV park."

"Pleased to meet you," said Roger, seconded by Kathy.

"Atha-hle," the woman replied, quickly adding, "That's a traditional Cocoye greeting."

"We were talking about native languages," offered Judy. "Willa was saying that the Cocoye language has survived all these years."

"It's true," said Willa. "I admit lots has been lost, but we Cocoye women can still chew out our husbands in our ancestral tongue."

"Impressive," said Roger. "Could you say something in your language? I'd like to hear it."

Looking pleased, Willa mouthed syllables that included grunts and other inflections missing in English.

"Thanks," said Roger. "What did you say?"

"I said I've got to get out of here if I don't want to miss my TV program." With that she said good-bye and left the store for the pickup parked outside.

After she was gone, while Kathy was getting milk and coffee and other groceries, Judy said to Roger, "I was telling her that the native language of Adelino and me is still alive too."

"Spanish isn't in any real danger of dying out," noted Roger.

Judy gave Roger a scathing look. "I didn't mean Spanish, I meant Nahuatl. The language of the Aztecs. It's still spoken down in Mexico, and while we don't know the details, there's no doubt that Adelino and I have Aztec blood."

Roger looked at her wide-eyed and said, "I'm sure you do, I'm sure you do."

Jenny Wilson was seated on a chair on the front porch of the Larkin home when Roger and Kathy returned. On other chairs beside her were Kathy's mother and father. "I was reading to them," said Jenny as she held up a book. It was *Harry Potter and the Sorcerer's Stone.* "Old folks like to be read to, same as kids."

Kathy's father didn't say anything, but her mother said, "That Hogwarts sounds like a nice place. Do we have Muggles here in Sweeney, Kathy?"

"Yes, Mother, we most certainly do."

As Jenny gathered her belongings and prepared to leave, she said, "I can drop by tomorrow too. Maybe we can take your folks to the barbecue. They'd like that."

Roger said to Kathy, "Actually, I was going to ask if you'd like to help me with the Rotary coffee table tomorrow. Like at the solstice. Seeing as how we're rodeo partners and all. Your parents could sit right by us. They'd probably have a good time."

"Sounds like a good idea," said Kathy. "Seeing as how we're rodeo partners and all."

As Roger started down the sidewalk, Kathy called after him. "Oh, by the way, I heard that Sam Jamison has agreed to take those puppies to his ranch near San Jon."

On the High Plains in August, one often told time by the height of the cumulus clouds that piled up in the sky most afternoons. It was monsoon season, when moist air from the Gulf of Mexico flowed northward, to be caught by hot air rising from the surface and driven upward, where condensation created massive cotton-candy formations, towering a mile high or more. Then, usually late in the afternoon, the weight of the condensing moisture all came crashing down in a cloudburst, if one was lucky, or a hailstorm, if one was not.

A couple of such midafternoon cloud formations were building to the east of Sweeney as Leland and other townspeople were finishing fencing off an area about fifty yards from the Rock. Leland noticed that Lee Harris and a couple of other Indian men had come over to help.

"Double strand it!" yelled Jim Biddle, who was supervising the construction. "Hell, triple strand it!" he yelled to the men who were stringing wire between fence posts sunk into the ground. "These ain't cows. Buffalo would as soon walk through a fence as sneeze at it."

Leland took a section of wire and secured it with a U-nail, then wrapped it around the post and secured it again. As he worked, his mind kept returning to the same thoughts. So S&S owns all this. Who in hell would have . . . I suppose we should have asked him if we could do this on . . . on his land. But Rudd said the old buzzard doesn't know he owns it, and his mind is in no shape to be burdened with such responsibilities, at least not yet. I know what Rudd means. I can't even get used to the idea of S&S having a mind.

"Snug 'em up!" yelled Biddle as the last strands of wire were strung into place. "I'll bring the animals first thing in the morning. No sense in getting them more stressed than is necessary. Buffalo don't handle stress very well."

Apparently S&S doesn't either, thought Leland, but then, neither do I.

He wandered off to see how the other preparations were going. Closer to the Rock, six men—two workers and four supervisors—were preparing the horseshoe pits. You can't have an outdoor barbecue without horseshoes.

Nearby, Rudd and Edward and other men, as well as supervisors, were muscling the huge, smoke-blackened barbecue grill from the back of a flatbed truck. You could barbecue an elephant on that damned grill, Leland observed. Maybe the town got it from a circus.

Still closer to the Rock, Judy and Adelino Baca were setting up their snack-and-souvenir tent. Leland noticed a rack proudly displaying Sweeney Weeney Water. Nearby hung T-shirts and ball caps, with Sweeney slogans on them. A few, he saw, had what seemed to be a crude representation of an Aztec stone calendar. What the hell is that all about?

At another tent several church members were putting out crafts for sale. Duck-shaped wooden weather vanes whose wings twirled in the wind. Framed pieces of embroidery reading "God Bless This Home." A paint-by-numbers portrait of a sad clown. Knit caps and mittens. Jars of jams and preserves. Tomorrow the plates of cookies and brownies and Rice Krispies bars would appear.

Next to the church tent was a huge canvas awning supported by aluminum poles; beneath were folding chairs and tables in no particular arrangement. Taped to one of the poles was a crude sign reading "Free shade." Set up to greet visitors was the Rotary Club's hospitality table with its coffee urn. Cups and coffee fixings would arrive in the morning, but Connie Nesbitt was taking no chances of missing early visitors; she'd already placed a stack of her real estate fliers on the table along with a sign saying "Take one."

Leland also noticed a microphone on the table and a pair of speakers perched on empty oil drums nearby. "Kathy's doing the announcing," Leland heard Roger say as he appeared carrying what seemed to be a bag of lime.

"We need an announcer?" asked Leland.

"Well, of course. How else are people to know when the horseshoe toss-offs are about to begin. You've got to admit she's good," said Roger with conspicuous pride.

"She is that."

"Besides," Roger continued, "Ron Suffitt wants to say 'a few words,' and without an announcer to run interference he might talk all day. You might want to say something too."

"Actually, I just might. By the way, what's with the lime?"

"Oh, just a little project Jim Biddle and I talked about. Should be fun."

"What kind of project?"

"Oh, nothing much. You'll find out tomorrow. I don't want to say anything now, spoil the surprise." And with that Roger strode off toward the buffalo area.

Nothing much, repeated Leland as he watched Roger leave. Why is it that every time he says that I get an uneasy feeling?

The truck depot in Tucumcari where Wayne Fall worked was busy as usual, but by swallowing his pride and asking a favor of a fellow supervisor, Wayne was able to leave work a little early, giving him extra time to pick up Harriet Moggs at the hospital.

The hospital orderly who had received her in the morning had said the doctor would see her as soon as possible, and they would take good care of her until Wayne returned. As the orderly guided her inside, Harriet had turned and looked at Wayne, fear and desperation on her face. "Don't worry, Harriet," he'd said, "they'll take good care of you. I'll be back for you later."

Now he parked his little car as close to the hospital's entrance as possible. When he went inside, he looked for the orderly he'd met earlier. Not finding him, he asked at the desk. "I'm here for Harriet Moggs." The woman behind the desk started to sift through files. "Older woman, with orange hair."

"Oh, her," said the receptionist. "Just a moment, the doctor wants to talk to you."

That boded ill, thought Wayne, as he sat on a long bench and thumbed through a rack of reading material. He had just started an article in *Prevention* magazine about the healthful benefits of molybdenum supplements when a young man in a white coat appeared and introduced himself as Dr. Fields.

Sitting next to Wayne he said, "You're here for Ms. Moggs. Are you a relative?"

Wayne hesitated, then said, "She doesn't really have any relatives. I'm her pastor."

"Good. She needs someone right now. We'll have to do more tests, but I'm afraid preliminary results suggest a bleeding ulcer, which in someone her age is a very serious medical condition. I don't know how long she's had this, but it appears to have gone beyond the initial stage and into complications. These include perforations of the intestine, hemorrhaging, and severe anemia."

"Oh, dear," said Wayne. "What should we do?"

"As I said, we'll need to see the results of more tests, but we can begin an antibiotic treatment that will help with infection. I suggested that she remain in the hospital for observation, but she's very resistant to that idea. I can let her go home tonight, but only on the condition that she stay in bed, and most important, that she take the medications I'm going to prescribe. Then I want to see her again next week when the lab results are in."

Wayne was flustered. This was more than he'd bargained for.

"Can you do that?" asked the doctor. "Otherwise, she'll have to stay here."

Wayne faltered. Finally he said, "Yes, I can." He actually did not know whether he could or not. He'd need help.

Soon after the doctor left, an orderly appeared with Harriet in a wheelchair. She looked paler and more fearful than in the morning. The orderly wheeled her into the parking area and helped Wayne load her into the car. "We'll see you next week," the orderly said with hospital cheer to Harriet. She gave no indication that she heard or understood him.

As Wayne started the car, he glanced at Harriet. She looked ghastly, her skin sallow. She could only stare blankly ahead.

It was only after they left Tucumcari and were driving across the empty plains that she finally spoke. "I think I'm pretty sick," she said. "That doctor is a nice young man, but he said I'm pretty sick." Her voice quavered; she was terrified.

"Yes, you are," said Wayne. He searched for comforting words. "But don't you worry, you're in good hands, and you've got good friends. We'll pray for you."

"That would be nice," she said feebly, then lapsed into silence.

Wayne noted that it was time for Pastor Pete's Bible Hour of Power Prophecy. "Would you like to listen to something on the radio?"

Harriet nodded weakly.

He turned on the radio just as Pastor Pete was beginning his sermon. As usual, the topic was sin.

"Sin, my brethren, sin is the cause of all the world's ills, and true Christians don't care about secular opinions, we don't care about what's in the newspaper, and we sure don't care about what fancy atheistic scientists say. All we care about is what God says. If them scientists had been paying attention to the Bible, they would have found out a long time ago what Christians have known for two thousand years. What's that? It's that sin is real and Satan is real and that the only way to be rid of sin is through Our Lord Jesus Christ. Did he not cast out demons when he went into Capernaum, as scripture tells us in Mark 1:21–27? And did he not give his twelve apostles the power and authority over all demons and to cure diseases, sending them out to preach the Kingdom of God and to heal, as it says in Luke 9:1–2?"

"Do I have demons inside me, Reverend?" rasped Harriet in an alarmed semi-whisper, as Pastor Pete thundered on.

Wayne hesitated. Why couldn't Pastor Pete have preached about money-changers today?

He looked at Harriet, who sat looking at him. "I thought it might be something with my chakras," she said, "but it sounds like it could be demons—what have I done to have demons inside me? Do I have demons?"

Wayne paused to listen to Pastor Pete. "Yes, my brethren, as we approach the End Times, Satan and his minions will be more active. They will go about the land, and only those armed with the Holy Spirit will be able to resist their temptations and cast out the demons that will corrupt all that is flesh." Normally, Wayne would have been muttering "Amen" every few seconds, but today Pastor Pete's words seemed hollow. It was easy to preach against sin and to quote scripture while speaking into a radio microphone, but dealing with an actual person, a member of the congregation . . . What would Jesus do? Wasn't Pastor Pete speaking for Jesus?

"I've tried to be a good person," Harriet pleaded, waiting for an answer.

June's words from last night came to Wayne: "Harriet needs you." Anger flared as he recalled their argument. But then the anger dissipated as quickly as it had come, for the answer he sought had come not from June nor from Pastor Pete but from his own mouth. To the doctor in Tucumcari he had said, "I'm her pastor."

"No, Harriet, you don't have demons. God loves you." And with that he reached over and turned off Pastor Pete.

"Hello, Rachel, good to see you," Joanie lied as she stood in the open doorway of her home. It had been a tiring day, helping Dave prepare for tomorrow's barbecue, and she had just poured herself a glass of wine in preparation for relaxing on the porch.

"Who is it, Mom?" Traci called from within the house.

"It's Rachel."

Traci almost immediately appeared behind her mother in the doorway. "Hi, Rache, what's up?"

Rachel was nervous, awkward, even for her. "I . . . uh, I came to ask about dollhouses." She didn't look directly at either of them. "I've never had a dollhouse," she added, as if in explanation.

"Neither have I," said Traci with thick sarcasm.

Joanie shot her daughter a dirty look, then said to Rachel, "Why don't you two wait here, and I'll get a few of my dollhouses."

Traci looked at her mother, as if to say, "How did I get roped into this?" but Joanie already was retreating into the house.

"So, you never had a dollhouse?" asked Traci. Rachel, as expected, was oblivious to the sarcasm.

"No, I've never had a lot of things other girls had, never was interested in them. I was more interested in reading and experiments and figuring things out. I still am. But I think a dollhouse would be kind of fun. At least, I'd like to see. As an experiment. You could have had a dollhouse, but you didn't—why?"

Taken aback by the question's directness, Traci stammered, "I don't know . . . I guess . . . I just don't know." She couldn't say the candid answer: "I didn't want people to think I was a nerd."

At that moment Joanie reappeared, carrying a large dollhouse, the English manor one. She ducked back into the house and came out with another one, the Swiss Chalet. Then another, the Victorian haunted house.

"There, that's a pretty good sample." She briefly described each one.

"A haunted house!" gasped Rachel. Then she added with skepticism, "You don't really believe in ghosts, do you?"

"She does," inserted Traci. "When I was little, there was an abandoned house out east of town, and she told me not to go in it because it was haunted."

Joanie glared at Traci. "That was just to keep you from trespassing and getting hurt." Returning her attention to Rachel, she continued, "Dollhouses aren't about reality, they're about pretending, about make-believe."

"Make-believe," repeated Rachel, clearly struggling with the concept.

"A dollhouse can represent anything you want. See, here, in this upper room." Joanie pointed to a window in the Victorian dollhouse. "This is where she appears."

"Where who appears?" asked Traci.

"Epithelia, the ghost. More than a century ago she was killed in this room by Lady de Montfort. Epithelia was the rightful heir to the house, but Lady de Montfort, her aunt, was covetous and jealous, so one night she attacked Epithelia with a knife in this room. Epithelia didn't die immediately, and before she did, she crawled to a wall where she used her own blood to draw a curse circle. Look, you can see it."

Eyes wide, both Rachel and Traci peered into the room. There, on a wall, a tiny red circle was drawn.

"Wow!" gasped Rachel.

"What's a curse circle?" asked Traci before she could catch herself.

"A curse circle forbids entry to all against whom it is directed. Almost immediately, Lady de Montfort began to experience pain and horrible visions whenever she slept in the house. She had to abandon the house she so much desired. She died in an insane asylum.

"Ever since then, Epithelia has remained in her house, and sometimes she returns to this room. You can always tell she's been there by the veil she leaves behind." And again Joanie pointed into the room. On the floor was a tiny swatch of white silk.

"WOW!" Rachel exclaimed. Then a skeptical look came over her face. "You made all this up."

"Of course I did," said Joanie. "That's what dollhouses are all about. Epithelia and Lady de Montfort aren't the only ones to live in this house. There are lots of stories here. Bright, happy ones. See that ball on the first floor, in the living room? That was left by the Gypsy juggler who came to visit the Pepper twins. This house is filled with stories. I made them up whenever I came to play with this dollhouse, or I'd rework old stories."

Comprehension, followed by wonder, spread across Rachel's face. "You just made them up . . ."

Joanie nodded.

"Mom," said Traci, "I have to admit that was pretty cool."

Joanie smiled.

"Do all these dollhouses have stories in them?" Traci asked.

"They do. That's why I like to keep old dollhouses—and why it's fun to get a new dollhouse."

"Can I get a dollhouse, Mrs. Daly?" Rachel pleaded, almost desperately. "Please?"

"Of course you can, Rachel. We can order one—or you can build one. What style do you think you might like?"

Without hesitation Rachel replied, "A planetarium. A haunted planetarium."

Traci rolled her eyes.

"Well, Traci," Joanie asked her daughter, "if you were to get a dollhouse, what would you get?"

"Who says I'd even want an old dollhouse?"

"Okay, fine." Joanie turned her attention back to Rachel, who was looking hurt.

"Actually," interrupted Traci, "I think I would like a dollhouse. Don't think I'll get serious about them, but it might be kind of fun, to have one to mess around with, now and then, you know . . ."

Rachel brightened. "What kind would you get, Traci?"

"A rock star dollhouse, you know, where there'd be a special room for the drugs, a hot tub filled with champagne, a pool to swim naked in—"

"Traci!" exclaimed her mom. Rachel's eyes widened in shock.

"Relax, just kidding. Actually, an English castle dollhouse would be kind of cool."

They continued talking about dollhouses while Joanie sipped the rest of her wine. Then as daylight faded, headlights appeared at the end of the street. "Uh-oh," said Traci. "Here comes Dad. I promised him I'd clean the kitchen."

As she got up to go in the house, she paused and turned to her mom. "I don't think you should keep those dollhouses in the attic."

"Why not?"

"The people in them will get lonely." Then she strode into the house.

"I've got to go too, Mrs. Daly," said Rachel. "Thanks for letting me get a dollhouse."

As Rachel marched down the sidewalk, she passed Dave, who had parked his pickup on the street.

"Hi, Mr. Daly, we've been talking about dollhouses."

"Huh?" But Rachel didn't pause to explain.

Just as she reached the street, Rachel turned. "Oh, Mr. Daly, I need to tell you, the Rock is sagging, it's going to fall over."

"*What?*"

"I measured its shadow on two different days at the same time and then used the Pythagorean theorem to calculate the angles and distances. They're definitely changing."

And with that she ran down the street.

The evening air was softening as Traci walked along Mangrove Street toward the Rock, but she was troubled. Both her father and mother had seemed distracted during dinner. Traci had hoped they would talk about the move to Santa Fe, or more specifically, that one of them would say something that would resolve the ambivalence she felt, but she was hesitant to initiate the discussion, especially as she wasn't sure what she wanted to hear. She certainly didn't want to be put on the spot herself. She had begun to realize that her opinion might be pivotal. Dad would vote to stay in Sweeney, Mom to leave. She would decide. Or maybe not.

Maybe her parents didn't really care what she thought. She knew that wasn't true, but the imagined injustice made her feel better nonetheless. Whatever she decided, she had to announce it soon; her father had to let Santa Fe know about the job by Monday.

All summer the girls had gathered after supper at the Rock, to hang out and to discuss things and decide what to do, or more often, to complain about having nothing to discuss or do. Lately, the girls had noticed that they weren't the only ones meeting at the Rock. Most evenings a squadron of little kids on bicycles zipped around it. They had created a ramp at the edge of one of the holes and launched their bikes up and over. Little dorks, Traci thought. A couple of young mothers wheeled their baby carriages there in the evening. And a few old fuddy-duddies gathered to sit on folding chairs and talk about the Good Old Days. Crusty old cheeses. What a town, Traci thought, where the community gathering place was a rock shaped like a dick. She imagined the boardwalk in Venice, California, or maybe the Pearl Street Mall in Boulder— or the Plaza in Santa Fe. So why was she so ambivalent about leaving?

Traci could see the Rock ahead when Rachel came alongside her with that long, geeky stride of hers. "Hi, Rache," Traci said limply.

"Your mom's cool," Rachel burbled, trying to be cool herself.

"Yeah, well, she has her moments." Then, changing the subject, she asked, "What are you going to do after you graduate next year?"

"Go to college. The school counselor says that with my grades and interest in science, I can pretty much go where I want." It was characteristic of Rachel that she said this with no hint of boasting.

"So where do you want to go?"

"I don't know. My dad says it'll depend on who makes the best offer. He's mentioned places like Princeton and MIT and Stanford." Then she paused. "I'm scared, Traci. I don't want to leave Sweeney, but I know I have to."

"You don't want to get out of Dweeby?" gasped Traci. "Most of us can't wait."

"Yeah, I know, and you're going to Santa Fe next year. But I'm not like you. You're cool, you'll fit in, but I'm afraid I won't really fit in anywhere but here. Here I fit in."

Traci struggled not to blurt, You do?

"Oh, Rache, you're wrong." Traci didn't say about what. "At a big university you will fit in, you'll find lots of other kids like . . . like you."

"From places like Sweeney? I don't think so."

"No, I meant kids who are smart and interested in science and all."

"But they still won't be from places like Sweeney."

To that Traci had no reply, so she changed the subject. "Rache, I haven't told this to anyone, but I'm scared too."

"You are?" Rachel gasped. "But . . . but, you're cool."

Traci wished Rachel would stop using that word.

"Thanks, Rache, but I've lived my whole life in Sweeney. I don't really know what's outside. I mean, I do, in a way, I've read magazines and watched TV, but I know that's not what it's really like. Think about it, I've never ridden a bus, or been in a subway or been to a rave. I don't know what people wear, or what music they listen to. I couldn't drive in a city; I'd get lost or have an accident. And I don't know the language of people my age. I don't think they say 'cool' anymore, but I don't know what they do say. I'll wind up just being a dweeb from Dweeby."

"But you're going to Santa Fe next year. You'll have a whole year to assimilate before you go off to college. The rest of us will go straight from Sweeney into the future. Aren't you excited about going off to Santa Fe?"

"Yeah, I guess so. I mean, yes, of course I am, but . . ." She left the sentence dangling. Only a dweeb would not want to leave Sweeney for Santa Fe, right? And did people her age still use the term "dweeb"?

Chapter Sixteen

☙ BARBECUE DAY BEGAN WITH A BANG. Precisely at 10:00 a.m., just as the parade was scheduled to begin, a loud explosion rocked the area, followed by the staccato of a string of firecrackers. No one knew who had set off the patently illegal explosives—Bare-assed Bob was suspected—but the effect was momentary mayhem. The livestock that had been assembled for the parade scattered, and it was nearly half an hour before they could be calmed and reassembled.

"This bodes ill," thought Leland, as he tried to coax Trixie out from beneath his pickup where she had retreated.

Finally he received the all-clear sign from Ron Suffitt, the official parade marshal, and he nodded toward Kathy waiting with a microphone at the Rotary coffee table. Then, after a preliminary squeal of feedback from the sound system, Kathy's amplified voice filled the area.

"Welcome, ladies and gentlemen, to the Sweeney Celebratory Barbecue to honor our visitors to town. I hope you paid no attention to the noise and commotion of a moment ago. That was just juvenile minds backfiring, nothing to worry about. We've got a lot of good food and good entertainment in store for you today, and we'll start it off with a parade, led by Sweeney's own Christie Herwig, rodeo queen of the plains, and her wonder horse, Sacajawea."

Kathy put the microphone down and turned to Roger. "Please, oh please, tell me that Abe Martinez and his urinating oxen won't be in the parade."

"Don't worry, they're busy with an irrigation project down south."

Standing on the sidewalk waiting for the parade, Traci put down her camera and turned to her friends. "Sacajawea? What's with that? I thought her horse's name was Fury."

"She changed it," said Heather. "She said Fury was a name for a cowboy's horse. Wanted something more Indian. She'll explain later. Quick, get ready, she's getting closer. We don't want to miss this."

Traci returned the camera to her eye. There, framed by the viewfinder, Christie rode resplendent, just as she had at the rodeo, though Traci noted that the tassels dangling from her elaborate cowgirl costume now were turquoise instead of red and gold. Part of the Indian theme, she surmised. With one hand Christie deftly handled the reins; with the other she carried a pole with the official Sweeney American flag, rippling in the breeze, like her long, blond hair.

Traci rapidly clicked the shutter button. She used the camera's zoom to focus on Christie's face—radiant, smiling with a joy that Traci knew came from the core of her being. And quite unexpectedly, Traci was overcome by deep melancholy, for she realized that probably never again would Christie be as happy and beautiful as she was in this moment.

Traci continued to click, almost desperately, determined to capture it for Christie before it faded. Then when Christie and Sacajawea went by, Traci stared after her. Sacajawea began acting skittish, and Christie frowned as she concentrated on controlling the horse. The moment had passed.

Sweeney, Traci thought. Sweeney had given Christie this. Whatever its shortcomings, however dweeby it was, Sweeney—and not LA, not New York, and not Santa Fe—had bestowed upon her friend this moment.

"Come on," interrupted Heather, breaking the mood. "Here comes the lizard."

"That was Christie Herwig and her purebred palomino, Sacajawea, folks. Let's have a big western hand for the two of them. And now, for something different, from straight out of the Jurassic, here's Joe Garcia and his pet. I mean, his pet's out of the Jurassic, not Joe." Through the microphone could be heard Kathy's voice asking, "Roger, what kind of creature is that anyway?" Then, "Joe Garcia, and his pet iguana. You sure don't see one of those every day, at least you hope you don't."

Joe Garcia tugged on a leash as the iguana waddled awkwardly behind him, flicking its tongue in annoyance at being the center of attention.

"Now, on a different scale," Kathy announced, "here's a brontosaurus, no, I mean, here's a John Deere backhoe, the biggest ever seen in Kiowa County, driven by Rudd Torgelson of Torgelson Farm and Ranch Implements and accompanied by . . . Edward."

Rudd was actually smiling as he steered the giant machine, while Edward, seated beside him and cackling gleefully, reached into a paper bag and tossed handfuls of penny candy to the crowd.

Leland turned to Nettie standing beside him and said, "There was a time not long ago when I'd have asked the health department to advise against eating any of that candy, but now I guess it's okay."

Nettie shook her head in wonder. "I never thought I'd see the day when S&S would be in a parade in Sweeney with all his clothes on."

Rudd's backhoe was followed by a combine made up to look like a grasshopper. Then came the livestock and pet procession: 4-H kids and their calves and lambs and rabbits, children with their dogs. Hank Thompson led his pair of Clydesdale horses down the street.

After the horses came Jimmy from the veterinary clinic, leading the old yellow dog that Kathy had seen two days before. The dog looked stove-up and pathetic. Around his neck he wore a sign reading, "Won't you be my friend?"

"Roger, you're shameless," Kathy whispered.

"Ah, come on, Kathy, give him a break, he needs one, give him a plug."

A moment later Kathy's voice boomed through the microphone, "Now here's Jimmy from the All Creatures Clinic with man's best friend who could use a friend himself. That dog's had some hard times, but haven't we all? I've met that dog personally, and there's a lot of good in him, and he's just waiting for a kind person to bring it out. If you're that kind of person, contact Jimmy or Roger at the clinic."

"Thanks, Kathy," said Roger. "I couldn't have done better myself." Kathy was unsure as to whether to take that as a compliment.

From behind her at the Rotary table Kathy heard her mother's voice. "That seems like a nice dog. Do we need a dog, Kathy?"

"No, Mother, we don't." To change the subject Kathy announced,

"And to illustrate the power of kindness, here comes Joanie Daly and her horse, Flicka, and their . . . their friend goat. That horse had been badly abused until Joanie took her in, and as you can see she's made a remarkable recovery to be here today."

Roger's mouth gaped open, then he said, "I see that horse has healed up nicely, both physically and psychologically."

Dave, standing by Roger at the Rotary coffee table, nodded proudly. "I was wrong—and Joanie was right. I told her there wasn't any hope for that horse, and I was wrong."

"You owe her now," said Roger.

"I do."

Traci, who had scurried along with the parade to photograph the lizard, was summoned by Heather. "Hey, Trace, come here, you've got to see *this*."

"What is . . . omigod!"

She was joined by her father. "Dad, did you know Mom was going to do this?"

"I suspected she might do something when I told her about the parade, but, no, I didn't know she was going to come with Flicka and the goat. That took guts, but it seems to be working out."

Dave started clapping and waving as Joanie and the animals paraded by. He turned to Traci. Overcoming her amazement, she also began clapping, joined by her friends.

Joanie held her head high and gave them a big grin. Traci suddenly remembered her camera and began shooting. "This is amazing, just freaking amazing."

At that moment, near the coffee table, Tom Binks said, "Wait a minute, I recognize that goat."

Roger immediately turned on him and barked, "No you don't. Trust me, Tom, you don't know that goat."

Taken aback, Tom stammered, "I guess you're right, now that I think about it, I don't know that goat."

Other participants paraded by. The members of the volunteer fire department perched on their polished antique fire truck. Agnes Norris and the officers of the Ladies Auxiliary of the Sweeney Grange. Roger turned to Leland and muttered, "The only club in history with more officers than members."

Old Tom Atencio and his accordion, playing something a musicologist would have said bore a resemblance to mariachi music.

And finally, the Indians. Kathy announced their appearance. "Ladies and gentlemen, today is a proud day for the Sweeney Barbecue Parade, because our guests, the Cocoye tribe, have graced us with a performance of genuine Indian dances and music, complete with authentic Indian costumes. Let's give them a big Sweeney welcome."

Uncle Billy, in his feathered headdress and beaded deerskin vest and leggings, led the procession, pounding vigorously on his drum. In a voice alternately wailing high and guttural low he chanted, occasionally joined by the Cocoyes behind him. They brandished gourd and turtle-shell rattles, and many had bells sewn onto their costumes. To the beat of the drum they stamped their feet and whirled, their beaded moccasins kicking up dust that rather than being an annoyance heightened the effect of an ancient ritual.

As Leland listened he found himself hearing the sounds as if they came from deep in the past, long before Sweeney, even long before Spanish explorers crossed the plains. He saw a small band of Indians around a campfire at night, drumming and dancing and chanting while the night wind carried sparks into the vast darkness of the prairie.

Lee Harris, who was not among the dancers, sidled up next to Leland. "Any of that authentic?" asked Leland.

"The music and the chanting," replied Harris. "And the dance steps. But the costumes and all . . . well, they make for a colorful display."

As the Indians paraded by, Nettie turned to Leland. "Do you see what I see?" She nodded to two outsize women parading beside the dancing Indians. One was Willa Cohen, wearing an Indian-style robe and a beaded headband, shuffling her feet to the drum's rhythm; the other was Iris Gerber, in a voluminous dress with big, non-Native swatches of red, pink, yellow, and blue. As she also shuffled to the drumbeat, she carried on an animated conversation with Willa.

Leland turned to Harris and whispered, "I didn't know we were going to have a fashion show."

Harris laughed. "Makes that lizard look stylish."

"Well, folks," Kathy's voice boomed over the microphone, "that was the Sweeney Celebratory Barbecue Parade, fun for humans and beasts alike. We've got a lot more for you today, lots of good food, a world-class horseshoe venue—and if I'm not mistaken, the plume of dust out yonder is Jim Biddle bringing in a few of his buffalo for everyone to see. Think of it, buffalo and Indians, back on the High Plains here in Sweeney, where the past and the future hold hands and do-si-do. Oh, and I've been asked to announce that our guests, the Cocoyes, will have their costumes and regalia on display over near the horseshoe pits and will be happy to talk about them and answer questions."

Damn but that was a good parade, thought Leland as the dust settled and people began to disperse. Sweeney did itself proud. With Trixie at his heels he wandered over to the Rotary Club coffee urn, where Dave Daly handed him a cup.

"That was impressive, really impressive," Leland said.

"Thanks," Dave replied. "I'm proud of her. What she's done with that horse is nothing short of miraculous."

"No, I meant the parade, though seeing Joanie and that put-back-together horse was truly inspiring."

"Oh, the parade. Yes, it was impressive. Everyone seems to be having a good time. And I noticed that many of the spectators weren't locals. Sweeney seems to be getting a reputation as a happening place."

Leland recalled the rodeo and Bare-assed Bob, and the solstice and Bare-assed Barbara. "Yeah, I guess we've acquired a reputation, all right."

Seeing Nettie at the church women's tables he strolled over. June and Wayne Fall were busy helping them set up. Nice to see him doing something useful for a change.

"Morning, Reverend, morning, June, morning, Nettie. That was a mighty fine parade."

"It was very nice," chirped June. She seemed in uncommonly good spirits. Then he noticed an electronic keyboard plugged into a cord snaking through the area. He looked inquiringly at Nettie.

She nodded almost imperceptibly before speaking. "You should come around later. June will be playing some old favorites."

"Does she know any Jerry Lee Lewis, maybe 'Great Balls of Fire'?" Nettie's scowl told him not to push it.

Leland smiled. He browsed the crafts tables, and bought an embroidered pot holder. "Man can't have too many pot holders," he said to Nettie.

She smiled. "Yeah, that's what I say about knitted tea caddies and why I've got maybe a dozen of them."

Still basking in warm feelings, Leland strolled over to the fenced pasture where he saw that the buffalo had been released. Three adults and a calf. They seemed to be drawing quite a crowd, especially toward the far end of the enclosure. He ambled closer. Then he heard Roger's voice at the center of the cluster.

"Step right up, folks, we've still got a few numbers left, but they're going fast."

What the hell? Elbowing forward Leland found Roger seated at a card table, taking money from people and handing them slips of paper. "What's going on?"

"Buffalo chip poker," Roger declared proudly. He motioned to the pasture where Leland saw a grid of sixteen squares marked with lime, each with a lime-drawn number in its center. "You pay your money, five bucks a pop, pick a number, then if a buffalo shits on your square, you win fifty bucks. The rest goes to the Sweeney-Cocoye Tribal Relocation Fund. Buffalo chip poker, it's the luck of the drop."

Leland's mouth dropped open.

Suddenly a man shouted, "Number ten, he crapped on number ten!" Leland looked into the pasture. Sure enough, a fresh buffalo pile lay steaming in the square marked ten. A man pushed forward waving a slip of paper that had number ten written on it. Roger took the slip, counted out five tens, and handed them to the man.

"How do you keep track of which squares have been recently . . . dropped on and which were selected previously?" Leland asked.

"Not a problem," said Roger. "Folks keep a pretty close watch, but we've got an official tally keeper." He nodded to where a man squatted on the ground with a big sheet of paper marked into a numbered grid corresponding to the pasture squares. Leland could see that a vertical line had been drawn with red felt-tipped pen in square ten. Now the man returned his intense focus to the enclosure. It was Edward.

"I'll be go to hell," Leland muttered in amazement.

"Step right up!" Roger shouted. "Numbers are going fast. It's for a good cause, and Biddle tells me those buffalo ate hearty this morning."

"Give me number eight," said a man. "I've got a feeling about that number."

Lee Harris stepped forward with a ten-dollar bill. "Give me five and seven. As you say, it's a good cause."

A woman that Leland recognized from cattle auctions in Clayton said, "I want number three if that's available. It's my lucky number."

"Come on, Leland," prodded Roger. "This is the best and most honest gaming around. No one put any laxatives in those critters; it's all natural."

As Leland's mind rose from the depths of dumbfoundedness he pulled a ten from his wallet. "I'll take number sixteen. And Trixie here will have number fifteen."

Putting the slips of paper in his back pocket, Leland walked slowly away. Trixie followed panting and grinning. Maybe fifteen is her lucky number, he thought as he shook his head.

Still shaking his head, Leland found himself back at the Rotary coffee urn. "You better refill this, Dave. I have a feeling this is not a one- or even a two-cup day." Then he nodded toward the buffalo pasture. "You know about this?"

Dave raised his hands in shocked innocence. "I had nothing to do with this. Not that I disapprove, mind you. No one's complaining. I hope they raise a whole bunch of money."

"How about you?" he asked Kathy, who was sitting on a camp chair beside her parents.

"Nope, can't say I did. But I admit I'm proud of Roger." Kathy paused. "Never in my life thought I'd say that. Creative. And I have a feeling good will come of this. What about you? Do you have a problem with it?"

"No, not at all." And as if to prove it he pulled the two slips from his pocket. "We're in the game too, me and Trixie."

They were interrupted by a roar from the buffalo area. "Number three!" a woman shouted. "I said it was my lucky number."

Leland shrugged. "Well, Trixie, I guess our crap detectors aren't working today. And just what *are* you grinning about anyway?"

Leland wandered over by the horseshoe pits. Kind of slow here, he observed. Normally the horseshoe pits were among the most popular sites at any community gathering, not because of the contestants necessarily but because of the side bets. The actual competition, aside from upstart challengers, usually was dominated by well-matched old-timers whom everyone knew. The old-timers were still here, but there were fewer spectators than usual. Competition from the buffalo, Leland supposed. That's okay, time for some fresh action. People had slowly been drifting away from the horseshoes for years, just as they'd been drifting away from Sweeney.

Leland found a longtime friend, Will Hopkins. "Five bucks says Abner Peck will come out on top."

"I don't know," drawled Will. "Ol' Scooter Henry's slinging some mean iron."

"You're on." They shook hands, and Leland ambled away. He wasn't about to bet on "Ol' Scooter," who he knew gobbled prescription painkillers, and he suspected they gave him an edge in a high-pressure sport like horseshoes. Leland felt that if Lance Armstrong could be tested for performance-enhancing drugs, so could Scooter.

Over the loudspeaker Kathy's voice boomed. "I'm told that the barbecue is ready, and a special barbecue it is, with your choice of beef or buffalo. Or both, for the committed carnivores among you. Ten bucks for all you can eat. Salad, beans, rolls, chips, and dessert. Iced tea or soda for a beverage. And if you find you've eaten too much, we've got our local vet here to take good care of you, just like he would a bloated horse."

Leland noticed that Iris Gerber and Willa Cohen were first in line.

With the opening of the barbecue, the horseshoers called a time-out, and most of the buffalo-chippers also drifted toward the food, though the game obviously continued. "You don't have to be present to win," Roger told the punters.

Turning to Edward, Roger said, "If you want to go get something to eat, I'll keep the tally."

Edward vigorously shook his head. "Nope, ain't leaving." He continued staring into the enclosure. Roger, however, noted that two of the buffalo had lain down.

A few people came by to purchase the remaining numbers. Then Kathy arrived, balancing three plates on her hands and arms. She put them on the card table. "What do you want to drink?" she asked.

"Coke," answered Edward. Roger asked for a cup of coffee.

Kathy left and soon returned with Coke, coffee, and iced tea.

"Thanks," said Roger. "I needed this."

"I thought you might. Hustling buffalo chips is hard work. How's it going?"

"Great, better than I expected. We've had four drops and sold out every time. That's $120 for the fund."

"I told Leland I was proud of you, and I am. I can remember the time when I could not imagine I'd ever say that."

"Thank you, Kathy," Roger said, with uncharacteristic soberness. "I can remember the time when I could not imagine it would mean so much to me."

Then, returning to a broad smile, he said, "You're a great announcer, you know, and to prove it that old yellow dog has a new home. Good announcers are always in demand. You could make decent money, which would help if you moved your parents to Albuquerque. Not that I want you to," he added.

Kathy started to open a new coffee can, looked at him, and said, "I don't think I'll be doing that, I mean the Albuquerque part. Mom and Dad have had a wonderful time today, even if they were a bit confused at times. Lots of old friends came by to see them. They've lived all their lives in Sweeney, mostly in the house where they are now. This is their home. This is where they belong." She paused. "Now, about that announcing, you say there's big bucks in telling folks to get ready for dust and horse shit?"

Roger and Kathy both laughed. Then they glanced at Edward. He still squatted on the ground, nibbling on his meal, his eyes fixed on the pasture.

Balancing a plate and cup, Traci walked to where her friends had gathered by the Rock. Christie, she noticed, was still in her parade costume. Sitting down, she turned to Christie. "You were great."

"Yeah," said Heather beamed. "And not just because you came right before that ugly lizard."

"Iguana," said Rachel.

"Whatever," said Kimberly. "Yeah, you looked great."

Christie started in surprise and beamed at Kimberly, who normally mocked Christie's western dress. "Why thank you, and you look great today too." Kimberly rolled her eyes and then smiled. She wore her standard Goth uniform of black-on-black.

"I don't think I've ever seen you more beautiful," Traci said, adding quickly, "and I've got the photos to prove it. I'll make you as many prints as you want."

Christie, moved by the compliments and noticing that Traci's eyes were moist, leaned over and hugged her. "I'm going to miss you when you move to Santa Fe."

Traci returned the hug, then said awkwardly, "Well, about that, I'm not going to be moving after all."

"Why not?" blurted Rachel, with characteristic tactlessness.

"Yeah, I thought that was settled?" questioned Heather.

"Well, it's complicated," Traci stammered, suddenly embarrassed.

"Does it have to do with your mom and that horse? Or maybe doll-houses?" asked Kimberly.

"Yes, and no," Traci replied. "I mean, Sweeney's been good for Mom and that horse." She paused. "And Dad wants to stay. He's really attached to this town." She paused again. "And . . . and, I'd miss you guys too."

There was an awkward moment, then Heather broke it by saying, "Aw, you just want to see if those cute Indian boys go to school here."

After eating, the girls wandered over to the buffalo chip area, where bettors had regathered.

"Ewww!" said Heather. "People standing around waiting for buffalo to shit—this is Dweeby at its worst! Are you sure you don't want to move to Santa Fe, Trace?"

Traci ignored the comment, concentrating on her camera equipment. Dorky and repulsive as the event might be, her instincts told her it needed recording. She meandered around the pasture's perimeter, taking close-ups of the buffalo, hoping, with severely mixed emotions, to catch one in the act of making someone a winner.

"Who're you with?"

With a start, Traci turned toward the voice. Approaching was a girl only a little older than she. Sunglasses hid her eyes. She wore a canvas adventure hat and a photographer's vest. An impressive camera dangled from her neck, and she carried a spiral-bound steno book.

"I'm Jennifer Tremali, with the *Sun*."

"Is that a newspaper?"

Exasperated, the girl sighed. "The *Quay County Sun*."

Her name was not familiar to Traci, though she recognized the *Quay County Sun* as the regional newspaper out of Tucumcari. Nodding toward Traci's camera, Jennifer repeated her question, "Who're you with?"

"I . . . uh, I shoot freelance, for *New Mexico Magazine*, sometimes,"

Traci stammered, not wanting to admit that she wasn't with any publication and in fact was just a Sweeney high school student.

"Wow!" said Jennifer. "Hey, isn't this just totally way beyond weird? I mean, when they asked me to, like, cover this one-horse event in the middle of freaking nowhere, I'm, like, whoa! I'm normally the city editor on weekends. But the guy who normally does the hayseed beat called in sick, so I was, like, stuck with it. How about you?"

"Oh, I'm kind of stuck with it too," answered Traci, a hint of resentment in her voice, "but it's not so bad, especially if you're, like, sensitive to people and their situations."

"But isn't this, like, just too much?" burbled Jennifer, oblivious to the gibe, then said, "Say, I've got a huge favor to ask, as one journalist to another."

"Yes?"

"Something's wrong with this piece of shit," she said, nodding toward her expensive camera. "I just can't get it to work right, had trouble with it before. Anyways, I'm screwed if I come back without photos, especially when my editor hears about this buffalo thing. Could you give me some of your photos, on, like, a memory stick? I've got one. I'll be sure you get a credit line. Please, as one journalist helping another?"

Traci hesitated. She suspected that the problem with the "piece of shit"—far more expensive and sophisticated than her camera—was that Jennifer didn't know how to use it. And she was resentful of Jennifer's patronizing attitude and her attempt to manipulate her. But she also figured it could do no harm, and a credit line, even in the *Quay County Sun*, perhaps could be useful someday.

"Okay, let me finish shooting, then I'll put some photos on the memory stick. And, yes, I would like a credit line."

"Oh, totally. Thanks, I really appreciate it." And with that Jennifer walked toward the betting table, presumably for interviews.

On impulse, Traci called after her. "One other thing, I'm going to give you a couple of photos of the parade queen on her horse, to have in case your editor wants to run something besides the buffalo. Her name's Christie Herwig."

"I've already got it," called Jennifer over her shoulder.

By late afternoon, the Sweeney Celebratory Barbecue was winding down. Little remained of the food, though Leland noticed that Iris and Willa continued grazing the scraps. In Africa they call them hyenas.

The horseshoe championship had been settled. Leland had already paid his debt to Will Hopkins. Old Abner just hadn't been up to his usual form today.

Tired and sated, people were beginning to drift toward their vehicles. Kathy Larkin had unplugged the Rotary Club's coffee urn and was cleaning it. The church women were tidying up their food and crafts area. Reverend Fall was helping them carry stuff to their cars. June was playing "As Time Goes By" on the keyboard.

Leland stopped and smiled. Quite a barbecue. Quite a summer. In just a few short weeks, everything had changed. For one thing, he and Grant finally came out of the closet in Sweeney. True, he'd kind of done it for Grant, but Leland knew Grant would approve. He recalled the old friends he'd seen today. He knew that everyone had heard about Grant's homosexuality, yet none had mentioned Grant, nor did they appear to be avoiding the issue. In fact, a few had asked about Grant, how he was doing.

Coming out of the closet. People talked about how city-dwellers didn't know their neighbors, but in places like Sweeney, shallow familiarity and routines allowed neighbors to slip into a different kind of anonymity. To hide in closets. Communities needed to be shaken up occasionally to make people really see each other—and to see themselves. Just look at Kathy Larkin. In just a few weeks she'd walked out of her prison and reclaimed her youthful vibrancy and humor. She'd reconnected with Roger in ways neither had expected.

So many changes set in motion by raising the Rock. Without it, S&S never would have emerged as Edward. Rudd would have grown old alone and bitter in his big empty house. Nettie was happier. So was June Fall, and in his own way so was Wayne. For better or worse, Dave and Joanie were going to stay in Sweeney. Even Traci had come to terms with the town.

And him? Nothing would bring Ruth back, but he'd brought Grant back. And he was at peace. A man could live his whole life waiting for the opportunity to make a difference, but it had come to him, finally, in the form of a quasi-indecent proposal from Roger.

Hell, if it hadn't been for the Rock, he wouldn't have Trixie, and that old yellow dog in the parade wouldn't have found a home.

As Leland ambled toward the buffalo pasture he noticed that even the bettors there were dwindling, though the buffalo themselves seemed more alert than earlier. Coming round from their afternoon siestas.

Actually, the buffalo looked downright agitated. They pawed the dirt with their hooves, they snorted through their flared nostrils, their lowered heads swayed back and forth almost in a threatening manner. They seemed focused on something outside the pasture, in the direction of the barbecue area. Leland glanced to see what it might be.

Prancing and dancing toward the pasture were Willa and Iris, waving their arms, whooping loudly, and then laughing even louder. But it was Iris's dress that most alarmed Leland. As large as a small tent, bright and gaudy, the fabric billowed tauntingly before the buffalo.

"Hey, Iris, Willa!" he started to call in warning, but he was too late. The buffalo charged.

The lead buffalo ran headlong into the fence. He was briefly entangled in the wire until the crush of the other buffalo behind him collapsed the fence, and they all were free.

Someone screamed.

Then Iris and Willa screamed, turned, and began running. Everyone started screaming. Jim Biddle cursed. "Gawdammit! GAWDAMMIT! Who spooked 'em?"

Kathy and Roger looked up from the coffee urn and saw Iris and Willa bearing down on them, pursued by raging, shaggy buffalo. Roger tilted up the table as a barricade, grabbed Kathy, and threw her behind it.

Just as the buffalo were closing on the two women, Reverend Fall ran between them and the animals, screaming, "Leave them be! I'm their pastor!" Then he sprinted off in the direction of the Rock.

The buffalo, thoroughly confused and a little terrified themselves, ceased pursuit of the women and also ran toward the Rock. Ignoring Reverend Fall, who had flung himself behind one of the boulders, they thundered past, their hooves making the earth tremble. They continued running, out onto the prairie, away from the humans, where finally they stopped. One of them lifted his tail, and crapped. "That's my number!" yelled someone who guffawed loudly.

But before anyone else could react, someone cried, "Look out! It's going to fall!"

The Rock, jarred by the stampeding buffalo, was indeed listing, slowly, then faster, until it struck the ground with a colossal *whump*.

All motion and conversation instantly stopped. Stunned silence. The buffalo were forgotten. All eyes stared as puffs of dust rose from around the Rock and drifted away in the breeze.

Then everyone rushed forward, except Iris and Willa, who wailed loudly as they lay on the ground, where Reverend Fall ministered to them.

Rachel Rowe ran up to Dave Daly. "See, I told you it was leaning. The mathematics proved it."

Dave could only shake his head. Roger and Kathy crawled from behind the coffee table. Leland and Nettie came forward and stared. So did Rudd and Edward. Everyone was in shock, as if a great chasm had opened in the earth and swallowed the town itself.

No one said anything. As shocking as the Rock's arrival had been, its collapse was worse, a kind of death. Everyone stood staring silently, solemnly, as if waiting for the Rock miraculously to right itself. When it didn't, they slowly wandered away.

Chapter Seventeen

◆ WITHOUT BOTHERING TO LOOK for traffic, Dave Daly stepped from the cracked sidewalk onto Main Street—and was almost hit by a car.

"Damned tourists!" he shouted and then recognized Iris Gerber as the driver of the huge, faded-green Oldsmobile about to nudge its way into one of the few remaining parking spaces near the Chick 'n' More.

Interesting, he thought, how a town meeting could be convened without anything officially being announced—no notices, no proclamations, just word of mouth. Yet Dave didn't doubt that everyone in Sweeney knew a public meeting was to be held this morning at the Chick 'n' More.

Rudd was entering now, with Edward in tow. There was Nettie with several friends from the Style Salon. As Dave stepped back on the curb to regain his balance, he saw Lee Harris, Chester and Willa Cohen, Uncle Billy, and several other Cocoyes and their families file into the restaurant. Judy and Adelino Baca were climbing out of their van. That meant they'd closed their store, but why not? Everyone in town was here—and not for a new special on the Chick 'n' More's menu. The people of Sweeney needed to talk

A week had passed since the barbecue, and everyone in town knew a moment of decision had been reached. Except for the raising of the Rock, which most townspeople had figured out had been accomplished by diesel and not aliens, all that had happened during this summer of

wonders—the nudists, the rodeo, the solstice, the Indians, the barbecue—all had been ad hoc, with no thought as to what to do next. But
with the Cocoyes' arrival and the Rock's collapse things had changed.
The town needed to grab the steering wheel.

Dave was just about to step back onto the street when, looking for
traffic, he saw Joanie walking toward him. Given her scorn for the
Rotary meetings, he hadn't asked if she might want to attend, but this
wasn't going to be a typical Rotary meeting. She was wearing blue jeans,
a western shirt, and the Stetson hat he'd bought for her soon after they'd
arrived in Sweeney more than seventeen years ago. A symbol of the
town she despised, she had never worn it.

"Nice hat. Don't tell me you're going to the Rotary Club meeting too?"

"Wouldn't miss it," she replied, ignoring his comment about the hat.
"If against all good sense we've decided to stay in Sweeney, I'd like to
have a say in what happens here. I hope you're happy, by the way."

The night following the barbecue, as the Daly family sat in their liv-
ing room, Traci had announced her decision to stay for her senior year.
Dave had known even earlier that Joanie had made her decision. On
Monday Dave had mailed the letter declining the teaching position in
Santa Fe. Nothing more was said in the family about the decision.

Was he happy? After the family meeting, he'd gone to the Rock and
asked himself that very question. He'd never fully answered why he was
so reluctant to leave Sweeney; he'd been so certain he wanted to stay
that he hadn't considered how he'd feel about all the doors the decision
would close. He'd expected the decision to sweep away all the ambigu-
ity he felt, but it hadn't. Sure, Sweeney had been more interesting lately,
but it wouldn't last. The Chick 'n' More would remain the only place for
food and coffee. He'd continue as the high school science teacher. The
plains would remain flat and monotonous. And in a year Traci would
be gone.

Still, he never doubted that moving to Santa Fe would have been
a disaster, at least for him. It probably would have been a mistake for
Traci too.

As for Joanie? He could only hope that with time she would become
more accepting of Sweeney. He vowed he'd do everything he could to
encourage that. She could adopt as many horses as she wanted. They
could travel. Whatever she wanted. He owed her.

"Am I happy? I suppose I am," he answered. He certainly wasn't about to taint the moment by admitting any misgivings. "I don't know what's ahead for us, or for Sweeney, but, yes, I am happy we chose to stay here, if only to see how this all plays out."

He paused, looked down, then directly at her. "How about you?"

"Yeah, I guess I am too. Flicka and I wouldn't have fit in at the Santa Fe Horse Park, with the dressage horses and the Olympic jumpers."

"I hope you don't think that means you fit in here, with S&S and Iris Gerber and the Chick 'n' More and all the other oddities."

"Actually, that's exactly what it does mean, but not in the way you think. When I lived in LA, I fit in there, but in the same way a grain of sand fits in on a beach." She paused. "Here people fit in like pieces in a jigsaw puzzle; without any one of them the picture isn't complete. It's a pretty weird picture we make up, but it's our picture."

It was a clever answer and accurate as far as it went. Following her conversation with Rachel and after Traci's announcement of her decision—and after Flicka and everything that had happened this summer—she had accepted, with surprisingly little regret, that she was fated to uncover the hidden virtues of Sweeney.

Dave smiled and shook his head. "And I was shocked by the transformation of S&S."

Joanie elbowed him in the ribs, "Come on, we don't want to be late for the meeting. And I reserve the right to change my mind."

They entered Chick 'n' More just ahead of Tom Binks and his wife and several other townspeople. Dave could not recall Binks going anywhere with his wife. The dining area had been cleared of tables, and chairs had been brought in from the Rotary Club's regular meeting room. As Dave and Joanie made their way to the few remaining chairs at the room's rear, Dave noticed Traci and her friends perched on a windowsill. She had her camera equipment out and ready to record the meeting. One of the Cocoye girls was sitting with them. Rachel Rowe sat with them too.

Helen the waitress bustled around, distributing cups of coffee. "It's on the house—no way am I going to try to keep track of all this. Any other orders will have to wait till the meeting's over."

Dave and Joanie took seats beside Roger and Kathy just as Ron Suffitt rose to his feet by the counter. He wore a freshly pressed white shirt, a tie, and a sport coat that Dave had last seen when he and Ron had posed for their senior class photo in high school.

Ron cleared his throat, then orated. "Ladies and gentlemen, fellow citizens of Sweeney, we have important matters of moment to discuss here today, and in solemn recognition of that I propose that we dispense with our normal meeting protocol, such as the reading of the minutes, the financial report, and committee reports. That is, unless someone has any objections."

"Hell no!" someone shouted. "Let's get into it."

"Well, not hearing any motion to object, I'm going to call upon our town manager, Leland Morton."

Ron sat, and Leland rose. He too appeared to have dressed for the occasion, his blue jeans having been freshly washed.

Leland looked out over the crowd. "Well, it's been quite a week. In fact, it's been quite a summer. Seems like a long time ago that a few of us were sitting at another Rotary Club meeting here in the Chick 'n' More, talking about how the Chick 'n' More was closing, folks were moving away, and Sweeney was dying. Well, as you can see, the Chick 'n' More is still open, people are still here, and Sweeney's still alive.

"In fact, there's even people who want to move here. I'm talking specifically about the Cocoye Indians, whom I assume you've all had a chance to meet. So before I go any further, I believe Lee Harris has a few words to say on their behalf." And with that Leland sat, and Lee stood.

"Atha-hle," he said in a self-consciously deep voice.

"That means 'greetings' in their language," said Judy Baca in a loud whisper everyone could hear.

Lee smiled. "Yes, we have been able to meet many of you, and we hope you've had a chance to get to know us. I think most of you are familiar with our history, living here on the plains a long time ago, then becoming displaced and forgotten, drifting from town to town through-out the West, wherever we could find work, going to LA, trying to stay alive as a people—not really too different from what you've been trying to do as a town. And like you, we were losing."

He surveyed the room. Most people just nodded their heads. A few frowned.

"Then we heard about Sweeney. We came here with the crazy idea that maybe we could get federal recognition as a tribe, establish a res-ervation, and open an Indian casino. A crazy idea, born of desperation. Just as crazy as the idea that raising up some rocks and digging a bunch of weird holes in the ground would cause the town to get noticed and somehow make a difference. Crazy ideas. Now before I continue, I'd like for Leland to fill you in on what's been happening this past week."

Lee sat, and Leland stood. The people were silent, waiting.

"Folks, something occurred last week that put Sweeney on the map in a way that I doubt any of us could have imagined. I'm talking about that buffalo-chip poker at the barbecue."

People exchanged puzzled looks. Joanie looked at Dave, who looked at Roger, who shook his head in bewilderment.

Leland continued. "I'm sure many of you saw the story and photos in the *Quay County Sun*. Well, the story and photos didn't stop with Quay County. Oh, no. They were picked up by the Associated Press and then other wire services and news organizations and the Internet, and they've been scattered all over the world."

Iris interrupted. "We were mentioned on the *Today Show*. They said Sweeney was Las Vegas on the plains, but people wouldn't be taking home souvenir chips like they do in Vegas. 'What happens in Sweeney stays in Sweeney,' they said."

Fred Yoder rose and held up a newspaper, the *National Enquirer*. "Look at this! There's a story in here that talks about Sweeney. We've done broke into the international press."

One of the church women spoke next. "I heard about it on the radio. The announcer was saying what a fine thing it was the town and the Indians were uniting in a common cause to keep their cultures alive. He said something about it being a good thing we didn't have elephants here. I don't know what he meant."

"I'm told it's all over the Internet," said Leland. "There are websites in India expressing concern that the buffalo be treated humanely, like cows over there."

"Hell yes, they are!" shouted Jim Biddle. "Only difference is we don't let 'em die of old age."

Tom Binks rose and in an uncharacteristically muted voice spoke. "Great, just great. First we attract attention because of a dick-shaped rock, and then we're known for buffalo shit!" He humphed for emphasis and sat down.

Several citizens began speaking at once, but Leland raised his hand for silence. "It's pretty clear we're all aware of what's been going on. This past week I've done little else but answer phone calls from TV stations and reporters and magazines and whatnot, all asking when the next buffalo-chip poker session will occur. And sure, we could stage another one, to cash in on our fifteen minutes of fame, but doing so would raise some legal issues, because gambling, even buffalo-chip poker, is illegal. About the only way we could have buffalo-chip gambling here is if it's on an Indian reservation, operated under state compact with a federally recognized tribe." He paused. "Lee, you want to take it from here?"

Leland sat, and Lee stood, taking time to hitch his pants up.

"Leland's right. The fifteen minutes of fame will last just about that long, but that's long enough to put Sweeney permanently on the gambling map. I'm not exaggerating when I say there are hundreds of thousands, maybe millions, of recreational gamblers across the country—across the world—who would love to stop by Sweeney just for the novelty of playing buffalo-chip poker. They won't come all at once, but they will come, week after week, month after month, year after year. They'll want lodging while they're here, they'll buy gas and food and other things, and they certainly will buy souvenirs, T-shirts and ball caps and—"

Judy Baca stood. "I'll tell you they will indeed buy souvenirs. Lots of 'em. What we sold for the Rock was nothing compared to what we'd sell for buffalo-chip poker."

Lee nodded and continued. "The economic impact of this crazy idea could be substantial, but it can't happen unless we work together, we the Cocoyes and you the people of Sweeney. I've been in touch with the Bureau of Indian Affairs and been told that with the publicity given to our history and how we need a reservation for our survival, there's a good chance we'd be granted federal recognition.

"I've been told by state officials there's a good chance we'd be granted a limited gaming compact—just for buffalo-chip poker, nothing else.

"But we need a reservation. Media coverage probably would help us find a patch of land somewhere that we could call a reservation, but we don't want it to be somewhere—we want it to be here."

He took a deep breath. "Sweeney welcomed us, made us feel at home. When we lived in LA our children were teased in school, made to conceal their Indian heritage. Here we're proud of it, and I'm told it's inspired some of you to discover a bit of your own Indian heritage. So we want our reservation to be in a community where we belong. We want to settle in Sweeney."

Lee was interrupted by loud applause and cries of "Hear! Hear!"

He raised his hands for silence. "Here's what we propose. If the town can grant us land for a reservation, we'll draw up an agreement specifying that any proceeds from buffalo-chip poker operations be shared equitably to our mutual benefit."

Lee sat, and Leland stood. "I've discussed this with Lee and also with state officials. I agree with everything he said. The arrangement will require a lot of trust and goodwill, but everyone knows that we've all got a lot to lose if it doesn't work—and a lot to gain if does. Now, is there any discussion?"

People clamored to speak, but Iris Gerber was first on her feet. "I say hell yes!" she said in a voice that filled the room. People cried "Hear! Hear!" Someone shouted, "Hell yes to what?"

"Hell yes to having these fine folks come and settle in Sweeney. They'll do our town a world of good, and I'd be happy to have them here even if they didn't bring in a penny."

Connie Nesbitt was on her feet and speaking even before Iris sat down. "It might work! This buffalo-chip poker thing just might work!" She was so enthused Dave feared she might hyperventilate. "It's just goofy enough to attract a lot of attention. And—trust me on this— gambling is *huge*. People will travel anywhere, even to a place like Sweeney, to bet. And while they're here, they'll get to know our little town, maybe buy property here."

Binks was next. "I'm with Iris. I'd be happy to have my Indian brothers move here—"

Most people exchanged questioning looks, though others just rolled their eyes.

"—even without the gambling. They're fine people. Some of them can get work with the gas company; they're planning on putting in a new pipeline and pumping station over near Conejo. I'm not sure about that buffalo-chip poker thing."

Roger stood to speak. "Regarding what Iris and Tom said, I agree. I think there's consensus here that we'd like to have the Cocoyes as part of our community—anyone disagree?"

Silence.

"That's what I thought. This is a good town, with good people. The issue isn't whether we want the Cocoyes here but how we can make that happen. And with all due respect to Tom, we can't make that happen with a few temporary gas company jobs. Nor can we keep our town alive with other such jobs. There's towns all over the plains that get a few crumbs from the gas company or the power company or the highway department—and those towns are still dying.

"I was the one who came up with the buffalo-chip poker idea, mostly just as a lark, but it's gone in directions I never imagined. I don't know whether this scheme will work, but as Shakespeare said, 'There is a tide in the affairs of men, which, taken at the flood, leads on to fortune,' and, folks, I think that tide is flowing up the arroyos of Sweeney. I think we should ride it out. I don't think any of us wants to wake up twenty years from now and wonder what would have happened if only we'd had the courage to take a chance. And we all know what future Sweeney is facing if we don't do something."

As Roger sat, almost everyone stood to applaud. When the clapping subsided, Reverend Fall arose tentatively. He looked about nervously, cleared his throat, and said, "I agree about the Cocoyes, but gambling is sin. I think scripture is very clear about that. Casting lots—"

"We're not casting lots," someone interrupted, "we're dropping dung."

Reverend Fall flushed; then, when the laughter subsided, he continued. "That's what I mean: irreverence. The Lord knows I want this town to survive as much as anyone. After all, I'm pastor of the church here, and Sweeney's people are my flock. I want us all to prosper. But gambling is sin, preying on human frailty. I think we should all pray for the good Lord's guidance on this."

Dave noted several of Nettie's cronies nodding their heads and mouthing the word "Amen," though not Nettie herself. Reverend Fall apparently saw them too, and, sensing that he should quit while he was ahead, sat down.

As Nettie stood to speak, she gave a subtle nod and a smile to Reverend Fall. Then she looked at the crowded room. "Our good pastor here is right: gambling is sinful. I'm not a proponent of gambling, never have been. But this isn't normal gambling. No one's going to cash out their children's college fund so they can place another bet at the buffalo pasture. No one's going to come here and lose their paycheck playing buffalo-chip poker. And we've heard Leland say that's all the state will agree to. We're not going to have slot machines and roulette wheels and green poker tables—unless you count the green grass of the buffalo pasture. And Roger's right, we've got to do something to keep our town alive."

When Nettie sat, Roger rose again. "Betting on buffalo-chip poker isn't a whole lot different from placing a five-dollar bet on horseshoes or a roping contest. We've all done it. This won't be Las Vegas.

"No, folks will come here just for the fun and novelty of it, and while they're here they'll get to know a little about the plight of people and towns out here on the plains. They can learn about the history of the Cocoyes, and about our history as well. We can have exhibits and pamphlets. We can have barbecues and rodeos and parades and Fourth of July celebrations. They can attend our community church. We can offer people the opportunity to visit a working ranch. Perhaps some of our fine old homes could have futures as B&Bs."

Then Jim Biddle stood to speak. "It only takes about four buffalo to deal a hand of buffalo-chip poker, so it won't directly affect my buffalo-ranching operation. But I think it could have an important indirect effect.

"Folks, buffalo are returning to the plains. I'm not the only buffalo rancher, not by a long shot. There's starting to be a huge demand for buffalo meat, because of how good and healthy it is. Having people come here to see buffalo in their native habitat can only benefit awareness of buffalo ranching. And if they eat a buffalo burger here at the Chick 'n' More, so much the better. Maybe they can buy frozen steaks at Judy and Adelinos's place. I'm with Roger; the actual betting's just a small part of what can happen here with buffalo-chip poker."

Murmurs of agreement rippled throughout the room, but everyone became suddenly silent when Christie Herwig climbed down from the windowsill. Today she wasn't dressed in her rodeo outfit but rather jeans, cowboy boots, and a white T-shirt with pink lettering that read, "Cute 'n' Tuff"—just another high school kid. Nervously, she looked around the room and began to speak.

"Most of my friends will be leaving Sweeney next year, to go away to school." She struggled to make her voice audible. "I'll be going away to school myself. Some of us won't be coming back, but I probably will, to keep the ranch. It's been in our family a long time. I never thought I'd say this" —she glanced at her friends seated behind her— "but I love this weird, dweeby place. It's been good to me."

She turned back to the crowd.

"Some of my classmates will want to stick around as well—if they can. But for that to happen, we need Sweeney to stay alive. We can't stay if Sweeney's going to be just another dying husk of a town like, well, you know.

"I've probably got more of a stake in keeping Sweeney alive than anyone else, and I say we give this Indian thing a try."

She ended, looking embarrassed. As she sat, her friends broke into applause, which spread throughout the room, intensifying her embarrassment.

When the applause died, a few other people spoke. All favored the Indians' proposal. A few asked questions. How would the proceeds be shared? What would they be used for? How many jobs would be created? Would they go just to Indians? Iris Gerber asked whether there would be buffet dinners, like in Vegas.

It was nearly noon when the discussion finally petered out. No vote was taken, for the town's consensus was clear: give it a try. Then Binks asked in a loud voice, "Where's this reservation going to be?"

All eyes focused on Leland.

"The logical place is where the buffalo-chip poker is now, on the land around those rocks at the edge of town."

"Who owns that land?" someone asked.

Leland hesitated. "Well, it's a citizen with deep family roots in Sweeney. Rudd, you want to answer that question?"

Without saying anything Rudd clomped forward, pushing a clearly uncomfortable Edward ahead of him. When the two reached the counter, Rudd turned, put his massive arm around the skinny man's shoulders, and in a firm voice said, "This here is the owner of that land, my cousin, Edward."

"Omigod!" someone gasped. "It's S&S!"

"How can this be?"

"S&S is a citizen?"

"His name is Edward," Rudd growled, "and don't you forget it." Edward himself looked terrified, as if he was facing a lynch mob.

"Edward inherited that land from his uncle, who was also my uncle, Morgan Torgelson, who acquired it as part of his share of the original Torgelson holdings when they first settled here. Until recently, neither Edward nor I knew about the family connection, but now we do. Edward is part of this community, same as I am—and I expect him to be treated as such. Right, Edward?" The scrawny man managed a feeble nod.

"I've talked over this Indian reservation thing with Edward, and we both agree that we want to do what's right for the town. We've discussed this with the Cocoyes, and they agree that the simplest arrangement would be for Edward to become a member of the tribe. He'd have to go through an initiation, but when it's all done he'll be a full Cocoye, and his land could then become tribal land and the reservation. Ain't that right, Edward?"

Again, Edward managed a feeble nod.

Tumult ensued. "Let's hear it for good old S&S—er, Edward." Applause erupted, and several people rushed forward to pat Edward on the back and shake his hand. Edward looked both elated and terrified, as if he'd been accorded the honor of serving as the town's human sacrifice.

"Well, I'll be damned," said Binks. "And him without half the Indian blood that I got."

Without waiting for the commotion to subside, Ron stood and in his official voice said, "I believe that takes care of all the outstanding business. Do I hear a motion to adjourn?"

"So moved!" shouted Roger.

"Seconded," said Leland.

"All in favor signify by saying aye," pronounced Ron. A few scattered ayes were all but lost in the commotion of people leaving, but they were enough for Ron to announce, "Meeting adjourned."

Suddenly Fred Yoder said loudly, "Wait, we ain't discussed the Rock and what we're going to do about it. Are we going to leave it just laying there?"

"Aw, to hell with it," someone said. To which someone else added, "Give it some Weeney Water and let it get up by itself."

And then the only people left in the Chick 'n' More were those waiting to order lunch.

After the meeting, Nettie approached Reverend Fall, who was standing by himself on the street corner. He tried to smile when she approached. Absent was his usual righteous indignation, replaced by resignation trying to morph into acceptance.

She put an arm around his shoulders. "I hope you don't take any of this the wrong way. You were right in there, gambling *is* sin. It's just that there's big sins and little sins, and betting on buffalo droppings is one of the littlest. You're the town's pastor, and I think there were folks who would have been disappointed if you hadn't said something."

"Thanks, Nettie. I think that's how I felt myself. I had to say something, even though my heart wasn't in it."

Nettie began walking. "Come on, Reverend, let's go to the church. There's more important things to work on now."

"Like what?"

"Like the church social to raise money for the home health care fund. You talked about it in church, remember? Raising money to pay someone to take folks without transportation to and from the clinic in Tucumcari. Everyone thought it was a great idea, so the ladies' auxiliary's been working on it. I know June's been practicing to play some good old-timey tunes, the kind people like, and you're needed to kind of lead everything. After all, you're our pastor."

Reverend Fall brightened. "Yes, I am."

Joanie and Dave walked homeward down Main Street. Already heat ripples rose from the pavement. Dave briefly worried about Joanie changing her mind about staying in Sweeney. She paused to remove her hat and wipe sweat from her forehead.

"Hey, don't do that! Don't you know that sweat's good for a cowboy hat? If that hat ain't sweat-stained, folks will be suspicious of you." He laughed.

She swatted him with her hat and asked, "Do you think the buffalo-chip thing will work?"

"Beats me. It's a crazy idea. Just like trying to rehabilitate Flicka was a crazy idea, just like most of what's been happening in this town lately has been crazy. It seems crazy ideas are the only kind that work around here."

"You're right. This place is just plain weird."

"It is that. Look, I've got to run an errand. I'll be home later."

As arranged, they met at Nettie's. Dave, Roger, Kathy, Leland, and Rudd. The original conspirators. Nettie found enough chairs that they could all sit around the kitchen table; then she went to the cupboard and brought out glasses and the bottle of Wild Turkey. She poured a generous amount in each glass. Raising her glass she said, "Here's to us. It's been a wild ride, but we hung on."

"To us," said Roger, as he and the others raised their glasses. "And to Sweeney. There's more to this old town than I ever suspected."

"But it took the weirdness at Indian Rocks to bring it out," said Dave. "It was the craziest idea I'd ever heard of, but as I was telling Joanie, crazy ideas are the only kind that seem to work here."

"What do you think the Indians will do with the Rock?" Kathy asked. "Actually, I guess we should ask Edward, since it's technically his. Rudd, any idea?"

"Not really. I suspect they'll just let it be. It'll go back to being Indian Rocks, like it was before. It's served its purpose. Its fame was fading anyway."

"But it won't be forgotten," said Dave. "My daughter has seen to that. The Rock and all that it led to has been well documented for posterity."

"It's kind of sad," said Kathy. "That Rock, once so important, now just an ordinary rock again."

"Well, not quite," said Roger. "As we left the Chick 'n' More, I overheard Judy Baca talking to Lee about putting a sign on the Rock. That way they can continue selling Weeney Water, which I understand is still a hot item. That Rock may rise again."

Epilogue

⟶ RACHEL WAS LATE DRIVING out of Santa Fe, and by the time she turned off I-40 at Exit 329 for Tucumcari the September sun already had begun to decline toward the horizon. Out of habit she quickly estimated the sun's angle and, factoring in the time of year, she performed rapid mental calculations and estimated that sunset would be in 1.5 hours. Plenty of time to drive to Sweeney. She could have simply looked at her watch, but what fun was that?

Tucumcari had changed little in the years since she last was here. It still was an appendage of the Interstate, its main street an intestine of restaurants, fast-food joints, motels, and truck plazas that sucked sustenance from the steady stream of traffic passing through.

As she drove her new, fuel-efficient station wagon onto NM 459, she saw a large sign beside the road:

Sweeney ahead
Home of the Cocoyes and Buffalo-chip Poker
It's the luck of the drop.

In the sign's upper left corner was painted a turquoise feather; in the upper right was a brown buffalo. She softly chuckled that at least the sign did not portray the "drop" part of its message.

The sign was relatively new, and as she drove on the highway she noted that it was recently paved. Apparently increased traffic warranted it. When she had lived in Sweeney the joke was that the highway was only resurfaced when the glaciers advanced.

Rachel smiled. The week-long conference at the Santa Fe Institute had gone well, spectacularly well, in fact, so much so that Mark, her husband, had been asked to stay an extra day to finalize some details of the proposal that the institute had agreed to back. He would join her in Sweeney tomorrow. Actually, she preferred returning by herself, not having to introduce Mark. She wanted to return to Sweeney as she had left it, as simply Rachel Rowe.

Rachel relaxed. She was in no mood to hurry, though eight years had passed since she had left Sweeney. The plains at this time of day were luminescent browns and ochres and yellows; in the distance cumulus clouds rose in gleaming white billows. The years spent in southern California at CalTech and then in New Jersey at Princeton's Institute for Advanced Study had deepened her appreciation of the High Plains. She sometimes wondered whether it was the vastness here—and especially the endless, horizon-stretching skies—that led her to study cosmology. Once a nighttime flight to New Jersey had taken her over eastern New Mexico. Below she beheld a seemingly endless emptiness, like the void of space, but just as in space tiny clusters of lights occasionally broke the darkness—ranches, tiny isolated communities. She had grown up in one of those tiny clusters of lights.

Sweeney. She couldn't say she'd missed it. She'd been too busy studying, navigating the tumultuous and complex new world she found herself in, too busy creating a career, falling in love, getting married, melding two careers. The last eight years had been like driving on an LA freeway at rush hour, demanding full concentration. Now she looked at the road ahead and behind: not a car in sight. She was at home, at peace.

Exactly 1.5 hours after exiting I-40, with the sun just touching the horizon, Rachel slowed for the bend in NM 459 that signaled the entrance to Sweeney. She could see that the black letters spelling the town's name on the municipal water tower had been freshly painted. The setting sun also illuminated a yellow-and-black sign that read: "Sweeney and the Cocoyes welcome you. Turn left on Main Street for Buffalo-chip Poker and the Visitor Center." Beneath it were arrayed the familiar smaller signs for the community's civic organizations.

Near those signs were a handful of commercial signs: the Chick 'n' More, the Baca Mart, "The Sweeney Diggs," apparently a bad-pun reference to Will Diggs's RV park and motel, Binks's Indian Souvenirs and Smoke Shop, Yoder's Barber Shop—could he really still be giving haircuts? The largest sign was one reading "Connie Nesbitt—meeting all your Kiowa County real estate needs." Rachel noted with concern that there was no sign for the Style Salon.

She drove down Main Street and turned onto the street where she once had lived. After she left, her father had surprised everyone by moving to Los Alamos, where he even more surprisingly had become a fixture at local coffee shops. Their home in Sweeney was still here. In fact, it had a large pickup in the driveway, a satellite dish in the front yard, and plastic children's toys scattered about. She'd always assumed that her house and her father would decay together.

Back on Main Street Rachel turned left, toward the visitor center. As she passed the Raylene Johnson Memorial Park she saw that someone still placed fresh flowers there. Ahead, the Rock lay where it had fallen years before. During her last year of high school there had been talk of resurrecting it, of making it a tourist attraction, but the talk had sputtered out in wrangling and indecision.

The buffalo-chip poker arena—according to the sign it was called that now—had been upgraded, with a much stronger fence. Four bored-looking buffalo nibbled on hay bales on the ground. Outside the fence rose a small tier of bleachers. For the players. Nearby was a raised covered shed overlooking the arena, doubtless for the official tally keeper. The bleachers were empty, and no cars waited in the dirt parking area. Not quite Las Vegas.

But lights were on in the visitor center. It was an elongated box, built of corrugated aluminum, redeemed from its resemblance to a railroad box car by the geraniums in the window boxes and the sunflowers planted beside the door. Arching over the door, like a rainbow, was a sign reading "Cocoye-Sweeney Visitor and Cultural Center"; a geometric design, vaguely Indian-looking and painted red, yellow, and turquoise, framed the letters. A Port-a-Potty stood discreetly at each end of the building.

As Rachel entered, the cluster of women watching television in one corner started and turned around, as did the white-haired woman who had been putting things away at the front desk.

"Rachel!" exclaimed Nettie, standing and coming around the desk to embrace her. "Rachel Rowe. Land's sakes, oh my oh my oh my. Hey, Iris, Willa, Inez, come over here, it's Rachel Rowe."

The three very heavy women lumbered across the room and also embraced Rachel, who had only the briefest acquaintance with Willa Cohen, and none at all with Inez.

"Well, I can't believe my eyes," blubbered Iris. Her hair had streaks of gray and she'd put on a few pounds, but otherwise she had not changed, certainly not her taste in clothing.

The three women's greetings left Rachel feeling she'd been mugged by walruses, and when she caught her breath she said, "This is my first trip back in eight years, and I'm dying to hear all that's happened."

"And so are we, dear, so are we," said Nettie. To Rachel Nettie looked smaller, frailer, older.

Rachel summarized the last eight years as quickly as the women would allow, then turned expectantly to them.

"So you're an astronomer," Iris said.

"Cosmologist," Rachel corrected, but Iris didn't seem to have heard.

"I follow the stars myself—I'm a Virgo, you know—and that lady on the daily TV star show said this morning that I should be prepared for surprises today—and now here you are."

"How's the Style Salon?" Rachel asked Nettie, changing the subject.

"Oh, I closed that three years ago. I was losing too many of my old customers to health problems—like poor old Harriet Moggs a few years ago. Do you remember her?"

How could Rachel forget? Harriet had been one of the main attractions at the solstice—until Rachel climbed on the Rock and became an angel. "I'm sorry to hear that."

"She died peacefully," said Iris, "and she died believing she was a goddess. I think she was looking forward to joining other goddesses on high."

"Nowadays," Nettie continued, "I come here, and I help Leland out a bit at the town offices. And I do a little coaching."

"Coaching?"

"Barrel-racing. Sometimes I go with Roger and Kathy when they're off doing their rodeo announcing and clowning thing. Funny, how even in this modern world getting beat-up and dusty in a ring with a bunch of animals is more popular than ever. Giving barrel-racing clinics isn't exactly big business, but it brings in a little extra money—and I'm sure not tempted to gamble it away here.

"They do it for the reasons I do, to get away and have a little fun. You know they got hitched, don't you? Her father died a few years ago. Her mother still lives in that big old house, but Roger and Kathy live near the clinic. She pays a couple of local women to help look after her mother."

At that moment, the door opened and a small, skinny man entered. "Evening, ladies," he said in a high, scratchy voice. He was dressed formally, with shiny cowboy boots, pressed pants, a white shirt buttoned to the top, and a bolo tie with a silver buffalo clasp. On his head was a top-quality cowboy hat. On his chest was pinned a name tag: "Buffalo-chip Poker. Official Tally Keeper."

"Evening, Edward," replied Nettie. "You should have come in sooner, didn't have to stay out there by yourself."

"Nope," he said, "if I'm on duty, I'm on duty, that's how it is."

"Well, good for you," said Nettie. "Edward, this is Rachel Rowe, you remember her, don't you?"

He extended his hand. Rachel was grateful that he didn't attempt a hug; even after all this time and him being cleaned up she couldn't quite face that.

"Edward only helps out part time," explained Nettie, "when Henry, Willa's cousin, can't be here. Edward's got other duties. He does most of the cleaning work at the B&B."

"The B&B? Sweeney's got a B&B?"

"Yep, Rudd turned that big old rambling wreck of a house of his into a B&B, fixed it up all neat and pretty, hired a bunch of Cocoyes to come in and help decorate, give it kind of an Indian theme. It's real nice. I haven't seen Rudd so happy since he was a kid."

"I'm having trouble imagining big, gruff Rudd in his grease-stained overalls greeting visitors to his B&B."

"He doesn't do the actual greeting himself, he hired Liz, one of the Cocoye girls, to do that, but he does seem to enjoy having a bunch of people in that old house again. Sometimes he'll sit in the kitchen with them and talk. He's got a collection of old comic books that he shows people who are interested—and you'd be amazed how many are."

The image of Rudd Torgelson talking about comic books was just too much, so Rachel changed the subject. "How's the buffalo-chip poker doing?"

"Well, as you can see, we're not exactly Caesar's Palace here." Nettie shrugged. "Actually, it's not been that bad, today's just a slow day. We do get a few people coming by, especially on the weekends. We've even had a few tour buses come through. And then there's the motorcycles."

"The motorcycles?"

"Yes. Seems it's quite a thing among motorcycle club members to have their machines go through a traditional Indian motorcycle blessing. Uncle Billy and some of the other Cocoyes really put on an impressive ceremony."

Rachel boggled at the oxymoron of "traditional Indian motorcycle blessing."

"And when we have a rodeo or a barbecue we get a real crowd," Nettie continued. "There's been talk of staging another solstice—you remember that, don't you, dear?"—Rachel only nodded—"but nothing's come of it. We'd have to raise the Rock for that to happen, and this time around no one would believe it was done by aliens."

"Besides, I imagine Reverend Fall would object," said Rachel.

"Oh, he's not here anymore. When their daughter had her baby he and June moved to the Northwest to be closer. He found work in a nice medium-sized town outside Portland, and he's pastor at a church there. I still get Christmas cards from June. They seem to be happy there." Nettie paused. "I don't think they miss Sweeney."

"We're still here," said Willa. "Us Cocoyes. And the town's still here. That's what counts. We never expected to get rich. We're living one day to the next—but we're still here. This is our home now."

"Oh, Rachel, I'm so happy to see you," said Nettie. "Let us show you around the visitor center. Willa, why don't you start with the Cocoye section."

Rachel followed the Indian woman to the half of the room devoted to the Cocoyes. A poster-board display explained the tribe's history, with emphasis on the centuries of living on the plains and none on Los Angeles. On a table beneath the display was a tape recorder. Willa proudly pushed the Play button to begin a recitation of Cocoye words and their translations. The voice was Willa's.

Nearby in glass cases were several arrowhead collections donated by ranchers. On a table were a feathered headdress, beaded moccasins, and Uncle Billy's drum. Nearby a placard explained that the name Sweeney was derived from words in the Cocoye language, *Tse 'ua nee*, meaning "place of rocks."

"I thought Sweeney was named for a place in Ireland," said Rachel.

"Could be," said Nettie archly, "could be."

"This is just awesome," said Rachel. Willa beamed.

"And now let me show you the Sweeney section," said Nettie as she ushered Rachel to the other half of the room. There was an old buckboard wagon beside a piece of rusted farm equipment that Rachel remembered once sitting behind the shed at Will Diggs's place before it became an RV park. A poster-board display outlined Sweeney history, with special prominence given to the rising of the Rock and the events that followed. Rachel recognized several photos that Traci had taken— Christie Herwig on her horse at the rodeo and the barbecue parade, Abe Martinez and his oxen, a blurry photo of Bare-assed Bob, Uther Pendragon and his druids, Liriodendra and her dancing goddesses, the White Wolf Apaches fleeing in panic from the calf, Traci's mother and her horse and the goat.

Looking at the photos, Rachel's eyes misted. It seemed so long ago, an almost mythic time, gone forever. She thought of the pain and humiliation she had endured in Sweeney, the loneliness and confusion. But that crazy summer changed everything. For the first time she found friends, for the first time she was accepted. Her senior year in high school had been fun, though the group's innocence had been shattered by Kimberly's unplanned pregnancy and sudden departure from town.

And she'd been wrong when she told Traci that at college she wouldn't find others from small towns like Sweeney. In a literal sense, that was true, but she'd learned that even within sprawling cities some kids grew up in "little towns."

She wiped her eyes, then looked at Nettie, who put her arms around her and said, "The past is never really dead, dear, and can return in so many unexpected ways."

The rest of the exhibit consisted of an old six-shooter pistol in a glass case, an antique telephone switchboard, a foot-treadle sewing machine, framed front pages of the *Sweeney Oracle and Independent*, and yellowed copies of the Sweeney town history, printed to celebrate the U.S. Bicentennial in 1976.

"Impressive," said Rachel, inwardly acknowledging that in many respects it truly was, that the town and the Cocoyes had risen to this level of self-awareness and pride.

"I'll be around for a couple of days," she said, as she started toward the door. "I'll stop by again. I'll bring Mark, my husband."

Edward, who'd been standing stiffly near a closet, said, "Be sure to stop by the buffalo arena. I'll show you around that too."

Wondering what exactly he would show her, Rachel smiled, nodded, and left.

The porch lights in the houses on Mangrove Street had just started to come on when Rachel parked her car in front of the Daly house. She got out, walked up the sidewalk, and knocked on the front door.

"Why, Rachel, what a pleasant surprise!" exclaimed Joanie when she opened it. "Come in, Rachel, come in. Traci's not in town, away on a photo shoot, and Dave's not here right now, but he'll want to see you. And I want to see you. Come in."

"Actually, I can only stay a minute right now. I'll be back tomorrow, I want you to meet my husband, who'll be coming then—Traci's met him—but there's something I can't wait to show you." And with that she turned, walked back to her car, and from the station wagon's back took what resembled an Erector set on steroids. She carried it to the porch and set it down. "There," she said proudly.

"It's . . . beautiful," said Joanie. "Uh, what is it?"

Rachel laughed. "I didn't expect you to know. It's a gamma ray observatory. See, here are the cryogenics laboratory, the stabilization beam housing, the ionization laboratory, the main control center, the sleeping quarters for the techs, the microprocessor module."

"Of course." Joanie laughed. "I'd recognize it anywhere."

"It's a dollhouse. I made it."

"A dollhouse? You made it?"

"Of course, it's not my only dollhouse, but I'm especially proud of this one. Look," she said, kneeling beside it, "this is where Sheila was working when she made her antigravity discovery." Rachel pointed a finger through the tiny window of the control center. Joanie peered in and saw tiny bits of paper scattered on the desk. "If you had a magnifying glass you could see some of the equations.

"The reason the papers are all scattered is that Karl, her arch-rival from the Max Planck Institute, had just broken in and attempted to steal them, but her dog, Boson, barked and warned her in time. See, here's Boson's house." She pointed to a tiny dog house by the control center. "Sheila fled, taking the crucial solutions with her. She went to the cryogenics laboratory, where she trapped Karl in a liquid nitrogen unit. After they thawed him out, he was never quite the same."

"Rachel," said Joanie in a hushed voice, "you made all this up. This whole story, you made it up."

"Yes," said Rachel proudly, "that's what dollhouses are for—make-believe. You taught me that. There are other stories in this observatory, and maybe I can tell them to you tomorrow, but I wanted to tell you this one, because of something you'll find out soon."

Joanie threw her arms around Rachel and hugged her. "Oh, Rachel, you have no idea how proud I am of you."

"Well, you always did have a gift for seeing the hidden potential in things. Like that horse . . . what was her name?"

"Flicka, She's still here, doing well. She's on her second goat though. When you come tomorrow I'll show her to you. Oh, I wish Traci was here."

"That's okay. We keep in touch. How's Mr. Daly?"

"He's fine. He retired from teaching two years ago. The time had come. We travel a lot. But he's still in what he calls . . . 'transition.' He doesn't really know to what. He loved teaching science."

"He taught me a lot. In fact, he led me to a career in science, astronomy. I remember when he would take his classes on nighttime field trips onto the prairie near Sweeney and talk about stars and constellations and planets and galaxies. Most of the kids just used it as an excuse to goof off, but I loved it. I never told anyone, but I used to walk out there by myself. You didn't have to go very far to get away from the city lights of Sweeney."

Joanie laughed. "No, light pollution isn't really a problem in Sweeney." A wistfulness passed over Joanie as she paused. "He still loves astronomy. Sometimes, like tonight, after he's finished hanging out at the Chick 'n' More, he just goes out on the prairie and watches the sky, says it makes him feel at peace. He'll find something to do with his retirement, eventually."

"Well, maybe that eventually will be sooner than he expects," said Rachel, and with that she hastily said good-bye, picked up her dollhouse, and walked back to her car, leaving Joanie standing bewildered.

Rachel was hungry. She hadn't eaten since leaving Santa Fe. And Sweeney still offered only one option for the hungry traveler: the Chick 'n' More.

"Rachel!" Heather squealed when Rachel walked through the door. "Rachel!" and with that Heather wiped her hands on her apron and scurried from behind the counter to embrace her friend.

At the counter sat an old man and a middle-aged man, both in western attire. "Hi, Rachel," said the old man as he rose to offer his hand, stepping over the dog curled around the stool. It was Leland and Trixie.

"Hi, guys," said Rachel. "I should have called ahead to let people know I was coming, but I wasn't completely sure I would be—and I didn't want anyone to go out of their way for me."

"That's thoughtful of you," said Leland. "As you can see, everyone in Sweeney is so busy they barely have time to wake up. Rachel, I want you to meet my son, Grant."

Grant stood and offered his hand. "Pleased to meet you. I've heard a lot about you."

Like his father, Grant wore faded blue jeans, a western shirt with pearl buttons, and a sweat-stained cowboy hat. And like many cowboys he wore a leather belt with a silver, wallet-sized belt buckle. Noticing Rachel looking at it, he said, "I won this in the steer-wrestling in a rodeo over in Logan when I was in high school."

Rachel smiled. "The only thing I won in high school was a science fair award. And I was the only entrant, except for a couple of junior high kids who brought in some stock-tank slime to put under a microscope."

As Grant sat back down, she noticed he mounted the stool exactly like his father, reinforcing the physical resemblance. She also noted that anyone seeing Grant would never suspect he was anything but another thirty-something cowboy.

"Grant here lives in Chicago, with his partner, Ray," said Leland. "Grant's a financial consultant there, and he comes out to Sweeney several times a year to visit and help manage the ranch finances and whatever money the town and the Cocoyes make off that buffalo-chip poker thing. We haven't made much, but we have been able to renovate some houses for low-income housing, and we've made a loan to help start up an Internet computer maintenance business that hires some local people, mostly young ones. You won't believe this, but the last census showed Sweeney had increased in population, the only town in Kiowa County to do so."

Leland paused. "I'm glad you're back, and I hope you're in the area next year. Ray is fixing to come visit, he's never been out West before, and I'd like to invite you to the barbecue we're going to have at the ranch. I don't know who all will be there, but Jim Biddle's donating a buffalo, and Rudd and Edward are bringing that huge barbecue rig. It'll be a lot of fun."

"I'd love to come; I'll make a point of it. In fact, I may have some friends and colleagues who also might like to attend, just to get a taste of the true flavor of Sweeney."

"You mean . . . Kiowa County's first gay-straight barbecue?"

"Exactly. What could be more quintessentially Sweeney?"

Just then Heather interrupted. "Rachel, you're spending the night at our place. Don't even think to argue. Eddie's out of town—he works for the electric company and gets called away a lot—and the kids are driving me bonkers. We've got a lot of catching up to do. Traci, when she calls, gives me general stuff about what you've been doing, but I want details, details."

Rachel took a seat next to Leland. "Well, then, you'd better get me a cup of coffee, and some food to wash it down with."

"My, my," said Heather brightly, "Rachel Rowe with a sense of humor. Well, I never . . ." And with that she bustled into the kitchen.

Leland looked at Rachel and said, "When Helen retired last year, she passed on her apron and her tactlessness to Heather."

"It's okay. How are you, Mr. Morton."

"It's Leland—and I'm doing well. Still working at the town offices. Nettie comes by to help me most days, though there's not really much to do. Toby, one of the Cocoye boys, helps out after school answering e-mails and updating the website."

"You still don't understand computers, do you?"

"Well, I wouldn't say that. I've made a lot of progress, it's just all those damned keys that get me confused—control, function, escape, and whatnot—but I'm working on it." He smiled. "What brings you to town, aside from a desire for fine dining?"

"I'll tell you tomorrow; it'll take a while. I'll stop by the town offices."

Leland looked puzzled.

At that moment Heather returned with a cup of coffee and a menu. "You got me so flustered I forgot to ask you what you wanted. At this time of day we don't have much but the special."

"I recommend the special," said Leland.

"I guess I'll have the special."

"One special!" Heather shouted back to the kitchen. "It's green chile stew made with buffalo meat."

Rachel, who was vegetarian, winced but said nothing. Instead she said, "Traci told me about you getting married to Eddie. I remember him, a nice boy, one of the Cocoyes. I'm married too. His name's Mark. You'll meet him tomorrow. "

"Oh, I know about you getting married. Traci told me. I wish she would find someone and settle down, but I have to admit I sometimes envy her and her photo assignments all over the world. She's away in South America right now. When she comes back here she talks about wanting to return and settle down, but I don't see it, at least not soon. While you're here you need to stop out and see Christie."

Rachel paused to blow on her steaming stew. To a vegetarian it was just plain revolting, but she had to at least attempt to eat it. She returned the conversation to Christie.

"She's married too, I understand."

"Yep, Lee Willis. They're at her family's ranch, but they're going to be building a place out on the Willis spread. She's expecting again, her third. I didn't know what she saw in him at first. I thought he was kind of a smartass—you know he turned out to be Bare-assed Bob? But the marriage has worked out pretty well."

"I'm happy for her. And Kimberly?"

"Kimberly's a mystery. She hasn't kept in touch. Couple of years ago her father died in a car wreck out on the Raton road, blind drunk, missed a turn. Mother moved away. Not much here for Kimberly, never was. I heard she's some kind of an artist up in Portland. I'd like to track her down sometime; maybe we could have a reunion or something."

"I'd like that too," said Rachel.

By the time Rachel had finished her meal and returned to her car, the day's afterglow had faded. All ten of Sweeney's streetlights were on. Heather didn't get off work at the Chick 'n' More for another hour. On impulse, Rachel drove to the end of town, toward Indian Rocks. Her intuition had been correct. Dave Daly's pickup was parked nearby, and she could make out his form perched on the large rock. She made a point of coughing as she approached, so as not to startle him.

"Hi, Mr. Daly. It's Rachel Rowe. Your wife told me you might be here." Not a complete lie.

"Rachel!" He started to climb down.

"No," said Rachel, "stay there. Do you mind if I sit and watch stars with you?"

"Only if you promise not to speak in equations. Traci has filled me in on your career."

"Thank you," said Rachel, some of the old awkwardness returning. "I mean, thank you for your teaching. It was those astronomy field trips you led that got me interested in astronomy. You were my favorite teacher."

"Well, thank you. And you were my best pupil."

They sat silently, awkwardly for a moment, then Rachel said, "That was quite a summer, wasn't it, Mr. Daly?"

"First, if you don't stop calling me Mr. Daly and start calling me Dave, like every other adult, I'm going to start calling you Dr. Rowe. Second, yes, that was quite a summer. I think that's why I like to come here to watch stars, because it was this rock we're sitting on that started it all."

"You started it all, you and the others."

"Well, it's no secret that we did some tinkering with the site here, those holes weren't really dug by aliens."

"I know. You did it with winches and pulleys, with an anchor point about . . . there"—she gestured into the dark toward a spot about fifty yards from the Rock—"with another anchor point over there." She indicated another spot, about 90 degrees from the first. "It would have been slow, tedious work, but with sufficient leverage and a couple of large power winches and some strong cable, it could be done. Of course, you would have used old carpet or scraps of Astroturf from the school's football field to protect the Rock and obscure the marks of the machinery. And digging the Mystery Holes with a router would have erased the indentations of the heavy equipment." She looked at Dave and grinned. "How am I doing?"

Dave stared. "Uncanny, just uncanny. So when did you figure all this out?"

"Oh, before the solstice. I knew that aliens hadn't done this, despite what everyone was saying. I haven't told anyone else."

"Thanks. Let's let this poor old rock keep a bit of its mystery. If you want, I can tell you who did it."

"I already know. Traci told me."

"Should have known. Actually, it was the whole town that made that summer; it was the town that came together and made everything happen."

A light breeze wandered by. Rachel inhaled deeply, savoring the subtle smells of the prairie. Interesting, how dryness could have a scent, how it picked up smells someone not familiar with the plains would not notice—the faint fragrance of sage, the scent of dust, the hint of cattle dung.

She turned again to Dave. "That was the summer I first had friends, though it didn't start out that way. I never thought it would begin with simulated puking in the high school auditorium."

"Rachel, I hate to tell you this, but even if you become the first person to go to Mars—which you could—you will never equal the legendary status you earned at Sweeney High through that mass regurgitation."

Rachel laughed. "When the Nobel Prize committee comes around, you won't mention that, will you?"

"Of course not."

Dave looked pensive. Rachel too lingered in the silence and then asked, "It was all worth it, wasn't it? I mean, the Rock and rodeo and solstice and barbecue and all?"

"It was indeed worth it. Sweeney's still alive, lives were changed, and for one glorious summer we all experienced splendid ridiculosity that will live in Sweeney's memory forever."

"Then why do you sound sad?"

Dave shrugged. "Anticlimax, I suppose. We really can't complain. Most towns like ours never come close to achieving what we achieved. It couldn't last, but we managed to keep Sweeney alive."

"That's important." She paused. "I told Traci that summer that I didn't want to leave Sweeney to go away to college, that I was afraid. She said she was afraid too. We both felt we'd be lost in the outside world. Well, we were wrong—and we were right. We did make our way in the outside world, but we never really left Sweeney behind. I like to think we were successful because we grew up in a secure nest. There aren't many secure nests anymore, and when towns like Sweeney die it's like a species of songbird going extinct."

They sat silently. Then Rachel pointed upward. "Andromeda's always been my favorite constellation."

"Why's that?"

"Because it contains the great galaxy, M31, the most distant object humans can see with the naked eye. You taught me that."

Dave looked upward and nodded.

"And because it's a prolific source of gamma rays and mu-mesons and could even help resolve some of the issues regarding dark matter."

"I didn't teach you that," said Dave looking at her.

"No, but you'll have to learn, you and the other people in Sweeney."

Then, looking at him she said, "Yesterday, at the Santa Fe Institute, a consortium of scientists from around the world agreed to compete for the world's largest, most powerful gamma ray telescope. It will be funded by the National Science Foundation, with possible additional funding from the European Organization for Nuclear Research. It will be a significant project, so the competition will be fierce, but I convinced the people in Santa Fe to consider Kiowa County as a site. It has clearer skies, less light pollution, and a more stable atmosphere than the other places being considered. But it's in the middle of nowhere, as someone put it, so Sweeney will have to convince the site reviewers that Sweeney can support such a project."

Dave's mouth dropped.

"As I said, the competition is stiff," Rachel continued, "so the town will really have to come together on this and show a lot of spirit and a willingness to accommodate changes and make the scientists feel welcome, but, let's face it, that summer proved Sweeney can do it."

Dave looked upward at the stars; then he turned to Rachel. "You're right, we *can* do it." He paused, and a moment later added, "Hell, yes, we can. Even if Bare-assed Bob stays retired. Maybe Indian Rocks can become a solar observatory. You don't suppose any of the scientists would be interested in joining our Rotary Club, do you?"

The End

Sweeney
Design and composition by Karen Mazur
Typest in Minion Pro with Eva Pro display